tary heroics, conniving politicians, devious agencies, a hijacked nuclear sub, lethal computer hackers, currency speculators, maniac moguls, and greedy mercenaries that rival Clancy for fiction-as-realism and Cussler for spirited action." —*Publishers Weekly* (starred review)

"Fans of Coonts and his hero Grafton will love it. Great fun." —*Library Journal*

"Coonts's action and the techno-talk are as gripping as ever." —*Kirkus Reviews*

"Thrilling roller-coaster action. Give a hearty 'welcome back' to Admiral Jake Grafton." —*The Philadelphia Inquirer*

HONG KONG

"Move over, Clancy, readers know they can count on Coonts." —*Midwest Book Review*

"The author gives us superior suspense with a great cast of made-up characters...But the best thing about this book is Coonts's scenario for turning China into a democracy." —Liz Smith, *The New York Post*

"A high-octane blend of techno-wizardry [and] ultra-violence...[Coonts] skillfully captures the postmodern flavor of Hong Kong, where a cell phone is as apt as an AK-47 to be a revolutionary weapon." —*USA Today*

"Coonts has perfected the art of the high-tech adventure story." —*Library Journal*

"Coonts does a remarkable job of capturing the mood of clashing cultures in Hong Kong."   —*Publishers Weekly*

"Filled with action, intrigue, and humanity."
—*San Jose Mercury News*

CUBA

"Enough Tomahawk missiles, stealth bombers, and staccato action to satisfy [Coonts's] most demanding fans."
—*USA Today*

"[A] gripping and intelligent thriller."
—*Publishers Weekly* (starred review)

"Perhaps the best of Stephen Coonts's six novels about modern warfare."   —*Austin American-Statesman*

"Coonts delivers some of his best gung-ho suspense writing yet."   —*Kirkus Reviews*

FORTUNES OF WAR

"*Fortunes of War* is crammed with action, suspense, and characters with more than the usual one dimension found in these books."   —*USA Today*

"A stirring examination of courage, compassion, and profound nobility of military professionals under fire. Coonts's best yet."   —*Kirkus Reviews* (starred review)

"Full of action and suspense…a strong addition to the genre."   —*Publishers Weekly*

Also in this series

Novels by STEPHEN COONTS

Nonfiction books by STEPHEN COONTS

STEPHEN COONTS'

DEEP BLACK:

ARCTIC GOLD

**Written by Stephen Coonts
and William H. Keith**

St. Martin's Paperbacks

This is a work of fiction. All of the characters, organizations, and events portrayed in this novel are either products of the author's imagination or are used fictitiously.

STEPHEN COONTS' DEEP BLACK: ARCTIC GOLD

Copyright © 2009 by Stephen P. Coonts and Deborah B. Coonts.

For information address St. Martin's Press, 175 Fifth Avenue, New York, NY 10010.

ISBN: 0-312-94695-3
EAN: 978-0-312-94695-1

Printed in the United States of America

St. Martin's Paperbacks edition / February 2009

St. Martin's Paperbacks are published by St. Martin's Press, 175 Fifth Avenue, New York, NY 10010.

10 9 8 7 6 5 4 3 2 1

PROLOGUE

Latitude 90° N
1445 hours

IT WAS, FEODOR GOLYTSIN THOUGHT, *like touching down on the surface of another planet.*

"Ostorojna!" Captain Third Rank Dmitri Kurchakov warned. "Careful! Reduce speed of descent!"

"Da, Kepitan," the helmsman replied.

"Vasily. Give me a readout on the depth below keel."

"Deseet' metrov, Kepitan," the diving officer replied. Ten meters.

Golytsin stooped to peer through the thick quartz window into the alien world beyond. Another planet, yes . . . a very *dark* planet. Blacker than the surface of far Pluto, for there, at least, there was a sun, if one shrunken and wan. Here there was nothing save the luminescence of the abyssal fauna, banished now by the light the submarine brought with her from above.

A dark planet, and a deadly one. At a depth of just over forty-two hundred meters, the pressure bearing down on each and every square centimeter of *Nomer Chiteereh*'s outer nickel-steel hull was almost two tons.

Muck swirled up off the bottom by the minisub's side thrusters danced in the harsh white glare of the forward lights, like drifting stars. Briefly, something like a worm, half a meter long and fringed with myriad legs or swimmerets, twisted through the unaccustomed light, casting bizarre and writhing shadows within the cold and watery haze.

Astonishing. Even here, four thousand meters beneath the ice, within this frigid eternal night, there was life.

The submarine was a new, experimental, and highly secret military model with the less-than-glamorous name of *Nomer Chiteereh,* "Number Four." Twenty-nine meters long and with a displacement of 150 tons, *Nomer Chiteereh* could reach depths of six thousand meters and could stay submerged for several days. A pair of external robotic arms operated from the forward observer's seat gave the tiny vessel considerable dexterity beneath the glare of her external lights. She could be handled by a crew of four, but there was space in the cramped and cold-sweating pressure hull compartment for four additional passengers . . . or a squad of elite Spetsnaz in the cargo bay aft.

Today, however, there was only Golytsin.

The submersible's sonar chirped, with ringing echoes. The diving officer read off the depth beneath the keel as they continued to descend, an almost mournful litany. *"Vaseem metrov . . . sem . . . shest' metrov . . ."*

"I see the bottom, *Kepiten,*" the helmsman reported.

Side by side, heads nearly touching, Golytsin and Kurchakov leaned forward and peered down through the second of the forward view ports. "There!" the normally impassive Kurchakov said. He sounded uncharacteristically excited. A dour and taciturn man by nature, he now seemed almost boyish.

White light glared against the blackness, highlighted by drifting bits of organic debris. The bottom appeared disappointingly flat and featureless, an endless gray desert of fine silt and decayed plankton.

Mingled with the chirp of the sonar, the litany continued. *"Chiteereh . . . tree . . . dvah . . ."*

"Halt descent!" Kurchakov ordered. "Maintain position!"

The submarine's side thrusters whined more loudly, gentling the beast to an awkward hover. The sharp increase in the thruster wash kicked up additional billowing clouds of fine silt from the bottom beneath the sub's keel, filling the night with brightly illuminated particles. *A blizzard*, Golytsin thought. A winter squall such as he'd once known in the St. Petersburg—no, the *Leningrad*—of his childhood.

"So where is our flag?" Golytsin asked, peering into the murk as it gently subsided. As he leaned forward, the light reflecting back from outside illuminated the web of blue lines etched into his arm and the back of his hand.

Kurchakov didn't reply at first. He was staring at Golytsin's tattoos. Then Kurchakov looked away and shrugged. "It could be anywhere, just a few meters away, beyond the edge of the light, and we'd miss it," he said. "Don't worry. We will drop another."

"No need, sir," the diving officer reported. "I have it on sonar. Bearing one-one-nine . . . range thirty-seven meters."

"Helm. Take us there. Slow ahead."

"Da, Kepitan."

In August of 2007, a pair of Russian Mir deep submersibles had reached this, the Arctic seabed at the North Pole. They'd taken readings, collected samples of the sea floor, and planted a large, rustproof titanium flag.

Since then, the Mirs had returned several times, taking further readings for the PP Shirshov Institute of Oceanology and extending Mother Russia's claim in this freezing wasteland. And today the Mirs were back, shepherding the much larger and more sinister *Nomer Chiteereh* to the cold, black depths of the Amundsen Plain.

An apparition emerged from the shadows beyond the light, broad rectangular, held above the muck by weights deeply imbedded in the sediment. As *Nomer Chiteereh* drifted forward, the colors emerged as well . . . the white, blue, and red horizontal bars of the Russian Federation.

"The Pole," Golytsin breathed. "The *real* Pole."

Not the imaginary point on the ever-drifting, ever-changing pack of ice four kilometers overhead, but the *actual* pole of the planet, on the seabed 4,261 meters beneath the surface.

A point now claimed by Moscow as a portion of the Eurasian landmass and part of the sovereign territory of the Russian Federation.

A point, Golytsin thought, that would very soon return the *Rodina*, Mother Russia, to greatness.

I

British Airways Flight 2112
JFK International Airport
1015 hours EDT

"SO, DOC, IS IT TRUE WHAT THEY say?" Kjartan Magnor-Karr said with a breezy insouciance as the two men strode down the boarding tunnel. "About you and Big Oil, I mean?"

Dr. Earnest Spencer scowled. "Young man, I haven't the faintest idea what you're talking about."

"This solar theory thing of yours," Karr said. They reached the entryway of the British Airways 747 and he grinned and winked at the welcoming flight attendant.

"Welcome aboard, sir," she said. She had the most gloriously pale blond hair. "May I see—"

Instead of his ticket, he flashed an ID at her, together with his special clearance. The ID, of course, was a fake. Despite what it said, he was not a special agent of the FBI, though the lie, the *legend*, as it was known in intelligence circles, occasionally was a useful fiction. Everyone had heard of the FBI; very few even knew there was such an organization as the National Security Agency. The clearance was real enough, however. It gave Karr permission to carry a firearm on the flight.

"Thank you, sir," she said. "I'll inform the captain."

"You do that, sweetheart," Karr told her.

He and Spencer filed aft and found their seats, located toward the rear of first class. For a few moments, the two men were preoccupied with putting their carry-on luggage in the overhead compartment and getting themselves settled in. Spencer had the window seat, Karr the aisle. As planned.

Spencer appeared ready to ignore the topic Karr had just raised, but the younger man persisted. "Aw, c'mon, *you* know, Doc. Everyone says the oil companies pay you to tell everybody that global warming is nonsense."

"Young man . . . ," Spencer began.

"Tommy."

"Eh?"

"Call me Tommy. All my friends do."

Spencer frowned at him in a way suggesting that he most assuredly did *not* consider Karr to be a friend. "Young man," he repeated. "If the oil companies were paying me, perhaps I could afford to buy their product. Secondly, global warming is not nonsense. It is real. All *too* real. My solar model simply demonstrates that human activities have little effect on the world's climate."

"Sure," Karr agreed. "So people can drive gas-guzzling SUVs all they want and not melt the ice caps, right?"

"Tell me," Spencer said, glaring at him over the top of his glasses. "Are *all* FBI agents as irritating as you?"

"Well—"

But Spencer had produced a copy of *American Scientist* he'd purchased at a kiosk inside the JFK terminal, and made a production of opening it and beginning to read.

"Jeez, Tommy!" a voice boomed inside his head. "Lay off the poor guy, how 'bout it?"

Karr chuckled in answer but didn't say anything out loud. Spencer glanced at him suspiciously, then returned to his magazine. Like all Deep Black field operatives, Karr had a minute speaker surgically implanted in his skull just behind his left ear, and he also had a microphone sewn into the collar of his pastel blue shirt. The transmitter hidden inside his belt linked him via satellite with the Deep Black nerve center deep beneath Fort Meade, Maryland, the Deep Black command center within OPS 2 known as the Art Room, to be precise.

"Everything look okay at your end?" the voice continued.

Karr glanced around the first-class cabin. Three other men in plain, dark suits had taken their seats, along with the other first-class passengers. FBI, all three of them, though all were taking care not to meet one another's eyes. The economy-class passengers were filing past, now. The agents surreptitiously watched each as he or she entered the plane and walked down the aisle.

"Mm-mm," Karr grunted the affirmative. It wouldn't do to have Spencer or the other passengers hearing him talk to himself.

"I'll take that as a 'yes,'" the voice said. The speaker was Jeff Rockman.

The last of the passengers, a frazzled-looking woman with two small and screaming children, herded her charges past Karr and into the aft section of the plane. The attractive blond flight attendant Karr had flirted with stood at the front, preparing to go into her spiel about oxygen masks and flotation cushions. She began with the usual admonition to turn off all electronic devices during the takeoff portion of the flight.

"Okay, we're gonna sign off for a while," Rockman told him. "Wouldn't do to get in trouble with the FAA."

"Mm-mm."

"And for the love of God, stop annoying Doc Spencer! He's not the enemy!"

Karr didn't reply, of course, but the statement brought a renewal of recurring questions. Just who *was* the enemy? Why would anyone want to kill Earnest Spencer and, perhaps more to the point, why was the threat serious enough that the NSA and Desk Three were involved? It was a waste of time, money, and vital personnel assets, having him here, pretending to be an FBI agent while babysitting an Ivy League professor type from the U.S. Department of Energy.

Well, at least he was off the Art Room's radar for a precious few moments. Aircraft navigation systems could be thrown off by signals from a field op's comm unit, hence the injunction to turn off all electronic gear during takeoff and landing. If anyone was going to try something stupid, this would be the time to try it, with the Art Room effectively out of the picture.

But save for the somewhat too-obvious watchfulness of the FBI guys, everyone in first class appeared to be acting with complete indifference both to him and to Spencer.

Karr caught the pretty attendant's glance as she chattered on into her microphone about wing exits and emergency landings, and winked.

He wondered if he would be able to get a phone number from her before they reached London.

DeFrancesa
Operation Magpie
Waterfront, St. Petersburg
0024 hours

Lia DeFrancesca took a moment to run the palm-sized lock scanner along the entire perimeter of the door and around the lock itself, its powerful magnetic field probing for wiring or other signs of hidden electronic devices. The digital readout remained unchanging, indicating the presence of iron and steel but not of electric currents.

Slipping the scanner into a thigh pocket in her black field ops suit, she produced a set of lock picks and began to work at the ancient padlock securing the door's hasp.

"Hurry; hurry," her partner whispered with fierce urgency. "If we're found . . ."

"Patience, Sergei," she replied. "We don't want to rush this."

She was having more trouble with the rust than with the padlock's mechanism. With a click, the lock snapped open, and she pulled it off the hasp.

A foghorn mourned in the damp night air. The warehouse loomed above the waterfront, overlooking *Kozhevennaya Liniya* to one side, the oily black waters of the southern mouth of the Lena River on the other. A chill and dripping fog shrouded their surroundings, muffling sound. Carefully she edged the sliding door open, but stopped after moving it only a couple of inches.

"What is it?" her companion asked. "What's wrong?"

She didn't answer immediately, but pocketing the lock tools, she pulled out a cell phone and a length of flexible tubing, as thick as a soda straw. One end of the tubing attached to the cell phone; the other she inserted into the partly opened door to the warehouse, turning the fiberoptic cable this way and that to let her peer around the corners. On the phone's screen, an image painted in blacks, greens, and yellows shifted and slid with the movements of her hand, giving her an infrared image of what lay beyond the door. She saw large open spaces . . . piles of crates . . . a trash can near the door . . . discarded junk . . . but no glow from warm-blooded humans lying in wait.

"Okay," Lia said at last. "It's clear."

Sergei Alekseev rolled the door far enough aside that they could enter. He was scared. Lia could almost smell his fear, could feel it in the way he stared and started at shadows, the way he moved, hunched over and rigid. Replacing the IR viewer, on the ground beside the door she placed a motion sensor, like several dozen button-sized devices she'd already dropped around the area. Only then did she extract a small flashlight and switch it on. "Which way?"

"Over here," Alekseev said, pointing. "I think."

"You'd better know."

"*Da*. This way."

Before moving deeper into the darkness, Lia tried her communicator again. "Verona," she said aloud. "This is Juliet."

A burst of static sounded in her ear, loud enough to make her wince. She thought she heard a voice somewhere behind the audio snow, but couldn't make out the words.

It would help if Romeo were here. Where the hell was he, anyway? With a small satellite dish on top of one of the surrounding buildings, they might have a chance of punching through this interference.

"Verona," she said again. "Juliet. Initiating Magpie!"

Again, static.

Damn. . . .

The Art Room
NSA Headquarters
Fort Meade, Maryland
1624 hours EDT

"What do you mean, we've lost her?" William Rubens demanded.

"We're just getting fragments, sir," Sarah Cassidy

replied from her console. "Her signal is intermittent. It might be the sunspots."

Rubens bit back a most unprofessional word. *Sunspots. . . .*

Desk Three's communications system depended upon a necklace of military comm satellites parked in geosynchronous orbit twenty-two thousand miles above the equator. Lia currently was working pretty far north—at sixty degrees north, in fact, the same latitude as the southern tip of Greenland. That meant that in the city of St. Petersburg, the comsats hung low in the southern sky, subject to interference from buildings, transmission lines, and any other horizon-blocking obstacles.

Add to that the fact that the sun was approaching the most active phase of its regular eleven-year cycle. Increased sunspot activity, solar flares, auroras in the highly charged upper atmosphere in the far north and south . . . it all meant that communications with field operatives could be a bit ragged at times.

But damn it all! He looked around the huge high-tech chamber known within the NSA as the Art Room, scowling at communications consoles and computer displays and satellite feeds. Hundreds of millions of dollars' worth of technology. What good was it all if it didn't *work?* . . .

"What about her backup?" he demanded.

"Romeo's not in position yet," Sarah told him. She indicated the big screen dominating one wall of the Art Room. It showed a highly detailed intelligence satellite photo of St. Petersburg's waterfront district, the southern shore of Vasilyevsky Island close against the southern estuary of the Neva River. A winking white point of light marked one of a line of warehouses along the wharf, together with the name "DeFrancesca" in white letters. A second white marker blinked several blocks away, on the *Kosaya Liniya*, accompanied by the legend "Akulinin."

"It's these buildings, sir," Jeff Rockman said. He used a laser pointer on the screen, indicating several tall warehouses and skyscrapers across the river on the south bank of the Neva. "They must be blocking her signal."

Rubens picked up a microphone. "Romeo. This is Shakespeare."

"Copy," a voice said from an overhead speaker, harsh with static.

"Where are you?"

"If you're in the Art Room, I assume that's a rhetorical question, sir," Akulinin replied. But he added, "I'm driving southwest on Kosaya. Just passing Detskaya."

Rubens glared at the satellite map on the wall above him, which mirrored Akulinin's description. *Damn it, Lia should have clapped a hold on things until her partner could get into position.* Alekseev, their Russian contact, had been too anxious, however, too skittish, and Lia had told the Art Room that she was going in, whether she had backup or not.

"We think Lia is inside the building. We're not getting a clear signal. We need you in place to relay her transmissions . . . and to watch for the opposition."

"Yes, sir." Akulinin's voice was momentarily garbled by static. Then, "I should be there in five minutes."

"Make it faster. I don't like the way this one is playing out."

Operation Magpie had been running rough since its inception. A good intelligence op *flowed,* like a carefully orchestrated ballet. Every operative had a place and a task, a precise and meticulously choreographed passage of a ballet. Of course, many of the dancers didn't even know they were performing—the local contacts, the informers, the marks, the opposition. The only way to keep them in the dance was for the operatives to *stay in com-*

plete control of the situation . . . meaning each of them was where he or she was supposed to be when he or she was supposed to be there, leading the unwilling and hopefully clueless participants in the drama through their steps and turns without their ever knowing they were onstage.

Of course things were bound to go wrong from time to time, but good operators could ad lib until things were back in control, back in the flow.

This time around, Rubens thought, someone had lost the beat, and now the situation was fast slipping into chaos.

The ballet, he thought, was fast on its way to becoming a brawl.

"What is the current position of Ghost Blue?" Rubens demanded. He didn't want to use that option, but . . .

Ghost Blue was an F-22 Raptor deployed hours ago out of Lakenheath. Stealthier than the F-117 Nighthawk, which it was currently in the process of replacing, more reliable than the smaller, robotic F-47C UAVs (Unmanned Aerial Vehicles), the F-22 had sophisticated avionics and onboard computer gear that allowed it to serve as an advance platform for ELINT, electronics intelligence, enabling it to pick up transmissions from the ground and relay them back to Fort Meade via the constellation of military comsats.

"Ninety-six miles west-northwest of St. Petersburg, sir," James Higgins replied from another console. "Over the Gulf of Finland, tucked in close by the Finnish-Russian border."

"Send him in."

"Yes, sir." Higgins hesitated. "Uh, that requires special—"

"I know what it requires. Send him in."

"Yes, sir."

Ninety-six miles. Ghost Blue would be staying subsonic to maintain his stealth signature, so that was seven and a half minutes' flight time . . . or a bit less to a point where he would be able to intercept Magpie's transmissions. Call it seven minutes.

Of course, this was a flagrant violation of Russian airspace and territorial sovereignty. At the moment, the Raptor was loitering unseen within Finnish airspace, also a violation of territorial boundaries, but not so deadly a sin as moving into Russian territory. St. Petersburg sat like a spider within a far-flung web of radar installations and surface-to-air missile sites, protecting dozens of high-value military installations in and around the city.

And if anyone could defeat U.S. stealth technology, it was the Russians. In 1999, Yugoslav forces had scored a kill, probably with Russian help, shooting down an F-117 with an SA-3 missile. The pilot had been rescued, but Yugoslav forces had grabbed the wreckage—and almost certainly turned it over to the Russians for study. The Russians, it was well known, were *very* interested in learning how to defeat American stealth technology.

Rubens had just kicked up the ante in an already dangerous game.

He reached for a telephone on the console beside him.

DeFrancesa
Operation Magpie
Waterfront, St. Petersburg
0025 hours

Well, they'd warned her she might find herself out of communications with the Art Room. There was nothing Lia could do about it now, however.

Like all Desk Three field operatives, Lia had a tiny speaker unit implanted in her skull just behind her left ear. The microphone was attached to her black utilities, while the antenna was coiled up in her belt. The system provided safe, clear, secure communications . . . usually. It was a bitch, though, when the technology failed.

Still, the satellite dish receivers at Fort Meade were a lot better as antennas than the wire in her belt. It was possible that they were receiving her back in the Art Room even if she couldn't hear them.

She would have to keep operating on that assumption.

What she couldn't rely on was the Art Room warning her of approaching threats.

She tried raising her backup. "Romeo, this is Juliet."

Nothing. And that *was* worrying. It meant she and Alekseev were on their own.

Alekseev had moved ahead and was searching the huge chamber now with his own flashlight. She could see stacks of crates, some covered in tarpaulins, looming out of the darkness.

But one large crate was off by itself, near the back wall of the warehouse. She could see words stenciled in bold, black Cyrillic lettering on the sides: *stahnka*.

Machine parts.

Akulinin
Operation Magpie
St. Petersburg
0026 hours

Ilya Ilyitch Akulinin peered ahead through fog and cold drizzle, past the monotonous beat of the rented car's windshield wipers. *Kosaya* came to a T at *Kozhevennaya Liniya*, and he turned the ugly little Citroën right.

That put him in a narrow canyon, with two- and three-story structures, most with façades of either concrete blocks or rusting sheet metal, looming to either side. Lia should be in the third warehouse in the row on the left side of the street; he pulled over to the curb and parked. He didn't want to get too close.

Akulinin was new to the National Security Agency and Desk Three. Born in Brooklyn, the son of naturalized Russian immigrants, he'd joined the Army out of high school and served as a Green Beret with the Army Special Forces, where his fluency in Russian had put him in great demand in joint operations with America's new ally, the Russian Federation. His had been among the first American boots on the ground in Dushanbe, Tajikistan, just prior to the 2001 invasion of Afghanistan.

Leaving the car, he dropped a button-sized sensor on the street, then walked across the street with casual nonchalance. If anyone was watching, they would see a tall, blond man in laborer's coveralls, carrying a large toolbox. Reaching a warehouse two down from the one Lia should be in, he stepped into the narrow junk- and garbage-littered space between two buildings and began looking for a way up. There was a ladder—or the remnants of one—but it began halfway up the side of the building. The rest had rusted away, or been stolen long ago.

Much of St. Petersburg's infrastructure showed the same advanced state of decay and crumbling collapse. Many of the buildings in this area were abandoned, and scavangers had long since stripped them of copper, lead, brass, and anything else they could pry loose, haul off, and sell.

He stepped over a pile of garbage and a set of rusted

bedsprings. Something large and furry squeaked as it scuttled from beneath an overturned two-legged chair.

At least, he thought, he shouldn't have an audience here tonight.

Except for the rats.

DeFrancesa
Operation Magpie
Waterfront, St. Petersburg
0027 hours

Removing yet another small gray case from a pouch on her combat blacks, Lia slipped a plug into her ear and held the device itself out in front of her. Instantly a staccato burst of clicks, harsh as the earlier static, sounded in her ear as numerals appeared on the small LED readout screen.

"Machine parts, my ass," she said.

"It is radioactive, yes?" Alekseev said.

"It is radioactive, yes."

"It is not harmful, I was told," Alekseev told her. "I was told—"

"Not harmful unless there's prolonged exposure," Lia corrected him. "So let's get this the hell over with and get out of here. Give me the pry."

"Huh? Oh, yes." He handed her one of the tools he'd been carrying at his belt, a short pry bar. She used it to jimmy up one of the boards on the crate's top with a sharp squeak of dry wood and bending staples, giving her a peek inside.

The crate was filled with what looked like thin sheets of metal, dull steel-gray, gleaming in the flash beam. *Bingo*.

But just to be sure . . .

Akulinin
Operation Magpie
Waterfront, St. Petersburg
0027 hours

Placing some more sensors, Akulinin emerged from the alley on a broad concrete promenade. The fog clung low and close above the black flow of the Neva. A thousand yards across the water lay a Russian Navy shipyard, but he could see no sign of it, not even a fog-shrouded light. Somewhere in the distance, a buoy-mounted bell clanged fitfully with the chop of the water, followed by the lowing of a foghorn.

Sticking to the shadows next to the line of dilapidated warehouses, he began making his way toward Lia's position.

When Ilya Akulinin had left the Army, shortly after his third tour in Afghanistan, he'd been approached by a recruiter with the the National Security Agency. The NSA was America's premier eavesdropping agency, and they, too, could use a man with his language skills, experience, and security clearances.

That had been just three years ago. After six months of training in Georgia and at the CIA's "Farm" at Camp Peary, near Williamsburg, Virginia, they'd put him at a desk listening to electronic intercepts from Russia . . . for the most part tracking the activities and the shadowy members of Russia's far-flung criminal underground.

Crouching beside a rust-clotted cliff of sheet metal, the southwestern wall of an empty warehouse, he paused to check his communications link with the Art Room. "Verona, this is Romeo," he called softly . . . but the answer came as a harsh burst of static. The surrounding buildings, concrete and metal, must be blocking the signal. He'd thought that perhaps here, directly next to the water, he would have a clean line of sight to a satellite, but evidently there were buildings across the Neva high enough to block the signal. He would need to get up high for a clear line of sight . . . and it would be better if he could deploy a small dish antenna and get a good lock on a comsat.

He touched his belt, changing frequencies. "Juliet, Juliet," he called. "Wherefore art thou, Juliet?"

"Knock it off, Romeo," was her response. Her voice was scratchy, with a lot of static, but he could hear her well enough. "We're almost done here."

"Where do you want me?"

"Sit tight. Everything's cool. Where are you?"

"On the ground, at the corner of the warehouse southeast of you, about fifty yards from your position."

"Stay put. We'll be done in a second."

"Roger that."

He waited. The damp breeze off the water made him shiver.

Akulinin had endured the boredom of a desk job for the next couple of years after his recruitment, until last month when out of the blue they'd asked him to volunteer for a routine but possibly dangerous operation in Russia. After almost two years of listening to recorded voices and filing ream upon electronic ream of reports, of *course* he'd volunteered.

He'd volunteered without ever having heard of Desk Three. And that had proven to be quite a revelation in itself.

The National Security Agency was *the* largest of America's intelligence agencies, and the most secretive, the least known. The old joke held that the letters stood for "Never Say Anything" or, more sinister still, for "No Such Agency." The NSA's charter had given it two basic missions—creating codes to ensure national security and breaking the codes of other nations. The few people who'd even heard of the organization assumed it handled nothing but SIGINT—signals intelligence—that it was a security-conscious band of mathematicians, programmers, cryptographers, and similar geeks who would never get their hands dirty on an actual black op overseas. *That* was the sort of thing left to the CIA. . . .

But the Deputy Director of the NSA, William Rubens, had approached him in one of the staff cafeterias last January and asked if he would consider transferring to the Agency's Desk Three, where both his language skills and his combat training and experience as a Green Beanie were badly needed. Some outpatient surgery to plant a communications device behind his ear, another month at a specialist school at the CIA's Farm, a quick series of briefings bringing him up to speed on something called Operation Magpie, and he'd found himself on a plane bound for Pulkovo International Airport.

And so far the mission had, indeed, seemed pretty routine. He and Lia had entered the country on separate flights, linked up in a seemingly casual encounter beneath Alexander's Column in the Palace Square in front of the Hermitage. That night, they'd picked up their special mission equipment where their support team had left it, in a well-hidden drop on the shore of a wooded lake in Primorskiy Park. Yesterday Lia had met with the furtive Sergei Alekseev in an out-of-the-way teahouse off the Nevsky Prospect while Akulinin had provided backup, listening in unobtrusively from a nearby table.

And Alekseev had brought them here.

But now things were turning sour. Akulinin had been supposed to be here forty minutes ago, before Lia and Alekseev even arrived, scoping out the dockyard and the approaches to the warehouse and setting up a satellite dish on top of a nearby building to provide reliable communications with the Art Room. No one had counted on his being stopped by that damned officious traffic inspector demanding to see his papers . . . or the need for him to bribe his way back onto the road.

Anxiously he watched the front of the warehouse, waiting for Lia and Alekseev to emerge. Smears of wet illumination from a couple of streetlights up on *Kozhevennaya Liniya* cast just enough of a mist-shrouded glow for him to see the main door and a line of loading docks above a parking lot.

Opening his workman's toolbox, he extracted his weapon—an H&K MP5K PDW—a compact little submachine gun chosen precisely because its fourteen-and-a-half-inch length would fit into a standard tool kit. He opened the folding stock and felt it lock, snapped in a thirty-round magazine, and dragged back the charging lever to chamber a round.

"Come *on*, come *on*," he muttered, half-aloud.

2

DeFrancesa
Operation Magpie
Waterfront, St. Petersburg
0029 hours

LIA USED AN AEROSOL SPRAY from a canister the size of a
lipstick to mist over one corner of the metal. She then
twisted the cylinder of her flashlight sharply clockwise.
The visible beam snapped off, but in its place, the wet
corner of the metal took on a magical green-blue lumi-
nosity, glowing brightly in the near darkness.

"What *is* that?" Alekseev asked.

"A solution of sulfonated hydroxybenzoquinoline,"
Lia replied, rattling off the tongue twister with practiced
ease. "It fluoresces in the presence of beryllium and an
ultraviolet light source." It was all the proof she needed.

"It is as I told you, yes?"

"Yes, it is. You did good, Sergei. Hold the board for me."

As Alekseev held the crate open, she took a final device from a pouch, a flexible bit of metallic foil the size
and thickness of a postage stamp, its surface precisely the
same dull gray as the beryllium shipment. Reaching gin-
gerly into the crate, she slapped the rectangle onto the
metal at one corner, pressing it hard to activate the sticky

side. Then she nodded to Alekseev, and he lowered the loosened slat, working the protruding ends of the staples back into the wood so that it was not evident that the crate had been opened.

She checked her cell phone, this time tuning it to the low-level signal emitted by the tracking device they'd just planted. When she sent a low-frequency RF signal, the microtransponder on the chip caught the pulse and flashed it back, a good, sharp signal.

"Verona, Juliet," she said, just in case they were reading her back at the Art Room. "We found the shipment. Tracking device is in place, transponder test positive. We're initiating our E and E."

Still, nothing but static.

They started for the front of the warehouse.

Akulinin
Operation Magpie
Waterfront, St. Petersburg
0030 hours

The sound of a vehicle engine startled Akulinin. It was coming from *behind,* moving toward him along the concrete wharf. He turned, crouching low to stay out of sight behind another pile of discarded rust- and rat-infested trash. One . . . no, two cars were approaching, driving up the wharf with their lights off. They raced past, then turned into the trailer-loading area in front of Lia's warehouse.

Not good. . . .

"Lia!" he called urgently. "Lia! We have company!"

Car doors slammed as men tumbled out into the night. He counted ten, five in each vehicle. It was tough to see in the dim light, but they appeared to be wearing civilian clothing. Reaching into the tool kit again, he fished out a set of OVGN6 binoculars, a compact handheld unit with two eyepieces but only a single light amplifier tube. Switching the unit on, he pressed it to his eyes.

Under LI, details sprang into sharp, close focus.

He could see their weapons. . . .

DeFrancesa
Operation Magpie
Waterfront, St. Petersburg
0030 hours

Lia and Alekseev were halfway back to the warehouse entrance when Akulinin's warning came through. An instant later, they heard the bang of car doors outside.

"This way!" Lia hissed, tugging at Alekseev's elbow. She moved off to the right, ducking behind the shelter offered by a stack of wooden crates. It took her a moment to realize that Alekseev hadn't followed her, that he was still standing in the open with a deer-in-the-headlights look to him.

A hollow boom echoed through the warehouse, followed by the sound of the main door sliding open. An instant later, the lights snapped on, the overhead lights first, then the glare of a powerful spot from the main entrance.

"*Stoy!*" a voice boomed from behind the light. "*Ktah v' takoi?*"

"*Nyeh strelyaii!*" Alekseev screamed, throwing his hands straight up in the air.

But Lia was already moving, plunging out of the light and into the shadows cast by stacks of crates to her right. She pulled her weapon from its holster, an accurized .45-caliber H&K SOCOM pistol fitted with an under-barrel laser sight and with the muzzle threaded to accept a suppressor. She was already pulling out the sound suppressor and screwing it down tight as more shouting sounded from behind her.

Alekseev, she thought, had been pretty damned quick to surrender, and she wondered if she'd been set up. It was possible. Alekseev was Desk Three's link to one of the local branches of the Organizatsiya, the Russian mafia.

It was the Organization that Desk Three was up against this time. That radioactive beryllium in the crate back there had come from a nuclear power facility in Rybinsk, stolen by members of the Russian mafia either in or working with the Russian military.

And the word was that the shipment had been sold to the highest bidder—which in this case happened to be the nation of Iran.

Beryllium possesses some interesting properties that make it invaluable within the nuclear industry. It doesn't absorb neutrons well, which makes it ideal as a neutron reflector and moderator in atomic piles. More significant, if the sphere of plutonium within a nuclear weapon is surrounded by a beryllium shell, preventing neutrons from escaping, much less plutonium is necessary in order for the weapon to achieve critical mass—and detonation.

"American!" a harsh voice snapped in English, echoing through the warehouse. "You cannot escape! Throw down your weapons and come out!"

Were the attackers mafia enforcers? Police? Or military? She had to find out. Moving silently, staying in the shadows, she worked her way around behind the stacks of warehoused crates, edging closer to the front entrance. There were several other doors to the building as well, she knew from her studies of the structure's blueprints before her deployment, but she also knew that those would be watched. She would have a better chance where the opposition had already entered the building.

Maybe. . . .

Akulinin
Operation Magpie
Waterfront, St. Petersburg
0031 hours

Akulinin watched as several of the men pushed through the open front door on the southeastern face of the warehouse. Others were spreading out to the left and right, moving to cover other entrances. He could hear shouting coming from inside, in Russian.

Through the light-intensifier binoculars, he could clearly see that the newcomers were wearing civilian clothing, which meant nothing. They might be OMON, MVD, or local militia, or they could be even Russian Army wearing low-profile civvies. The weapons they carried were definitely military-issue assault rifles, however, AK-74s and AKMs.

It was also distinctly possible that they were Organizatsiya enforcers. Alekseev had been a member of one of the major organized-crime groups, the Blues, but when Desk Three approached him, had been willing to help in exchange for asylum for himself and his family.

"Lia?" Akulinin called over the tactical channel. "You reading me?"

"Yeah." She sounded out of breath. "Who *are* these guys?"

"Not sure. They're wearing civvies . . . with military weapons. Are you okay?"

"So far. Stay put. I'm trying to reach the southwest door."

He swung his night-vision device in that direction. "You've got two goons outside," he told her. "Just waiting."

"Can you take them down?"

"Not without alerting half of St. Petersburg." The

MP5K did not have a sound suppressor, unlike some of its larger and more cumbersome cousins. Besides, the range to those two sentries was better than seventy yards . . . a hell of a long range to tap someone with that weapon. To make matters worse, a sheet-tin storage shed built just off the corner of the warehouse was partially blocking his view. He couldn't be sure there were *only* two men there.

"Copy," Lia said. "Wait a second. . . ."

The Art Room
NSA Headquarters
Fort Meade, Maryland
1632 hours EDT

"Ghost Blue is now inside of Russian airspace," Rubens said. He held the telephone handset to his ear while looking up at the big screen above him. The map's zoom had been pulled back to show the entirety of the St. Petersburg area, from Primorsk on the Gulf of Finland to Kirovsk, twenty-five miles east of the city. At this scale, the white pinpoints marking Lia and Akulinin had merged into a single point on the southern point of Vasilyevsky Island; a new flashing icon had just appeared at the extreme left, moving in across the Gulf of Finland on a heading straight for St. Petersburg.

"Is there any sign of a reaction from the Russians?" Dr. Donna Bing wanted to know.

"Not so far, ma'am," Rubens replied.

"The President will have to be informed," the National Security Director said. She sounded angry, and Rubens knew she had cause. Ghost Blue had been built into Magpie from the beginning as a backup in case of unforeseen technical difficulties, but no one had actually expected that option to be put into play.

The big danger was that Bing would use this in her power-play shenanigans against Desk Three. She'd tried it before.

"How long before the plane is over the city?"

"It won't actually overfly the city, ma'am," Rubens replied. "It will orbit about ten miles out, out over the Gulf of Finland. That should be close enough for them to pick up our agents' transmissions. He should be at his loiter point in . . . five more minutes."

"I don't like this, Rubens," Bing told him. "Not one damned bit. We have no business putting a military aircraft that deep into Russian airspace."

Rubens, always the diplomat, did not point out that the United States had no outwardly legitimate business putting human agents into Russian territory, either . . . or that both Russia and the United States had a very long history of intruding into each other's territories when they needed to do so.

Of course, both countries had long used all kinds of assets to keep tabs on each other, from human agents to spy satellites to submarines to ELINT and reconnaissance aircraft. Of those various means of gathering intelligence, though, aircraft made the people in Washington the most nervous.

No doubt the shoot-down of Captain Francis Gary Powers' U-2 over Sverdlovsk in May of 1960 had something to do with that.

"Ghost Blue knows what he's doing," Rubens told the National Security Director. "He'll know if he's being picked up by the St. Petersburg air defense net, and he has means by which he can evade any hostiles."

A rather sweeping generalization, that. Rubens wasn't trying to be misleading, but he *was* oversimplifying to a rather alarming degree. So very much could go wrong in an op like this one. It was impossible to predict how it would come together.

Or fall apart.

"Your tail is riding on this one, Mr. Rubens," Bing told him. "Keep me in the loop."

"Yes, ma'am."

But Bing had already hung up on him.

He glanced at Rockman as he replaced the handset. "We'd better tell Dean, too."

Pistol Range
Fort Meade, Maryland
1633 hours EDT

Charlie Dean squeezed the trigger twice in rapid succession, tapping off two rounds, the bangs echoing down the white-painted room. Two shots, two hits . . . squarely at the center of mass and less than two inches apart.

Recovering, he shifted his aim, gripping the pistol firmly in the classic Weaver stance, right hand holding the grip at full extension, finger lightly caressing the trigger, left hand cupping and holding the right. Accuracy in the Weaver stance depended on the interplay of forces as he pushed with the locked right arm and pulled with the supporting left.

Two more shots, two more hits, this time in the target's head.

"Target left!" a voice growled from beside and slightly behind him. Dean shifted instantly, bending his left elbow slightly to pull his right arm into line with a second target, ten yards beyond and behind the first. Again, two taps at the center of mass, followed by a third . . . and then the slide on his .45 locked open.

Raising the muzzle, he hit the magazine release and

dropped the empty magazine, before racking the slide once more to make sure the firing chamber was empty. "Clear!" he called.

Behind him, Gunny Mark Strieber mashed his thumb down on a button, and the two targets, each bearing the head and body of a vaguely human-shaped black silhouette, whined toward the firing line on their overhead tracks.

"Not bad, Marine," Strieber said. "Not too shabby at all, in fact. A bit of spread on your third group."

Both of the center-of-mass shots on the second target had struck within the inner kill zone, but they were a good five inches apart. His final shot was low, on the line between head and throat. He'd rushed it.

"Yeah, but he's still dead, Jim," Dean replied, parodying a well-known line from an old science fiction show on TV.

Strieber ticked a box off on the clipboard sheet he was holding. "I'll give it to you. *This* time. . . ."

The Fort Meade pistol range was empty at the moment, except for the two of them. Dean set his weapon—a classic Colt .45 1911A1—on the table in front of him, muzzle pointed carefully downrange, along with the empty magazine. He then pulled off his hearing protectors. The devices were decidedly high-tech, with active feedback to block out sharp sounds like gunfire while permitting ordinary speech.

"So do I pass my quals?" Dean asked Strieber.

"You could use some improvement on the OC," Strieber replied, paging through the sheets on his clipboard. Then he shrugged. "Still, for such an *old* jarhead, I'd have to say you're holding together pretty damned well."

"Ah, you *young* Marines don't have a clue."

"Cry me a river, Grandpap."

Both Dean and Strieber were former Marines—within the fraternity of the Corps, there was no such thing as an *ex*-Marine—and that fact alone created a shared camaraderie, even though his experience in the service had left Dean somewhat bitter.

Dean had been one of Desk Three's field operatives for over a year now. Strieber was employed by the National Security Agency as what was euphemistically known as a military expert consultant—which in his case translated to range boss at the NSA's Fort Meade training center.

This particular range boss, Dean thought, got a particularly savage enjoyment out of ragging Dean about his age. Some of the comments hit a little too close to the mark sometimes. Dean was in his early fifties, now, and getting through the Fort Meade OC—the obstacle course—had been a major challenge, despite his daily routine of exercise and running.

"Charlie?" a new voice sounded in Dean's skull. "This is Rockman."

"What's up?" Dean asked. Strieber raised his eyebrows but said nothing. He was used to Desk Three operators suddenly breaking into one-sided conversations, apparently with themselves. "I'm not even supposed to be on duty."

"The DD told me to let you know," Rockman said from the Art Room. "We've got a . . . situation here."

"What kind of—"

Dean stopped, forcing down the sudden upwelling of cold fear. While Desk Three would be engaged in any number of ongoing operations on any given day, there were two well into their active phases that were of particular interest to Dean because both involved very dear friends. Right now, Tommy Karr would be somewhere out over the North Atlantic, helping escort some high-level government scientist or other to a conference in London. And Lia . . .

"Lia," he said. "Is she okay?"

"You'd better get down here, Charlie. She's out of contact. She may be in trouble."

Dean bit off an unpleasant word, then forced himself

to relax. Lia was a superb agent, well capable of handling herself in almost any situation imaginable.

But he didn't like it. He'd argued point-blank with Rubens when he'd found out Lia was going to Russia. The new guy being paired with her was *too* new, too inexperienced. Dean wanted to go instead.

But Rubens had pointed out that Dean's yearly quals were due and that there wasn't time to wait while he worked his way through the battery of tests, physical drill, and proficiency exams. *Damn* the bureaucrats, anyway. . . .

"Excuse me, Gunny. The master's voice."

"I hear you, Marine," Streiber said, gathering up Dean's equipment. "Go. I'll check your gear out."

"Thanks."

"*Semper fi*, Charlie," the former Marine said, his voice grave. He must, Dean thought, have read something in Dean's voice, or in his eyes.

"Yeah. *Semper fi*."

He hurried toward the door.

DeFrancesa
Operation Magpie
Waterfront, St. Petersburg
0034 hours

Lia hunkered down in the darkness between two walls of crates, watching and listening. From here, she could just glimpse several armed men moving past the opening to her hidey-hole, could hear more shouting in Russian.

She didn't speak the language, beyond a few rough-and-ready tourist survival phrases like "Good morning" and "Where is the women's restroom?" and she didn't have her communications link with the Art Room for a running translation. Still, it sounded like they were demanding something of Alekseev, and it sounded like Alekseev was talking, talking all too willingly.

The fact that one of the newcomers had already identified her as an *American* told her that the mission had been compromised, quite likely by Alekseev. Two people breaking into a warehouse on a St. Petersburg waterfront? With crime and looting as bad as they were in the city, how would the newcomers know foreigners were involved, much less Americans?

No, someone had talked. And she was pretty damned sure she knew who.

Keeping low, she found a side passageway through the labyrinth of crates, one taking her closer to the main door. Emerging from the warren, she crept over to the southeastern wall of the warehouse, keeping to the shadows. She could see one of the bad guys now, twenty feet away, standing with his back to the open door. He was visible to her in profile, holding an AKM in his right hand, gesticulating with the left as he shouted something to the others. *"Gdeh ona? Skarei! Skarei!"*

She studied him carefully. He had a distinctive face, scarred and weathered, with a cruel mouth revealing blackened teeth when he shouted.

A garbage can sat just this side of the open door, next to a clutter of janitorial tools—a push broom, a rusty bucket and a mop, a pile of filthy rags. She thought she'd noticed the can when she'd peeked in through the fiber-optic surveillance device.

The garbage can was overflowing with trash, its round, handled lid perched atop the pile precariously. She edged along the wall, moving closer.

"Il*ya*?" she called softly, giving the name its correct pronunciation, with the accent on the second syllable. "Ilya, do you copy?"

"I hear you."

"I'm close to the main door . . . on the southeastern wall. Is anyone outside?"

"Yeah. Two goons with AK-74s. They're standing to either side, their backs to the wall."

"Can you take them?"

She heard a long pause as he studied the situation. "Yeah. They're about fifty yards away."

"Don't do anything until I tell you to."

"You're the boss."

Yeah. I'm the boss. And if I get out of this alive, I'm going to have a hell of a time explaining to my boss. . . .

Rising from her crouch, she moved toward the garbage can. . . .

Ghost Blue
Two miles north of Ostrov Kotlin
0034 hours

Major Richard K. Delallo eased back on the Raptor's throttle, bringing the powerful twin Pratt & Whitney F-119-PW-100 thrust vectoring turbofans back to a purring near idle. According to his navigational display, he'd just passed the island of Kotlin, with its naval base at Kronshtadt, to his right. At fifty thousand feet, dense fog carpeted the waters of the Finland Gulf beneath him. He could just make out the diffuse glow of city lights beneath the fog ahead, eerily peaceful and quiet. Overhead, auroras flamed and shifted like pale, utterly silent ghosts.

His radio and radar receivers, however, showed a much busier picture. Pulkovo Airport was loudest, with traffic control radars banging away to the southeast, but he could distinguish the thready pulse of military search radars as well.

Nearest and most worrying was the big Kronshtadt

SAM-2 site on Kotlin, just eleven miles away, but there were several naval bases in and around St. Petersburg itself, all on the lookout for exactly this sort of incursion.

No one was targeting him, though, and none of the signals suggested they'd picked up Delallo's Raptor. The F-22's actual radar cross section was highly classified but was widely assumed to be somewhat smaller than that of a sparrow.

He put the Raptor into a gentle, banking turn right and switched his receivers to the highly classified frequencies used by NSA operatives on the ground.

A man's voice came through. ". . . about fifty yards away."

"Don't do anything until I tell you to." That was a different voice, a woman's voice.

"You're the boss."

Delallo opened the com feed channel to Fort Meade.

DeFrancesa
Operation Magpie
Waterfront, St. Petersburg
0034 hours

Lia's biggest advantage at the moment was that damned light the bad guys were waving around. It was a handheld spotlight with a pistol grip, and a civilian with an AKM slung over his shoulder was using it to try to penetrate the shadows deeper inside the warehouse. Any dark adaptation these people had possessed when they'd entered the building had been shot to hell by now. Lia was still in deep shadow in her combat blacks, though she would have to emerge into the glare of the overhead lights to reach the door.

The two Russians were less than ten feet away now,

their backs to her. Beyond, she saw Alekseev and two more Russians. She could hear the shouts and crashes of yet more Russians moving through the labyrinth of crates.

Silently she stepped up to the garbage can, grabbed the lid by the rim, and hefted it. Moving back a few feet, she gauged the distance to another pile of warehoused crates on the far side of the main door, pulled her arm back, and flung the round lid hard, whirling it like an underhanded Frisbee.

The lid sailed past the door, rising, arcing, falling . . . then struck the top of the far row of crates with a boiler factory clatter.

Instantly gunfire erupted inside the echoing cavern of the warehouse, as one of the men with Alekseev opened up with his AKM on full-auto.

"*Tudah!*" the man with the spotlight screamed, swinging the beam to the northeastern end of the warehouse. He pointed. "*Tudah!*"

Another Russian joined in, spraying the northern corner of the room, sending up clouds of whirling splinters.

"*Stoy!*"

"*Nyeh shevileetes!*"

"Now, Ilya!" Lia called. "Take them out!"

She lunged forward.

Akulinin
Operation Magpie
Waterfront, St. Petersburg
0034 hours

Gunfire thundered from inside the building. Akulinin had been holding his MP5K on the Russian to the left of the entrance, waiting for Lia's command. It was an awkward stance. The MP5K was a ridiculously stubby weapon, even with the shoulder stock locked open, and Akulinin was trying to brace it with his left hand on the small hand-grip beneath the almost nonexistent barrel. Leaning into the recoil, he tapped the trigger, loosing a three-round burst with a sharp, harsh clatter.

Fifty yards was the upper end of the weapon's effective range, meaning he had perhaps one chance in two of hitting his target. The range was too great for trying a finesse shot at head or center of mass. Instead he aimed low, with the expectation that muzzle climb would throw at least one or two of the three rounds into the target.

Both of the outside sentries were in the process of turning as he fired, distracted from the sudden gunfire inside. The man on the left seemed to stumble as he turned, then sagged, clutching at his side as he dropped to his knees. Akulinin had already shifted his aim to the man on the right, drawing a bead and triggering another three-round burst.

The man on the right, apparently not hit, went to his partner's aid. Akulinin took aim again and tapped off two more bursts. The man staggered, slammed backward into the half-open sliding door, and crumpled to the ground. The wounded man on the left slumped into an untidy heap.

"Two down outside the door," Akulinin reported.

"Check fire!" Lia called. "I'm coming through!"

DeFrancesa
Operation Magpie
Waterfront, St. Petersburg
0035 hours

For just an instant, every armed man in the warehouse was turned toward the northeast end of the huge room, some of them firing with wild imprecision, weapons blasting away on full rock and roll.

"Prekrazhenii ogeya! Prekrazhenii ogeya!"

From five feet away, Lia put a bullet into the back of the head of the man with the spotlight, her pistol emitting a harsh *chuff* as it fired. She was so close she didn't even need to watch for the red blip of laser light marking the impact point.

She fired as she moved, holding the SOCOM pistol two-handed and stiff-armed as she tapped off two more rounds at the first target, then shifted to the man next to him. That man was just beginning to register the fact that the guy with the spotlight had been hit, the front of his skull blossoming in a nasty red burst of blood, bone, and tissue. The second man turned, mouth gaping, hands fumbling at his assault rifle . . . and pitched backward as two of Lia's rounds slammed into his throat and upper chest.

Then she was through the open door. Two bodies lay sprawled on the concrete; she leaped over one and bounded across the open parking lot.

"*Stoy!*" another voice called, not from straight behind, but from behind and to her right. "*Slushaisya elee ya budu strelyaht'!*"

She kept running.

3

**The Art Room
NSA Headquarters
Fort Meade, Maryland
1636 hours EDT**

GUNFIRE, MUFFLED BY DISTANCE, boomed and rattled.

"Now, Ilya! Take them out!"

"Two down outside the door."

"Check fire! I'm coming through!"

The words emerged from the overhead speaker, and Rubens felt an inward sag of relief. Ghost Blue was picking up Magpie's transmissions and relaying them through the satellite net to the Art Room.

"Someone's yelling at her to stop, to obey, or he'll fire," Ivan Maslovski said from his console, several stations away. He was one of Desk Three's Russian specialists, brought in to provide linguistic support for Magpie. "Should I translate?"

One of the advantages of the implanted com system used by Desk Three operatives was that an agent in the field didn't need to speak the local language. Someone listening in from the Art Room could provide a running translation and even lead the agent through a simple but appropriate response.

"No," Rubens said, shaking his head. "I think she gets the general idea."

The big map on the main display screen had been re-sized again, zooming in on two warehouses, some storage sheds, and the concrete wharf along the river. Lia's icon was moving south across the open parking and loading zone between the two warehouses; Akulinin was at the corner of the warehouse to the south.

Two new pinpoints of light, red this time, marking presumed hostiles, appeared on the satellite map. The ground sensors placed by Lia during her approach to the warehouse picked up sound and motion over a wide area and transmitted the data back to Fort Meade, where the enormous computational power resident within the Tordella Supercomputer Facility translated raw data into moving points of light on a map.

"Lia! Ilya!" Jeff Rockman said at his console. "Two hostiles, southeast of the big warehouse!"

Sounds of gunfire erupted from the speaker. "I see them," Akulinin replied. "Lia, *drop!* . . ."

Akulinin
Operation Magpie
Waterfront, St. Petersburg
0036 hours

Akulinin had risen to a half crouch, still holding the tiny MP5K tucked in against his shoulder. Lia, running straight toward him from the main warehouse entrance, was almost between him and the hostiles emerging from between the warehouse and the shed. One of the gunmen opened fire with his AK, the sharp *crack-crack-crack* echoing across the parking lot. Bullets slammed into sheet metal somewhere above Akulinin's head.

As he shouted, "*Drop!*" Lia fell to the pavement in what must have been a painful slide, hugging the ground as the gunmen behind her sprayed rounds above her. Akulinin had a clear shot, now, at one of the Russians as he emerged from between the two buildings at a dead run. With luck, he thought he'd knocked Lia down and didn't yet know Akulinin was there.

Akulinin tapped the trigger, hitting the man with a three-round burst high in his chest, knocking him backward with a wild flailing of his arms. "Three down!" he called.

Fort Meade, Maryland
1636 hours EDT

Dean climbed into his car, backed out of the parking spot, and all but peeled rubber as he left the pistol range, pulling on to Rochenbach Road and accelerating toward the towering structure visible on the wooded Maryland horizon ahead. He had to show his ID at a gate—even inside the far-flung confines of Fort Meade, security gates and checkpoints kept casual civilians and Army personnel out of the ultra-secure zone set aside for the NSA complex.

In a way, the NSA was the tail wagging the dog. Fort Meade sprawled across over some six thousand acres of the Maryland countryside between Baltimore and Washington, D.C. About nine thousand active-duty military personnel were stationed here, along with about six thousand civilian dependents in base housing, but the NSA employed over thirty thousand civilians. In fact, the Army post at Fort Meade had been scheduled for closure in the 1990s and ultimately had remained active solely to support the NSA's activities. That huge complex ahead, the large, pale ocher office building, the two black-glass, ultra-modern monoliths behind it, and the tangle of smaller buildings in between, was called the Puzzle Palace, a moniker once applied to the Pentagon but now reserved solely for the NSA's headquarters.

"Rockman?" Dean called over his radio. "I'm en route. Anything new?"

There was a worrisome pause. Then, "We're back in touch with them," Rockman said. Dean felt a surge of relief, but the feeling was overturned almost immediately by Rockman's next words. "She's in a firefight. Wait one . . ."

Dean fumed and pressed down harder on the accelerator. He turned left onto Canine Road, which put the towering ten-story monolith of the NSA's headquarters building on his right, beyond several acres' worth of parking lots.

A gunfight was the worst possible news. No matter what Hollywood cared to depict in the way of James Bond and other fictional spooks, in Lia and Dean's line of work, firefights rarely took place. In fact, a firefight could *only* mean that something had gone seriously and drastically wrong. He hadn't been briefed on her mission—such operations were kept tightly compartmentalized and shared strictly on a need-to-know basis—but he knew she was in Russia and that her op involved going in, planting something, and leaving again, all without alerting the locals.

If there was shooting, the op had been compromised.

Another turn, and Dean arrived at a parking lot outside a nondescript building sheathed in metal, almost in the shadow of the titanic edifice of the headquarters building itself. Inside was another security check . . . and an elevator ride, plunging deep into the bedrock beneath the facility, and two more security checkpoints after that, both requiring handprint, voiceprint, and retinal scans.

One curious feature about the NSA facility at Fort Meade: there were no visible room numbers, no corridor names, nothing to help any visitor who didn't know exactly where he was going.

They didn't make it easy to access the Art Room.

And with very good reason.

Akulinin
Operation Magpie
Waterfront, St. Petersburg
0037 hours

The second gunman ducked behind the corner of the shed, then emerged to trigger another burst of full-auto fire at Akulinin. He was almost invisible against shadows unrelieved by the pale light from the lone street lamp on Kozhevennaya. Akulinin waited, aiming at the point where he'd seen him last; two seconds dragged past, and then he saw movement, a dark shape as the Russian half-emerged from cover once again.

Akulinin squeezed the trigger again and the dark mass vanished. "Art Room!" he whispered. "Did I get him?"

"Both targets are down," Rockman's voice replied in his head. "They're not moving. Can't tell if they're KIA or not."

The sensors scattered by Lia around the building early in the op could pick up remarkably faint noises—breathing, footsteps, even heartbeats at a close enough range. The NSA computers would keep painting the targets where the devices sensed them, only letting the icons fade away some minutes after *all* motion and sound from the target ceased.

They would have to chance it. "C'mon, Lia!"

He kept his weapon trained on the corner of the shed as Lia scrambled to her feet and dashed for cover. As she reached his position, several more armed men began spilling out of the warehouse through the main door.

There was no time for carefully aimed bursts. He thumbed his weapon's selector switch to full-auto and mashed down the trigger, sending a second-long volley into the gaping door.

One Russian crumpled on the spot as the others pulled back and bullets banged into the sheet-metal sliding door. Then Akulinin's weapon ran dry, the slide locking open as the final spent cartridge spun away into the darkness and clinked against the wall to his right.

"You okay?" he asked.

Lia nodded. She was rubbing her arm. "A little scraped up. . . ."

"C'mon. Before these clowns get themselves organized!" Taking her elbow, he guided her past a tangle of discarded and rusted machinery, leading her back toward the alley through which he'd approached the waterfront a few minutes before.

"How about it, Jeff?" he asked aloud. They stopped just short of the alley as Akulinin pocketed the empty clip from his weapon and snapped in a fresh magazine. "Anybody waiting for us around the corner?"

"We're not picking up any movement in the alley or near the car," Rockman's voice replied. "Hostiles are coming out of the warehouse now . . . but cautiously."

They ducked into the entrance to the alley and made their way northeast, emerging again on Kozhevennaya Liniya. After a careful look up and down the street and at the staring, empty windows of the buildings towering around them, they crossed the street at a casual stroll to the parked white Citroën. Lia climbed into the back while Akulinin slid in behind the wheel.

"*Damn!*" he said.

"What's the matter?" Rockman and Lia answered in almost perfect unison.

"My toolbox," he said, glancing back across the street. "I left it back there."

"Leave it," Lia told him. "The opposition is going to be all over that waterfront."

"What's left in the tool kit?" Rockman asked.

"The OVGN6," he said. "Some rope and climbing gear. Some spare mags for the H and K. Some ground sensors." He hesitated. "And the satcom."

That last was not good. The AN/PSC-12 com terminal with its two-foot folded satellite dish was a compact and extremely secret unit small enough to be carried in a small briefcase—or a workman's toolbox. The black box attached to the terminal contained computer chips and encryption codes that the National Security Agency emphatically did *not* want to fall into unfriendly hands.

Stupid! Akulinin told himself. *Careless, sloppy, and stupid! . . .*

"We've alerted your support team," Rockman's voice said. "They'll try to make a recovery when things quiet down."

"What the hell kept you anyway, Ilya?" she demanded as he started the ignition and pulled out into the street.

"Traffic inspector," Akulinin replied. "He flagged me over just before the Exchange Bridge and demanded to see my papers. The bastard kept me there cooling my heels for half an hour before he finally agreed to accept a five-hundred-ruble fine for my, ah, violation."

"Five hundred rubles," Lia said. "About what . . . twenty dollars at the current rate? I didn't realize the local cops were such cheap dates."

Akulinin drove slowly up the road, passing the warehouse that had been the focus of Operation Magpie. A number of shadowy figures were visible in the parking lot . . . more than he'd seen originally exit the two cars on the wharf. An open-bed truck was parked on the road in front of the warehouse, suggesting that reinforcements had arrived. How many goons had he and Lia been facing, anyway?

He kept his eyes on the road ahead, not looking at them, and they, apparently, didn't connect passing traffic on the street with their quarry. By deliberately driving at a sedate and unhurried pace toward, then *past* the hunters, rather than pulling a U-turn in the middle of the street and rushing off in the opposite direction, Akulinin might throw off any would-be pursuit.

It was a bit of tradecraft Akulinin had learned only recently, during his induction into the secret ranks of Desk Three, and he didn't yet entirely trust the psychology behind it. What if the opposition had people in some of the surrounding buildings, watching the street? What if they'd seen him and Lia emerge from the alley and get into the car? A quick call over a walkie-talkie from a hidden lookout and that whole pack of Russian gunmen could be swarming after them in an instant.

He drove with one hand, the other gripping the MP5K on his lap, out of sight but ready for action.

Several of the men glanced at the Citroën as it cruised past, but there was no other reaction.

"Okay, I guess they didn't track us," he said.

"They're not pros," Lia said. "All muscle, no brain."

He set his loaded weapon on the seat beside him, relaxing slightly . . . but only slightly. "Your fancy duds are in a bag on the floor of the backseat," he told her.

"I see it."

For the next several blocks, Akulinin was treated to the sounds of tantalizing rustles, snapping elastic, and shifting movements in the backseat. Determined to maintain a professional bearing, he kept his eyes rigidly on the road, not even checking the rearview mirror.

Professional or not, though, nothing said he couldn't try to *imagine* the scene at his back. Lia was an extremely attractive young woman. . . .

Soon Kozhevennaya came to a T at Bol'shoy Prospekt, and Akulinin turned left, then began hunting for the entrance to a parking lot. The cruise ship terminal was just ahead. The atmosphere of their surroundings, he noticed, had changed dramatically, clean, well kept, well lit, and open, where only a few blocks away the decrepit warehouses and abandoned machine shops brooded over fog-shrouded darkness.

St. Petersburg, Akulinin knew, depended these days upon making a good impression on tourists for its economic survival.

Pulling the Citroën into an empty space in the parking lot, Akulinin took a moment to peel off his worker's coveralls. These went on the floor under the passenger side seat, leaving him in a suitably tacky short-sleeved shirt that fairly shouted "American tourist." The MP5K, along with Lia's SOCOM pistol, went under the seat. Pulling a small stack of papers and booklets from the glove box, he stepped out of the car. Lia was transformed, wearing a pale blouse displaying significant cleavage over a short black skirt and heels, with a sweater over her shoulders to keep off the night chill.

Gallantly he held out his elbow. "It's been a lovely evening out on the town, my dear. Shall we?"

"I don't go out with Romeos," she told him, smiling. "At least . . . not with *any* old Romeo. . . ."

Together, they started for the building entrance that would take them through to the cruise ship.

Ghost Blue
Ten miles west of St. Petersburg
0056 hours

Dick Delallo was holding his F-22 in a gentle right turn above the Gulf of Finland when the threat receiver lit up and the warning tone sounded over his headset.

"Haunted House, Ghost Blue," he called. "The Oscar Sierra light is lit. Do you copy?"

"Ghost Blue, Haunted House," came over his headset. "Copy. You are clear to get out of Dodge. Over."

"Ah . . . roger that." He was already tightening his turn, trying to identify the source of the threat. "On my way back to the barn."

"Oscar Sierra" was a pilot's inside joke, using the phonetic alphabet letters for *O* and *S* to represent the words "oh, shit." It meant someone was painting him with a target acquisition radar and that a missile launch could be imminent.

The signal from the threat radar, though, was weak and intermittent. The frequency suggested that he'd been briefly painted by the acquisition radar code-named Spoon Rest by NATO, which meant they were trying to target him with an SA-2 Guideline.

Guideline was the NATO reporting name for the Lavochkin OKB S-75 surface-to-air missile—ancient by the standards of modern military technology but still deadly. Gary Powers' U-2 had been downed over Sverdlovsk in 1960 by a barrage of fourteen SA-2 missiles, a barrage that had also managed to take out a MiG-19 trying for an intercept.

Just because Delallo was being painted didn't mean the Russian radar operator could see him. In fact, the operator probably didn't. The whole point of stealth technology was to prevent the energy of the threat radar from returning to the emitting dish, rendering it blind. Still, the pucker factor for Major Dick Delallo was rising.

Operation Magpie
Waterfront, St. Petersburg
0058 hours

Akulinin and Lia walked up a low concrete ramp toward the entrance to the cruise ship wharf. The ship, the North Star Line's *St. Petersburg 2,* was tied up on the pier just beyond the high chain-link security fence, her lights ablaze stem to stern, like beacons promising refuge and safety.

To get to that promise, they needed to go through the security checkpoint and customs. A pair of Russian MVD police eyed them suspiciously as they approached.

"Good evening!" Akulinin called in his most jovial dumb tourist's voice. "Some fog out tonight, huh?"

One of the men pointed his weapon, an AKM, at Akulinin's chest. "You stop, please," the man said in thickly accented English. "Passports."

Akulinin and Lia both handed their passports over.

The guard grunted as he looked at the stamps, then added, "Your other papers. ID. All."

When these were produced, the guard went through them with microscopic attention while the other watched the two with a sullen expression.

"Your papers not in order," the first said after an interminable examination.

"Why?" Akulinin said, putting on his best naïve-American expression of surprise and confusion. "What's the matter?"

"Our papers were perfectly in order before," Lia said. "What the hell is going on?"

"Papers not in order," the Russian said, his broad Slavic features betraying no emotion. "You come with us."

"We're alerting Mercutio," Rockman's voice said in Akulinin's ear . . . and presumably in Lia's as well. "Stall them."

Stall them, Akulinin thought. *Right. Maybe I should do a little soft-shoe? . . .*

"Mercutio"—Romeo's best friend in *Romeo and Juliet*—was running Magpie's support operation in St. Petersburg, the stage crew behind the scenes who let Lia and Akulinin play their roles. The support team was on board the cruise ship, which was serving as a kind of impromptu safe house for the op.

Of course, in the original *Romeo and Juliet* Mercutio had been killed in a duel.

Akulinin hoped to hell it wasn't going to come to that.

Ghost Blue
Twelve miles west of St. Petersburg
0058 hours

Major Dellalo pushed the throttle forward as he brought the stick back, sending the F-22 higher and yet higher into the thin, cold air. The SA-2 Guideline had a range of about thirty miles and a ceiling of sixty thousand feet. Thirty miles from the SA-2 site on the western end of Kotlin Island would reach to the far end of St. Petersburg to the east and halfway back to the Finnish border to the west.

His F-22 had two advantages if the Russians could actually see his plane and target it—speed and altitude. The top speed of the F-22 Raptor was classified, of course, but his baby could crowd Mach 2.5 and have knots to spare. Her service ceiling was sixty-five thousand feet.

It should be possible to get above a Guideline's reach, and while he couldn't outrun one—the SA-2 had a velocity of about Mach 3—the speed of his Raptor would make it nearly impossible to catch if the missile was launched from a stern position.

His major disadvantage at the moment was the fact that Kotlin Island, with its SAM base, lay only eight miles ahead, and perfectly blocked his route back to international airspace out over the Baltic Sea. If they wanted to, they would get at least one clear shot at him.

How had they spotted him? His radar screen showed a number of targets in the immediate vicinity, all at lower altitudes. Most of them were civilian aircraft, but a few had the characteristic signatures of Russian military aircraft. A JOINTSTAR E-3 Sentry AWACS over the North Sea was feeding him data on possible threats. There were two radar returns that worried him in particular . . . streaking in over Vikulova, from the south. The Sentry was identifying them as MiG-31s.

His threat receiver lit up again, and this time it stayed lit and he heard a high-pitched warble in his ears, which meant that the threat radar had switched to a high PRF tracking mode. So the Russians did see him, after all.

"Haunted House, Haunted House, Ghost Blue," he called. "Oscar Sierra, repeat, Oscar Sierra. They have a lock."

"Copy that, Ghost Blue."

He suppressed a momentary flash of anger. It would be nice if "Haunted House," the radio handle for the op controllers at Fort Meade, had something *constructive* to say.

The warning tone wailed away incessantly. A launch, a dim flash of light in the gloom immediately below . . .

By lowering a wing he could see the exhaust plume of the missile climbing through the fog, its exhaust illuminating the white haze below. A second missile rose close behind the first, followed by a third.

He was still climbing, passing through fifty-four thousand feet.

It was time to go balls to the wall. He slammed the

Raptor's throttles full forward, angling his thrust to increase his rate of climb.

Behind and below, the missiles began angling toward their high-flying target.

The question for tomorrow, Dick Delallo thought, was how did the Russians see this stealth aircraft? The pressing question of the moment, however, was how to avoid being shot down.

The Art Room
NSA Headquarters
Fort Meade, Maryland
1658 hours EDT

Charlie Dean walked past an Army sentry at the door and stepped at last into the Art Room, his glance taking in the dozens of technicians and communications specialists huddled over consoles around the room, the numerous monitors, and the huge central display on the back wall. Currently the main display showed a satellite map of a large city, but he couldn't tell, offhand, which city it was. A river snaked in from the right, then split to flow to either side of a large triangular island. Major highways were highlighted with yellow or white lines.

Two time readouts glowed in the upper right corner. It was 1658 hours Eastern Daylight Time; wherever Lia was at the moment, it was just before one in the morning.

Radio chatter sounded from speakers overhead.

"Haunted House, Haunted House, Ghost Blue. Oscar Sierra, repeat, Oscar Sierra. They have a lock."

"Copy that, Ghost Blue."

William Rubens looked up as Charlie Dean walked in. "They're okay," he told Dean without preamble. "*She's* okay."

"Good to hear it," Dean replied, keeping his voice neutral. Rubens knew that he and Lia were close, but neither of them wished to say so aloud.

Dean was afraid that someday someone higher up the bureaucratic chain of command would declare that his and Lia's relationship was somehow unprofessional. In the modern, Orwellian world, the illogical, whimsical boundaries of political and sexual correctness could be redrawn overnight.

"Jeff said they were in a shoot-out?"

Rubens nodded. "Things went bad. We think our contact was a dangle."

The word was tradecraft slang for someone deliberately exposed to a hostile intelligence service in order to lure that service's agents into a trap or a compromising position.

"For? . . ."

"Not now, Dean," Rubens said, his voice brusque. "We've still got a . . . situation."

Dean almost asked if the situation involved Lia but managed not to say anything. He knew Rubens well enough to know the Deputy Director would fill him in when—and if—he needed to know.

"Launch! Launch," an anonymous voice said over the speaker. Dean could hear the stress behind the words. "I've got three missiles coming up, probably Guidelines. Maneuvering . . ."

Dean understood Rubens' curtness better now. If an NSA asset—in this instance meaning an aircraft somewhere over the Gulf of Finland off of St. Petersburg—was being shot at, that was a serious situation indeed. The bad old days of the Cold War were long gone, but that didn't mean there weren't occasional problems with America's new ally the Russian Federation. In the global arena, more often than not, Russia still reverted to her old role as America's adversary. In fact, in some ways it was tougher now.

In the Cold War, at least, you knew the Russians were the enemy. Nowadays, they were nominal allies in the War on Terror, as long as their cooperation didn't interfere with their own agenda, such as dominance of the former Soviet republics, or the struggle for influence in the Middle East, or the developing international crisis in the Arctic . . .

Jeff Rockman was looking up at the big screen. Dean watched him a moment, then walked over to the coffee mess tucked away against one wall. He returned a moment later with two cups full. He set one on Rockman's workstation desk.

"Hey, Charlie. Thanks."

"Who's shooting at whom?" Dean asked, looking up at the display. It was, at the moment, singularly unhelpful, showing a swath of satellite-revealed sea and land from Estonia to Finland. A white icon labeled "Akulinin and DeFrancesca" was blinking on the waterfront in St. Petersburg. Another, marked "Ghost Blue," was drifting slowly north a few miles off the coast of Kotlin Island.

Rockman glanced at him, then back at the board. "The Russkies just popped three SAMs at our comm relay aircraft. It's getting a little tight over there."

"Sounds it." He could see three icons marking the SAMs, now, painted in by the computers running the display. They were swiftly closing the range between Kotlin and Ghost Blue. Other icons showed in the area as well, some orange, meaning unknowns, others red, meaning confirmed potential hostiles.

" 'Russia shoots down American aircraft inside Russian territory,' " he said, mimicking a newscaster's voice. " 'Details at eleven.' The old man's a bit worried about the publicity, you know?"

Dean did know. The National Security Agency and Desk Three were successful only insofar as they could elude the spotlight of public awareness. The encounter over the Baltic could well mean *big* trouble for the Agency.

Especially if the opposition managed to shoot the plane down.

As for the pilot hanging it all out for God and country at the top of the world . . . well, Charlie Dean thought, these Art Room chess players were pretty focused on the big picture. If the pilot got bagged, they would cry tomorrow. Or perhaps next week.

Ghost Blue
Two miles northeast of Ostrov Kotlin
0059 hours

Major Delallo waited until the missiles were trailing him. He was passing fifty-eight thousand feet, now, but the trio of Guidelines was closing faster than he could climb. It was going to be damned close.

Past fifty-nine thousand feet. The missiles were five miles below him, still coming strong at three times the speed of sound.

Delallo had a tactical choice. He could keep climbing, hoping to get above the SAMs' operational ceiling, and hope to hell the Russians hadn't packed a surprise into those three birds, like some extra altitude. Or he could turn into the missiles and try to force an overshoot. The good news was that his F-22 was much more maneuverable than the missiles.

A major factor was those two MiG-31s back there. They were climbing, too, and coming fast. The MiG-31 Foxhound was the best interceptor in the Russian arsenal, and it could both outclimb and outrun the F-22. It would not be a good idea to let them get too close.

Delallo gauged the right moment, then popped chaff, hauling around on the stick and vectoring his engines sharply in a grueling, high-G Herbst maneuver.

The Herbst maneuver—also known as the J-turn—was only possible for high-performance aircraft like the Raptor. You needed post-stall technology, meaning vectored thrust engines and advanced computer-operated flight controls to manage a high enough angle of attack to pull it off. As he brought his nose around and down, his velocity fell off dramatically. The missiles were closing quickly— he could see their exhaust plumes out of the corners of his eyes as he concentrated on flying his plane.

An alarm sounded as he went into a stall; only his vectored thrust engines, delicately handled in sharp, precise movements, kept him properly oriented. In seconds he had the aircraft on a new flight path, down and into the missiles, which were about sixty degrees off his nose. He was forcing them into a maximum rate turn, a maneuver he knew he could win. Accelerating now at full throttle and assisted by the relentless pull of gravity, he was past the first Guideline before it could even begin to alter course . . . then past the second, then the third. All three had failed to hack the turn.

Now he eased off the throttles and made a gentle turn back toward his original heading, still descending and accelerating past Mach 2.

Grunting hard against the savage, crushing pressure of the G-load, Dick Delallo automatically swept his eyes over the threat indicator panel. It was blank.

So he was surprised when a missile he had neither seen nor known was tracking him exploded twenty feet below his right wing. Surprised? It was the shock of his life. After the flash and thump that rocked the plane, the surprise was that he was still alive.

4

Operation Magpie
Waterfront, St. Petersburg
0059 hours

A BRIGHT, SILENT, SMALL FLASH briefly flared in the western sky, somewhere above the fog, but no one on the ground saw it.

The guard was deep into his perusal of Akulinin's papers. Akulinin had the feeling that these guys weren't exactly the MVD's finest. More like armed postal clerks, trying to decide if he needed more stamps.

"You need pay special tax," the guard said, waving Akulinin's Russian visa.

As if that were news! "Okay, okay," Akulinin said. "*Skol'ka?* How much?"

The two guards exchanged a glance; Akulinin could see the avaricious smiles shielded behind their eyes. "Eight hundred rubles," the first said.

Akulinin nodded. "I can take care of that." He reached for his billfold.

"No," one of the guards said, gesturing with his AKM. "You come with us. Pay at—what is word? At office."

"Listen, Ivan," Akulinin said, throwing some swagger into his voice and manner. "Our papers are fine. You're just trying to shake us down for a little *vzyatka,* am I right?" He deliberately mispronounced the word, which was Russian for "bribe."

The guards' faces hardened. "You come." There was no mistaking the threat behind the words. *"Now!"*

The Art Room
NSA Headquarters
Fort Meade, Maryland
1659 hours EDT

"I'm hit!" Ghost Blue's voice called. "I'm hit!"

Dean stared at the flashing icon marking a point just north of Kotlin Island in the Gulf of Finland, the coffee in his mug forgotten. He could hear the ragged edge of stress in the pilot's voice.

The controllers in the Art Room, all of them, remained silent. Dean could almost feel the oppressive sense of helplessness as the drama played itself out on the other side of the world.

"Damn it," Sarah Cassidy said from a nearby console. "I *told* them they should use F-47s!"

Dean said nothing. Like every other branch of the American intelligence community, the National Security Agency had for years been working toward what Dean considered to be an impossible goal—the ability to conduct operations with a complete lack of risk for human operators. Spy satellites, remote sensors, unmanned aerial and submarine drones—billions of dollars had been spent over the past few decades to reduce the possibility of human casualties to zero.

The same mentality had haunted the Pentagon for decades now as well. Was it possible to fight a war relying solely on robotic weaponry, smart bombs, and invisible aircraft, to win a war without the images of body bags on the nightly news to remind the people at home that victory always came at a price?

Within the intelligence community, the list of serious intelligence failures over the past few years only emphasized the fact that all the spysats in orbit couldn't provide the same depth and detail of data as a single well-placed human agent, HUMINT as opposed to SIGINT.

That, in fact, had been a large part of the philosophy behind the creation of Desk Three. The NSA was the principal agency responsible for America's SIGINT capabilities, but there were times when you needed *people* on the ground, down and dirty.

Or, in this case, in an F-22 Raptor above the icy waters of the Gulf of Finland.

"Okay . . . okay, I've got it . . . ," the voice said over the speaker. Dean could hear the whoop and buzz of alarms in the background. "Starboard engine's out, but I've still got control. Heading for Waypoint Tango Bravo."

"Ghost Blue, Haunted House," Rockman said, touching a microphone transmit switch. "Be advised that there are two, repeat, two targets closing on you. Probable Foxhounds. Over."

"Yeah, I got 'em on the gadget. I'll be over international waters before they catch me."

"Copy that. Good luck, Ghost Blue."

The answer was unintelligible.

"Sir!" Cassidy called out. "We've lost Magpie's signal!"

Ghost Blue had been relaying radio communications from the Magpie team but must have now moved out of range.

"That's okay," Rubens replied from another console down the line. "We're getting their signal through Mercutio and the safe house."

"Who's Mercutio?" Dean asked, joining Rubens.

Rubens looked up at Dean, then back to the big display.

"One of our agents," Rubens said with cryptic understatement. "He's in charge of the backup team for Magpie."

"Where the hell are they, anyway?"

"At a commercial dock in St. Petersburg, Vasiliev Island. They've been detained by MVD guards at a customs checkpoint—"

"I thought you said they were *safe*?"

"Comparatively speaking. Mercutio is moving in now to get them through to the safe house."

"Safe house?"

"A cruise ship tied up at the dock. Lia and her partner are posing as tourists. They're close enough to the ship now that we're getting their personal com transceiver signals boosted through from a satellite dish on the ship." He shook his head and sighed. "It was a close one tonight, Charlie."

Tonight. Dean smiled at that. It was, in fact, just past five in the afternoon. Rubens was so attuned to the mission in St. Petersburg right now that he was thinking in terms of it being past one in the morning.

"So why *did* they decide to use a Raptor?"

"My call," Rubens told him. "We've been having real problems with communications in high latitudes lately. Sunspots. A live pilot gave us better flexibility."

Dean nodded. It was as he'd suspected. Desk Three often used unmanned drones like the F-47C to relay radio communications and datanet streams from operations on the ground, but sometimes you needed the human element.

"Do we have an ID on the opposition?"

Rubens gave him a sour look. "Hardly. Lia and her partner weren't exactly in a position where they could stop and take pictures. Best guess at the moment is that they're Russian mafia."

"Oh, joy."

Dean's first op with Desk Three had been in Siberia—

that had been where he'd first met both Lia and Tommy—so he knew a little about the Russian mob. Any intelligence agent inserting into modern Russia had to know at least a little about the Organization, if only because he *was* going to find himself working with them, one way or another.

"Tambov group?" he asked. The Tambovs were the largest and arguably the most dangerous of the Russian Mafia groups in St. Petersburg.

"You're going to tell us."

"Oh?"

"I'm sending you to St. Petersburg, Charlie. I want to know who set us up . . . and what they were after."

"When do I leave?"

"ASAP. Briefing tomorrow morning, oh–nine hundred hours, Green Room. You'll get your legend then. We'll have a commercial flight booked for you by tomorrow afternoon."

"Then I guess I'd better pack." He looked up at the large display. "Cruise ship, huh? Sounds great. I know Lia could use a vacation."

"She won't be there for long."

"Oh? Why not?"

"Because the Russian Mafia tried to take her down tonight, Charlie. She managed to get away, but the opposition is tough . . . tough, capable, and determined." He turned a cold gaze on Dean. "I want to know exactly what the hell's going on over there. And I want our people safe and out of there. You hear me?"

"I hear you."

"Good."

Dean listened to the concern in Rubens' voice. The old man didn't usually show his worry, not this clearly, at any rate.

Dean wondered just what it was he was about to get himself into.

Operation Magpie
Waterfront, St. Petersburg
0101 hours

Akulinin considered his options—which weren't many and weren't good. Every sector of life in modern Russia was dominated by corruption, from ordinary citizens on the street to the highest ranks of government and industry. These two customs guards, almost certainly, were engaged in a bit of opportunism—shaking down a couple of rich American tourists who happened to be alone on the waterfront in the middle of the night.

It was just possible that something more was going on here, that the guards were part of the ambush back at the warehouse and that Akulinin and Lia were about to be turned over to the mafia. That didn't feel like the answer, though. These two, he was certain, were just looking for a little graft.

But why did they want to take the Americans someplace else?

They couldn't afford to be taken out of sight. If these guys *weren't* in with the mafia, they might be soon, once the word went out on the street that the two Americans had escaped. It could be a pretext to rob the two of them. Or . . .

He glanced at Lia. She *was* a most attractive woman. . . . These two bastards might have something else in mind besides money.

The watch phrase for all intelligence agents was "low-key." You never called attention to yourself, and kept a carefully tailored and very low profile. Still, there were times when it paid to be as loud and as obnoxious as possible.

He folded his arms belligerently. "I'm not goin' *any-where,* fella!" he bellowed, his voice echoing from the walls of nearby buildings. "I know my rights! I am a citizen of the United States of America, and you can't tell me where to go or what to do!"

Startled, both MVD guards took an awkward step back. Akulinin stepped forward, crowding them, jabbing an angry forefinger at them both. Their English probably wasn't up to deciphering more than a word in three, but it was clear that Akulinin's emotion needed no translation.

"What kind of country are you running here, anyway? I demand to see the American consul! I demand to see your commanding officer! I demand—"

Psychologically, the tables had turned. The guards still had the assault rifles, but the large American, screaming into their faces, had the advantage.

"*There* you are, my friend!" a second booming voice called across the pier from the *St. Pete 2*'s gangway. "What has been keeping you, eh?"

James Llewellyn strode toward the customs checkpoint, an impressive figure in a heavy trench coat and a goatee that Lenin himself would have been proud of. Llewellyn was in his sixties, with a deeply lined and weathered face, but he moved with surprising strength and self-assurance. One of the MVD guards turned, raising his weapon, apparently grateful for the interruption, and barked, "*Stoy!*"

Llewellyn, Akulinin knew, was Welsh—normally he worked for the National Security Agency at the Menwith Station in Yorkshire—but his Russian was excellent. More, his understanding of Russian psychology was excellent.

"*Nyeh kulturnii!*" he snapped at the guard in Russian. "*Do you know who I am?*"

He waved an open wallet at them, presumably flashing an ID. Both MVD guards came sharply to attention.

For the next five minutes, Llewellyn reamed both

guards a variety of new bodily orifices. In his role as an American tourist, Akulinin had to pretend he didn't understand a word, but he listened with genuine admiration as Llewellyn—code name Mercutio—discussed in vivid detail the guards' mysterious parentage, lack of breeding, improper upbringing, nonexistent education, subhuman intelligence, and utter lack of culture, never once repeating himself and never once actually telling the two just exactly who he was supposed to be. The Russian syllables, thick as glue, flowed from his lips in an uninterrupted and uninterruptible torrent.

"These are my friends!" he said at last, gesturing at Lia and Akulinin. "My very special friends! They are coming with me! *Vih panimayiti?*"

"*Da, grahjdaneen!*" both guards stammered. "*Panimayu!*"

"Get your papers," Llewellyn said in English, still glaring at the two guards as if he could nail them in place by sheer force of personality. "Start for the ship."

Lia snatched up passports and ID, then touched Akulinin's shoulder. "Move it!" she said, her voice a harsh whisper. Together, they walked past the checkpoint, past the pier facility with its shabby hotel and gift shop, and onto the wharf. As they walked up the pier toward the gangway, Akulinin felt an intolerable itch building between his shoulder blades; if the guards decided to start shooting . . .

Llewellyn remained to have a few more choice words with the MVD guards. When Akulinin glanced back, he saw a sheaf of Russian currency changing hands as Llewellyn paid their "tax." He then turned and strode after them, his trench coat billowing after him like a cape.

Once on board the ship, Akulinin allowed himself to begin to relax. "Was that a shakedown?" he asked Lia. "A simple extortion? Or something more?"

"I don't know," Lia said. She looked at Llewellyn as he joined them. "How about it, Lew? Was that random, or were they after us?"

"Hard to tell," Llewellyn replied. "*Probably* random . . ."

"But you never can tell in this game," Lia said, completing the thought. "Thanks for coming to our rescue."

Llewellyn grinned at them. "The new kid here was doing pretty well on his own. You did exactly right, son. The Russkies respect authority. Step on their toes until they apologize. If you throw your weight around, chances are they'll cave."

"Yeah," Lia said. "Either they cave or they'll shoot you." She seemed to sag a bit. "Where are our staterooms?"

"I'll show you. But . . . don't get too comfortable. The word from the Art Room is you'll be on the move again soon."

Akulinin leaned against the ship's railing and studied the vista ashore. A more depressing location for a cruise ship dock would be difficult to imagine. The facility was brightly lit, but hemmed in by ancient apartment buildings, close huddled and clotted with shadows, and industrial complexes, rusted, decrepit, and cloaked in night.

In the parking lot, two men approached the rental car Akulinin had acquired that afternoon—part of Mercutio's cleanup team. They would drive the vehicle someplace safe and get rid of the incriminating evidence—weapons and clothing—hidden inside.

He looked to the right, toward the southeast. The warehouse district they'd just escaped from lay just beyond the port's security fence.

"Can I help with the post-op cleanup?" Akulinin asked. He was still thinking about the equipment he'd left behind. *Stupid, stupid, stupid. . . .*

"We'll take care of it," Llewellyn told him. "I need to

take you two down to the communications center. They need some data back at the Puzzle Palace."

"Does it have to be tonight, Lew?" Lia said. "I'm dead on my feet."

"Tonight, Lia. There'll be time for rest later." He turned and led them toward a companionway ladder descending into the ship.

Ghost Blue
Approaching Waypoint Tango Bravo
0119 hours

Major Delallo stuffed his nose down and raced toward the surface of the sea. He only had one engine, but he had it wide open and was using gravity all he dared. Down he went into the gloomy night, trying to get against the surface of the sea, where he would find some measure of safety from his pursuers. He just might make it. He allowed himself that much hope, at any rate.

A worrisome thump began sounding from somewhere aft, causing the aircraft to shudder and buck. He'd been supersonic when he took the missile. Now, as the thumping became louder and the instrument panel jiggled and danced, he automatically retared the throttle and let his speed bleed off as he tried to assess the damage to his mount. The missile's detonation had peppered the Raptor with shrapnel, knocked out one engine, and played merry hell with his avionics. The slipstream might be peeling back a piece of the aircraft's fuselage, and that might make for a bright, easy target on hostile radars.

He loved the Raptor, an astonishing piece of advanced aircraft engineering. Its one weakness, though, was a variation on the Murphy Effect. When things went wrong with the aircraft, *everything* went wrong, and in the worst possible way.

In February of 2007, Delallo had been one of six pilots ferrying a flight of F-22s from Hickam Air Force Base to Kadena, Okinawa. The moment they'd crossed the international date line at the 180th meridian, the computers on all six aircraft had crashed, taking out all navigational systems and most communications. It had been good weather and broad daylight, thank God, and the flight had managed to form up on their tankers and make it back to Hawaii. Forty-eight hours later, the problem had been fixed and the flight had continued, but the incident had been a nasty reminder of how complicated these systems were. The F-22's software ran to something like 1.7 *million* lines of code, most of it concerned with data processing for the incoming signals from the aircraft's sophisticated radar systems.

Right now, he was getting squat from the radar—both the AN/ALR-94 passive receivers and the AN/APG-77 AESA, or Active Electronically Scanned Array. His navigational systems had crashed as well, leaving him as in the dark as he'd been that afternoon over the central Pacific.

The one electronic system that appeared to be working was his SAS, or Signature Assessment System, which threw up warning indicators when wear and tear on the aircraft had degraded its low radar signature to something the enemy could detect. Of course, the warning indicators might themselves be a glitch in his failing electronics . . . but he didn't want to count on that. *Something* was thumping hard against the side of the aircraft aft, like the monotonous beat of a flat tire on pavement.

The aircraft shuddered, the thump growing savagely more severe. The aircraft was completely fly-by-wire, with three flight-data computers that actually flew the aircraft. All his stick and rudder controls did was make inputs to the computers. They were doing all right just now, but if the structural damage exceeded the computers' ability to cope, or the control throw available, he was going to tumble out of the night sky.

He was down to four thousand feet now and still descending. Where were those MiGs? His gadgets were silent—which probably meant they were damaged—although it might mean the Russian jocks had headed home for the night.

Delallo searched the darkness behind him as he keyed his radio. "Haunted House, Haunted House, Ghost Blue," he called.

No response. If a data stream was still going out, it wasn't registering on his almost nonexistent instrumentation.

Well, at least he was going in the right direction, west. Waypoint Tango Bravo was inside Finnish waters, a few miles south of Kotko. A support vessel was there. If necessary, he could bail out and hope for a pickup.

That, however, was an option he didn't want to have to use. Those black waters, patchy with streamers of fog, were frigid even in late spring. Not even his flight suit would keep him alive for long, and with his navigation systems out, finding the support vessel would require outrageous luck.

Still looking aft, he saw a flash high and behind him, at four o'clock.

The northern sky flamed and shimmered with the cold glow of aurora. His eyes searched the deep twilight. . . . Now he saw it, a streak of fire in the night.

A missile contrail, a thin white thread arcing around to intercept him.

Oh, shit! There was no way his crippled Raptor could manage the maneuvers necessary to evade an incoming air-to-air missile.

He grabbed the lanyard for his ejection seat and yanked up hard. . . .

St. Petersburg 2
Waterfront, St. Petersburg
0230 hours

Lia was exhausted. She'd been at it for an hour and a half, with no results yet. She was ready to pack it in.

"Anything, Lia?" Rubens' voice said in her ear.

She leaned back in her chair and looked around the stateroom, a fairly luxurious suite booked under the name Stevens but occupied by Llewellyn. It was the "communications center" only by virtue of the laptop computer set up on a desk in the corner.

A cable ran from the back of the laptop to a suitcase-sized unit beside the desk, the hardware necessary to link Lia's computer to a satellite dish above the cruise ship's bridge. A black-box encryption device guaranteed her that her connection to the NSA computer center back at Fort Meade was secure.

The laptop was open. Prominently displayed on the flat 19-inch screen were front and profile views of a bearded, rumpled-looking man with watery eyes. He might have been a thief . . . or, just possibly, an unshaven accountant. A third photo showed a candid surveillance shot of the same person, taken in a crowd on a city street.

No.

"Nothing so far," she said. She was alone in the room. Llewellyn was off somewhere with his cleanup team, while Akulinin had gone to his stateroom to get showered and shaved.

She pressed the enter key, and another face came up on the screen. A big man with an ugly scowl.

No.

Enter.

"I'm not sure we're going to find him this way," she

told Rubens. "How many mug shots of Russian Mafiya big shots do you have, anyway?"

"About a thousand," Rubens told her.

Another face, small, thin, and mean. He looked like a school bully Lia once had flattened on the playground.

No.

Enter.

She'd been through about half of the database already, focusing on those members of the Russian crime syndicates known to be operating in and around St. Petersburg.

No.

Enter.

"This is getting us absolutely nowhere," she said.

"It's important that you look through these pictures while impressions are still fresh in your head," Rubens told her.

No.

Enter.

With a start, she recognized the next face—the man with bad teeth she'd seen in the warehouse.

5

Airport Hilton
Heathrow Airport, London
0815 hours GMT

THE POUNDING ON THE DOOR woke him.

Tommy Karr was on his feet next to the bed before he was fully awake. It took a moment for him to remember where he was. London. He was in London. The pretty flight attendant had agreed to have dinner with him, and they'd spent a pleasant evening chatting over espressos in a coffee shop. *What was her name? Julie. Yeah, Julie . . . something.*

"Hey, Karr!" a voice called from the hallway. The pounding sounded again. "We've got to get moving!"

He went to the door and peered through the spy hole. It was Payne, one of the FBI agents, blue suit, sunglasses, ear wire, and all. Karr opened the door partway. "Yeah?"

"Get dressed, lover boy. We're rolling in ten."

"Be right there."

Minutes later, shrugging into his sport coat, Karr walked through the hotel lobby at Dr. Spencer's side. Agents Payne and Delgado were with them. Agent Rogers was bringing the rental car around to the parking garage pickup.

"I trust you had a . . . pleasant night?" Delgado said, smirking.

Karr considered several ribald replies but then simply shrugged. "I slept okay."

He knew the three Federal agents were about as thrilled to have him along as he was to be there. There'd been, Karr understood, quite a squawk out of the FBI overseas department when they'd learned the National Security Agency wanted to include an agent on Spencer's security team. Karr's presence implied that someone higher up the totem pole didn't think the FBI could handle the job . . . or, possibly, it was just another inside-the-Beltway turf war. The Bureau's director had finally agreed, but only on condition that the FBI agents—the real agents—had operational control and final responsibility for Spencer's security . . . meaning, among other things, that Delgado, Payne, and Rogers would be solely responsible for Spencer's safety at the hotel, sharing shifts in his suite.

Which was how Karr had found himself at a posh airport hotel with an evening free for socializing with a pretty flight attendant. He smiled to himself. Maybe the three Bureau suits were just jealous.

★   ★   ★

In the hotel lobby, a woman sat on one of the overstuffed leather sofas, watching from behind a copy of *The Sun*. As the four men—including her date from the evening before—strode across the polished marble floor twenty feet away, she felt a delicious shiver of excitement. Those men, she'd been told, were Russian spies posing as Americans, and MI5 had recruited her, *her*, Julie Henshaw, to help in the surveillance.

The young man, Tommy, had been engaging, charming, and smart, not at all the image of your typical Russian spy. He'd actually seemed quite nice.

But as the four walked through the double glass doors into the hotel garage, she reached into her handbag and extracted a cell phone. Punching out a memorized number, she held it to her ear. "They're on their way."

And she replaced the phone, mission accomplished.

★　★　★

According to the itinerary, Spencer was scheduled to give his talk at Greater London's City Hall, in the speaker's hall popularly known as London's Living Room. He was one of a number of speakers attending the European Summit on Global Warming, a prestigious event sponsored by the Royal Society. London City Hall was located on the south bank of the Thames close by the Tower Bridge, a straight-line distance of just sixteen miles, but a considerably longer and more indirect drive by way of London's tangled roads and highways.

"Okay, George, this is Gordon," Karr said, using the communicator hidden in his collar. George and Gordon were handles sometimes used by the Art Room and agents in the field; they came from the name of the Civil War officer who'd given his name to Fort Meade—General George Gordon Meade. "We're on our way to the garage. How are we doing?"

Marie Telach's voice came back in Karr's ear. "We've got you, Tommy. We're picking up feeds from the hotel security camera. Wave!"

Karr glanced up and saw the small security camera mounted up near the ceiling and grinned . . . but decided not to wave as well. They were supposed to be keeping a low profile, after all.

"Switching to the camera in the parking garage," Telach told him. "All clear outside the doors."

Through the lobby, down some steps, and out through two sets of glass doors to the parking garage, where Karr spotted the second camera.

This, he knew, was the reason Desk Three had been roped in on a simple security detail. The National Security Agency possessed a remarkable asset in its ability to monitor electronic links of all kinds virtually worldwide: Any place where security cameras existed—like that one mounted atop the garage attendant's shack across the driveway—the Agency's signal-monitoring staff could trace the feed, duplicate the signal, and essentially peer over the security system personnel's shoulders. It provided an extra layer of security for high-risk targets such as Dr. Spencer.

Karr still wasn't sure why Spencer was considered so important but had by this time reconciled himself to the fact that someone thought him to be worth Desk Three's time, attention, and resources. He felt he'd gotten off to a bad start with Spencer yesterday and hoped he could smooth things out this morning.

A few minutes later, Rogers drove the rented black Lincoln up to the door and the three climbed in, Delgado in front with Rogers, and Payne and Karr in the back, to either side of Spencer. Karr was momentarily startled to see the driver seated on the right, then remembered where he was.

"Okay," Karr said as they pulled out of the garage. He glanced at the surrounding traffic, checking for possible tails. "We're rolling."

"Give us some video, will you?"

He pulled a small device from his jacket pocket, the size of a thimble, with a glassy lens on the narrow end. He stuck the base against the seat in front of them.

"Smile, Doc!" he said conversationally. "You're on *Candid Camera*!"

"Very funny," Spencer replied. "Are these melodramatic measures really necessary?" He sounded somewhat scornful.

"Beats me," Karr replied cheerfully. "If we're lucky, we won't find out."

The car pulled out onto the street, made several turns, and picked up the M25, heading north.

"Seriously, Doc," Karr said after a few moments. "I'm sorry if I rubbed you wrong yesterday. I really *am* interested in what you have to say."

Spencer was going through some papers in his briefcase, which he had open on his lap. "Will you be at my presentation?"

"Of course."

"Then you'll hear what I have to say then."

"Yeah, well, I'm curious, though. My . . . people have been having some communications problems lately, y'know? And they were blaming sunspots. I wondered if that was what you were talking about, you know, with this solar model theory of yours."

Spencer studied Karr for a moment over the top of his glasses, as though considering whether the agent was serious or setting him up for some kind of practical joke. "The solar model," he said finally, "is simply an updated and extremely detailed computer simulation, which incorporates far more data than climatologists have had access to before. It demonstrates once and for all that humans really have very little impact on such a large and complex system as global climate. And . . . No, the oil companies are *not* paying me for my opinion."

"Look, I was out of line with that crack, Doc. And I apologize."

Spencer seemed somewhat mollified. "Accepted."

"So, this theory of yours. You're saying global warming is from the sun becoming more active?"

"Essentially. You may know that the sun goes through an eleven-year cycle which oscillates between more and less activity. We're coming up on the next solar maximum in the next year or two, and so there *has* been an increase in sunspots, which *do* cause interference with communications here on Earth.

"However, what I've been looking at are cycles of much greater magnitude . . . hundreds, even thousands of years. According to the computer model I've developed, the warming we are experiencing now is perfectly natural, and not a product of human carbon dioxide production through industry or fossil fuel emissions. In fact, it demonstrates that much of the rise of carbon dioxide in the atmosphere over the past century is due to warming temperatures, which release CO_2 from the oceans."

"So . . . the rising CO_2 levels are caused by global warming, but global warming is not caused by rising CO_2. . . ."

"Precisely."

The car swung around a gentle curve, threading its way through a major junction to pick up the M4 near Thorny, heading east toward the city. It was a gloriously clear late-spring day in apparent defiance of the tradition that British weather was always cold and wet.

Karr and Spencer chatted amiably for the next ten miles, discussing global climate change. Occasionally Karr turned in his seat, checking the traffic behind. There was one vehicle, a white Mazda, that was nagging at his awareness.

"So, global warming might be a *good* thing?" Karr asked.

"I know," Spencer said. He chuckled. "Absolute heresy. People committed to the gloom-and-doom scenario really don't like to hear about that part. But higher levels of carbon dioxide mean accelerated plant growth, worldwide. Bigger crops. Expanding forests. Longer growing seasons. Canada and Siberia, especially, could begin producing bumper crops of corn and wheat. But, somehow, the news media doesn't seem to feel that *good* news is worth broadcasting."

"Tommy?" Marie Telach's voice said in his head. "This is George."

" 'Scuse me," Karr said, holding his left hand up to touch his ear. He reached into his inside jacket pocket and pulled out a cell phone. "Gotta take a call."

"I didn't hear it ring."

" 'S on vibrate. George? . . . Go ahead." He held the cell phone to his ear, pretending to talk on the phone. It was a useful fiction that avoided unnecessary explanations about high-tech and high-secret gadgetry.

"You seen the white car on your tail?" Telach asked.

"The one that picked us up in the front of the hotel?" Karr replied. The vehicle, a white Mazda, double-parked in front of the hotel entrance, had dropped in on the Lincoln's tail as they'd pulled out of the parking garage. "Yeah. I've been watching him."

"Think you can give us a close-up?"

Karr glanced back. Traffic was growing heavy as they entered the outskirts of Greater London. On the M4, the other vehicle had fallen back to a comfortable distance, but now, as they skirted a traffic circle and plunged into West London, the Mazda was following closer, only about thirty feet off their back bumper.

"Sure thing." He turned and aimed the cell phone over the back of the Lincoln's rear seat. The unit appeared to be an ordinary camera phone, but when he adjusted the lens and pressed the imaging key, the picture that came up on the phone's display was far sharper, with a much higher resolution, than ordinary commercial cell phone cameras. Karr touched another button on the keypad, and the image grew brighter, with higher contrast. The sky and the surrounding buildings were washed out in the glare, but the people in the Mazda were clearly visible.

"What *are* you doing?" Spencer asked.

"Getting some snaps for the family back home."

He touched another key, and the camera zoomed in for a close-up—tight enough that he could image the individual faces of each of the four people in the car, three men and a woman.

"Hold it steady a sec," Telach told him as the phone transmitted video in real time via satellite back to the Art Room. "Can you adjust to get a better angle on the guy in the back? Okay. Got 'em all. Have they made any threatening moves?"

"Nah." Karr turned the camera slightly, studying the man in the left-hand front passenger seat. He was young, dark complexioned, and serious looking, and he was holding a cell phone against his ear.

Karr brought the phone back to his ear. "Who are they?" he asked.

"Don't know. But we'll run the video through our database and see if we can pick up some matches."

"Looks like the guy in front's talking to a friend."

"That woman in the back isn't your, um, little friend from last night, is she?"

Karr felt himself flush. He'd thought he'd disconnected from the Art Room channel before they'd figured out he was spending the night with someone. His night with Julie hadn't been against regulations, exactly—the FBI agents had been responsible for Spencer's safety in his hotel room—but there were some back at the Puzzle Palace who might see last evening as an unprofessional mingling of business and pleasure.

"No," he said at last. He couldn't see her well, since she was partly blocked by the driver, but Julie was blond while this woman was a brunette. "She's not."

"Just checking," Telach told him. "Your secret is safe with me."

Yeah . . . and five or six others who were pulling Art Room duty last night, Karr thought. "Okay. Bye." He snapped the phone shut and pocketed it.

"I take it we're being followed?" Spencer asked. Payne started at that, then turned to look through the back window.

"Possibly."

Spencer looked disgusted. "That's what I just don't understand about this. Who would want to kill me?"

"Your work is pretty controversial, isn't it, Doc?"

"Yes, certainly. The Royal Society is going to have a fit when I give my talk today, because they've bought so completely into the gloom-and-doom scenario. And plenty of others in the field hate my guts because I'm threatening their grants. But this is *science,* damn it! Scientists don't go around *killing* each other when they disagree!"

"Gives a whole new spin to the idea of peer review, doesn't it?" Karr glanced back again. The Mazda had dropped back a little but was still on their tail as they continued east on the Great West Road, now the A4. The Thames River was just a block to the south. They glimpsed stretches of it from time to time through factories, row houses, and commercial properties.

"We're honestly not sure, Doc," Karr said. "But the word on the street over here is that someone wants you dead . . . one of the environmentalist groups."

"That's ridiculous. Who? Greenpeace?"

"Almost. Ever hear of a group called Green*world*?"

"Certainly. A militant-activist spin-off from Greenpeace. Started in . . . I don't know. Oh-five?"

"Two thousand six, actually."

Karr didn't say more. The NSA had a long history of tangling with Greenpeace. Back in July of 2001, Greenpeace protestors had stormed the NSA station at Menwith Hill, in Yorkshire. Later, the NSA had supposedly eavesdropped on Greenpeace members while looking for international terror links . . . and ended up in an involved lawsuit with the ACLU over domestic spying and abuse of power. The court case eventually had been settled in the Agency's favor, but there was no love lost between the two organizations. In 2006, some of the more vocal members of Greenpeace had split off to form their own organization—a far-left environmentalist group called Greenworld that embraced the lunatic-activist fringe too violent and extremist for the original Greenpeace.

"Are you saying Greenworld wants me dead?"

"Those blog death threats were by individuals with a Greenworld connection," Karr said. "And the e-mail of some of the Greenworld members we've been keeping tabs on indicates they were *very* interested in your itinerary."

"Are you saying the FBI has been reading their electronic mail? Isn't that . . . I don't know, *illegal*?"

"Like some of your work, Doc, some of it is . . . *controversial*."

Karr didn't want to open that particular can of worms, not here, not now.

For now, it was enough to get Spencer where he needed to go, without interference from the people in the Mazda behind them.

The Art Room
NSA Headquarters
Fort Meade, Maryland
0405 hours EDT

With a five-hour time difference, nine in the morning Greenwich Mean Time was four in the morning in Maryland. Marie Telach leaned back in her chair and rubbed her eyes with the heels of her hands. *God,* she was tired. . . .

Telach was, in fact, the Art Room supervisor, answering only to William Rubens himself when it came to directing missions in the field from the Deep Black ops chamber. Rank doth have its privileges, and she wasn't required to stand night duty.

Tonight, she'd chosen to stay on. Things had been insanely busy since yesterday afternoon, with not one but *two* major ops going down simultaneously—Sunny Weather and Magpie. Of the two, Sunny Weather was, so far, completely routine. No one really expected any problem there until later today, if then.

But Magpie had gone seriously wrong. Communications had failed, two field agents had come *that* close to getting caught or killed, and the F-22 deployed to fill in the communications gap had been spotted and downed. Telach had worked through the evening processing data coming through from Lia in St. Pete, trying to identify one of the gunmen she'd met, then helped coordinate the search for Ghost Blue. She'd finally sent Rubens home around eleven—all but ordering him to go home and get some sleep—but elected to stay on herself, working through the night. A little after three in the morning, Tommy Karr had checked in from London, and she'd been running him as he rode in a rented car into the heart of London.

She'd spotted the car following Spencer's vehicle through the video bug Karr had planted on the seat. Karr had transmitted a series of still and video images from his cell phone, which Telach had in turn relayed to the Vault.

Now, however, she found herself staring at a new window opened on her computer screen. The Vault had come through.

The Vault was Deep Black's database, containing an enormous volume of information—much of it video or still photos, together with police records, surveillance reports, and debriefing notes—all gleaned from a variety of sources all over the world. Despite the name, which sounded like something completely passive, a storage space, perhaps, the Vault was a far-flung computer network that maintained active links with other criminal and terrorist data banks, including those run by the FBI, Interpol, and Mossad. In fact, the Vault's very first international link some years ago had been with Komissar, the huge computer network at Wiesbaden run by what then had been the West German police.

Of course, the Germans hadn't realized at the time that they were sharing all of that data on international terrorists with the National Security Agency.

The Vault operations center, located down the steel-paneled passageway from the Art Room, possessed, like the Art Room itself, deeply buried fiber-optic links with the Tordella Supercomputer Facility half a mile northeast of the NSA headquarters building. Telach had submitted the best of Karr's photographs of the four people in the car following him. For almost thirty minutes, the Tordella super-Cray computers had crunched through the images, comparing hundreds of separate elements—the distance between eyes, the shapes of noses and chins, the angles of cheek bones, the arcane geometry of facial planes and their relationships with one another—looking for matches among the hundreds of thousands of photographs in the NSA's memory stacks and, when necessary, those of other military and police networks worldwide.

She clicked on the window and saw the results of the search.

Damn. . . .

She checked the time again—0410 hours, just past four in the morning. She didn't want to wake him . . . but Rubens was going to want to know about this.

She reached for the secure phone.

Tooley Street
Approaching London City Hall
London
0912 hours GMT

"What the hell is going on up there?" Rogers said from behind the Lincoln's wheel. "A parade?"

"Uh-uh," Karr said, leaning forward so he could see through the windshield in front. "Looks to me like some kind of protest."

After cutting through West London on the A4, they'd picked up the Strand in front of Nelson's Column in Trafalgar Square, crossed to the south side of the Thames over the Waterloo Bridge, and, with only one missed turn, made their way across Southwark to Duke Street Hill, close by the London Bridge, picking up Tooley near the London Bridge City Pier. According to the GPS mapping program in the car, they were a block south of the Thames and within a hundred yards of the entrance to the underground parking for City Hall.

The street, however, was clogged with protestors.

It looked, Karr thought, like a bad flashback to the street protests of the sixties. Hundreds of people, most of them young, but including folks old enough to have protested against the Vietnam War, surged along Tooley and gathered in massed crowds along the sidewalks. Several buildings appeared to have been taken over wholesale; American flags, flying upside down, were much in evidence, as were a variety of handheld signs. "Independence from America!" was a popular bit of signage. So were "Global Warming Is Real" and "Save Our Planet." Some of the marchers carried Greenpeace signs or placards bearing the Greenpeace logo. Some were awkwardly dressed in bulky costumes meant to represent factory smokestacks or oil-drilling rigs.

"All of this for you, Doc?" Karr asked.

"I shouldn't think so," Spencer replied. "I'm hardly the *only* voice of sanity at the symposium."

"Yes, but you were the voice singled out on that blog for silencing," Karr pointed out.

The London Environmental Symposium, he knew, had attracted a lot of attention in the world press. The United States was under increasing international pressure to ratify the Kyoto Accords, which required signatory nations to accept mandatory limits to greenhouse gas emissions— carbon dioxide, in particular—in order to halt or slow global warming.

Of course, putting caps on such emissions would also put a cap on the economies of member nations. Billions of dollars were at stake, along with industrial growth, employment levels, and the very standards of living for first-world nations such as the United States and Great Britain. Britain had signed and ratified the Protocols; the United States had signed them, but that signing had been a purely symbolic gesture, since they carried no weight until they were ratified by Congress.

Dr. Spencer was spokesman for a point of view seen as heretical by the environmentalists, that global warming and cooling were functions of solar output, and human activity affected climate little, if at all.

"I don't see any Greenworld signs," Payne said.

"I don't think they're that much into peaceful demonstration," Karr said. "But you can bet they're here." Turning in his seat, he glanced at the vehicles behind. Odd. The white Mazda had turned off somewhere within the past block or two, after staying on their tail all the way from the airport.

"Doc, I suggest you get down on the floor."

"Mr. Karr! Really! I—"

"Do what he says," Payne said. The FBI man sounded nervous. "Get down and out of sight."

Grumbling, Spencer complied. The back of the Lincoln was roomy enough—just—for him to find enough space to scrunch down on his knees, his head between Payne and Karr and below the level of the windows.

Rogers leaned on the horn, then pounded on it. Reluctantly, people in the crowd parted ahead, allowing the Lincoln to move slowly forward. Embattled London bobbies helped; several were visible in the crowd, trying to get the people off the street. One pointed at the Lincoln and waved them ahead.

"There's the entrance," Payne said. "Thank God."

They turned left off of Tooley Street and descended a ramp leading to the garage. Before vanishing underground, Karr had a glimpse of London City Hall.

It was one of the oddest buildings Karr had ever seen, like a black-glass and steel egg tilted backward from its perch above the river.

Karr had read about the thing as part of his mission briefing. Opened in 2002 as a part of the More London development of the area near the Tower Bridge, it had originally been intended to be an immense sphere suspended above the Thames, but later design changes opted for a more conventional anchoring on solid ground instead. Native Londoners referred to it as Darth Vader's helmet, a misshapen egg, or a titanic human scrotum, and the Mayor of London himself had called it a glass testicle. The design, Karr had read, was supposed to be make the building energy-efficient by reducing its surface area, and at some point in the future, the London Climate Change Agency was supposed to attach solar cells to the exterior.

Inside the structure were housed the offices of the Mayor of London and the Greater London Authority, or GLA. A spiraling walkway circled all the way up the building's ten stories just inside the darkened transparency of its curving surface, giving access to the top-floor meeting and exhibition space known as London's Living Room.

From this angle, Karr thought as the garage entrance blocked the structure from view, the building seemed a dark and forbidding presence and not living room–like at all.

Behind them, someone with a megaphone was leading a chant: "USA, CO_2! USA, CO_2. . . ."

And the crowd's mood, Karr thought, was damned ugly.

"Gordon, this is George," Telach's voice sounded in his ear.

"Go ahead," he replied. He knew from the sound of her voice that he wasn't going to like this.

6

Rubens' Office
NSA Headquarters
Fort Meade, Maryland
0525 hours EDT

WILLIAM RUBENS EMERGED from the elevator on the ninth floor of the NSA headquarters building and walked down Mahogany Row, past the Agency's executive offices. At the far end, behind a blue door set into a blue wall displaying the Agency's shield, was Room 9A197—though of course it was not marked as such—the offices of DIRNSA, the Director of the NSA.

Next to the DIRNSA suite was Rubens' smaller office. He slipped his key card into the lock to his suite, put his hand inside the shrouded keypad to type in a code entry, and opened the door. Five swift strides took him through his secretary's office—she wasn't in, yet, the lucky bitch—and up to his office door.

Inside, he pressed a control to reduce the polarization of the large window that made up one wall of his office. The window was double paned, not for reasons of energy efficiency, but to foil certain high-tech eavesdropping equipment that used laser beams to translate vibrations on window glass into intelligible conversations.

The window looked west across the still night-shadowed Maryland countryside. Traffic on the Baltimore-Washington Beltway was light but picking up with the beginnings of rush hour. Beyond, streetlights illuminated the parking lots within an industrial park housing a number of businesses and defense contractors—every one of them connected via various black budget links with the NSA.

It was, Rubens thought, an enormous and endlessly complex empire. Sitting down behind the desk, he pressed his thumb against a reader, then booted up his computer.

He'd spent the past twenty minutes going through the mandatory security checks at multiple stations on his way up, but these last few security measures were second nature. Rubens himself had ordered the implementation of several of them and would sooner have broken an arm than the protocol of NSA security procedures.

After a moment, his screen display lit up with the NSA logo—an American eagle, a flag-bedecked shield on its chest and on a blue background, grasping a large key in both sets of talons. Above was the legend "National Security Agency" and below, the words "United States of America."

Rubens yawned. He'd not gotten much sleep before Telach had phoned him at home. The information she had was classified level red . . . which meant that it was not to leave the confines of NSA headquarters. He could have had her transmit the data to his home computer—there was a secure dedicated line for just that purpose—but . . . protocol.

An icon was winking at the bottom of his screen, indicating a waiting live message.

He touched a key. "Yes?"

Marie Telach's face appeared in a window on the display. "Mr. Rubens?"

"Yes, Ms. Telach. God . . . you look terrible. Up all night?"

"Yes, sir."

He nodded. She'd said something about staying over when she'd unceremoniously shooed him out of the Art Room last night.

"So . . . what's up?"

"I thought you would want to see these, sir," Telach told him.

A second window opened on his screen. Faces stared out at him from simulated file folders on the display.

There were four people in all, three men and a woman, each with his or her own electronic dossier.

"Sunny Weather picked up a tail when they left the hotel at Heathrow," Telach told Rubens. "That was about two hours ago. Agent Karr managed to transmit high-res images of the driver and three passengers. We ran them through the Vault and, well, this is what popped up."

Rubens clicked on the top file, opening it on his screen. There were a number of photographs inside, most of them obviously candids, a long PDF file with pages of text, and a brief video. Among the photos were the full-face and side images of police mug shots.

" 'Jacques Mallet,' " he said, reading the introduction of the text file. " 'French. Joined Greenpeace in 1993. Arrested by the Sureté, '94, for trespassing during protests outside a French nuke submarine base . . . and again in '95 for trespassing at Muruoa.' " The French had conducted hundreds of nuclear weapons tests at Muruoa, in French Polynesia, over a thirty-year period that ended, finally, in 1996. Greenpeace had been active in protesting those tests.

He kept reading. " 'Co-founded Greenworld in 2005 after a split with the Greenpeace committee. . . . ' "

There was more, lots more, but he clicked to the second file. " 'Yvonne Fischer. English. Greenpeace in '98.

Arrested in 2001 for her part in the protests at Menwith Hill. Greenworld, '06.' " One surveillance photo showed her perched precariously atop a chain-link fence, waving a Greenpeace flag. Several of the huge, white golf ball radomes of Menwith Hill were visible in the landscape behind her.

He clicked again. " 'Kurt Berger. Germany. Recruited straight into Greenworld, 2007. No police record, but surveillance photos have placed him repeatedly with hardcore Greenworld agents.' " *Click.* "And . . . 'Sergei Braslov. Russian.' " His eyebrows arched high on his forehead. "Well, well, well. . . ."

"I thought you'd be interested in Braslov, sir," Telach said.

"Soviet Army in the eighties," Rubens said, skimming the PDF file's intro. "Rank of major. Served in Afghanistan, wounded twice, won the Order of Lenin . . . as well as the Order for Service to the Homeland in the Armed Forces, Second Class. In '87, he moved to the GRU . . . more awards and decorations, promotion to colonel . . . then transferred to the MVD in '91."

Rubens stared at the file for a long moment, his forefinger tapping absently on the mouse as he scanned through the document. "It says he joined Greenpeace in December of '98. . . ." He glanced at Telach's face, waiting patiently in the other window on the screen. "But under the name Johann Ernst. False ID and papers."

"We think he was a plant, sir," Telach said.

"Of course. An agent provocateur. Why else would a high-ranking member of the Russian Federation's Ministry of Internal Affairs join an international organization like Greenpeace?"

The Soviets might be gone, but the dark labyrinth of Russian power politics continued to churn as it had since the days of the czars.

Greenpeace International, so far as Rubens was concerned, was a gadfly, though a well-meaning one. They'd racked up some impressive environmentalist victories worldwide . . . in the campaign to reduce unnecessary whaling, for instance. If they were an annoyance for the industrial West, however, with their protests against nuclear power and industrial pollution, they were doubly so within the borders of the former Soviet Union. There, the nation's disintegration had left a festering morass of environmental problems—toxic waste spills and dumps, radioactive zones, dying seas and rivers, and abandoned rust-belt factory complexes, a situation driven to crisis proportions by a fast-disintegrating infrastructure, the breakdown of authority, local wars, and rampant corruption.

Greenpeace International had opened an office in Moscow in 1989. Since that time, Greenpeace Russia had conducted a number of protests within the country—against the resumption of nuclear testing on Novaya Zemlya, against a pipeline near Lake Baikal, against the illegal timber trade with Finland. With a long tradition of nonviolent protest and confrontation, the organization had for almost twenty years struggled to call world attention to the fast-worsening environmental situation within the Russian Federation.

And they'd scored some important successes with their David-and-Goliath tactics. For the most part, however, the Russian authorities maintained the same gray, grim, and stolidly monolithic presentation of absolute control as their Soviet predecessors. News reports and photos only rarely made it out of the country or had much of an impact among native Russians.

In 2006, some of the more radical elements within Greenpeace had split off to form a new group.

Greenworld was smaller than Greenpeace, more secretive, more elusive, but at the same time, more confrontational. During the past couple of years, they'd staged several massive protests in Great Britain, Belgium, and Russia, grabbing a lot of media attention with flashy banners, hurled rocks and bottles, and mass arrests. Where Greenpeace insisted on using purely nonviolent means to get its message across, Greenworld was not quite so fastidious. Several of its members had been arrested for sabotaging an oil refinery in England, and in 2007 the car-bomb death of a German industrialist had been blamed on the group, though no arrests had been made. The NSA had been maintaining a file on the group, which appeared ready and willing to use terrorist tactics, unlike its parent organization.

One week ago, a routine NSA electronic intercept had picked up a blogger's page that talked about assassinating Dr. Spencer at the Environmental Symposium in London. The blogger was a London teenager . . . but the kid had a police record. He'd been arrested for his part in the Menwith Hill affair and, five years later, had joined Greenworld.

The tidbit had been passed up the bureaucratic totem pole inside the Washington Beltway and ultimately trickled back down to Rubens' desk. The State Department was taking seriously the possibility that Greenworld was going to try to kill Spencer.

As a result, Rubens had initiated Operation Sunny Weather, assigning Tommy Karr to the FBI team escorting Spencer to London and back.

"Braslov," Rubens said, reading further, "was one of Greenworld's founders?"

"We think so, sir," Telach told him. "We don't have much intelligence on Greenworld's inner workings, but we know that 'Johann Ernst' was a close associate with Peter Strauss and Emily Lockyear, who were the official founders."

"And here he is tailing Sunny Weather." Rubens considered this for a moment. "Have you passed this tidbit on to Karr yet?"

She shook her head. "No, sir."

"Let him know who he's dealing with. I—" Rubens stopped in mid-sentence. "Uh-oh."

"Sir?"

Rubens had been leafing through the electronic pages of Braslov's file. He'd come to a photo of the man, grainy and poorly focused, obviously a surveillance photo taken of Braslov at long range, but clear enough to show a ragged scar on the left side of his face. He appeared to be standing on a beach, laughing. With him were a pretty, bare-breasted blonde in red bikini briefs and an older man with a bushy mustache. Both men wore swim trunks and short-sleeved shirts, both shirts open enough to reveal a number of tattoos on their torsos as well as their upper arms.

"Who is this?" Rubens asked, clicking and dragging a square over the second man. "Do we have a positive ID?"

Telach's eyes shifted as she studied her own monitor, then typed in a command at her desk. A new window opened on Rubens' display, filling up with text and photos.

"Yes, sir. Grigor Kotenko."

"That," Rubens said slowly, nodding, "is what I was afraid of. And these tattoos on Braslov's chest?"

Telach nodded. "I ran those through the Vault as well. It's difficult to make out details, of course. But it looks like both men are sporting eight-pointed stars on their chests in blue ink."

Mafiya, then . . . the Organizatsiya. The Russian mafia made extensive use of tattoos to convey a wealth of data about a person's rank, reliability, and criminal history. Often the tattoos were acquired in prison or within the

Russian gulag, where the rubber heels of shoes were melted down and mixed with soot and urine to produce a characteristic blue ink. The eight-pointed star indicated a very high rank within certain Mafiya groups.

This was not good. Not good at *all*.

The Green Room
NSA Headquarters
Fort Meade, Maryland
0912 hours EDT

Individual rooms and corridors within the Puzzle Palace might not be outwardly named or numbered, but human nature being what it was, unofficial names continued to arise as needed. The Art Room was one such necessity; the Green Room was another, one of a hotel's worth of meeting rooms, briefing rooms, and auditoriums where face-to-face business within Crypto City could be conducted.

Dean took a seat at a long oval table that was already fairly well occupied. The walls—painted a pale shade of hospital green, hence the name—were hung with photographs of presidents and NSA directors past and present, and an American flag and a flag bearing the NSA seal flanked a large flat-panel wall screen at the head of the room.

He didn't like these gatherings. Once, Rubens had tried to keep them small and informal. Things went a lot faster that way. Cleaner. More efficient. Lately, though, these sessions had begun resembling the dog-and-pony shows put on at the Pentagon, with staffers, officers, and assistants all trying to grab face time with the Deputy Director. There was even an Air Force general at the table this morning, a man named Blakeslee, who was a Pentagon liaison because of the presence of the F-22 in Operation Magpie. Several of the people present, Dean knew, were lawyers, there solely to present opinions on any legal risks the Agency might be facing.

Black ops, espionage, electronic eavesdropping. Hell, *everything* Desk Three did was illegal in one sense of the word or another. What was the point of having lawyers at a briefing, for Christ's sake?

A number of low-voiced conversations were taking place as people continued trickling into the Green Room and taking their seats. Voices in the chamber took on an oddly muffled quality. Like similar spaces within the CIA headquarters at Langley and in the Pentagon subbasements, the room was electronically isolated from the outside, with armor plating thick enough to shield the occupants from a near miss by a small tactical nuke.

"Before we begin," Rubens said, standing at the head of the table, "I have some news. We've confirmed that Ghost Blue went down in the Gulf of Finland last night as a result of enemy action. We believe the pilot ejected, but so far, search efforts have been unsuccessful. We're continuing the search through the daylight hours over there, of course, but as of oh–three hundred this morning, the pilot has been logged as missing, presumed dead."

Dean leaned back in his chair, a sigh escaping as he sagged. *Damn . . .*

"Has there been any word from the Russians?" Greg Paulson asked. He was chief of staff for the current Director of the NSA and would be especially sensitive to possible political repercussions.

"I gather a protest was filed this morning with our embassy in Moscow," Rubens told him. "I'll be going in to talk with . . . people about the situation later this afternoon."

"People," Dean thought, meant either the National Security Advisor or the President himself. There would be brutal questions, perhaps a formal investigation. Dean did not envy his boss.

"We can always blame UFOs again," John Jacobin, one of the lawyers, pointed out.

There was a subdued chuckle from several of the men and women seated at the table. More than once, going back to the years of the Cold War, NSA and CIA incursions over Russian territory had been spotted but remained unidentified. The long-running popular mania over supposed alien spacecraft in the airspace of both the United States and Russia had on several occasions proven surprisingly useful.

"We don't yet know if the opposition got a good look at our aircraft," Rubens said mildly. "It's not really important, one way or another."

But Dean knew it *was* important. A critical failure on an intelligence op inside Russia would inevitably spawn serious interagency trouble down the line. The CIA, especially, didn't like the fact that the NSA was trespassing on what it considered its turf, its particular area of responsibility. Hell, they'd been trying to shut down Desk Three or get it transferred to their Directorate of Operations ever since its inception.

"What *is* important," Rubens continued, "is that we secure our people over there, get them out safe, resolve Operation Magpie, and follow through with Operation Blue Jay. Miss DeFrancesca has provided us with a vital link between Magpie and Blue Jay. We need to take advantage of this before the trail goes cold." He nodded to one of the men at the table. "Mr. Ryder, if you please?"

Tom Ryder was the designated briefing officer for the morning's meeting, a small and fussy analyst from the Russian Section. He stood up, took his place behind a lectern at the front of the room, and used a handheld remote to bring up an image on the large flat-panel screen on the wall behind him.

The man's face was shown full-front and profile, with numbers and Cyrillic lettering on a board in front of him. Two more photos showed what appeared to be surveillance photos of the same man—on a street corner and at a table in a restaurant. The face was lined and heavily scarred. The photo taken in the restaurant showed him with his mouth open, displaying black and uneven teeth.

Ryder cleared his throat, then launched into his presentation without preamble. "Victor Mikhaylov," he said. "Agent DeFrancesca positively identified him as the leader of the gunmen at the warehouse. Mikhaylov, we believe, is the number-one enforcer for *this* man, Grigor Kotenko."

Kotenko's photographs replaced those of Mikhaylov. Where Mikhaylov had the look of a street rat, a thug, Kotenko looked smoother, more urbane, a businessman, perhaps, or a lawyer, with a thick walrus mustache and a cold-eyed squint.

"This guy's a real piece of work," Ryder said. "When he was eighteen, he was sent to a gulag for armed robbery, kidnapping, and rape. While there, he made some important contacts within the Leningrad criminal underworld, and when he got out four years later—with the help of a wealthy uncle in the Organizatsiya—he went to work for Vladimir Kumarin as an enforcer. We believe he was the triggerman in a particularly brutal murder—of Peter Talbot, an American hotel entrepreneur who was shot ten times at point-blank range on a metro platform . . . while surrounded by six hired bodyguards, no less. Seems Talbot had refused to 'share' his partnership in a new hotel chain over there.

"Since then, however, Kotenko has gone from enforcement to administration, working his way all the way up to the top echelons of the Tambov organization. After Kumarin's arrest by Moscow officials in 2007, Kotenko may have moved up to the number-two or -three position in the gang's leadership, though reports indicate that Kumarin is still running things from prison.

"So if Kotenko is involved, it means we're dealing with the Tambov Gang."

"This is the so-called Russian mafia you're talking about?" an Air Force colonel in Blakeslee's entourage asked.

"One branch of it, sir," Ryder replied. "And there's nothing 'so-called' about it. The Russian Mafiya is an extraordinarily large and complex organization made up of many groups, some in alliance, some mutually hostile, all more or less in competition with one another.

"The Tambov Gang was formed in 1988 by two men from the Tambov Oblast, Vladimir Kumarin and Valery Ledovskikh. They started out by providing protection to businessmen in what was then Leningrad. Today, the Tambov Gang is the most powerful organized-crime element in St. Petersburg, numbering at least six hundred hardcore members, and thousands of occasionals. They are known to control outright over one hundred of the city's industrial enterprises, including the Petersburg Fuel Company, which maintains a monopoly on all fuel bought and sold within the city. Their membership roster includes members of both the state Duma and the St. Petersburg Legislative Assembly."

"Nice to have friends in high places," Dean murmured.

Ryder ignored the interruption. "Desk Three became concerned with Kotenko's activities when one of our sources reported that he had sold some five hundred kilograms of beryllium sheeting to an agent of the Iranian government. The beryllium sheets had been discarded by a nuclear reactor facility at Rybinsk, and were mildly radioactive when they were stolen. Reportedly, they were destined for a freighter of Liberian registry, which would have taken them to Bandar 'Abbas.

"Currently, Desk Three is running two distinct operations in Russia aimed at the Tambov Gang—designated Magpie and Blue Jay. Magpie was intended to track the stolen beryllium to Iran. Our agents would plant a small transponder chip on one of the sheets—a device the size of a postage stamp, colored and textured to be indistinguishable from the beryllium itself. It would have given us some insight, we hoped, into the Iranian nuclear program . . . especially insofar as their attempt to manufacture fission weapons is concerned.

"Yesterday, our agents succeeded in planting the tracker. However, they were discovered, and we don't yet know if the opposition has found the tracking device, or if they've guessed what we were up to.

"Grigor Kotenko, we believe, is behind not only the beryllium sale to Iran but another major Tambov operation . . . which is the target of Operation Blue Jay. We have learned that they are attempting to gain control over Russia's oil and natural gas industries."

"Just a minute," General Blakeslee said, interrupting. "Where's the Russian government in all this? Where's the *military*?"

"That, General, is part of the problem." Ryder held up his hands, clasping them together with fingers intertwined. "Government and organized crime are like this. Over there, the Organizatsiya is how things get done. It was that way under the Soviets. It was probably that way under the czars. It's much, much worse now. As for the military . . . many of the Organizatsiya's members are ex-military or -KGB. A lot of military personnel were cut loose when the Soviet government fell, remember. As a result, there's a kind of old-boy network in modern Russia that includes the military, the government, *and* the organized-crime syndicates. We believe that over eighty percent of all Russian businesses either are controlled outright by organized crime or, at the very least, pay a cripplingly large percentage of their profits to the syndicates for 'protection.'

"This has had a terrible effect on the Russian economy. People over there are actually yearning for the good old days when the Soviets had everything controlled and orderly. Of course, the criminals were active under the Soviets as well, but in a state-run economy, the problem was pretty well hidden. Now, it's out in the open and clearly out of control."

Ryder continued his presentation, but Dean listened with only half an ear. He knew most of this already. He'd seen the moribund state of the Russian economy firsthand . . . the poverty, the hopelessness on the faces of people in the streets and on the subways, the dead factories and boarded-up shops, the crumbling facades in a state without enough free money to rebuild the infrastructure, to say nothing of launching into new business ventures.

Ryder spoke for another ten minutes on the threat of the Russian mafia, touching on the sales of weapons to terrorist groups, the suspected theft of nuclear weapons and materials, the destabilizing effect the Organizatsiya was having globally. He mentioned, to a few chuckles, the sale of a Russian Tango-class diesel submarine to a Colombian drug cartel in the late nineties. The sale had fallen through, thank God, when the Colombians, thinking the plan just a bit *too* ambitious, had backed out. Had the sale been completed—just $5 million would have purchased the submarine and a trained crew of twenty for a year—the Cali Cartel would have been delivering multi-ton loads of cocaine and heroin to the California coast, completely eluding the web of land-, sea-, and air-based radar guarding the southern approaches to the United States.

"But we know the Russian mobs have been delivering other military hardware to Colombia for over a decade," Ryder continued. "Thousands of automatic weapons, millions of rounds of ammunition, at least two military helicopters, and a number of advanced surface-to-air missiles that are going to make our interdiction efforts in South America extremely difficult. The point is . . . the Russian Mafiya thinks big, *very* big, they have more money than God, and they don't give a damn who they deal with or what the consequences might be."

The Russian Mafiya, Dean thought, had an overly developed sense of drama. He found himself thinking about various supervillain groups in spy fiction—Ian Fleming's SPECTRE or even Thrush in the old *Man from U.N.C.L.E.* TV series, comic-book criminal organizations bent on world domination.

The Organizatsiya, evidently, was coming uncomfortably close to matching those fictional villains in the real world in the sheer scope and scale of their ambitions.

An hour later, the briefing over, Dean was ushered into Rubens' office. "Well, Mr. Dean, you now know more about the Russian mafia than you really cared to know."

"It still seems a bit odd, sir," Dean replied, "going up against a bunch of criminals instead of a government."

"In this case, it's tough to draw a line between the two," Rubens said, booting up the computer on his desk. "In any case, we have you booked on a flight to London this afternoon, Dulles, fourteen thirty."

"And then on from there to St. Petersburg," Dean said, completing the thought.

"No," Rubens said. "There's been a change in plans."

Dean felt an unpleasant tickle, centered in his gut. "I

thought I was supposed to join Lia and her partner in Russia."

"DeFrancesca and Akulinin are safe enough for the moment, and our organization inside St. Petersburg is arranging to smuggle them out of Russia within the next twenty-four hours. Right now we're more concerned about the potential threat to another of our assets. An entirely different operation."

Rubens turned his monitor so Dean could see the screen, which displayed a grainy and slightly out-of-focus photograph of a laughing, half-naked blonde, Grigor Kotenko, and another man, lean, his hair buzz-cut short, his shirt open to reveal a number of blurry tattoos.

"The man on the right," Rubens said, "is Sergei Braslov, former Red Army, GRU, and later MVD. A Russian working for the CIA snapped this photo through a telephoto lens at a Black Sea resort last summer. Our agent on Operation Sunny Weather encountered Braslov a few hours ago in London. He appears to have infiltrated an environmental activist group, Greenworld."

"Excuse me," Dean said. "This Braslov . . . is he still MVD? Or is he with the Tambov Gang? Who's he working for?"

"That," Rubens said dryly, "is what you are going to find out. As Mr. Ryder pointed out at the briefing, it's sometimes difficult to tell whether an individual over there is with the government or with the crooks, and where their loyalties lie. However . . ." He touched a lectern control, dragging a square around Braslov's upper torso in the photo, then enlarging the picture, in effect zooming in for a close-up of the man's partly revealed chest. Dean could just make out the blurred blue shapes of several tattoos on the man's skin.

Rubens used his mouse to bring up an overlay of straight lines, resolving and clarifying the tattoos. "Within the Russian Mafiya," Rubens said, "tattoos comprise a rather complex symbolic language, a code, if you will. This image isn't clear enough for a complete translation, but computer enhancement allows at least a partial reading.

"Here—" A pointer darted across the screen, indicating a large tattoo over Braslov's solar plexus. "A crucifix. It signifies a 'prince of thieves,' someone with a high ranking within the organization. Above the crucifix . . . a crown. That means the wearer is a *pakhan,* the leader of a thieves family. Think of a Sicilian Mafia don, the head of one of the Five Families.

"And above the crown . . ." The pointer shifted to a blurred mark beneath Braslov's throat. "An eight-pointed star, sometimes called a *chaos star*. Another rank insignia. It means Braslov is a member of the very highest levels of Russian organized crime.

"From this, we can infer that Braslov is a member of the Russian Mafiya, most likely one of the Moscow families. If he's socializing with Kotenko at a Black Sea dacha, it's possible that we're seeing evidence of some sort of alliance. Braslov's direct involvement with Greenworld suggests some sort of disinformation campaign, but we're not sure of that yet. Braslov may be there in his official capacity as an officer of Russian Internal Security . . . or he may be there as a key player with the Mafiya . . . or he may be there for *both*.

"You, Mr. Dean, are going to make contact with Braslov in London. You'll have Mr. Karr already there, as backup. 'L' Section will provide you with a small bugging device and remote transmitter that will allow us to eavesdrop on Braslov's conversations. We're particularly interested in what he is doing as an agent inside of Greenworld.

"I can't stress this strongly enough, Mr. Dean. The Russian Mafiya is an extraordinary threat in today's world. It has already demonstrated its potential for destabilizing nations and economies worldwide, and might well do so on a global scale. We need to know what's going on over there—if there is an alliance between the St. Petersburg and Moscow gangs, if the Russian government is in on such an alliance, and just what it is that they're up to."

Dean slouched back in his chair, then nodded. "Yes, sir."

He was worried, frankly, about Lia. From the little he'd heard so far, Lia and Akulinin had come up against the St. Petersburg mob and bounced. It hardly seemed credible. Desk Three routinely took on national governments—China, North Korea, Syria, Russia—and emerged victorious. It didn't seem possible that a gang of common criminals could best the Agency's field operators.

And that thought, Dean decided, highlighted the problem. Members of the Russian Mafiya, whatever else they might be, were *not* "common criminals." They were smart, they were wealthy, they were powerful, they were as well armed and as well equipped as some small countries, and they were well connected with members of their own government and with powerful people in the governments of other countries.

Underestimating these people, Dean decided, could have decidedly lethal consequences.

7

TOMMY KARR WALKED OUT onto the broad observation platform that encircled the uppermost floor of London's City Hall.

The Thames lay spread beneath him, gray-green and dotted with pleasure craft and barges. An ancient light cruiser, the HMS *Belfast,* now a museum, lay tied up to the City Pier to the left, on the near bank almost at his feet. Beyond her, the clean, modern lines of the new London Bridge spanned the river, in front of the thrust and bustle of London's business district and the far-off blue dome of St. Paul's. To his right, downstream, rose the Tower Bridge, older and more conventional beneath its twin supporting caissons and towers that looked like the squared-off steeples of Anglican churches.

The bridge architecture fitted in perfectly with the sprawl of medieval castle walls, turrets, towers, and cupolas directly across the Thames from City Hall, the infamous Tower of London.

Closer at hand, the demonstration had spilled into the park and waterfront pier directly below City Hall, filling it as far as the near end of the Tower Bridge, perhaps 150 yards away. Karr was looking down on a sea of people and brightly colored banners. Occasionally megaphone-directed chants rose the ten stories to the observation promenade, but mostly the noise was little more than a distant, subdued rumble.

"Anything new on the telly?" he asked aloud.

"Nothing on CNN or the networks," Jeff Rockman's voice said in his ear. "BBC Two is carrying a lot of footage, though. It's big news in Europe, at least. We've spotted you three or four times, now, when the cameras zoomed in on Spencer."

Karr grinned as he turned from the sprawling city panorama. "Hi, Mom," he said. He could see a couple of media types nearby, a sharply dressed woman with a mi-crophone and a shirt-sleeved partner with a minicam, filming the delegates.

The meetings had broken for an afternoon recess. A number of delegates had spilled out onto the promenade outside or wandered off to the building's restaurant. The symposium had been going for more than four hours now and already generated several spirited, even acri-monious debates between various of the attendees. A Nigerian delegate had been ejected, loudly shouting that caps on emissions were tantamount to racism, a means of strangling the economies of third-world nations. Sup-posedly, the Kyoto Accords exempted developing coun-tries from the stringencies of limiting their industrial emissions, in effect requiring industrial nations to pay a tax on their behalf. There still seemed to be a lot of misunderstanding on that point, however, generating a widespread sense that the developed countries were ei-ther patronizing the third world or strangling it—take your pick.

The entire issue was now so bound up with politics,

money, and shrill invective that it was nearly impossible for mere *facts* to make themselves heard.

Dr. Spencer, standing just outside the broad glass doors, appeared to be engaged in an ugly confrontation with a distinguished-looking Brit, a member of the Royal Society, if Karr remembered correctly.

"Nonsense!" the silver-haired delegate sputtered. "Your data, sir, are contrived and inaccurate! Nothing can be clearer from the record than that the increased temperatures of the past century and a half are due to increased industrial emissions. *Human* emissions!"

"Bullshit!" Spencer snapped back. "The total effect of the sun on Earth's climate is *overwhelmingly* greater than anything we can do to add or detract!"

"Sheer moonshine, sir! You have no proof—"

"I have all the proof necessary, Sir James, *if* you're willing to pull your head out of your ass and listen to a dissenting view for a change!"

"*Doctor* Spencer! I resent—"

"Well, I must say they're getting on famously," someone said at Karr's side.

"If they don't kill each other first," Karr replied. He looked the other man over . . . a nondescript, older man with white hair and the air of a banker, perhaps. Karr had seen him earlier that morning in the conference hall, standing off to one side, and assumed he was a delegate to the symposium.

"Randolph Evans," Rockman's voice whispered in Karr's ear. "GCHQ. He's one of us."

Karr extended a hand. "You're Randolph Evans, aren't you? GCHQ?"

Evans took his hand. "And you're Kjartan Magnor-Karr. 'Tommy.' NSA."

Karr grinned. Government Communications Headquarters, or GCHQ, was Great Britain's equivalent of the NSA.

An agreement dating back to 1947 called the United Kingdom–USA Communications Intelligence Agreement, usually shortened to "UKUSA," had forged an unusually close and highly covert alliance aimed at intercepting and decoding electronic intelligence all over the world. If GCHQ wasn't a branch of the NSA by now, it was the next best thing . . . a full partner in global espionage and SIGINT.

He didn't bother asking Evans what he was doing here. If the operative was here on an op, he wouldn't discuss the fact any more than Karr would. Karr could guess what GCHQ was interested in this afternoon, though.

"A lot of very noisy people down there," he commented.

"Indeed. Greenpeace. Greenworld. Several other environmentalist groups. They seem to think the world's governments aren't moving fast enough."

"All in all a good thing," Karr said, nodding. "When governments move quickly, *that's* when ordinary people need to start worrying."

"As when they make the trains run on time?"

"Exactly. Or promise 'peace in our time.'"

"Ouch. Touché."

Karr nodded toward the confrontation near the doors. "Who's the silver-haired gentleman threatening to throw Dr. Spencer off the roof?"

"Ah. Sir James Millvale. Distinguished member of Parliament. Highly respected Senior of the Royal Society. Environmental scientist. And thoroughly peeved that people like your Dr. Spencer may be about to turn the tide of official opinion against the idea that people are to blame for global warming . . . *after* he and his party rammed through some rather expensive and deucedly inconvenient emissions standards here in this country. Millvale and his allies will look like fools, lose professional standing, power, prestige. They have everything to lose, so they have stopped listening."

"That's supposed to be our fault?"

"Well, you Yanks do have the reputation for kicking over the apple cart. Boston Harbor, 1773?"

"You're still carrying a grudge? You people have *such* long memories. . . ."

Evans chuckled.

Before he could reply, however, Rockman interrupted over Karr's communications system. "Hey, Tommy? Looks like some trouble is developing downstairs."

"Excuse me," Karr told Evans. "I have a call."

He didn't know if Evans was cleared to know about the highly secret communications implants used by Desk Three operators—for all Karr knew, GCHQ agents used the things as well—but pulling out a satellite phone and holding it to his ear gave him plausible cover with the surrounding crowd of guests and delegates as he spoke with Rockman.

"Jeff? What's up?"

"We're monitoring the situation through BBC Two and the security cameras inside the building," Rockman said. The NSA, it was said, could tap into *any* security camera system worldwide, especially if the system was part of a computer-monitored network. "The crowd outside just exploded. About fifty of them muscled past the security guards at the main entrance. That seems to have been a distraction, though, because when the guards started struggling with them, about fifty more vaulted a set of barrier fences and entered the building through a side door."

"Are they armed?"

"Not that we can see," Rockman replied. "But you may be about to have company."

Frowning, Karr said, "Excuse me," to Evans and pushed

through the wide glass double doors into the building's tenth-floor lobby. Leaning over a railing, Karr could look straight down the center of the staircase spiraling up the inside of the building, all the way to the entrance floor. Shouts and wild yells echoed up the staircase, along with the magnified thunder of running feet coming up the steps. It looked like the mob was up to the third floor already . . . no, the fourth.

Returning to the promenade outside, he signaled Delgado and Payne, who were flanking Spencer as the American continued arguing with Sir James. With things apparently peaceful enough, other than Spencer's disagreement with the locals, Rogers had wandered off to find the cafeteria and get something to eat.

"Some of the protestors just jumped the security barriers," Karr told the two FBI agents. "They're on their way up. We need to get Sunny here someplace safe."

"Inside," Delgado suggested. "In the speakers' area. There's a green room."

The green room was a place for delegates to rest and hang out without being pestered by the news media or other noisy types. Karr nodded. The room had one entrance, which could be easily defended.

Still, he didn't want to overreact. When Greenpeace activists protesting the Star Wars initiative had broken through the security perimeter at Menwith Hill a few years ago, they'd used similar tactics. A few, designated "hares," had cut through the fence and run across the compound, drawing off the security guards. Then the main body, designated "rabbits," had swarmed over the fence, climbed communications towers, and raised banners. They'd stayed long enough to pose for the media cameras, some of them wearing outlandish costumes representing ballistic missiles, before being evicted or, in some cases, arrested and carried off to waiting police vans for trespass.

Most likely, the activists downstairs were going to try to crash the symposium's party, shout some slogans, maybe hang up some banners, and grab some high-quality airtime on the evening news.

But they couldn't afford to take chances, not with the death threats against him. They closed in on Spencer.

"Excuse me, sir," Payne told him, interrupting a diatribe by Sir James. "We have a situation. If you would come with us . . ."

"I *beg* your pardon, young man," Sir James said. He was furious, his face bright red. "We are having a private discussion!"

"You can discuss things with the mob, sir," Karr told him. "They're on their way up!"

"Eh?" Sir James stopped, listened, then scowled. "My word. What *is* that ungodly racket?"

"We have them on the eighth floor," Rockman said. "They just pushed past a couple of security guards like they weren't even there. More of them are coming in through the main doors now, too. Looks like this thing was *planned*."

"We may not have time to reach the green room," Karr told the FBI agents. "Come on. Over here."

Delgado was holding his earphone in place, talking rapidly to Rogers over a needle mike beside his mouth. Karr heard him say, "Get the hell back here!"

Karr led them back from the glass doors, putting a number of confusedly milling delegates between them and the oncoming mob. Moments later, the doors swung open and a large number of activists spilled out onto the sight-seeing platform.

Most, Karr saw, were young people—teenagers or twenty-somethings. They had the somewhat trendy-shabby look of protestors everywhere, wearing jeans, sandals, T-shirts, and, among the males, at any rate, lots of facial hair. Many were chanting: "USA! CO_2 USA! CO_2!" Karr saw signs and waving banners, clenched fists and raw emotion.

Security guards and London bobbies burst through the door after them, but there were too many protestors scattering across and around the encircling promenade. Five protestors emerged from the tenth-floor lobby of the GLA carrying a cumbersome sixty-foot-long bundle, bright green and tightly rolled up. They hauled it to the safety railing at the edge of the promenade, which canted sharply inward over the walkway, and began muscling their burden over the side. Others formed a barrier between the five and the police, who in short order were surrounded by a mob of chanting, shouting protestors.

Delegates to the symposium were scattering everywhere, running protestors among them. The situation was completely chaotic, completely out of control. Tightly wedged in around Dr. Spencer, Karr and the two FBI agents backed their charge away from the confrontation.

The five protestors had everyone's attention now. They'd anchored their heavy bundle to the top railing of the safety fence around the promenade, locking it in place with chains and padlocks sewn into the heavy material. When they released the bundle, it tumbled out over the slanted railing, then down the side of the building with a sharp crack, an enormous green banner hanging from the building's top floor.

From this angle, Karr couldn't see what was on the banner, but he could guess . . . something about a green world and no global warming, perhaps. The protestors now were ganging up on the police and security guards. People were screaming and running.

"Hold it!" Delgado yelled. He had his sidearm out and had pivoted to aim it back in the other direction, behind Karr. "Drop it! *Drop it!*"

Karr spun. Several protestors had come all the way around the promenade, circling it clockwise as Spencer and his guards backed around counterclockwise. One of the protestors, oddly on this brilliant late-spring morning, was wearing a heavy overcoat. That was damned strange. . . .

With a sense of dawning horror, Karr saw the man pulling something out from under the coat . . . a weapon . . . an Uzi submachine gun . . . raising it to his shoulder. . . .

Spencer was between Karr and the gunman . . . no, the gun*men*. Another activist nearby had a pistol in his hand, was aiming it at Spencer.

Karr lunged, plowing into Spencer from behind and the side with his shoulder, a football block that sent the American scientist sprawling. Karr hit the deck of the promenade, his Beretta out of its shoulder holster and gripped two-handed as he slid over smooth concrete.

The man with the Uzi was the greater danger in terms of sheer firepower; the man with the pistol was already drawing a bead on Spencer. In an instant's instinctive decision, Karr swung his Beretta to aim at the one with the pistol, squeezing the trigger in a fast double tap.

The gunman fired in the same instant. Karr felt the sting of concrete chips slashing his cheek. The activist with the coat and the Uzi opened up on full-auto, sending a stream of slugs slamming into Delgado, then sweeping the chattering weapon around, trying to hit Spencer.

Spent brass cartridges tumbled and flashed in the sunlight. Delgado was falling; Payne was aiming his weapon in a stiff Weaver stance, firing into a third gunman, no, a gun *woman*. . . .

Karr shifted aim as he got his feet underneath him, throwing himself between Spencer and the attackers, firing into the guy with the submachine gun as he moved. As he came to his feet, however, he felt something like a hammer slam into his side . . . then again, hard against his chest.

Part of him knew he was hit, though there was no pain . . . not yet. He kept squeezing the trigger as he fell and turned, sending round after round into the gunman, slamming against the railing, dropping to one knee.

Two more hammer blows . . . and a terribly wet *crunch* against his throat. Karr felt himself falling, the Beretta gone, spinning off into space. Damn it, he couldn't *breathe!*

He tasted blood, salty and hot.

Tommy Karr collapsed as the darkness descended, engulfing him. . . .

**The Art Room
NSA Headquarters
Fort Meade, Maryland
1035 hours EDT**

"Jesus!" Rockman stared at the big display screen, which currently was showing a number of TV monitors. On one, the earnest, too-perfect makeup of a BBC anchorwoman stared from the screen as she mouthed unheard words into her microphone. Another screen showed the view of another camera, aimed up at the green banner unfurling ten stories above the Thames. The banner, so huge it could easily be read from the ground, showed the Greenworld logo, together with the words "Save Our World!"

But Rockman and the other runners in the Art Room were staring at one of the other monitors, this one tapping into a security camera mounted in the ceiling of the overhang above the outside sightseeing promenade around London's Living Room. The scene was one of incredible confusion, of an enormous, surging crowd struggling hand to hand with the police. Gunfire had panicked the mob, sending it scattering across the observation deck.

But in the background . . .

"My God!" Sarah Cassidy shouted. "They *shot* him! *They shot him!*"

Jeff Rockman couldn't believe what he thought he'd just seen . . . Tommy Karr catching a full-auto blast from the gunman's Uzi, exchanging fire, then falling backward against the guardrail before crumpling to the concrete deck.

Spencer was on his hands and knees, looking dazed but apparently unhurt. Karr had thrown himself between the gunmen and the scientist, had probably saved Spencer's life. One of the FBI men was down; another was on one knee, his pistol locked in a two-handed grip and swinging wildly back and forth as he looked for another target, another threat. He was screaming into the needle mike at his mouth, calling for backup.

The third FBI agent entered the picture from behind the foreground a moment later, weapon drawn. And Evans, the GCHQ agent, was there as well, also armed.

But too little, too late. All three tangos—in his mind, Rockman had immediately reverted to the code term meaning "terrorists"—all three, two men and a woman, were down. The woman appeared to be wounded, was trying to get up. Evans pushed her down again as Rogers kicked her handgun away. More backup arrived, London bobbies and several in plainclothes . . . MI5.

Payne was checking the motionless form of Delgado.

"Call Rubens," Rockman said.

"He's . . . he's in a briefing," Ron Jordan said, his voice shaking. "He can't be—"

"*Call Rubens!*"

Desk Three had lost agents before. The NSA had lost

agents and operators many times since its creation in the late 1940s. But the loss of another agent was never easy.

The loss of a *friend* was much worse.

**More London Center
Near the GLA Building
1435 hours GMT**

Directly adjacent to the black, leaning egg shape of the GLA, some fifty meters to the southwest across the tree-lined pavement of a park known locally as Potter's Field, loomed a brand-new office building, the More London Center, housing a bank, an insurance firm, and a number of government offices that had not fitted in with London City Hall or the Greater London Authority. Hours ago, Sergei Braslov had used a back stairwell and a stolen passkey to gain entrance to a maintenance door leading out onto the roof. Twelve stories up, the roof let him look down onto the outside promenade at the tenth floor of the GLA building. By climbing a ladder up onto the top of the small rooftop structure housing the building's air-conditioning system, he gained a bit more elevation . . . and a perfect shot.

Braslov carried with him a black, leather camera bag, as well as various ID proving him to be a cameraman with the BBC. If anyone happened to be on the More London Center's roof, Braslov could flash the ID and claim he was looking for a good vantage point overlooking the fast-developing riot below. Inside the bag, however, was not a minicam, but a high-powered rifle broken down into four pieces, a weapon originally designed for use by the Soviet Spetsnaz, the Russian equivalent of the American Special Forces. It was a matter of two minutes' work to snap or screw the pieces together, chamber a round, and peer through the telescopic sight into the crowd on the GLA building's promenade deck.

At a range of just under fifty meters, he could hardly miss.

He'd not fired the weapon, however . . . and didn't plan to do so if he could possibly help it. Mallet, Berger, and Fischer, simpleton dupes, the lot of them, had done exactly as he'd coached them over long, patient hours during the past week, finding Spencer, rushing in as close as possible, and only then pulling out their weapons and opening fire. Braslov was ready with the sniper's rifle if necessary, if none of the three succeeded in hitting anything, but at point-blank range, they were almost certain to hit someone.

That they appeared to have missed Spencer mattered not at all. They'd killed one, perhaps two of Spencer's bodyguards.

It would be enough.

There was one final task Braslov had set for himself, however. None of the three, after his coaching, had expected the bodyguards to be armed, and, as a result, all three of the Greenworld attackers were now down. Two were almost certainly dead, but the third, the woman, was still moving, a puddle of blood spreading on the concrete beneath her and soaking through her T-shirt. He shifted his aim until the crosshair reticules in his scope centered on her head. A squeeze of the trigger and the only person on the GLA observation deck who knew exactly what had happened would be dead.

It was a difficult shot, however. The surviving bodyguards and several GLA security personnel were clustered around her, and she was partially blocked from his view by the back-slanting safety railing at the edge of the deck.

No, he decided. *Too risky.* Shooting the woman would alert the security forces that a fourth shooter was in the game. They might even spot him and call in support before he could get clear of the building.

Fischer was done for, shot in the stomach and chest several times. Even if she survived, she didn't know enough to be a threat to Braslov, or to the Organizatsiya.

Moments later, paramedics arrived, and they began strapping Fischer onto a gurney. The window of opportunity was past.

Thoughtful, Braslov disassembled the rifle and stowed the pieces back in the camera bag. Only then did he pull out a satellite phone and punch in a number, opening an encrypted line.

"Rodina," he said. Motherland. Mother Russia.

"We're watching BBC Two. Excellent work."

"One of our agents still lives. I cannot get a clear shot, however."

"She knows nothing. We don't want to reveal your presence. That might tell the opposition too much."

"That was my thought." He hesitated. "Perhaps it is time to activate Cold War. The two . . . incidents should take place close together, for maximum effect."

"We agree. A ticket and new identity papers are waiting for you at the embassy. You fly out tonight."

"Good. Until tonight, then."

Utter pandemonium reigned throughout the GLA building and in the surrounding parks and waterfront. It was simplicity itself to walk down the stairwell and let himself out onto Potter's Field. Terror-stricken people continued to flee the area, spilling out of the GLA building and into the surrounding park. Police were arriving now, many in heavy combat gear, but no one took notice of the lone cameraman with a BBC ID badge clipped to his shirt.

He looked up at the enormous green banner for a moment, hanging ten stories above his head, smiled, then mingled with the fast-thinning crowd and disappeared.

8

Met Remote One
Arctic Ice Cap
82° 30' N, 177° 53' E
1910 hours, GMT − 12

KATHY MCMILLAN PULLED the edges of her hood closer to her face. The temperature was only just below freezing, but the wind was shrill and biting. The windchill, she thought, must be down around zero, Fahrenheit.

Forty years ago, an American astronaut had described the surface of the moon as a "magnificent desolation." This, she thought, must have been what he'd felt. The landscape in every direction was utterly flat and almost featureless, save for occasional small upthrusts and pressure ridges, none more than a few feet high, and randomly scattered patches of ice melt. The sky was a searing, featureless blue, the sun a heatless white disk suspended above the southern horizon. In every direction there stretched a barren white icescape, pocked with shallow craters filled with icy water, broken here and there by darker leads.

Scarcely five hundred miles away, in *that* direction, lay the North Pole itself.

Met Remote One was an unmanned meteorological drift station established on the Arctic ice cap three weeks before. There wasn't a lot there—a slender tower with an anemometer, a surface instrument package for measuring temperature, barometric pressure, humidity, ice thickness, and other data, and a GPS and a dish antenna for measuring ice drift and transmitting the information to Ice Station Bravo, some eighty miles away. The whole setup required minimal maintenance; the three American scientists were essentially employing the met station's presence as a useful excuse . . . an alibi.

Somewhere off toward the north, about seven miles away and just barely over the horizon, was Objective Toy Shop, an amusing reference to their proximity to the North Pole and Santa Claus. While the NOAA expedition at Ice Station Bravo was out here on the ice to monitor changes in climate and ice thickness, Yeats and McMillan were here specifically—and secretly—to have an up-close look at the Toy Shop.

"Hey, Mac! Quit playing tourist and give me a hand, here," Dennis Yeats said. He and Randy Haines were beside one of the sleds, wrestling with the Unmanned Underwater Vehicle.

"Sorry." She tore her attention away from the barren panorama and crunched through soft ice to join the others. She carried an M-16 slung over her shoulder. All three of them were armed—a necessary precaution against the possibility of polar bears. Unslinging the weapon, she stowed it on the supply sled behind Haines' snowmobile, then joined the others.

"Did you get through to Bear One?" she asked.

"Yeah," Haines told her. "*And* to Asheville. A freakin' miracle."

Communications had been frustratingly intermittent lately. Maybe things were finally starting to break their way.

The three of them had driven out across the ice in three

snowmobiles, each towing a sled with supplies and the special equipment. Yeats' sled carried the Orca, eight feet long and weighing over a quarter of a ton, while hers carried the cable reel and support gear. The two men had just finished stripping the protective plastic sheet off the cradled Orca and were readying the sleek black and red device for launch.

McMillan was the Orca's technician. Approaching her sled, she first double-checked to see that the ice brakes were solidly set. Then she took several minutes to hook up the guidance wire, stringing the thin length of fiber-optic cable from its spool on her sled across to the receiver on the Orca's dorsal surface and attaching the other end to a small handheld control unit. The connections made, she switched on the power for a final prelaunch check.

The readouts on her control panel all showed green and ready.

"We're set to go," she told them. "I've got feedback and control. Ready to cut the hole?"

"We're on it," Haines told her.

One hundred yards from the met station, they'd found a patch of ice melt, a circular depression in the surface filled with milky green water, where the ice was thin enough to have nearly broken through to the ocean beneath. The ice here was about three meters thick; at the center of that depression, it might be as thin as a few centimeters.

Yeats now trudged toward the edge of the depression, carrying a small, tightly wrapped satchel. Reaching back, he flung the device far out over the water. It hit with a splash, sinking gently about three-quarters of the way toward the depression's center.

"Okay!" Yeats called, hurrying back from the depression's edge. "Let's blow it!"

"And three," Haines said, holding a small transmitter in his gloved hands, "and two . . . and one . . . and *fire!*"

A column of water and chunks of ice geysered into the cold air with a solid *thud* that they felt through the soles of their heavily insulated boots. The water and spray subsided, leaving a large dark spot at the bottom of the depression.

"Breakthrough!" Haines called.

"Right," Yeats said. "Launch the baby."

"Watch your feet!" she called. "Don't get caught in the cable!" McMillan touched a control on her board, and the cradle supporting the Orca at the depression's edge began rising on powerful hydraulics, tipping the UUV's tail high, the nose down. In seconds, gravity took over and the Orca eased forward on its rails, slammed hard onto the ice belly down like a huge and ungainly penguin, and swiftly slid into the water. It reached the dark patch, nosed over, and vanished, trailing the slender wire behind it.

The large spool of fiber-optic cable mounted on McMillan's sled played out rapidly with a faint hissing sound. An age ago, in what seemed now like another life, Kathy McMillan had worked for Raytheon on the ADCAP torpedo for the U.S. Navy. Five years ago, she'd come to work for the National Security Agency, bringing her experience—and her security classification—with her. For the past year, though, she'd been seconded from the NSA to the CIA and had been working with the Company's Directorate of Science and Technology to fine-tune the Orca for CIA operations worldwide.

The Orca was actually quite similar to the wire-guided torpedoes used on board U.S. submarines—considerably smaller, lighter, and slower, of course, and lacking a high-explosive warhead, but powered by batteries, driven by pumpjet propulsors, and remotely piloted over its two-way data feed. McMillan had about ten miles' worth of cable on her spool, though it didn't look bulky enough for that.

Her handset looked like a video gamer's control box, with a pair of inch-long joysticks, one for left-right-up-down, the other for controlling speed. Touch-pad controls handled the sophisticated array of underwater sensors and cameras into its nose. Headlamps set into the Orca on either side of the nose cast an eerie, cold-white light ahead, illuminating swirling clouds of gleaming white motes in the vehicle's path. McMillan was getting a clear picture on her small display—a deep blue-green and featureless haze, with an oddly wrinkled and rugged ceiling of white overhead.

"How's she look?" Yeats asked, coming up beside her.

"We're beneath the ice," she told him. "On course, fifteen knots. We'll be there in about half an hour."

"Good. I don't want us to hang around here longer than we have to."

"Relax. They don't even know we're here."

"They would've heard the explosion," Yeats told her. "Sound travels underwater, you know."

"Yes, Dennis," she said in her most acid, yes-dear tone. She hated it when men patronized her. "I know something about sonar, okay?"

"Oh, yeah. All that work for the Navy."

"And I also know that it's almost impossible to track underwater sounds under the ice. They heard the explosion, all right, but they won't have a clue as to where it came from, or how far away it is. So far as they know, it was something echoing in from the oil derricks off the North Slope."

Minutes passed. The fiber-optic cable continued unreeling from its drum, vanishing into the hole in the ice. On her monitor, the bottom side of the ice raced past overhead with a flicker of fast-shifting shadows. Twice she adjusted

the Orca's depth to avoid looming pressure ridges—
inverted mountain ranges plunging down into the black.
This part of the ice cap, though, was fairly uniform and relatively thin. Maybe, she thought, the environmentalists had
something after all; the ice cap *was* thinning rapidly from
year to year. A couple of years ago, for the first time since
such things could be checked, ice-free water had actually
opened around the North Pole itself.

Then she thought of the Greenworlders back at the
main camp on the ice and dismissed the thought. That
bunch of screwups couldn't be right about the time of
day, much less something as dynamic and ever-changing
as the Arctic.

She felt a shudder pass through the ice beneath her
boots.

"What the hell was that?" Haines asked.

Yeats eyed the hole uncertainly. "Dunno. Maybe we
should move back from the edge a bit, though. We
might've used too big a charge."

Another shudder was transmitted through the ice, a
solid shock. "Nah, it's not that," Haines said. "That's not
like ice breaking. More like a thump from underneath."

"A whale, maybe?" Yeats suggested.

Haines gave Yeats a sour look. "No."

"We should probably move the sleds back a bit anyway," McMillan told them. "Just to be safe."

"Right," Yeats said. "I'll—"

And then the ice was shuddering and bucking so hard
that Haines fell down, and Yeats and McMillan both
grabbed hold of the edge of the sled to stay standing.
There was a roar, like avalanche thunder, and the ice between the party and the met station began to heave and
buckle skyward.

McMillan's first thought was that a pressure ridge
was forming . . . but the buckling and upthrust contin-

ued. Blocks of ice toppled backward and slid down the growing mound, and then something like a smooth, black cliff appeared above the center of the mound, rising slowly.

"Submarine!" McMillan screamed. "It's a fucking *submarine!*"

The conning tower, or sail, as submariners called it, continued to loom slowly above the ice, which was rising and cracking now to either side of the structure as the submerged vessel's hull ponderously broke through to the surface. As more of the structure came into view, she noted that the sail was rounded and sloped both fore and aft, giving it the streamlined look of a teardrop. That was emphatically not an American design. It was almost certainly a Russian boat, probably a Victor II or III, nuclear powered, with about eighty men on board.

"It's Russian!" she called to the others. "Quick! We've got to ditch the gear!"

She rammed both joysticks on her controller full forward, sending the UUV into a vertical dive. Then she released the ice brakes on the equipment sled and locked the cable reel. Immediately the tough plastic wire snapped taut and the sled began to slide, slow but steady, toward the hole in the ice.

It hurt, destroying a $4-million piece of hardware like this, but the team was under orders to be careful not to let it fall into unfriendly hands.

She just wished they'd had a chance to get close enough to actually see what the Russians were doing at Objective Toy Shop.

"Shit!" Yeats said. "C'mon, Randy!" The two of them released the brakes on the second sled, unhooked the snowmobile, and began sliding the empty cradle toward the ice-melt depression.

The submarine had come to rest, surrounded by huge,

cracked blocks of ice. A figure, made tiny by comparison with the huge vessel, appeared at the top of the sail. A second figure appeared next to the first a moment later . . . and a hatch behind the sail broke open to disgorge a line of men, all in heavy parkas, all carrying assault rifles.

"*Stoy!*" a voice boomed from the sail over a loudhailer. "*Nyeh sheveleetess!*"

"How's your Russian?" Haines asked.

"He's telling us to halt, to not move," McMillan told them.

The sled with the reel of cable was well out into the ice-melt depression now. It hit the black opening and vanished with a splash. The sled with the Orca cradle was in the depression but not moving.

There was nothing that could be done about that.

"*Brahstee arujyeh!*"

"He wants us to drop our guns."

"I suggest we do what they tell us," Yeats said, stepping away from the snowmobile, unslinging his assault rifle, and dropping it on the ice. Carefully he raised his hands.

Heavily armed sailors were clambering down off the submarine's deck now, using a long extending gangplank to cross the broken ice. In another few moments, the three Americans were being herded back toward the surfaced submarine.

In the hard, blue sky overhead, a pair of Russian helicopters circled, apparently searching for other trespassers. One of them was gentling toward the ice ahead.

A sailor behind her nudged her hard with the muzzle of his rifle. "*Skarei!*" Quickly.

Hands up, she stumbled forward.

Just possibly, she thought, they were about to see the Toy Shop up close after all, without any high-tech help from the Orca.

Rubens' Office
NSA Headquarters
Fort Meade, Maryland
1035 hours EDT

Rubens sat alone in his office, staring out across the Maryland countryside. The morning rush hour was long since past, and traffic on the Baltimore-Washington Parkway was light and brisk. *All those people,* he thought. *All those people with no idea that we're at war. . . .*

From William Rubens' perspective, that war had little to do with terrorism, or with oil, or with specific geographical locations such as Iraq and Afghanistan. It was, instead, a war between the forces of civilization and the barbarian night, a last-ditch stand against the ultimate night that had been clawing at the light of culture and rationality and science for as long as such concepts had been understood. The storming, dark passions of National Socialism; the stolid gray and monolithic rigidity of the Soviets; the shrill sloganeering, the witch hunts, and the petty sabotage of the more ignorant branches of political activism; the mindless embrace of God's will as excuse for any act of bloodshed, stupidity, or bigotry . . . all were, in Rubens' mind, aspects of the same darkness, the same ancient and abyssal evil that threatened to tear down all that Humankind had built, all that was decent and civilized and safe.

It was a war the National Security Agency had been fighting since 1953 . . . and Desk Three since its inception only a few years before.

And it was a war in which good men and women died.

In the early years of the Cold War there'd been no satellites, no huge and ultra-sensitive listening stations, no means of eavesdropping on the Soviets short of actually flying up to or even across their borders in deliberate acts of trespass intended to get them to turn off their defense radars and other electronic networks and record the results. It had been a deadly game, one played across decades, and there had been casualties. A still-classified number of unarmed reconnaissance aircraft had been shot down, some inside the borders of the Soviet Union, others well outside, over international waters.

And now, even with satellites and high-tech sensors and all of the toys and gadgets meant to make covert ops foolproof, sterile, and safe, good men and women died. Despite all the acts of Congress, all the black programs of the military, there simply was no way to get the job done without risk.

As at the headquarters of the CIA in Langley, there was a wall downstairs in the NSA tower, a wall set with gold stars, some with names, many without . . . a star for every NSA employee to be killed in the line of duty.

Tommy Karr dead? It didn't seem possible.

There would be a memorial service, of course . . . but later. For now, the rest of them had to carry on.

For now, the information would be kept tightly compartmentalized. Dean knew, but he would be carrying out the investigation in England now. Rubens had already arranged for Dean's flight to Russia to be canceled and put him on a flight to London instead—the same flight, in fact, that Karr had taken. What the hell? It was worth a shot.

Rubens also had transmitted orders to have Lia and Akulinin meet Dean in London, but they would be kept out of the loop on Karr's death for now. Need-to-know . . . and Lia, especially, would be emotionally sensitive to the news. Rubens didn't want to break it to her while she was still, in effect, inside enemy territory.

Several facts had become clear already. Desk Three knew who the killers were. Randolph Evans, a GCHQ operative who'd been nearby when Karr was killed, had flashed digital photographs of the three terrorists back to the Art Room.

Right now, three digital photographs were displayed on Rubens' monitor. The three had been positively identified as Jacques Mallet, Kurt Berger, and Yvonne Fischer, the three Greenworlders Karr had spotted and photographed on the trip in from Heathrow. Mallet—the one with the overcoat and the assault rifle—and Berger both were dead. Fischer was on her way to a London hospital with multiple gunshot wounds; she might live. If she did, she was going to have a visit from Dean. Rubens wanted answers.

Another fact, and a worrisome one. The Russians were behind the Greenworld strike in London. Their motives weren't clear yet—maybe Dean could come up with something there—but Sergei Braslov had been photographed with the Greenworld killers that morning. A careful search of TV broadcasts and security camera shots of the protest mob outside the London City Hall, using feature-matching software to pick faces out of crowds, had so far failed to turn up an image of Braslov. That didn't mean he wasn't there, but it did suggest he'd remained back and out of sight.

It felt like Braslov had been running the three assassins, sending them in to kill Spencer while the local security forces were occupied with the Greenworlders putting up their silly banner. Rubens had flashed a strongly worded request to GCHQ: *find Braslov.* The Russian was the key to what had just happened on the observation deck outside London's Living Room.

A question remained, though: assuming Braslov had put them up to it, why had three political activists agreed to go on what amounted to a suicide mission? Dean had already had the files pulled on all three, and it didn't make sense. Fischer, Berger, and Mallet were upper-middle-class college graduates. All three had been employed, and Berger had a family back in Germany.

The Frenchman, Mallet, reportedly had a passionate hatred of all things American, and he also had a drug problem—heroin. Those might have offered handles by which Braslov had maneuvered the man, but had they been enough to make him commit suicide by bodyguard? Berger was a confirmed socialist, but he appeared to be a hanger-on, a follower, not someone who would risk being shot over a difference in ideologies.

The woman, so far as could be told from her arrest record, was a passionate neosocialist ideologue who despised oil companies, global conglomerates, and capitalism. She saw herself as a freedom fighter at the barricades, joining the downtrodden masses in their righteous struggle against the robber-baron overlords of the planet, a worldview helped along by the fact that she was carrying sixty thousand pounds of credit card debt.

According to the bank records pulled in through the NSA's far-flung computer nets, both Berger and Mallet were deep in debt as well. Might that be the common link, the handle Braslov had used? Their bank records didn't show any large deposits, but money might have been placed in new accounts under false names, or even into Swiss accounts.

The fact remained, the three assassins had launched an attack that had all but guaranteed their deaths or, at the very least, arrests for murder. Money, even lots of money, wasn't much of an inducement if you couldn't enjoy it. The three weren't fanatic jihadists seeking eternal life. What in hell had Braslov promised them in order to get them to attack Spencer?

Dean felt like he was juggling, and he was beginning to lose the rhythm. Russia, England, plus the administrative and political threat here at home to Desk Three, with the loss of that F-22 *and* the death of a Desk Three agent.

And of course it all had to hit at once.

Rubens checked his watch and sighed. Soon it would be time for him to head inside the Beltway for his three o'clock appointment with Wehrum. *Damn.*

He wasn't looking forward to this.

CFS *Akademik Petr Lebedev*
Arctic Ice Cap
82° 34' N, 177° 26' E
2215 hours, GMT – 12

Kathy McMillan sat on the narrow bunk in a ship's cabin, waiting.

They'd brought her here several hours ago, she thought, though she wasn't sure of the time. They'd taken her watch, along with her boots, parka, and other cold-weather gear, and most of her clothing, and unceremoniously shoved her in here. Through the single tiny, round porthole, she could see the ice outside; at this time of the year, however, the sun never set but circled endlessly above the horizon.

How long before they miss us back at the camp? she wondered.

She tried not to think of the corollary . . . that even when they missed the three-person team, what would the rest of the expedition be able to do about it?

Their captors had hustled them across the ice to one of the helicopters and flown them across the ice to a large ship with the name *Akademik Petr Lebedev* picked out in Cyrillic letters on the bow. A civilian ship, then, probably one of the fleet of exploration and science vessels the Russians used for Arctic surveys and research. Two other ships were visible nearby, an icebreaker and what was probably a transport of some kind. She only had a glimpse of the activity on the ice around the three ships, but the Russians appeared to have constructed a small base and there were stockpiles of supplies and carefully shrouded equipment everywhere.

The Toy Shop indeed. What the hell were they building?

Once on board the ship, they'd herded the three Americans belowdecks, taking their things and putting them in three separate cabins. McMillan had tried pounding on the door and shouting, but after a while her voice was raw and her hands sore, so she'd been waiting quietly ever since.

She heard a rattle at the door and came to her feet. Half a dozen ill-formed plans flitted through her thoughts—of knocking down whoever was coming inside and racing for the deck—but common sense won out. Where the hell could she go, barefoot, wearing nothing but a T-shirt and panties?

The door swung open, and a tall, blond, rugged-looking man stepped inside. Behind him, she could see a guard, a man in a Russian naval uniform, holding an AKM assault rifle.

"Good morning," the man said in almost faultless English. "How are we doing?"

"*We* are demanding to be allowed to talk to an American consul," she said. "*We* are protesting being captured and dragged here by your goons! We were engaged in a scientific—"

"We were spying, darling," the man said evenly. "The captain of our submarine got excellent video footage of you scuttling your equipment on the ice. What was it . . . an unmanned undersea rover? A robot submarine?"

"I am part of a NOAA survey expedition," she told him. "We are mapping and measuring the thinning of the ice cap, and monitoring ice drift."

"Indeed. And you seem to have drifted into Russian territory."

Russian territory. McMillan bit back a harsh laugh. "I hate to break it to you, Ivan. These are *still* international waters."

The Russian claim was utter nonsense, of course . . . sheer political posturing and muscle flexing. The NOAA ice station had been deliberately, almost ostentatiously, constructed on the ice over international waters. Over the past month, however, the ice cap's normal clockwise drift—as much as twenty-five or thirty miles in a single day, depending on winds and currents—had carried the station across the antemeridian, the 180-degree longitude line, and, according to the latest Russian claims, at any rate, into Russian territorial waters.

No one was taking the Russians very seriously, of course. In the summer of 2007, they'd pulled a kind of high-tech publicity stunt, sending a couple of their Mir three-man minisubs to the bottom of the Arctic Ocean at the North Pole, some twelve thousand feet beneath the ice. They'd planted a large titanium Russian flag at the bottom and operated a kind of ultra-exclusive tourist service, ferrying several people able to pay the eighty-thousand-dollar fare to what they were calling the *real* North Pole.

The flag planting was solely symbolic, of course . . . but the Russians were trying to make something more of it. According to the way they read the map, their territorial waters, by international treaty, extended two hundred miles from their continental shelf. They were trying to make a case for the undersea Lomonosov Ridge, which extended out from the Siberian landmass almost all the way to Greenland, as a part of their continental shelf, a declaration that allowed them to claim fully half of the Arctic Ocean, including the North Pole and as far over the top of the world as the 180th meridian, as their sovereign territorial waters.

The whole matter was due to be adjudicated by the United Nations within the next couple of years, but in the meantime, the Russians had been doing a lot of saber rattling.

And the West had been rattling back. Canada and Denmark, especially, weren't about to let the Russian claim go unchallenged, and the United States was weighing in as well. As barren and cold as the ice cap was, various geological surveys conducted by both the United States and several other nations suggested that fully 25 percent of the world's as-yet-undiscovered oil and gas reserves might lie beneath the floor of the Arctic Ocean, a staggering bonanza of fossil fuels that might power the industrial nations for another century or more. If the Arctic Ocean remained for the most part international waters, anyone with the technological know-how could tap those petroleum reserves. Russia wanted to grab the bear's share of that treasure for herself, a move that could revitalize their creaking post-Soviet economy and make Mother Russia once again a major force in the modern world.

The NOAA station had been set up at least in part to reaffirm the United States' commitment to the Arctic Ocean being international waters. And McMillan and Yeats had come along with their own agenda, of course.

"What is your name?" the man asked, his voice disarmingly pleasant.

"Katharine McMillan," she told him. There was no harm in admitting that much, and the truth would be safer than a lie.

"Katharine. And my name is Feodor Golytsin. I work with a private corporation called Siberskii Masla."

McMillan had heard of it. The name meant "Siberian

Oil," and it was less a private corporation than it was an arm of the Russian government.

"And who," Golytsin continued, "are you working for?"

"NOAA," she replied. That was a lie but a completely plausible one. A check of NOAA's personnel files *would* show her listed as an employee. "That's the National Oceanographic and Atmospheric Administration."

"I know what NOAA is," the Russian said. "I suspect, however, that you are, in fact, CIA or possibly DIA. NOAA doesn't usually have access to such high-tech equipment as what we saw you dumping into the ocean. *Or* such a need for secrecy. You will tell me the truth."

"I've told you the truth. Go screw yourself. You have *no* right to—"

"*Right* does not enter into the picture, Katharine. Not here." He looked thoughtful. "If you choose not to cooperate, we have several possible courses of action."

Suddenly Golytsin reached out and grabbed her, yanking her close and spinning her around so he was holding her from behind. She shrieked and tried to hit him, but he was strong enough to clamp his arms down over hers and hold her immobile. She tried kicking his kneecap, but he lifted her off the deck and grabbed her left breast, hard.

"Let go of me, you bastard!"

For answer, he squeezed her, painfully, through her shirt. She shrieked, "*Stop! Let me go!*"

"There's the crew of this ship, for instance," he continued, ignoring her squirming and her shouts. "One hundred twenty-eight men on board the *Lebedev.* Another one hundred fifty on the *Taymyr.* Perhaps fifty on the *Granat.* And for most of them, it has been a *very* long time since they've seen their wives and girlfriends. You are an attractive woman, Katharine. For them, you might have considerable . . . entertainment value."

"Go to hell, you sick bastard!"

He released her suddenly, shoving her hard across the cabin. She tumbled into the bunk and lay there on her back, panting.

Golytsin took a step forward and bent forward, looming over her. "But I imagine even you would lose your appeal after a time. How long would it take, do you think? A month? Two? If we then decided you were worthless, that we needed to dispose of you, I might order you dropped into the ocean alongside this ship. Just how long do you think you would live? The water temperature here is actually a bit below freezing—minus two, maybe minus three degrees Celsius. The salt content, you know. You might survive, oh, two or three minutes.

"Or . . . better still, if we dropped you on the ice out there, somewhere. Even if we chose to return your cold-weather gear, how long before you froze to death, do you think? There are lots of very hungry polar bears out along the edge of the ice pack, hunting for seal. Do you think you would still be alive when the bears found you?

"In any case, Katharine, your body would *never* be found. *Never.*"

"I'm telling you the truth!" she yelled. "I'm with NOAA! I'm—"

Golytsin captured her jaw with one hand, silencing her, holding her head motionless. For a horrible moment, she was forced to look into his eyes. She was *certain* he was about to . . .

Then he released her. "But not yet," he told her. "I'll give you some time to think about your options, mm? But I suggest, Katharine, that you not test my patience."

He turned, strode to the door, and was gone. She heard the lock click behind him.

She lay on the bunk, still breathing hard. She was terrified—there was no other way to describe it. She was convinced that the bastard would do whatever he needed to do to get information out of her . . . rape, beatings, torture . . .

When she'd joined the National Security Agency, she'd done so as a technician, a very skilled and highly trained technician. The idea of being sent out into the field had been ludicrous; hell, as far as she knew, the NSA didn't even *have* field agents. And when she went over to the CIA, that had strictly been a temporary technical assignment.

How the hell had she let them talk her into fieldwork? This wasn't supposed to happen!

She began reviewing her options. Not one of them, she found, was at all pleasant.

9

Ice Station Bear
Arctic Ice Cap
82° 24' N, 179° 45' E
0125 hours, GMT – 12

EIGHTY-FIVE MILES FROM THE *Lebedev* and twelve time zones away from London, another storm was coming in. Dr. Chris Tomlinson could see it in the dark band of clouds just beginning to shroud the southwestern horizon in shadow, could feel it in the icy bite of the freshening wind. He finished wiping the rime ice from the anemometer high in the met tower and awkwardly clambered back down the narrow ladder. It was a thrice-daily chore shared by the odd mix of personnel here at the ice station. The anemometer and other weather instruments were mounted on the fifteen-foot tower to keep them clear of wind and spray at ice level, but they still tended to accumulate a thin layer of ice under the incessant spring wind.

The sun hung just above the southeastern horizon, wan and pale and as seemingly devoid of warmth as a silvery full moon.

In a more civilized clime, 0130 was the middle of the frigging night. Late in May at these latitudes, a month before the summer solstice, the sun never set but circled the horizon slowly clockwise with the turning of the Earth. With no real day or night, the actual time scarcely mattered, so the team ran on Eastern time. The National Climatic Data Center was in Asheville, North Carolina, and it was easier to coordinate work and communications schedules with everyone on the same clock.

Tomlinson carefully stepped off the ladder, his thick boots crunching lightly on the ice. Lieutenant Phil Segal was waiting for him at the bottom—his safety buddy, present just in case. Personnel were encouraged to go about in pairs or teams when they left the shelter of the Quonset hut that served as the small base's living quarters. Tomlinson had seen for himself how fast the wind could kick up sometimes, and when it mixed with fog or blowing snow, whiteout conditions could set in so fast that someone outside could become hopelessly lost just a few short feet from safety.

"Looks like we're fixing to have a blow," Segal said, looking up at the anemometer, now wildly and freely spinning in the breeze.

Tomlinson looked up at the instrument. "Ah. Thirty knots. Hardly worth the notation in the log."

"Tell you what, though," the NOAA officer said with a nasty chuckle. "Next time we send the tree huggers out here, right? Let them enjoy some of this here global warming first hand!"

Tomlinson laughed, but without much feeling. Like the other *official* personnel stationed here, he had little patience with their . . . guests, the five kids from Greenworld. What the bloody *hell* did they think they were trying to prove up here?

Kids? He snorted. Hardly. The youngest was in her mid-twenties, the oldest thirty-something. But the ten regular station personnel, three NOAA officers and seven scientists with the National Climatic Data Center, were here with a genuine purpose. The Greenworld bunch was up here grandstanding, nothing more. They claimed to be filming a documentary for PBS, but during the past week they'd done more grousing and bellyaching than camera work.

The two men trudged across the ice toward Bear One, the main hut. All told, there were four main structures in the camp and several smaller sheds and supply buildings, all of them flown up here slung beneath the belly of CH-47 helicopters and assembled on the ice. The largest, dubbed Bear One, was the center of the tiny, isolated community's life and warmth. Near the building's door, an American flag, already ragged in the constant wind, fluttered from a piece of pipe raised as an impromptu flagpole.

Officially, the place was the NOAA Arctic Meteorological Station Bravo, but the men and women currently living here called it Ice Station Bear . . . a tribute, in part, to a pair of old Alistair MacLean thrillers with similar names, plus just a bit of gallows humor drawn from the latest spate of international one-upmanship with the Russians. Wrangel Island was just 760 miles distant, directly due south, and Mys Shmidta, the nearest Russian military base and staging area on the Siberian mainland, about 150 miles beyond that.

The Russian specter had been looming quite large in the tiny community's thoughts lately. At least every other day, jet aircraft, military aircraft out of Mys Shmidta, had overflown the station, flying low enough to rattle the hut's walls. Sometimes, the already-chancy radio communications with Asheville were blotted out by what Commander Greg Larson thought was Russian jamming.

And, of course, for the past week they'd been repeatedly warned that they were trespassing and must leave Russian territory at once.

What a crock, Tomlinson thought. The Russians were trying to intimidate them into leaving. He wondered what the hell it was they were hiding eighty-some miles over the northern horizon and if Yeats and his people had managed to get a good look.

Three members of the NOAA expedition had left yesterday, taking three of the snowmobiles east to Remote One, an unmanned weather station seventy miles across the ice. Theoretically, they were checking the instrumentation and taking some ice-thickness readings.

The thing was, everyone in the expedition knew that Yeats and McMillan were spooks for the CIA, though that particular tidbit had not been shared with the Greenworld visitors. They also knew that Yeats, McMillan, and Haines—a genuine climatologist but also an expert on traveling over the Arctic ice—had gone to Remote One more to snoop on the nearby Russian base than to check instrument packages.

Currently, the surest bets making the rounds among the scientists were that the Russians were prospecting for oil. Everyone knew they wanted to claim half the Arctic Ocean as their own in order to get at the oil and natural gas beneath the sea floor.

Yeats, McMillan, and Haines should have been back by now. There'd been a brief message five hours ago—and not a word since.

Tomlinson suppressed a shudder. Something was wrong. He could feel it. They were going to have to send another team out to learn what had happened to the first. He wished they could send the Greenworld kids.

We don't need this shit, he thought, bitter. *Missing people, hostile Russians . . . and we have to babysit, too.*

He wondered if the ecology nuts had come here because the Russians wouldn't let them go to their base instead.

Ecology nuts. Tomlinson had little respect for people who made sweeping and hyper-dramatic claims without solid scientific evidence backing them up. A number of high-profile organizations—organizations such as Greenpeace and Greenworld and the Sierra Club—wanted to keep this frozen wilderness pristine and the petroleum resources below the ice untapped. *Tree huggers,* as Tomlinson and his associates thought of the five unwanted visitors to the base, though there wasn't a single tree for them to hug within the better part of a thousand miles. Their agenda didn't have a chance, no matter how many polar bears they'd been able to film out on the ice. You couldn't stop progress . . . or the power of the almighty dollar.

What did the Greenworlders think they could accomplish by finagling a visit to Ice Station Bear?

He knew one thing. They wouldn't have been here at all if one of them hadn't been the daughter of a New England congressman. Raymond C. Cabot had been pulling strings at NOAA and the Department of Commerce for a month, getting permission for Lynnley Cabot and her four friends to take this little junket into the frozen north. Tomlinson wondered if Cabot was just a doting father who couldn't say no, or if he saw a way of making political capital. Cabot was a Democrat and liked thumping the environmentalist bible loudly and often. Maybe he thought a docudrama of his darling daughter in a parka would help him with his next campaign.

Tomlinson followed Segal through the door into the hut, letting the wind bang it hard behind him. The Quonset hut's interior was surprisingly cramped, given the exterior size of the thing. Half was partitioned off into sleeping quarters, with the women's area sequestered off behind a curtain at the back. Another curtain hid the chemical toilet and the tiny portable shower stall; most of the walls and available free space was occupied by boxes—food and scientific instruments. The opposite end was devoted to the radio set, two computer workstations, and the meteorology instrumentation. Clothing hung drying from various overhead hooks and hangers, creating a cluttered, humid forest of textiles. Social life inside the community was defined by the space around the stove and heater. Most of the people were there, at the moment, looking up at the sudden explosion of cold and wind from outside.

"Hey, we thought you were the Russians," Tom McCauley said. He was a heavyset North Dakotan with a twisted sense of humor, who'd first used his degree in meteorology to get a job as a TV weatherman, but who later moved to Asheville to take a job with the National Climatic Data Center.

"*Nyet, tovarisch,*" Segal said, grinning as he threw back the hood of his parka. "*Ya nyeh Ruskii.*"

"Too bad," Fred Masters said. He was playing cards with two other climatologists and slapped a card down on the table. "We were hoping you would save us from our Greenpeace friends, here."

"That's Green*world,*" Lynnley Cabot said, sounding disgusted. "Jackass."

"Sorry, sweetie," Masters replied, picking up another card. "From here I can't tell the difference."

"Ah, it's easy, Fred," Susan Fritcherson said, picking up the discarded card. "Greenpeace wants to save the whales. Greenworld wants the whales to inherit the Earth."

"They'd do a better job running the world than we have," Ken Richardson, the ostensible leader of the Greenworld group, put in.

"Pipe down, all of you," Commander Greg Larson said. He was the senior NOAA officer and the expedition team leader. "I've told you yahoos before . . . we don't have the room for that kind of nonsense. Or the patience."

The bickering subsided, as it had to. The Greenworlders had been told in no uncertain terms that this base was under NOAA's jurisdiction and therefore under *military* jurisdiction. They would obey the regulations and the orders given by the NOAA officers . . . or they could start walking the 650 miles across ice and open water to Point Barrow.

NOAA was a scientific agency under the aegis of the U.S. Department of Commerce. Most of its employees were civilian scientists and administrators, but about four hundred of its personnel made up the NOAA Corps, one of America's seven uniformed services. All were commissioned officers, wearing uniforms similar to those of the U.S. Navy.

Tomlinson stripped off his parka, boots, and snow pants, hung them on a wall hook, then squeezed into the tiny galley area to pour himself a cup of coffee. That was one good thing about this place; there was always a large pot more or less fresh brewed, and if your standards weren't too high, it was pretty good. He'd only been outside for ten minutes, but there was ice laced through his mustache and beard.

"You get through to the Center yet, Bill?" he asked the man currently at the radio. Lieutenant Bill Walters was the third NOAA officer on the team, a communications specialist.

"Nah," Walters said, pulling the headset off his head and tossing it on the desk. "Our Russki friends are being too noisy right now. And the solar interference is worse than yesterday, too."

"Cold out there, Chris?" Masters asked.

"Not too bad. About minus two Celsius. But it's going to get colder. Another squall's coming in."

"Is it going to be . . . bad?" Jenny Cicero, another member of the Greenworld delegation, asked. She sounded scared. When a full gale was blowing outside, the Quonset hut walls shook and pounded as though giants were plying it with jackhammers. Such a storm had hit a few hours after the Greenworlders had arrived last week, and Tomlinson had thought they were going to have to ship Cicero back to Point Barrow in a straightjacket.

Welcome to the Arctic, kids, he thought.

"Nah," Fritcherson told her. "Twenty below . . . wind at fifty knots. Heavy snow and icing. Piece of cake."

"Is Yeats going to get his people back here before it hits?" Larson asked. "That's what I want to know."

"Don't know, sir," Walters said. "They have a satcom with them, but . . ."

"Maybe we should take a couple of snowmobiles out to look for them," Tomlinson suggested.

"Not yet," Larson replied. "I don't want more people running around out there and maybe getting lost in a whiteout." He sounded worried.

"They have GPS," Fritcherson pointed out. "Even if they can't get through the radio interference, they can navigate by satellite."

"Keep trying to raise them on the satcom," Larson told Walters.

"Yes, sir. But our regular frequencies are full of garbage." He listened for a moment. "I think the Russians may be holding some kind of military maneuvers out there."

"Nothing to do with us," Larson said. "Keep at it."

"Yes, sir."

Larson looked around the crowded room. "Where's Benford?"

"Sacked out, Skipper," McCauley told him, jerking a thumb over his shoulder toward the curtained-off bunks. "Said he was wiped."

Larson scowled but said nothing. Tomlinson could guess what was going through his mind, however. The five Greenworlders were *very* unwelcome guests. They ate the expedition's food, put a strain on the sanitary facilities, took up valuable space both with their bodies and with their baggage, and brought a nasty air of politics and confrontation into the tiny and tight-knit world of the NOAA climate research expedition, all without bringing a single useful skill to the camp. Oh, there was make-work enough—cleaning, cooking, stowing or unpacking gear, even taking turns cleaning the ice off the outside sensors—but it simply wasn't enough compared with what they took. In Arctic exploration, no less than if this had been a scientific expedition to Mars, *every* person had to pull his or her weight. There was no room for freeloaders.

Tomlinson wondered what the Connecticut congressman had paid in the way of a contribution to the Climatic Data Center to get them to foist these five on the expedition. They were supposed to be filming some sort of documentary, and for the first few days they'd done nothing but get in the way with their cameras and sound equipment and inane questions. Lately, though, they'd pretty much kept to themselves.

The trouble was, space was at such a premium in Bear One that they still got in the way.

Benford in particular was a monumental pain in the ass. The guy started arguments with the team personnel, had to be chivvied to perform even minimal chores, and maintained an all-round sour and unpleasant attitude that already had affected the station's morale.

Well, it wouldn't last forever. The freeloaders had been here a week and were scheduled to be here for another two weeks more, until the next scheduled supply flight up from Barrow. When the tree huggers were gone, the ice station was going to feel a *lot* roomier.

Tomlinson had to squeeze past three of them, Cabot, Cicero, and Steven Moore, to reach an empty chair by the heater.

Yeah, he couldn't wait for them to be gone.

Harry Benford lay in his narrow bunk, face to the wall and his privacy curtain pulled across the open side, but he wasn't sleeping. He'd heard the bickering a moment ago. *Good. Keep up the pressure. . . .*

In his hand, pressed up against his ear, was what looked like a transistor radio, the size of a pack of cigarettes. It tuned to only a single channel, however, one reserved for military transmissions.

The static was terrible, reception lousy, and atmospherics squealed and wailed as he listened, but twice a day at the same times he always sought the privacy of his bunk, the toilet, or outside in order to listen for five minutes.

And today, finally, the signal he'd been listening for came through.

He'd been wondering if it would ever come. There wasn't much to it, a man's voice repeating the same word over and over: "Rodina . . . Rodina . . . Rodina. . . ."

Quietly Benford turned off the receiver and slipped it under his mattress.

It was time for the sleeper to awake and carry out his mission.

Offices of the National Security Council
The White House, Washington, D.C.
1638 hours EDT

"The President," George Francis Wehrum said in a cautiously neutral tone, "is *furious.* I should tell you that Dr. Bing is recommending a complete restructuring of the intelligence hierarchy."

Rubens kept his face impassive. It was, actually, no worse than he'd been expecting, especially after he'd been kept waiting for over an hour before being ushered into the Presence. "With respect, Mr. Wehrum," Rubens said carefully, "this is scarcely the time for recriminations, for petty politics, or for . . . personal vendettas. The situation is serious."

"We know that. That's why Dr. Bing considers it necessary to take certain steps."

"By refusing to let me do my job?"

"There is some question at this point if you are the best man for the job. It may be time to restructure your agency to some extent." He shrugged and almost managed to look embarrassed. "You *must* know that this has been coming for some time."

Rubens took a deep breath. "Mr. Wehrum, this is not about turf wars between the NSA and the CIA. One of my best field agents is dead. We believe the Russian mob had a hand in it, though we don't yet know why. I intend to find out."

Wehrum dismissively waved a hand. "I'm not talking about that. When you conduct covert operations of the sort your Desk Three so enjoys, you *will* suffer casualties. You know that. I am referring to the loss of a three-hundred-and-thirty-nine-million-dollar aircraft and its highly trained Air Force pilot. That F-22 was over Russian territorial waters, where *you* sent it. Dr. Bing intends to conduct a full investigation into the reasons you made that decision, and its consequences."

Rubens sighed. This was getting him nowhere. "May I see Dr. Bing?"

"Dr. Bing is in a closed session with the President and with the DNI and the D/CIA."

That stung. "I should be there."

"You should not. The DNI will inform you when—*if*—it is necessary for your department to have administrative access to POTUS."

DNI—the Director of National Intelligence. Nominally the head of all U.S. intelligence agencies, James Fenton was known to favor a sharp streamlining and redefining of American intelligence. "D/CIA" referred to the Director of Central Intelligence, the head of the CIA, Roger Smallbourn. Smallbourn was a political hack, but one with aspirations identical to Fenton's; his Deputy Director of Operations, Debra Collins, had been trying to take Desk Three out of the NSA's organizational chart and fold it into the CIA since its inception. Within the tangled world of the inside-the-Beltway jungle of D.C., wars were won or lost, careers saved or lost, over direct access to POTUS, government slang for the President of the United States.

Rubens grimaced. "If they're discussing the future of the NSA or Desk Three—"

"Actually, they're discussing the Russian ice-grab," Wehrum said. He sounded smug, with a touch of amusement to his voice and the way he shrugged. "It has *nothing* to do with you. Nothing whatsoever."

Rubens scowled at the other man for a moment. That last bit of information—about the Russian crisis—had been both purely gratuitous and utterly vicious. Wehrum had no business mentioning the President's agenda, but he'd done so, it seemed clear, solely to let Rubens know that he was in the doghouse at the moment.

Wehrum was Bing's senior aide within the National Security Council and, therefore, an extremely powerful man. The NSC, currently consisting of about one hundred staffers working out of one of the concrete-walled lower levels of the White House basement, was responsible for hashing out defense and foreign policy issues before they reached the President's desk. The National Security Advisor—a title generally abbreviated as "ANSA," for "Advisor on National Security Affairs," in order to distinguish it from the acronym for the National Security Agency—briefed the President on all potential international problems and, during times of crisis, ran the White House Situation Room. Where the Chairman of the Joint Chiefs was, by law, the President's chief advisor on military matters, the ANSA was responsible for a whole range of diplomatic, economic, and intelligence issues as well as military ones.

By mentioning the DNI, Wehrum was not so subtly reminding Rubens that the Director of National Intelligence was the director of all U.S. intelligence agencies. And by mentioning the D/CIA, Wehrum was reminding him that the CIA felt that it had the right to manage the lion's share of American intelligence and that the NSA should be restricted to its historic purview of SIGINT.

Put another way, Washington functioned on funding and on size. The NSA was the largest of America's intelligence agencies and received the biggest chunk of the funding pie. The CIA had been looking for ways to cut into that pie slice for a long time.

Rubens was close to making a bitter retort, but he clamped down on the surge of anger. Damn it, he could feel his blood pressure rising, a red heat climbing behind his eyes.

Within Washington, the man who determined where the paper went and, even more, who decided who got to talk face-to-face with policy-makers such as the President or the ANSA was the man who ruled, who controlled the *real* power within the government. The former ANSA, George Haddad, had been a close personal friend of Rubens', a mentor and a confidant. His death had been devastating personally for Rubens.

It had also profoundly affected Rubens' career and possibly the future of Desk Three as well. He was used to having direct personal access to the President; now, though, Rubens could feel himself being shouldered aside, ignored, sidelined . . . and possibly even reduced to the role of official scapegoat.

But venting his anger here and now would get him nowhere. If Rubens had learned one thing in his years of public service, it was that patience was almost as valuable in this town as face time with the President.

So Rubens forced himself to relax. A longtime practitioner of Hatha Yoga, he let his mind momentarily settle into a place of calm, watching as he drew in a deep breath from the belly. Through breath control alone, Pranayama, it was possible to control the blood pressure . . . and the deep-seated fury within.

He released the breath and, with it, the rising knot of anger.

"Very well," he said after a moment. He opened his eyes to find Wehrum staring at him curiously. "Please inform Dr. Bing that I do wish to see her at her earliest convenience. Shall I give you my report on Operation Magpie?"

Wehrum shrugged again. "You can send it as an e-mail attachment. I'll see that it gets to the proper desks."

Another slap, a means of telling him quite distinctly that his report wasn't important enough to warrant discussion or close consideration.

"I also wish to discuss future operational plans." That

was something that *did* have to go through Bing, at the very least.

"Dr. Bing has instructed me to inform you," Wehrum said, "that *all* Desk Three operations should be put on hold for the time being. It is possible that Operation Magpie will be detailed to another agency." He hesitated. "Why 'Magpie,' anyway?"

"I beg your pardon?"

"Why'd you name the operation Magpie?"

"Our Russian ops currently share a bird theme," Rubens said. "Magpie, Blue Jay. We've found a connection between those two, by the way, and we think it's important."

"Oh?"

"'Augurs and understood relations have,'" Rubens quoted, "'(by magotpies and choughs and rooks) brought forth the secret'st man of blood.'"

Wehrum smirked. "What's that supposed to mean?"

"*Macbeth*," Rubens said. "Act three, scene four. *Magotpies* are what we call magpies today. The King was referring to things in nature revealing a man's bloody secrets."

"If you say so. In any case, I suggest you start making whatever arrangements you need to make to bring your 'magotpies' home."

Rubens considered this. "We're doing so now. There are still some loose ends to tidy up in St. Petersburg, however."

Again, a dismissive wave. "Whatever. I don't need to know the details. But you should be prepared to hand the operation in all respects over to Debra Collins. I suspect that's where this is going. I can't imagine them allowing your Desk Three to continue operating while an investigation is under way. What other irons do you have in the fire?"

"Several. Blue Jay is investigating the Russian mafia, which appears to be making a serious effort to take control of Russian petroleum resources. And Sunny Weather involves the protection of a scientist at a symposium in England." He decided not to add that there was now a strong link between the Russian ops and the attempt to kill Spencer in London. "That's the one where we just lost an agent."

"Not my concern." Wehrum sniffed. "If I were you, I would simply get my house in order and await further instructions. Someone on the DNI's staff will, no doubt, be in touch with you on the details soon."

Wehrum reached for a file lying in his in-box and flipped it open, effectively ending the interview.

A most unsatisfactory interview, from all perspectives. Rubens was furious as he left Wehrum's office. There'd been nothing in this meeting that could not have been handled more efficiently by e-mail or phone.

As Rubens pulled out of the secure underground parking lot and turned left on Fifteenth Street, he was considering his options. Clearly, Bing, Smallbourn, and Collins were going to use the F-22 shoot-down as a reason to remove Desk Three from the aegis of the NSA and, quite likely, to demand Rubens' resignation as well.

If that was the way it had to be, so be it. Rubens disliked Washington inner-circle politics, hated them with a white-hot passion, in fact, that frequently had him wondering if retaining his position as the NSA's Deputy Director was even worth it. Only two things had kept him at this damned job for as long as he'd been here—his loyalty to the agents working for him and his rock-solid belief that Desk Three *was* making a difference in a very dangerous, very twisted world.

Whatever happened, he was not going to abandon his people.

First things first. Dean was on the way to London and would have to take over the investigation of Karr's death. And Magpie needed to be pulled out of Russia.

But something was nagging Rubens, something sinister. What was the connection, through Sergei Braslov, between a scientist working on global warming and the Russian mafia? Why did they want Spencer dead? And what was their link with Greenworld?

Rubens was determined to follow those questions through for as long as they let him.

And to hell with what anyone *in Washington thinks.*

10

Ice Station Bear
Arctic Ice Cap
82° 24' N, 179° 45' E
0205 hours, GMT − 12

HARRY BENFORD STEPPED OUT into the bitter wind. The clouds on the horizon, during the past day, had spread across most of the sky, blotting out the wan and heatless sun and causing the temperature to drop by a good ten degrees. Snow snapped along with the stiffening breeze, stinging the exposed skin of his face. His breath steamed in quick-paced puffs, quickly stripped away by the wind.

God, I hate this place.

God, in fact, had very little to do with this forsaken corner of the planet, at least in Benford's heartfelt opinion. It was amusing to remember that the lowest circle of Hell, according to Dante's *Inferno,* was not fire but ice, that Satan was pictured as a devouring monster trapped in eternal ice.

Hell indeed.

But Golytsin had promised Benford money, a *lot* of money, to play spy. Payment was due when he completed this mission—half a million dollars American deposited untraceably in a Bahamian bank. At the moment, though, he was wondering if it was worth it, if he should have held out for more.

Up ahead, just visible through the layers of horizontally blowing snow, Larson and Richardson had reached the garage and were going in. Benford heard the yapping of the dogs as the door opened.

"The garage" was what they all called the building, a large shed twenty yards from the main building. Inside, along with propane tanks, spare parts, stored food and gasoline, were the expedition's snowmobiles—three of them, now that Yeats had the other three out on the ice— as well as the kennel holding the expedition's dogs. While snowmobiles provided excellent mobility over the ice cap, the expedition had brought along a sled dog team as well, a bit of a belt-and-suspenders precaution against the possibility of mechanical breakdown. Arctic conditions were appallingly tough on mechanical devices. One of the chores assigned to the Greenworld visitors was the daily routine of thawing out chunks of meat, then throwing them to the dogs.

Benford reached the door, hesitating. He was carrying a canvas satchel tucked under his arm and didn't particularly want to have to explain what was in it. Extending from one end of the bag was a heavy, four-foot-long pry bar. He took a long look around, but no one else was visible, no one following from the Quonset hut, no one else out on the ice. Back in the main building, several of the team members were preparing to go out on the ice. There'd still been no word from Yeats or the other two expedition people, and Larson had finally decided that a run by snowmobile out to Remote One was necessary. Yeats and his people should have been back, now, long before this, and the storm would make their survival problematical.

Benford eased the door open and stepped inside the garage. It was chilly inside—he could still see his breath with each cold exhalation—but warmer than the bitter cold of the wind. The dogs yapped and bawled. Richardson was near the door, opening up the locker that contained slabs of thawed meat; Larson was a few feet away, pulling a five-gallon container of gasoline off of a rack. As was usual, they were arguing.

"I'm *not* disputing global warming, damn it!" Larson snapped. "But there's no proof yet, one way or another, that we have anything to do with it!"

"Proof? What proof do you need?" Richardson snapped back. He was a young man, in his twenties, and passionately opposed to the injustices of the world. "The industrial revolution comes along and *bang*! Temperatures go up. Carbon dioxide goes up. Summers start getting hotter—"

"An oversimplification, Richardson. Back in the seventies there was a scare that the climate was getting colder, remember that?"

"That was before my time."

"Kids." The word was a snort. "Yeah, well, there was a downturn in global temperatures from the fifties through the seventies that suggested we were on the verge of a new ice age. The point is, we don't know. All we can do is gather data at this point, which is why we're up here in the first place." He looked past Richardson as Benford stepped inside and pulled the door shut behind him. "Oh, Benford. What do *you* want?"

"I just came out to help. Thought I could give a hand fueling the snowmobiles."

Larson looked surprised, then shrugged beneath his heavy parka. "Suit yourself. Here." He passed Benford the container of gasoline, then turned to reach for another one.

"How many are we fueling up?" Benford asked, shouldering the bag so he could take the can. "All three?"

"Just two. I want to leave one on reserve in case something happens to the rescuers. We'll leave one plus the dog team in reserve. Just in case . . ."

He didn't elaborate, but Benford heard the worry in his voice. Fifteen people at this outpost . . . three of them now missing. Communications with the mainland were dodgy at best, and it was two weeks until the next supply flight was due in. Commander Larson was having to do some nasty juggling with his assets, trying to find the three missing personnel without leaving the remaining twelve at risk.

Larson handed Benford the second container of gasoline, then nodded down the concrete aisle toward the other end of the building. "Go ahead; get started with the fueling. I'll be with you in a minute and we'll do the mechanical checkout."

"Right."

As he lugged the gasoline past the cacophony of the dogs, he could still hear fragments of the argument at his back.

He paid no attention. The philosophical divide between the scientists and the Greenworlders had reached a fever's pitch during the past few days. Benford had added a little fuel to the fire here and there, helping to enflame the debate, but it had scarcely been necessary. The scientists resented, deeply and angrily, the Greenworld presence here. For their part, the other four Greenworlders felt the scientists were all but betraying the human species by downplaying the world-threatening dangers of major climatic change. Richardson and that little rich bitch Cabot, in particular, were convinced that the climatologists all were deep in the hip pockets of Big Oil, that they were being paid to downplay the immediacy of the global threat.

Benford didn't buy any of that himself. He'd joined

Greenworld because the people represented by Feodor had sought him out during his trip to St. Petersburg two years ago and offered him a proposition, quite literally an offer he couldn't refuse.

He wished now he had refused it. Things were getting entirely too nasty, too risky personally. The trouble was, he'd gotten into this mess step by tiny step, had never seen ahead of time where the bastards were leading him.

Two years before, he'd been a very junior sales rep for Wildcat Technologies, a Houston-based firm that manufactured high-tech drilling equipment for the petroleum industry . . . especially for certain highly specialized deep-ocean drilling rigs.

In 2006, Benford had been sent to Russia with a WT sales team to negotiate a $500 million deal. A Russian petroleum company was interested in the new robotic drilling rigs that could actually work on the seabed itself, and the order for a single test rig alone would have guaranteed Wildcat's success.

Unfortunately, doing any business in Russia at all these days was an ongoing exercise in frustration, unforeseen expense, and delay. The Russian mafia had its hand in everything—including in the Russian petroleum industry, it turned out—which meant they had to be paid off before any negotiations could even begin. That half-billion-dollar deal would cost 10 percent, an extra 50 million, just to get to the talking stage, and there'd be another 10 percent in fees, bribes, and special considerations for each consignment shipped into the country.

And Wildcat Technologies, frankly, was on the ropes. They'd developed the Deepsea platform over the past ten years at considerable expense, and they'd overextended on the loans needed to begin production. So far, though, none of the big global petro companies had shown more than an initial and passing interest. The Canadians were intrigued, but there were some governmental barriers there on both sides of the border . . . and way too many rumors that Mobil and Exxon both were working on their own versions of the Deepsea drilling technology.

The Russians could make or break Wildcat Technology with this one order, and that extra 10 to 20 percent on the red side of the ledgers might well have killed the entire deal.

And then Benford had met Masha.

Maria Antoninova. She'd been one of the interpreters for the sales team in Russia, blond, leggy, and drop-dead gorgeous. They'd flirted, harmlessly enough . . . and then one evening after a particularly discouraging round of negotiations with the reps from Russian Petro-Gas, he'd come back to his hotel room to find her naked and waiting for him in the bed.

The next morning she'd told him that she might know some people who could help.

And, in fact, Feodor had been *most* helpful. The barriers, the difficulties, the need for yet another round of high-level approvals and special payments, all had vanished as if by magic. Benford had been able to secure several signatures in particular that had opened up a whole new world of possibilities for Wildcat, including no less than Putin's signature on a long-term agreement for continued sales and service that would guarantee Wildcat's survival for the next decade.

It hadn't hurt that the unexpected turnaround had transformed Benford, the very junior member of the sales team, into Houston's fair-haired boy, with promises of a big raise and bonuses that would set him up *very* well in the years ahead.

And all he'd had to do in exchange was make a promise to join a bunch of tree-hugger freaks out to save the planet . . . and maybe do a little job for Golytsin later on, when the time was right. Where was the harm in that?

Joining Greenworld had been simple enough. Apparently, the Russians already had people—sleepers, they called them—planted inside the organization, though Benford still had no idea what interest the Russians could possibly have with the environmental activists. He'd joined the American branch of Greenworld by contacting one of their agents in California and happily gone back to work in Houston for more money than he'd dreamed was possible. Not only that, but it turned out, just by chance, that Masha was now working in Houston for a travel agency and she'd wanted to keep seeing him. Benford was married already, but Masha hadn't minded in the least seeing him as his mistress while he stayed married to Georgette. Life had been good. So *very* good.

Benford reached the far end of the aisle, set down the gasoline, and looked around. Yeah, this would work okay. And he might not get another chance, not one as good as this, anyway. Both Larson and Richardson were here, with no one else around. There wouldn't be a better time.

He was terrified. Could he go through with it?

He had to. That was the problem. He *had* to. There was no other way out.

Benford had thought he was home free. As a member of Greenworld, he received a certain amount of junk mail and computer spam, but he hadn't been expected to *do* anything. He'd not even had to attend any meetings. Then, just five weeks ago, his contact had phoned him and told him it was time to make good on his promise.

When he'd learned what was involved, what was expected of him, he'd done his best to back out and renegotiate the deal. Three weeks in the Arctic . . . God, there was a *reason* he liked living on the Texas gulf, despite the mosquitoes and the cockroaches. And what they wanted him to do . . .

He'd tried to get out of it; he really had. He'd threatened to go to the authorities and blow this filthy thing wide open. But it seemed the bastards had been filming him and Masha in that hotel room through a one-way mirror, both that first night and on some of their subsequent trysts over the two years since.

If he didn't do precisely what he'd been ordered to do, Georgette would find out about Masha. Worse, his bosses at Wildcat would receive convincing documentation suggesting he'd been feeding the Russians highly proprietary information on Deepsea drilling technology, passing it through Masha to Moscow.

It meant utter ruination—losing his wife and his job and his overpriced house with its pool and hot tub and expensive back deck. It meant blacklisting in the industry and a very expensive lawsuit, and probably criminal charges and jail as well.

But if he did this thing, just this one thing, his handlers would turn him loose. He'd have the negatives of him and Masha *and* the incriminating documents to do with as he pleased. And he'd have a half-million dollars besides.

Yeah . . . an offer he couldn't refuse.

The whole thing didn't make an ounce of sense. The Cold War was over, right? The Russians were friends now, friends and business partners. It wasn't like they were asking him to steal military secrets or betray his country or anything like that.

But to actually *kill* someone . . .

Golytsin had explained with great care why he had to do this, and do it this way. A simple murder wasn't enough. The murder had to look like it had been committed by one of the NOAA officers. Otherwise, it would all

be for nothing . . . and Benford would lose everything
he'd worked for since leaving college.

He didn't like the idea of murder, but it wasn't nearly
as bad as the alternative. . . .

British Airways Flight 2112
200 miles southeast of Nova Scotia
1710 hours EDT

Charlie Dean sat in 7A, a window seat in tourist class,
looking down on the brightly sunlit waters of the western
Atlantic. *Tommy . . . dead?*

No. God damn it, no! It made no sense whatsoever.
Tommy Karr had been a good agent, but more important,
he'd been a *lucky* agent. At times, it had seemed like nothing could touch the exuberant young giant with the un-
kempt blond hair and unfailing grin.

Everyone back at NSA headquarters had been shaken
by the news . . . no, *stunned.* It just didn't seem possible
that Tommy was gone.

Damn it, this was going to hit Lia hard. Her relationship with Karr had been a thorny one, full of jabs and put-
downs and outright arguments at times, but Dean knew
she liked and respected the guy, despite the sometimes
acid banter.

Somehow, it made it even worse that Rubens had left
the job of actually telling Lia to him, a job Dean was *not*
going to enjoy. On the other hand, of course, it would
have been worse if she learned about the death through
other channels—a radio call or a terse e-mail from headquarters. Dean understood why she hadn't been told
while she was still in the field.

But *God,* this was going to be hard.

Almost as hard, just possibly, as identifying the body,

picking up Karr's effects, and arranging to have him shipped back home.

"How about you then, sir?"

"Eh?"

An attractive blond flight attendant was leaning over him. "Something to drink, sir?" She had a lovely British accent.

"Um, no. Not right now. Thank you."

"You just give me a ring if there's anything I can get for you."

"Right. Thanks."

This was the same flight Tommy had been booked on a couple of days ago.

Rubens himself had rescheduled Dean's flight. His trip to St. Petersburg was off, he'd been told. Instead, he would catch a shuttle for the quick hop up to JFK, and there catch British Airways Flight 2112, part of the regular transatlantic service between New York and London.

Dean was used to sudden changes in orders and schedules, often with no explanation . . . but Rubens had explained this one carefully.

Tommy Karr . . . dead?

Dean had wondered at first why they'd insisted on putting him on the same flight Karr had taken, but it did make sense. As Rubens had told him, "Don't take anything for granted, Dean. This thing is big, bigger than we've been seeing. I'd like you to talk to the flight crew, the flight attendants, maybe see if any of them remember Karr."

Dean wondered if this attendant had waited on Karr, if she even remembered him? He looked at her name badge.

Julie.

After she was gone, Dean brought his hand up to his jaw and pretended to rest his head, using his hand to block his mouth from view. "You guys on the air?"

"We're here, Charlie," Rockman said back in the Art

Room. His voice was fuzzy and indistinct, with bursts of static. Sunspots, they'd told Dean. Communications were going to be patchy in spots for the next several months.

"Just wondering. Did Tommy have any conversations with the flight attendants the other day? Something you folks might have picked up?"

"Sorry, Charlie, you're breaking up. Say again after 'Tommy.'"

He repeated himself, trying to speak distinctly while keeping his voice low enough that none of the other passengers would overhear.

"Okay," Rockman said. "Got it. I was running Tommy during his flight, but Sandy was handling him later on, at the hotel. I do know he was chatting one girl up on the plane, though. Took her back to his room after he got in, in fact."

"Got a name for her?"

"It'll be in the transcripts. I can check."

"Do it, please."

"Hang on; I'm calling it up. You got something?"

"Not really. Mostly just wondering if someone on the flight crew remembered Tommy, y'know?" He was also remembering that someone had followed Tommy from Heathrow Airport all the way into downtown London. He wasn't sure why yet, since the ambush had taken place the next day at the symposium, but Karr hadn't picked up that tail at random. They'd been waiting for him on the street outside the Heathrow hotel. That strongly suggested a chain of contacts, picking him up and handing him off.

"Yeah. Okay . . . I have it here. 'Julie.'" There was a pause as Rockford read the transcript. "Wow. Looks like they were going at it pretty hot and heavy until Tommy shut down his comm system. Don't have a last name on her here, but we could check British Airways records and see who's scheduled for that flight."

"Not necessary. Probably not even important. But I may see what she knows."

Besides, it would give him something else to think about than his upcoming reunion with Lia.

Ice Station Bear
Arctic Ice Cap
82° 24' N, 179° 45' E
0538 hours, GMT – 12

The snowmobiles rested on their wooden racks at the far end of the aisle. The barking of the dogs was so shrill and loud, Benford could hardly hear himself think. Which, as he thought about it, wasn't a bad thing at all. Damn it, how had he gotten himself into this? . . .

He set the gasoline cans down, then reached into the canvas shoulder bag. Inside were two items—the pry bar, stuck halfway out of the bag, and a heavy canvas belt with a black holster dangling from its length. Holding the bar in one hand, he set the belt and holster on the floor.

Benford stepped back, moving into a niche formed by stacks of supply crates, which placed him out of sight. Holding the pry bar in both hands, he hefted it, getting the feel of its weight.

"Commander Larson!" he shouted. "Can you come here?"

There was no answer. Peeking around the corner of the crates, Benford could see both Larson and Richardson at the far end of the building, their backs to him. The damned dogs were making so much racket, the men couldn't hear him.

This was bad. He was sweating, now, and his heart was pounding. He hadn't anticipated the possibility of not being heard against the racket.

"*Hey!*" he screamed, bellowing as loud as he could.

Startled, the dogs stopped barking for just a few seconds, long enough for him to shout, "*Commander Larson!*"

The barking started up again, but not as loudly, for now. Benford heard Larson moving just behind the sheltering corner, heard him say, "What the hell?" as he found the gun belt on the floor. That holster was Larson's own, holding his 9mm service Beretta. Benford had taken the weapon from Larson's personal locker hours before, along with a loaded magazine, hiding them in the satchel. "Benford! What the hell is this?"

In the next moment, Larson came into clear view as he stooped over the holster, reaching for it, his head at about the level of Benford's waist.

Benford had been gripping one end of the pry bar with both gloved hands, holding the bar to one side and low, next to his leg. As Larson bent over the holster, Benford swung the bar, pivoting, coming around hard and up, across his body, the pry bar first catching Larson awkwardly on his arm but then slamming up into his face.

The blow was clumsy. Benford was badly positioned, squeezed in as he was behind the stack of crates, and he'd almost squandered the swing by accidentally striking Larson's arm first. Still, Benford managed to hit the man squarely enough and hard enough to knock him over, sending him toppling against the crates, a few of which came tumbling down on top of him as he collapsed in a sprawl on the decking. Larson's face was gushing blood from a broken nose, his hands and legs moving feebly. The dogs went berserk. One husky, easily over a hundred pounds, slammed itself against the chain-link fencing of the kennel.

Stooping, Benford checked the NOAA officer. Larson was unconscious and bleeding heavily.

Quickly Benford dropped the bar, peeled off his gloves, and picked up the holster, fumbling with the catch until he could open it and draw Larson's Beretta. Benford fished the magazine from the satchel, nudged the end into the grip, and slapped it home, dragging the slide back and letting it snap forward, chambering a round.

Now came the really tough part . . . except that Benford felt surer, more confident, now that he'd taken the first irrevocable step. Holding the weapon in his right hand, he turned so that it would be hidden behind his body. "Richardson!" he screamed. "Richardson! Come here! Something's happened!"

No response. Cautiously Benford peeked around the corner of those crates still stacked after Larson's fall, looking for the other Greenworlder.

Richardson was not in sight.

God! Benford was close to screaming with frustration and growing panic. Where had Richardson gone? A moment later, though, the door opened again and Richardson reentered the garage, carrying another armload of frozen meat from the ice locker outside. Benford almost sagged with relief. *"Richardson! . . ."*

Richardson heard him, saw Larson on the floor under a spill of heavy crates, and came at a run.

"Jesus, Harry! What happened?"

As Richardson pulled one of the crates off of Larson's twitching form, Benford brought the Beretta up in one smooth motion and squeezed the trigger.

The explosion of sound momentarily silenced the dogs, but as Richardson toppled backward, they began barking more wildly than ever, the noise so shrill it almost masked the second shot.

Richardson collapsed in an awkward sprawl.

His eyes wild, Benford looked from one man to the other, checking the scene, looking for loose ends. Okay . . . this would work. Just one more thing, the final and convincing argument . . .

He pushed the muzzle of the handgun against his upper arm, trying to position it in such a way that it would miss the bone. He needed a flesh wound as a convincer. He hesitated, though, fearing the pain, fearing even more what would happen if this went wrong.

Squeezing his eyes tight, he tried to make himself pull the trigger . . . tried . . . failed . . . then tried again. Damn it, he had to do this. . . .

The third shot came as a complete surprise. Almost, he'd decided to try to get by with the story alone, without the self-inflicted wound, but then his finger slipped and the gun went off. To his surprise, there was little pain, at least at first, but it felt as though someone had just slammed a hammer against his arm. The shock staggered him, and he dropped to his knees.

Don't lose it, he told himself. *Focus! Focus!*

He had a handkerchief in his pocket. For a moment, he was stumped, needing to wipe down the pistol but suddenly aware that his left arm and hand simply weren't working. He managed to get the cloth free, however, and wiped the oily surface of the weapon. He doubted anyone would be in a position to check for fingerprints up here, but he wasn't taking any chances. The gun wiped clean, he dropped it on the floor next to Larson, then pocketed the handkerchief.

A final check. Larson and Richardson had been arguing about *here.* Larson had drawn his weapon and shot Richardson twice, killing him. Benford had seen it all happen and had picked up the pry bar . . . from *that* shelf. Larson had shot at him but only wounded him just as Benford had swung, knocking Larson out.

Yeah. It all fitted.

Golytsin hadn't told him how to carry out the murder, of course, but had stressed that whatever Benford did, he *had* to make it look as though one of the NOAA officers had killed one of the Greenworlders. Everything, Golytsin had told Benford, depended on his making the scene look convincing.

Larson was still alive. Benford could hear him trying to breathe through the blood still pouring from his savaged nose. Benford considered hitting Larson again, killing him . . . but decided that would be harder to explain. Then . . . *damn*! The gun belt! He'd almost missed that detail, almost forgotten. Stooping, he slid the belt under Larson's torso, immediately wishing he'd remembered to do this before he'd shot himself in the arm.

Finally, though, the belt was on, and Benford was able to click it shut with one hand. His left arm was starting to hurt now, a dull, throbbing ache, and blood was starting to seep through his parka. It felt like he might have hit the bone after all. He was starting to feel dizzy. Fishing out the handerchief again, he pressed it over the seeping wound.

Benford took a couple of minutes to collect himself, breathing hard . . . then made his way to the door and banged out into the cold.

It was snowing harder now as he raced back to the main building.

"Help! Everyone, help! Murder! Help! . . ."

11

City Morgue
London
1045 hours GMT

CHARLIE DEAN FOLLOWED EVANS and the morgue attendant deeper into the chill of the morgue. Fluorescent
lights hung overhead, and the green-painted concrete
block walls added a depressing air to the place. The attendant walked up to one of the stainless-steel doors in one
wall, checked his clipboard, then opened the vault and
hauled the steel slab into the room.

They already had Karr in a black body bag, the zipper
halfway open, the man's eyes staring up at the lighting
fixtures overhead. Some cold inner part of Dean was operating on pure automatic, letting him note the wounds—
a number of deeply purpled bruises around half a dozen
holes in his friend's chest and upper abdomen, and a terrible gash that had opened the left side of his throat from
jaw to collarbone.

Christ. . . .

"That's him," Dean said simply. He looked up at the
attendant. "I'd like to see his effects, too, if I may."

The morgue attendant shrugged and nodded. "Sure

thing." He seemed to be nothing so much as bored and . . . was he chewing *gum*?

"Friend of yours?" Evans asked as Karr's body slid soundlessly back into the recesses of the locker.

"Yeah."

"I'm sorry. He seemed like a good chap."

"What the hell is that?" Dean demanded. "British understatement?"

"I only met him a few moments before the attack," Evans said. His mouth twisted unpleasantly. "The two of us were joking about the Boston Tea Party."

Dean drew a deep breath. Evans had met him at the airport and driven him into London late last night, putting him up in a hotel a short walk from the Tower of London and just across the river from the bizarre black egg of a building where Tommy Karr had been killed. However much Dean wanted to lash out at someone, it wasn't Evans' fault that Tommy was lying dead on a morgue slab.

"I'm . . . sorry," Dean said. "Didn't mean to snap."

"Not a problem. I know what it's like to lose a mate."

Yes, I imagine you probably do, Dean thought, but he said nothing. As one of the senior British officers at the Menwith Hill listening station, Evans had been on the front lines of European SIGINT for a good many years. Listening in on other people's radio and telephone conversations didn't seem like a dangerous occupation, but over the years there *had* been all too many incidents.

People had died. Good people, like Tommy.

" 'Ere's his kit, sir," the attendant said around the wad of gum. He gestured toward a table with several plastic-wrapped packages on it. "We bagged it and tagged it, like we was told."

"Thank you." Dean sorted through the packages, wondering what he was looking for. Karr's shoulder holster and Beretta were in one bag, his wallet, a set of house keys, two pens, some loose change in another, wristwatch and sunglasses in a separate bag. Same for his passport, an airline weapons permit, an FBI ID card, a driver's license, and a number of pocketed receipts. Karr, Dean knew, never wore jewelry, rings, or other accoutrements unless they were needed for a particular legend on an op. One bag held a small collection of technological odds and ends . . . a cell phone; a fiber-optic lead; what appeared to be a PDA; a couple of button-sized objects that Dean recognized as small, sticky-backed surveillance cameras; the clip-on microphone Karr would have been wearing beneath his shirt collar, a part of his personal communications hookup with the Art Room.

A few of the tools of the trade.

His clothing made up a rather larger bundle. Slacks, coiled-up belt, shoes, socks, underwear. Shirt, tie, and jacket, all of them soaked with dark blood.

Keeping his emotions firmly in check, Dean reached into a jacket pocket and pulled out a PDA identical to the one in the bag on the table. Evans raised his eyebrows but said nothing as Dean switched it on and began passing it over each of the bags of Karr's effects. Several LEDs lit up as he passed it over the package containing the phone, mike, and cameras.

" 'Ere," the morgue attendant said. "What's that?"

Dean didn't reply but continued moving the PDA above Karr's things. When Dean passed it over the bag containing the blood-soaked shirt and jacket, the LEDs flashed again. "Hello there," Dean said, half-aloud. "That's interesting."

"What do you have?" Evans asked.

"Not sure yet." Setting the device on the table, Dean pulled the plastic wrapping open, giving him access to the clothing inside. Picking up the device again, he checked, the shirt first and, when nothing happened, began checking the jacket.

He got a strong signal there . . . strongest at the back of the collar.

Dean bent closer. This part of the jacket was saturated with blood, but he rolled the collar up, peering closely at it, trying to ignore the sticky-sweet smell. A moment later, he straightened up, holding between thumb and forefinger what appeared to be a black pin with a round head.

The pin set off the LEDs when he tested it; the jacket now gave no response.

"Circuit checker?" Evans asked.

Dean nodded. "Puts out enough of a magnetic field to get a signal back from an electronic circuit. Someone slipped this into Karr's jacket. He was bugged."

"His date from the night before?"

"I'd put money on it," Dean replied. He was thinking fast. His talk with Julie on board the British Airways jetliner had been disappointingly unproductive. The young woman had indeed remembered Karr on her last flight but had point-blank refused to admit meeting with him later. That in itself wasn't suspicious, of course. Even when Dean had flashed an ID badge identifying him as FBI, she'd had no reason to go into intimate details about her having spent the evening with the tall, blond passenger she'd met that afternoon.

But at some point between his having caught that flight out of JFK and being picked up by a tail near Heathrow, someone had slipped that pin invisibly into the fabric of Karr's sport coat, inserting it beneath the collar where it could not be seen. The pin, Dean was certain, would prove to be a short-range transponder, a tracking device that allowed someone to follow him through city traffic.

He was also certain that a microscopic examination of the device would identify it as of Russian manufacture. The KGB had used such devices twenty years ago; presumably the Sluzhba Vneshney Razvedki, Russia's modern Foreign Intelligence Service, or SVR, still did. Desk Three had similar devices, even smaller and more surreptitious.

Pulling a small specimen bag out of his jacket, Dean deposited the pin and returned it to his pocket. He would take no chances with this piece of evidence being lost.

"We need to pick up Julie Henshaw," Dean said. "Flight attendant on British Airways Two-one-one-two, JFK to Heathrow. She was the last person to be with Karr before he left for the GLA building with Spencer."

"You think she's in on this?"

Dean shrugged. "We know Karr had dinner with her the night before he was killed. We know he walked out of the hotel with three FBI agents and Spencer and there was a car double-parked outside the hotel, waiting for them. They follow them closely, then vanish in downtown London. But a few hours later, three of the people in that car show up at the GLA building with weapons."

"She slipped that pin into his clothes?"

Dean nodded. "Maybe she pretended to adjust his collar, or something."

"I'll pass the word to MI Five then." He shook his head. "Not sure if we'll get any action, though. Things have been crazy since the attack."

"I can imagine."

At the hotel last night, Dean had switched on the TV and found nothing but special news reports on the terrorist attack at the Greater London Authority, complete with endlessly recycled film clips of the huge green banner unfurling from the observation deck overlooking the Thames and several maddeningly jerky and motion-blurred segments from news cameramen in the crowd on the deck itself.

Desk Three, he knew, was going through all of those

film clips frame by frame, hoping to find more clues. So far, though, all they had was the testimonies of some badly shaken eyewitnesses, two dead and one critically wounded tangos, one dead FBI agent, and the body and effects of Tommy Karr.

Greenworld already was being indicted by commentators on both sides of the Atlantic for embracing assassination as a tool for global activism. Whoever had decided to try to kill Spencer had made a serious mistake; where Greenpeace was notorious for its Gandhi-esque program of peaceful confrontation, Greenworld was now known worldwide as the organization that sent young people armed with Uzis and handguns after politically unpopular scientists.

What the hell had they been thinking?

Dean was beginning to suspect that he was seeing some kind of double cross and an intricate game of multiple layers. The Russians had their hand in it, were probably the major players. Sergei Braslov and the presence of the pin-shaped tracking device in Karr's jacket proved that.

So what did *they* have to gain from the attack?

Dean didn't know, but he was determined to find out.

Dean arranged for the packages of Karr's clothing and other effects to be sent by special courier straight back to Fort Meade. His body would be flown out aboard an Air Force transport to Dover, Delaware. If possible, Dean planned to be on that flight, to accompany Tommy back to the States.

First, though, Dean had other business here in England. "I think we're done here," he told Evans after he'd signed the last form arranging for the flight to Dover.

"Right then," Evans said. "Care for a flight up to Yorkshire?"

"I'm looking forward to it," Dean told him. "I've never been to Menwith Hill."

"I hope you like golf in a *big* way then," Evans told him with a wry smile.

He didn't find out what Evans meant until some hours later.

Rubens' Office
NSA Headquarters
Fort Meade, Maryland
0915 hours EDT

The National Security Agency maintains listening posts all over the world.

The largest are those at Menwith Hill in Yorkshire, England, and at Pine Gap, in central Australia, but there are many others—at Bad Aibling, Germany; at Misawa Air Base in Japan; at Akrotiri, Cyprus; at Guantánamo Bay, Cuba. A world-girdling network of extraordinarily sensitive electronic ears, teasing radio whispers out of the static of the sky and processing them into intelligible data.

At Point Barrow, Alaska, the northernmost tip of the United States, a station called POW-Main broods over the cold, gray waters and ice floes to the north. Originally part of America's Distant Early Warning system, or DEW Line, the center had been refurbished in recent years, with part of the base turned over to the NSA for use as a SIGINT-gathering site. Now, instead of watching for the appearance of Russian ICBMs rising above the cold horizon, some of those antennas, at least, were set to gather radio signals emerging from Siberia—most especially from the Russian air bases at Mys Shmidta, Anadyr, and Provideniya.

There'd been a lot of radio traffic bouncing off the ionosphere lately, and all of it had been duly recorded at POW-Main, then relayed via satellite to Fort Meade. Most was destined for Langley and the Pentagon, but some of it had looked interesting enough for the Desk Three analysts to take a first look. Intelligence coming in from this site was given the distribution code "Powerhouse."

Two Powerhouse transcripts had just arrived on Rubens' desk. One, originally in a Russian Air Force cipher easily decrypted, had come from Mys Shmidta. The other, transmitted in the clear and in English, had come from a tiny and remote climate-monitoring station on the Arctic ice cap. Both intercepts would be routed according to standard protocols, the military intercept to the Pentagon, the other to the State Department, and both to CIA headquarters at Langley. However, there was someone else who he felt should see these.

What he was about to do was highly irregular . . . and might even be interpreted as a breach of security. The current political situation, however, left him few options.

Turning to his computer, he began composing an e-mail.

Menwith Hill Echelon Facility
Yorkshire, England
1510 hours GMT

Two hundred miles north of London, eight miles west of the city of Harrowgate, lies the NSA listening station at Menwith Hill. Dean and Evans had boarded an RAF helicopter, a venerable Westland Wessex Mk. 2, at London City Airport for a bumpy and noisy three-hour flight to what once had been RAF Yeadon and was now Leeds Bradford International Airport. A car and driver had been waiting for them as the helicopter lifted off once more on its way to the big RAF base at Dishworth, farther north.

From there, it was a twelve-mile drive over winding roads through rolling Yorkshire cow pastures and farmland, passing through tiny English towns along the way with names such as Otley, Farnley, Bland Hill, and, Dean's favorite, Pool-in-Wharfedale. They were driving north on the B6451 and were just topping a rise at the intersection with Bedlam Lane when the Menwith Hill Echelon Facility first came into view.

Golf balls. Titanic golf balls . . .

The place looked utterly alien, completely otherworldly set among the gentle green hills of Yorkshire. Dean had shrugged off Evans' comment about golf earlier but got the joke now. The immense dimpled white spheres were simply radomes, lightweight shells that masked the dish antennas within, protecting them from the weather and preventing casual observers outside from knowing exactly where the antennas happened to be pointed. Two identical structures, a big one and a little one both painted gray, crowned the south wing of the HQ support building at Fort Meade just above Herczog Road, and there was a solitary white one on the ground half a mile away, not far from the HQ satellite uplink facility. But here the huge white golf balls grew in abundant profusion, appearing, then vanishing again behind folds in the moor, then rising once again. Dean counted twenty-five of the things, the largest well over one hundred feet across, but there might have been more. He'd seen photographs of the place and thought he'd known what to expect, but the reality was absolutely breathtaking.

Technically, Menwith Hill was an RAF base, but in fact the 560-acre complex had been taken over by the NSA in 1966. Also known as NSA field station F83, it was home to the GCHQ, the British counterpart of the NSA, and a number of Brits, like Evans, worked there. By far the largest population at the base, however, was American, most of them civilians—mathematicians, engineers, computer programmers, technicians, linguists, and analysts—with the NSA.

Desk Three, Dean knew, maintained a suite of offices here, somewhere within the vast warren of underground chambers and facilities hidden beneath the looming white golf balls.

Past a long stretch of chain-link fence topped by curls of razor wire and patrolled by armed men with dogs, they turned right into the sandbagged main gate, where unsmiling British soldiers scrutinized their IDs, checked files displayed on computer monitors, and made phone calls to the main security office before finally waving them through. They passed two more security checkpoints on their way to the underground part of the facility, with backscatter X-ray scans, handprint readers, and, finally, retinal scans. Only then did they receive badges. Security here was at least as tight as it was back at Fort Meade.

Ilya Akulinin and Lia DeFrancesca were already there, waiting for them in a basement conference room.

"Dean!" Lia cried, jumping up from her chair and rushing to meet him.

Her presence startled him. He'd known he would be meeting them here but hadn't been told they'd already been brought out of Russia. He was torn by pleasure at the sight of her . . . and the sudden memory of what he needed to tell her.

Dean took her in his arms and squeezed her close. "Hello, Lia." God, she smelled good, *felt* good. . . .

She pulled back, sensing something in his mood, and searched his face. "What is it? What's wrong?"

He glanced at Akulinin, who was standing nearby, uncertain. Dean didn't know the new kid very well, but he'd been in the field with Lia, and that counted for something.

"Do you two need some time alone?" Evans asked.

"No," Dean said, deciding. "It's just . . . Lia, I have some bad news. Tommy is dead."

Her eyes widened. *"No. . . ."*

"There was a protest yesterday at a conference in London where he was escorting an American scientist. We think the Russians—possibly the Russian mob— infiltrated the protestors and started a riot in order to carry out an assassination. Tommy saved the scientist, but . . ."

"The Russian *mob*?" Lia repeated. "Why—"

"Who's Tommy?" Akulinin asked.

"Another Desk Three agent," Dean told him. "And a friend."

"God. I'm sorry to hear that." Akulinin came closer, reaching out to put a hand on Lia's shoulder. "Were you guys close?"

Dean felt a stab of jealousy as the kid touched her. Totally irrational, he knew, but totally human as well. He swallowed it.

"We were friends," Lia said, pulling back a step to face Akulinin. Tears glistened in her eyes. "We worked together in the field quite a few times." Grief was already hardening in her face into something else, Dean noted. Determination. And anger.

"Well," Akulinin said, "that just sucks rocks."

Lia ignored the comment. "Why would the Russian mafia want to kill Tommy?"

"We're not sure they did," Dean told her. "Like I said, they were trying to kill an American scientist, a Dr. Spencer. He was a Department of Energy climatologist speaking on global warming. There'd been some death threats, I gather, and Rubens assigned Tommy to help escort him to London and back."

"That makes no sense. Since when did Desk Three begin providing bodyguard service? Why not a U.S. marshal? Or the FBI?"

"I don't know."

"And what does the Russian mob have to do with global warming, anyway?"

"We think the Russian mafia is trying to discredit Greenworld, and maybe some of the other environmental groups as well," Evans put in. "Greenpeace. The Sierra Club. The Russian MVD might be trying to make them look like terrorist groups."

"We don't know why," Dean added. "Yet."

"Not Tommy . . . ," Lia said, shaking her head. She moved back into Dean's embrace. "Not Tommy . . ."

"Maybe these two should have some time alone," Akulinin told Evans.

"Sure," the British agent said. "C'mon. I'll buy you coffee."

"They *have* coffee in England?"

"Menwith Hill," Evans replied, opening the door, "is *not* England."

★　　★　　★

Hours later, Lia and Dean lay in each other's arms, in bed. After a light dinner at the station's cafeteria, Evans had escorted them to three adjoining rooms in the base housing block reserved for short-term visitors to Menwith Hill, but Lia had come to Dean's room as soon as Evans had said good night and departed.

It had been such a long time. . . .

Their lovemaking had carried an urgent, almost desperate edge to it, however. Lia did not want to believe that Tommy was gone.

She'd not cried. She would *not* cry, though she admitted to herself that she might, later. For now, she needed to know every detail of Tommy Karr's death.

"I honestly don't know that much," Dean told her, his

face just visible in the darkness next to hers. "Rubens called me while I was at Friendship, waiting for a flight out to meet you in Russia. Apparently it's all over the news here, but I haven't had a chance to catch it."

"I wonder which mafia group was behind it," she said.

"We could call the Art Room, easily enough."

She thought about the mikes and transmitters, currently switched off and discarded with their clothing on the other side of the room. "No," she decided, snuggling closer. "Tomorrow."

Restlessly his hand caressed her bare hip. "Evans has scheduled a briefing for us tomorrow morning," he told her. "Maybe we'll learn more then."

"Assuming they know *anything* back at the Puzzle Palace," she replied. "I'm wondering if it's the Tambov group, though. We're pretty sure that's who we were up against in St. Petersburg. They're coming down a lot more aggressively than in the past. Big schemes. Wild, high-risk, high-gain operations . . . like selling radiation shielding to Iran."

"I went through a briefing on the Russian mob the other day," Dean said. "The protestors who killed Tommy were working with a Russian MVD colonel named Braslov. And he's been linked with the Tambov organization." He looked at her in the dark. "Are you thinking your op and Tommy's were up against the same people?"

"It could be. I don't see the connection, but it could be."

"Selling beryllium plating to Iran's nuclear program and assassinating climate scientists. I don't see a link." He thought for a moment. "Of course, what has Washington in a dither right now is the fact that the Tambov group is also supposedly trying to corner Russia's petroleum industry. There's a lot of oil and natural gas prospecting going on in Siberia right now . . . and speculation about untapped energy reserves in the Arctic." He broke off, silent for a moment. She could almost hear him gnawing on the problem.

"Maybe that's the link," he said after a moment. "The Russians have been trying to stake a claim to half of the Arctic Ocean since 2007, claiming their territorial waters extend all the way to the North Pole. Greenworld and the other environmentalist groups would raise one hell of a stink if the Russians started sinking oil wells and building pipelines up there."

"True," Lia said. "But the Russians wouldn't be able to do that. Put oil wells in the Arctic, I mean."

"Why not? It'd be simpler than building an offshore drilling platform. Just build your tower, drill through the ice, then extend your cutting head through water and into the sea floor, just like they do in the Gulf of Mexico or the North Sea."

"No, Dean. Absolutely impossible."

"Why?"

"Because the Arctic ice is *moving,* dummy," she told him, smiling to rob the words of their sting. Then she realized he probably couldn't see the smile, so she let her hand glide down his torso, gently stroking him. "It drifts with wind and current. I don't know how fast, but the whole ice cap moves. Build an oil rig on the ice, send the drill head down to the sea floor . . . and in a few days or weeks or whatever . . . *snap!*"

"Oh. Yeah. I think I remember reading about that somewhere."

"If the Russians want to look for oil in the Arctic Ocean, they're going to have to wait for the ice cap to melt."

He chuckled. "You think global warming is that bad?"

"The ice cap is getting smaller and thinner every year," she told him. "Last I heard, if things proceed at the same rate they've been going over the past couple of decades, all of the Arctic ice will be gone—it'll all be open ocean—by 2060."

"Huh. I had no idea."

"Most people don't. The whole global-warming thing has become so politicized that it's tough to know what's real and what's hype."

"The Russians are known for thinking pretty far out into the future," Dean said, thoughtful. "I could see them planning for when they could build conventional offshore drilling rigs after the ice is gone. Still, fifty-some years? That's kind of a long shot. And right now no one can agree if global warming is real or just a temporary fad, if humans are causing it or it's part of a natural cycle. I can't see the mafia gambling on something like that."

"And they wouldn't give a damn about the environmentalists half a century out, either," Lia said. "If the mafia is behind it, that suggests a short-term goal as well. Those guys don't wait fifty years for a return on their investment, you know?"

"Even governments don't think that far ahead," Dean admitted. "So what's the answer, do you think?"

She sighed. "I don't know. The Art Room said Ilya and I were going to be on hold for a while. There's some sort of political crisis on back at the Palace. You know anything about it?"

"Not much. An F-22 was shot down over the Gulf of Finland in support of your op. Did you hear about that?"

"A little. Did they find the pilot?"

"Not that I've heard. But the scuttlebutt at Fort Meade was that Desk Three might get into trouble for losing an F-22 instead of a UAV."

" 'Scuttlebutt'?"

"Sorry. Marine and Navy slang. Means rumor or gossip."

"I like it. Damn, the Russian op just went to hell, didn't it?"

"They didn't tell me much. What happened?"

"Our contact turned on us. There was an ambush . . . and a firefight. Ilya lost his kit, including some rather sensitive black ops gear."

"Shit!"

"There's a sanitizing team in there now, trying to recover it. The two of us got clear of the operational area, then almost got picked up by the MVD." She shook her head slightly. "I've had the . . . I don't know, the feeling that we've been set up right along, that the opposition was always a step or two ahead of us the whole way."

"I can't imagine the Russian mafia deliberately playing games with the NSA," Dean said. "I mean . . . they're *just* criminals."

"Yeah, and it's dangerous to underestimate them, Charlie," she told him. "A lot of them were KGB and GRU before the Communists lost power. They had some pretty specialized knowledge and equipment, and it all went to the highest bidder."

"Kind of like all the jokes about out-of-work Russian nuclear scientists. 'Will sell nuclear secrets for food.' "

"Exactly. And the gang leaders themselves, even if they're not tied in with Russian intelligence or the military, well, they had to be damned tough and smart, and they had to have some pretty good connections just to survive under the Soviets, to say nothing of building an underground criminal empire. They're also . . . I don't know how to say it. Less constrained than the Soviet government was."

"How do you mean?"

"The Soviet government had a nuclear arsenal big enough to wipe out the planet."

"So did we."

"Right. But neither we nor the Soviets used that arsenal, because no one can win a nuclear war. Okay?"

"There were a few people who thought we could," Dean put in. "But MAD—Mutual Assured Destruction—worked as a deterrent, sure."

"The Soviets were as careful as we were to make sure nukes didn't get into the wrong hands, because if they screwed up, it would come back to bite them in the ass."

"Okay. . . ."

"Don't you see? The Russian mafia doesn't care! Oh, they don't want to see the world blown to bits. That would be bad for business. *But they don't have the obligation to provide for their country's welfare that the Soviets had.* You can see that in the way the mobs are strangling the Russian economy today. Capitalism doesn't stand a chance so long as the mobs are bleeding businesses over there dry."

"So . . . you're saying the mafia is more likely to do crazy stuff."

"Exactly. During the Cold War, we were worried about Soviet adventurism, about all those times they played brinksmanship games and created international crises. The Cuban Missile Crisis. The invasion of Czechoslovakia. The invasion of Afghanistan. Those were the times when things *were* dangerous, when the missiles *might* have flown. The Tambov Gang, the Blues, all the other Russian mobs . . . all they want is money, power, and to come out on top of the heap. If Colombian drug lords get their very own submarine, if a reactor melts down in the Urals and wipes out a city, if Iran gets a nuclear weapon and obliterates Israel, what's it to them? They may not even care if Russia's economy tanks, because they've been going international lately in a big way. Ask Ilya about the Mafiya in Brighton sometime."

"Brighton?"

"He's American. His parents were immigrants. Brighton Beach is near Brooklyn, in New York, and it's where a lot of Russian émigrés settled. They call it Little Odessa. For ten, fifteen years, the Mafiya has been moving in there, big-time. They're *everywhere*."

"Somehow, I never thought of Desk Three as being crime fighters," Dean said.

"In some ways the Russian mobs are as much of a threat as al-Qaeda," she told him. "Maybe more."

"Are you sure you're not just making it personal?"

"What do you mean?"

"I don't know. I can hear the anger in your voice. Like you want to go back over there and kill them all. For Tommy."

"No," she told him. "I *am* going back . . . one way or another. But when I do, it will be for *me*."

She drew him closer then, trying to lose herself in his arms. "C'mere, Marine," she told him. "I'm going to scuttle your butt. Again."

12

Menwith Hill Echelon Facility
Yorkshire, England
0930 hours GMT

THE NEXT MORNING, DEAN and Lia were in Menwith's Deep Centre, a high-tech underground chamber that was the equivalent of the National Security Agency's Black Chamber or the Art Room. After having breakfast with the two Americans in Menwith Hill's cafeteria, Evans had led them through several checkpoints and down into the sanctum sanctorum, a steel-and-concrete-reinforced cavern that, its designers believed, would have withstood a near-direct hit on the surface eighty meters above by a fair-sized nuclear weapon.

The facility had much in common with the Art Room, Dean decided, right down to the banks of computer workstations and consoles and the ranks of monitors, though the large screen dominating one wall was absent.

Echelon II was the code name for the current NSA/GCHQ program to collect electronic signals out of the air worldwide, process them, and send them on for analyses. Menwith Hill, in particular, was tasked with eavesdropping on all of Europe, as far east as the Urals.

Local legend had it that Menwith Echelon scooped up

all radio, telephone, fax, and Internet communications in Europe . . . but then, local legend also had it that the NSA was studying little gray aliens held within the underground complex, which supposedly was an English version of the notorious American Area 51 in Nevada. Exactly how much of Europe's electronic gossip was actually recorded was, of course, a closely guarded secret.

But there were no aliens so far as Dean could discover.

"I'd like you two to meet someone," Evans told them, leading them to a particular cubicle in a room filled with cubicles off the main control room. An attractive young woman stepped out to join them. "Charlie, Lia, this is Carolyn Howorth—'CJ' to her friends. She's one of our best linguists down here."

"Pleased to meet you," Dean said, shaking her hand. "What language?"

"Russian, at the moment," she told him.

"She's heading up our Russian desk right now," Evans said. "But she's also our best Japanese linguist."

That told Dean something about Menwith's electronic reach. Apparently they weren't limited to Europe after all.

"We've been putting together some intercepts from the other day," she told him. "Randy here thought you should hear this."

She led them back into her cubicle and entered a string of characters into her workstation. "This is from four days ago," she said. "A satellite phone exchange, apparently originating from within a few meters of the GLA building a few minutes after the riot in which your friend was killed broke out. The conversation was encrypted, but we've known this particular encryption key for some time."

"Rodina," a voice said from a speaker.

Carolyn translated. " 'Motherland.' We think that was a code word, identifying the speaker."

Another voice replied, also in Russian, as Carolyn provided a running translation.

" 'We're watching BBC Two. Excellent work.'

" 'One of our agents still lives. I cannot get a clear shot, however.'

" 'She knows nothing. We don't want to reveal your presence. That might tell the opposition too much.'

" 'That was my thought. . . . Perhaps it is time to activate Cold War. The two . . . incidents should take place close together, for maximum effect.'

" 'We agree. A ticket and new identity papers are waiting for you at the embassy. You fly out tonight.'

" 'Good. Until tonight, then.' "

The connection was broken.

"Braslov," Dean said. "The fourth man in the car that tailed Tommy from Heathrow."

"We think so," Carolyn agreed. "We've recorded some other communications previously with voiceprints that match this one, and which we suspected were Sergei Braslov. We can't prove it yet, but we believe that he's our man."

"Who is he speaking with?"

"Grigor Kotenko."

"Ah," Dean said. "The Tambov Gang."

"At the time of this conversation," Carolyn told them, "Kotenko was at his personal dacha on the Black Sea. We have quite an extensive voice-intercept file on him now."

"The agent he mentions," Dean said. "That must be the woman Tommy shot during the GLA attack. What was her name?"

"Yvonne Fischer," Evans said. "We have her under close arrest at Barts—that's St. Bartholomew's Hospital, back in London. She hasn't regained consciousness as yet. Still listed as critical."

"Sounds like the bad guys aren't concerned about her giving us anything useful."

"That would be a typical op for GRU or KGB back in the bad old Soviet days," Lia put in. "Use some poor schmuck you recruit off the street, don't tell him jack, program him to do a dirty deed that can't be traced back to you."

"Might've been a false-flag recruitment," Dean said. False-flag was spook-speak for recruiting agents by convincing them that you worked for someone else, someone of whom they approved.

"Any idea where Braslov is now?"

"We know he caught an Aeroflot flight out of Heathrow that night. Pulkovo."

"St. Petersburg," Lia said.

"And there he caught a Sakha Avia flight out of Pulkovo to Yakutsk."

"Yakutsk? That's out in the middle of Siberia."

"Right the first time," Carolyn said. "Unfortunately, we have no one on the ground there and Misawa hasn't picked up any relevant intercepts, as yet." Misawa was an NSA listening station in Japan, one of the largest Echelon bases, in fact, in the world. "We think he had another destination after that, but we don't know where."

"What is that 'Cold War' Braslov mentioned?" Dean asked. "The way he said it, it sounded like a secret operation of some kind."

"We may have another piece of that puzzle," Carolyn told them. She typed at her keyboard for a moment, queuing up another intercept. "This came out of Misawa four days ago, about four hours after the GLA attack. After picking up the intercept from Kotenko, we put an electronic tracer on him that would flag any call with that particular encryption key. Here it is."

"Rodina," a voice said, Kotenko's.

Another voice responded in Russian. " 'Well, it's been a long time, Grigor,' " Carolyn translated. " 'We thought you'd forgotten us.'

" 'Never, my friend. You are far too important for our plans. Cold War has commenced.'

" 'Has it, then? That's good news.'

" 'Osprey is on his way to you. He should be there within—' "

A blast of static interrupted the conversation.

"We can't make out what came next," Carolyn said. "Communications have been erratic of late, and the speaker's location is at an extremely high latitude. What we have is only a fragment."

"Osprey," Dean said. He looked at Evans. "Braslov, do you think?"

"It's possible."

"So who is Kotenko speaking with?"

For answer, Carolyn typed at her keyboard again, bringing up a file on her screen. A photograph showed a ruggedly good-looking man, blue-eyed, blond-haired. Dean could just make out a piece of a tattoo on his chest.

"Another Russian mafioso?" he asked.

"His name," Carolyn told him, "is Feodor Golytsin. Formerly Soviet Navy—specifically their submarine services. He was court-martialed in 1986 for speaking out against Soviet military policies in Afghanistan. He spent four years in a gulag, where, yes, we believe he made connections with the Organizatsiya. However, in 1995 he took a job with Gazprom."

"Gazprom?" Dean asked. "That's natural gas?"

"Gazprom," Carolyn told him, "is the largest natural gas company in Russia . . . and by some measures the third-largest corporation in the world. With its oil-producing subsidiary Gazprom Neft, it's also the third-largest producer of petroleum in the world, after Saudi Arabia and

Iran. It started off under the Soviets as a state-owned sub-sidiary, of course, but has been operating as an independent corporation since the mid-nineties. Today, a dozen Eastern European nations all depend on Gazprom for natural gas. The European Union gets twenty-five percent of its natural gas from them."

"But there are concerns that the Russian Mafiya is trying to take over the Russian petroleum industry," Dean said. "So if what you say is true, that means Gazprom."

"There've been a number of corruption scandals involving Gazprom in the past. Our Russian desk believes that Golytsin is part of what we think of as a Mafiya beachhead within the corporation."

"An ex-submariner," Dean mused. "That suggests some interesting possibilities."

Arctic oil exploration would almost certainly require submarines.

He was beginning to think he knew where Braslov had gone out of Yakutsk.

Executive Cafe
K Street NW, Washington, D.C.
1225 hours EDT

It was two days after his unsatisfactory interview with Wehrum.

Rubens sat at a small table set up outside of a popular Washington sidewalk café, waiting for Barbara. She was late. She'd promised to meet him for lunch at noon, but so far only strangers had passed on the sidewalk or on the other side of the street, through McPherson Square.

He enjoyed watching people, and the table gave him the perfect vantage point. A few had been quite exotic—including one silver-goateed individual with a black and red cape streaming from his shoulders, plus any number of people in saris, turbans, caftans, or other foreign dress. Washington was truly *the* international city, with Embassy Row only a few blocks to the north, and hordes of international tourists descending on the Mall, the White House, and the monuments. It was a gorgeous spring day, and the tourists were certainly out in force.

The White House was an easy six blocks away, down Vermont Avenue and past Lafayette Square. He wondered what was keeping her . . . then decided the question was nonsense. He knew what Barbara's schedule was like these days. And he expected that the e-mail he'd sent her yesterday afternoon had stirred things up a bit there.

There she was, cutting across McPherson Square and breaking into a near jog across K Street, as fast as her platform heels would permit her. Barbara Stahl was an attractive woman in her forties, with PhDs in both international studies and economics. She was the senior Russian specialist currently serving on the National Security Council.

He stood up as she neared the table. "Hello, Barbara."

"Hi, Bill. Sorry I'm late."

"Not at all. Waiter!"

"Get for yourself, not me. I have to get right back."

"I'm sorry to hear that. Coffee, perhaps?"

"Thank you." She took a seat. "Things are not so quietly going nuts back there. Full-blown crisis mode. But I did need to see you."

He sat down opposite her. The waiter came up and Rubens ordered coffee for the two of them. "Your e sounded stressed."

"Mm. And your e-mail has stirred up a hornet's nest."

"I was afraid it might."

"I'm not on the eyes list for Powerhouse intercepts," she told him. "Why the hell did you do it? Damn it, Bill, are you *begging* to get canned?"

"It's not that bad."

"Not that bad? Twenty years in federal prison and up to half a million dollars in fines? You don't call that bad?"

"As Deputy Director of the NSA, I have some leeway," he told her. "Not a lot, but some."

"Are you saying you make the rules, so you can break them?"

"No. But I reviewed your security clearances and made sure you were cleared for Powerhouse-level documents before I sent that e."

"If Dr. Bing finds out, she could have those clearances revoked. And God only knows what they'll do to *you*."

"Barbara, overclassification of sensitive material is as dangerous in this job as underclassifying it, maybe more so. The whole point of intelligence is making sure the people who need to see something actually do see it. You won't get in trouble with your boss over your level of security; trust me on this. As for me, well, they can play those games with me later. Right now, it is important, *imperative*, that the President knows what's going on up in the Arctic. Those intercepts went to Langley, but I don't trust them to see the whole picture. Or to put it into the pickle."

"The pickle" was D.C. insider-speak for the President's Intelligence Checklist, a daily ten-page newsletter prepared by the Director of Central Intelligence for the President on overnight developments of five or six items of immediate presidential concern. CIA headquarters at Langley was sometimes called "the pickle factory" for that reason.

"You're just pissed that you don't have POTUS access through George Haddad anymore."

That hurt. He frowned, sitting back.

"I'm sorry, Bill," she said, seeing his expression. "I shouldn't have said that. But you've got to know that every time you try working through the back doors in this city, you're stepping on toes. *Powerful* toes."

"And sometimes working through back doors and stepping on toes is the only way to get anything done. Look . . . did you do as I asked?"

"Yes. I was in on the briefing on the Arctic situation this morning, and I brought up the intercepts. I have to tell you, though, both Bing and Collins were there, and they were *furious*."

"I can imagine."

Presidential briefings tended to be carefully scripted affairs, with no digressions from the planned agenda. Rubens had asked Barbara to interject a new issue into the session, bringing up the Powerhouse intercepts as hot new intel just received from the NSA . . . which was true, as far as it went. But to bring up something not already on the agreed-upon list of topics was a serious breach of protocol.

"I didn't say where the message had come from. I just said 'a highly placed intelligence source.' "

"They'll guess. It's okay. I was expecting that. Did it get *you* into trouble, departing from the agenda like that?"

"No. Not yet, anyway, though Dr. Bing did tell me she wants to have a chat with me." She grimaced. "First, though . . . the President wants to hear those intercepts for himself."

"Good."

"This afternoon."

Rubens' eyebrows went up at that. "That was fast."

"Do you have them?"

He reached into his jacket pocket and extracted a small, flat case, half the size of a credit card and a little thicker, a data storage device similar to an iPod, but with more memory and the ability to link into computer networks. He handed it to her, and she slipped it into her handbag.

"So what's the word on the Russian ice-grab as of now?" he asked her.

"Canada and Denmark are both screaming bloody murder. They're dispatching warships."

"That bad?"

She nodded. "That bad. The President has decided to send a couple of subs into the region as well. The *Ohio* and the *Pittsburgh*."

That news startled Rubens. It represented a major, and very serious, escalation in the growing crisis.

The *Ohio* was a relatively new addition to the U.S. special ops arsenal. She'd started out as a ballistic missile submarine, a "boomer" in naval parlance, but with the end of the Cold War, she and several other SSBNs had been targeted for decommissioning in order to adhere to treaties requiring a reduction in ICBM platforms in the post-Soviet drawdown.

Instead of being scrapped, however, four excess boomers had been converted into SSGNs, guided-missile submarines equipped to carry out covert Special Forces operations. The *Ohio* and her sister boats could carry over sixty SEALs or other special ops troops, as well as over 150 Tomahawk cruise missiles with either conventional or nuclear warheads.

The other sub, the *Pittsburgh*, was a Los Angeles–class attack boat and would be operating under the Arctic ice as the *Ohio*'s escort. The deployment was an indication of just how sharply the situation up there had deteriorated over the past week.

The waiter returned with their coffee. Rubens thought about what this new wrinkle might mean for the NSA and Desk Three.

"You and your people are still in rather bad odor in the White House basement," she told him. "Collins has been pushing to take over Desk Three."

He smiled. "Nothing new there." Debra Collins could be a most . . . determined woman.

"The President put his foot down this morning," Stahl continued. "There will be no talk of another reorganization within the intelligence community until after the crisis is resolved, one way or another. And the investigation of the F-22 shoot-down incident is on hold."

Rubens' heart quickened a bit at that. President Marcke had always been a staunch supporter of Desk Three. And why not? The team had produced good results in the past. And Marcke's administrative philosophy tended to run along the lines of "if it ain't broke, don't fix it."

For the past few weeks, though, Rubens had been cut off from presidential access.

"I'm glad to hear that," he told her. "But what do you—?"

"Listen, Bill," she said, interrupting. "You have friends in the Administration, at the Pentagon, and in the NSC, and they all know that Collins and Bing are using the situation to pull off a fast hatchet job. But those two will be talking to their friends on the Hill, and that could be bad for you. Even the President won't be able to help you if this ends up in front of a Senate Investigations Committee."

"I understand that." Even if things were to go well, a congressional investigation could prove disastrous. Neither Rubens nor the NSA worked well under the spotlight of publicity. He could win the battle and find he'd lost the war if some details of Deep Black and Desk Three became public.

"The President wants you to get solid intel on what the hell is going on in the Arctic," she told him. "Do that and maybe he can derail Bing and Collins on the F-22 thing."

"We've been passing the relevant SIGINT up the chain right along," Rubens said. "Our Alaskan listening post, especially, has been picking up a lot, despite the bad atmospheric conditions lately."

"So why did you send it to me?"

He shrugged. "Like I said. The President needed to know."

"Have you seen an analysis of this stuff?"

"No. Remember, we just collect. Other agencies do the analysis."

"Give me a break, Bill. We both know it's not that clear-cut. If it were, Desk Three would be totally useless."

That was true enough, at least as far as it went. The NSA by design gathered and decoded electronic intelligence—SIGINT—and distributed it to agencies and departments that needed it: the CIA, the State Department, the Pentagon, the National Security Council. For the most part, though, they did not analyze it, again by design. A cell phone intercept from a known terrorist leader, data on an electronic funds transfer in Lebanon, and the recording of a landline conversation between Paris and Beirut might all be reported to the CIA, but it was *not* the job of the NSA to put together the jigsaw pieces and predict a terrorist attack against American tourists in France . . . a situation that the NSA's signals intercepts had helped prevent just last year.

But, as Barbara had pointed out, things weren't that simple in reality. The NSA gathered such a huge volume of electronic information in the course of a single day that a certain amount of analysis was necessary just to determine what was important and what was garbage. And once Desk Three had come online and begun operating all over the world, it made more sense to pull hard data out of the NSA's own networks than it did to wait for the CIA or the State Department to crunch the numbers and return the SIGINT in usable form.

Operation Magpie was a good example of this. A CIA request for help in tracking a possible theft of contaminated beryllium in Rybinsk had gotten things rolling, but NSA signals intercepts had picked up details of a sale to Iran, of Grigor Kotenko's involvement, of the use of a Liberian freighter to make the transfer, and on the location of the beryllium in a St. Petersburg warehouse. While all of that information had been passed on up the intelligence distribution network, as always, Desk Three's own analysts had worked on it as well, assembling the complete picture that had allowed Rubens to send Akulinin and DeFrancesca to St. Petersburg in order to find the beryllium shipment and plant the tracking device.

If Rubens had waited for the analysts at Langley to get back to him with the complete picture, he'd still be waiting.

"Let's just say," Rubens told Barbara after a moment's thought, "that I don't usually see the raw data when it comes in. There's way too damned much of it . . . and it takes time to massage it into something useful. I *do* know there's been a lot of radio chatter out of Mys Shmidta over the past couple of weeks and lots of high-energy RF jamming. POW-Main has been keeping an eye on it. Looks like military maneuvers, probably routine. I was only marginally aware of the details.

"But when we intercept, first, a call for help from a NOAA ice station—something about a civilian being murdered by a NOAA officer—and then a few minutes later we pick up Russian military transmissions discussing orders to seize that base and take the people there, American citizens, into custody . . . yeah. Someone figured out what it meant, and they made sure I saw it."

"What I'm about to tell you is classified, Bill," Barbara said.

"Of course."

"The base in question is NOAA Arctic Meteorological Station Bravo."

"Sure. A NOAA climate research station a few hundred miles north of Mys Shmidta."

"That's it. Three NOAA officers, seven scientists, and five kids with Greenworld."

That caught his attention. "Greenworld?"

"Yes. One of them is a congressman's daughter, heavily involved in environmental issues."

He closed his eyes. He could just imagine it. A too-young, too-rich, and too-well-connected WASP princess, most likely, with the politics of Jane Fonda and the common sense of a Christmas tree ornament. "Shit."

"Just so."

"What the hell is Greenworld doing up there?"

"Filming a documentary on global warming," she said. "But they're not our concern at the moment. Two of the expedition scientists are CIA officers."

"Christ. This just gets better and better."

"Three days ago, three members of the expedition—Randy Haines, Kathy McMillan, and Dennis Yeats—set off across the ice, ostensibly to check a remote met station. Haines is a meteorologist and an experienced Arctic hand, but Yeats is CIA and McMillan is NSA. She's a tech specialist, seconded to the CIA."

"Okay, I'll bite. What is the Agency doing in the Arctic?"

"About eighty miles northwest of Station Bravo—they call it 'Ice Station Bear,' by the way—there is a surface Russian expedition. Three ships, the polar icebreaker *Taymyr*; the *Akademik Petr Lebedev*, a civilian geological research vessel; and a support ship, the *Granat*. Five months ago they took up their current position, and have been station keeping ever since. Satellite reconnaissance shows they're building something, building something pretty big, in fact, but we haven't been able to determine what it is."

"So the Agency sent a couple of spooks out for a look-see, is that it?"

She nodded. "The remote met station was set up in a particular spot on the ice. A deliberate spot."

"What . . . close enough that they could approach those ships?"

"The ice up there is constantly moving," Barbara said. "Over a hundred, hundred-fifty miles a week. The Russian ships cut through the ice to reach a specific set of coordinates, and they've been maintaining station on top of those coordinates ever since."

"So . . . the ships are staying put, and the ice is moving around them?"

"Exactly. The *Taymyr* keeps breaking up the ice around the *Lebedev* and the *Granat*. Over the past few weeks, the remote met station has drifted with the ice almost five hundred miles. It's less than ten miles from the Russian position now. Yeats and McMillan hoped to launch a UUV three days ago to give them an up-close look at what was going on, underwater."

A UUV—an Unmanned Underwater Vehicle. Desk Three had similar devices in its arsenal, which allowed an underwater inspection of enemy ports, harbors, or ship bottoms from a safe distance . . . as much, say, as twenty or thirty miles. The CIA's device was probably similar to a small wire-guided torpedo with a ten-mile range and cameras and other sensors instead of a warhead. The whole assembly, UUV plus miles of control wire and a remote piloting unit, would have been small enough to carry on, say, a sled towed by snowmobile. At the met station, they would have dropped the UUV in through a hole in the ice and wire-guided it to the objective, allowing for an underwater reconnaissance impossible for satellites, for men on top of the ice, or for something as large and as intrusive as a submarine.

"You said 'hoped to,'" Rubens pointed out. "They didn't make it?"

"They reached the met station. They established a satellite relay and reported that they were about to launch the UUV. Then the relay went bad. We haven't heard from them since."

"Sunspots."

"Communications at high latitudes have been god-awful lately."

"Tell me about it," Rubens said. "That's why things went so wrong in St. Petersburg."

"The Russians have been jamming, too. Anyway, there's no sign of our people at the remote station, and they're long overdue back at Ice Station Bear. It's possible that the Russians spotted them and picked them up. And now you get an intercept that claims our people are murdering each other up there on the ice . . . and the Russians are moving in because this is happening on *their* territory."

"It smells like a setup."

"Maybe. The Russians *might* have all of our people in custody now, including a congressman's daughter. But we don't know."

"No ideas what the Russians are doing up there? Drilling for oil, maybe?"

"The water is too deep in that area for conventional drilling-rig technology," Barbara told him. "Over twenty-five hundred feet. But they're up to *something* on a big scale."

"Can the Danes or the Canadians help?"

"Maybe. But the President wants answers, and he wants them soon . . . sooner than other countries are going to be able to get anything up into that region. That's why he's thinking about you and Desk Three."

"That's most gratifying . . . but I imagine Debra Collins is going to have her own ideas about that."

"The President's exact words were, 'I want to talk to Rubens. If his people can't get me what I want, nobody can.'"

"I see."

"Besides, one of the missing people is *yours.*"

He nodded. "Kathy McMillan. Although she's working for the Agency right now."

"Is she Desk Three?"

"No. She works for the NSA's tech department." The vast majority of the NSA's employees were technologists, computer programmers, and mathematicians. In fact, the NSA had more mathematicians working for it at Fort Meade than any other single employer in the country. Deep Black ran only a handful of agents like Dean or DeFrancesca.

Or Karr.

As a result, Desk Three was stretched to the breaking point right now.

"But you're right," Rubens continued after a moment. "She belongs to us, we're going to take care of her."

"I imagine the Company feels the same way," Barbara said carefully, using insider-speak for the CIA. "But they're stretched pretty thin right now."

"And we're not?" Still, there was an opportunity here. If Deep Black *could* get the missing Americans back—all of them, of course, not just the NSA technologist—it would weigh heavily in Desk Three's favor.

He despised thinking of the situation as a kind of game played with numbers and accounting ledgers, but an agency's worth, or the worth of its individual people, came down to just how effective they were at getting the job done.

Not that such thinking went far these days in cutting the deadwood out of the pile in this town. He looked at his watch.

"So, when does the President want to see me?"

"You have a three o'clock appointment tomorrow afternoon," she told him. "And both Bing and Collins will be there."

"Oh, joy." But he'd expected that. Both women would be jealously guarding their own respective turfs.

And he would be guarding his.

Ice Station Bear
Arctic Ice Cap
82° 24' N, 179° 45' E
1340 hours, GMT – 12

"Damn it, Bill!" Lieutenant Segal was frantic. "Can't you raise *anyone*?"

Bill Walters shook his head, one earphone pressed up against his ear. "Nada," he said. "Nothing but static . . . and Russian jamming. They're on every frequency now."

Outside, the wind gusted with the freshening gale. Behind its keening they could hear the *bang-bang-bang* of the storage shed door, slamming in the wind. Most of the base personnel—NOAA and Greenworld—were crowded together at one end of the Quonset hut as Walters tried to establish contact with the outside world. At the other end of the room, near the curtains leading to the women's bunk space, Susan Fritcherson and Dr. Chris Tomlinson sat with the unconscious Commander Larson. Tomlinson had bandaged the injured man's head and made sure his breathing passage was clear . . . but there wasn't much more he could do. Larson needed to be in a hospital, and soon. *Soon.*

"Are—are they coming, do you think?" Harry Benford asked.

"Who?" Fritcherson demanded.

"The Russians, of course."

Tom McCauley turned and glared at Benford. "Why? What's it to *you*?"

"Well, it's obvious, isn't it? I mean, we need to get the commander to a hospital, and if we can't raise our own people—"

"Just shut the hell up and stay out of the way," Fred Masters told him. "You've done enough damage."

"Look, I didn't mean to hurt him that bad! But it's like I said . . . he shot Ken, and then I thought he was gonna shoot me, too, and I—"

Lieutenant Segal whirled and advanced on Benford, fury in his face and clenched fists. "You slimy little bastard!" Segal shouted. "Isn't it convenient that there was no one else there to back up your story! You know what I think? I think *you* shot Richardson and then you clobbered the skipper to cover your tracks!"

"That's ridiculous! Why would I do something like that?"

"Why would a man with sixteen years in NOAA and a wife and two kids just up and shoot a guy? Huh?" Segal reached Benford and grabbed the man by the throat. "Answer me that, you little prick!"

"He hated us!" Benford cried, pounding at Segal's hands. "Let me go, you big—"

"Break it up, you two!" Masters shouted. "Both of you! Stand down!"

"*This* is the criminal, Fred!" Segal said. "This little bastard right here!"

"Let him go, Phil. He's not worth it."

Segal shoved Benford hard, slamming him back against the wall as he released him. "No. He's not."

"Larson *did* have it in for all of us Greenworld people," Lynnley Cabot said. "We all saw it!"

"*Commander* Larson wouldn't have shot anybody," Fritcherson said. "I don't believe Benford's story, not for a second. But it won't do us any good arguing about it. Save it for the trial."

"I didn't kill anybody!" Benford screamed.

Tomlinson was about to snap back a reply, but he stopped, his mouth open. There was a new sound rising above the wind outside . . . a deep, almost throbbing rumble, punctuated by the unmistakable crack of breaking ice. "What the hell is that?" he asked.

The others were listening now, too.

"Pressure ridge," McCauley said. "Ice coming together, buckling, creating an upthrust."

"*We have to get out of here!*" Cicero cried. She bolted for the door.

"Don't go out there!" Masters shouted.

Steven Moore reached out and grabbed her arm, pulling her back. "Just . . . chill!" he said. "Don't panic! Everything's going to be okay. . . ."

"It sounded pretty close," McCauley told the others. "We should check it out."

The sounds from outside had stilled, save for the blustering of the wind.

"I'll go," Tomlinson said, rising. Pressure ridges could form anywhere on the ice, at any time. It wasn't likely, but if one decided to come up underneath the Quonset hut, the base could be torn apart, leaving them without shelter in the storm.

Fortunately, it sounded like whatever it was had stopped. . . .

The door banged open. Surrounded by swirling snow and a blast of frigid wind, a heavily bundled man stepped into the hut.

Cicero screamed. McCauley started, then reached for a rifle leaning against a nearby wall. For a moment, Tom-

linson wondered if an American expedition had come up
after all . . . but the assault rifle in the man's gloved hands
was wrong—orangewood and ugly black metal, with a
curved, banana clip magazine.

A Russian AKM.

"Be still," the intruder barked in accented English. "All
of you! Be still!"

A second man pushed his way inside behind the first.
Both of them wore fur caps with the earflaps down. The
first kept his assault rifle pointed at them; the second held
a small but deadly-looking military pistol.

"What the hell are you—," McCauley started to say.

"Silence!" the man with the pistol shouted. "Hands up,
all of you!" He aimed the pistol at McCauley. "You! Stand
back from that weapon!"

Hands raised, McCauley did as he was told. Through
the open door, in the wan light of the never-setting sun,
Tomlinson could see other Russian soldiers and, beyond,
the sheer, smooth black cliff of a submarine sail, rising
vertically up from the broken and jumbled ice.

"This . . . territory," the man with the pistol said, "is
the sovereign territory of the Russian Federation, and you
are here illegally."

"Get over yourself, Ivan," Walters said. "This ice isn't
yours until the UN says it is. In the meantime, this is an
American outpost—"

"Not anymore," the Russian said. "We . . . understand
that a crime has been committed here. A crime on Russian territory. You will all come with us until this matter
can be properly settled."

"This man is badly injured," Tomlinson said, pointing
at Larson. "Can you get him to a hospital?"

The man gave a short, sharp nod. "*Da.* There are . . .
medical facilities where we are going. He will be taken
care of. Get your winter gear. Quickly!"

Stunned, the Americans began doing as they'd been told. As he donned his parka, though, Tomlinson glanced at Benford. The man seemed relaxed, now, almost at ease.

Tomlinson saw him slip something beneath the mattress of Steven Moore's bunk.

What the hell was going on?

13

Oval Office, the White House
Washington, D.C.
1508 hours EDT

"THE PRESIDENT WILL SEE YOU NOW."

The three of them had been waiting on benches set against the walls of the main corridor of the West Wing, Collins, Bing, and Rubens. None of the three had spoken a word when they'd arrived separately half an hour earlier, but Rubens could feel the chill in the air, the psychic sharpening of knives. For his part, Rubens had leaned back on the bench and focused on a relaxation mantra, calming himself. If these two harpies were going to descend on Desk Three, he wanted to be able to respond with cool logic, not a storm of emotion.

As the secretary held the northwest door of the Oval Office open, they stood and, still without a word to one another, entered the historic room.

All three had been here before, of course. The ancient grandfather clock against the northeast wall still clucked quietly to itself. The familiar portrait of George Washington still glowered down from over the fireplace on the room's north wall, the rosy-cheeked figure still looking as though his mouth hurt. Swedish ivy, grown from cuttings in a series going back to President Kennedy, adorned the mantle itself while, elsewhere, Remington bronzes of horses and western themes graced tabletops and niches in the walls.

President Marcke sat behind the familiar Resolute Desk . . . so named because it had been made from the timbers of a British frigate, HMS *Resolute,* a gift from Queen Victoria to President Hayes in 1880 and brought out of storage a century later by President Carter. That touch seemed appropriate to Rubens now. They would need to rely a lot on their British counterparts if they were going to have a chance at getting a team back into Russia anytime soon.

James Fenton and Roger Smallbourn both were already in the room, standing before the desk. A third man stood near the east wall, the only uniform present. He was Admiral Robert Thornton, the Deputy Director of the Defense Intelligence Agency.

Rubens was surprised to see them, but he could feel the startled shock of both Bing and Collins; obviously they'd not been expecting the DNI or the D/CIA to be here, *the* top two men in U.S. intelligence. As for the number-two man in the DIA, Rubens could only imagine why he was here as well. It was almost unprecedented, having this many top spooks together in the same room at the same time.

"Ladies," President Marcke said, looking up. "Charlie. I would like to know what the hell is going on."

"I . . . I'm not sure what you mean, Mr. President," Bing said.

"I mean how the hell this mess could have exploded in the Arctic and no one in U.S. intelligence was aware of anything going down!"

"Sir, we were aware of ongoing developments," Collins said. She spoke with a crispness that might have been meant to convey cool efficiency, but Rubens could hear her gears shifting in her mind. "We had two officers up there with the NOAA expedition with orders to determine what was going on at that Russian base. It was all there in your pickle a couple of weeks ago."

"Your two officers have been captured by the damned Russians, along with a number of American civilians and NOAA personnel. The Russians say they're being interned for the time being, pending a resolution of the status of their territorial claims in the Arctic."

"In other words," Fenton said, "they're holding them hostage to ensure that we go along with Moscow's agenda. They particularly want our assistance in reining in the Canadians and the Danes."

"You're kidding," Rubens said.

"Unfortunately, I'm not." Fenton gestured at a paper on Marcke's desk, closely typewritten beneath the richly decorated letterhead of the Russian embassy. "Their ambassador gave us official notification this morning. Very politely worded, of course. But it amounts to a ransom demand just the same."

"Publicly, we've been staying out of this brouhaha up north," the President said, "and Moscow seems to have taken that as acquiescence on our part. They may see hostages—though they'd never actually call them that, of course—as a guarantee of our active support."

It made sense in a weird way. Normally, the United States would have sided immediately with Canada, her old ally to the north, but in this recent exchange of confrontation politics over the Arctic, the U.S. had been keeping an uncharacteristically low profile. Cynics, both inside the Beltway and those writing op-ed columns, had pointed out that America had her own territorial ambitions in the Arctic. The North Slope oil fields provided just a glimpse of what riches might yet be hidden beneath the seabed north of Alaska.

The Russians might think that Washington's support at the United Nations would resolve the issue in their favor. Holding a few Americans as "guests" while their legal status was determined might nail things down just that much more firmly.

"This situation has been brewing since the Russians planted that damned flag at the North Pole in '07," the President went on, "and the intelligence community has let me down big-time. Why the hell didn't we see this coming?"

"Sir, in all fairness, our assets are stretched rather thin," Bing said. She glanced at Thornton. "Between Iraq, the nuclear situation in Iran, Pakistan, and North Korea, *and* trying to contain al-Qaeda—"

"I don't want fucking excuses, Donna!" the President said, his voice rising to a shout. "You people have been so busy playing Beltway power politics, trying to upstage each other, trying to cut each other out, pissing on the boundaries of your own turfs, you're not delivering the results I need! This thing came out of nowhere and bit me in the ass, and I don't like that one damned bit!"

"Sir," Fenton said into the shocked silence following the presidential outburst, "you already have my recommendations for streamlining U.S. intelligence. It may be that by eliminating certain inefficiencies—"

"Inefficiencies my ass," the President said. "I'm going to start eliminating some of the political deadwood around here and see what *that* does for inefficiencies!" He glared at them from behind the desk for a moment before continuing in a calmer voice. "Now, I'm going to say this just once. We are, all of us, on the same side, tough as it may be to recognize that fact sometimes. I want you people to stop the infighting and play nice. Pull together. Produce results I can use. Or I'll fire the lot of you and put in people who give me what I need! Do I make myself clear?"

A mumbled chorus of, "Yes, sir," rippled about the

room. Rubens was surprised at the outburst, surprised and pleased. Marcke tended to present a laid-back and folksy outward charm that was both disarming and ingratiating, a tool he'd used to superb effect when it came time for rounding up votes, both at the polls and on the Hill. Only rarely was a steel core revealed beneath the country-boy demeanor, so rarely that the man was often castigated by the press for being wishy-washy.

"Okay? We're on the same page? Good." The palm of his hand slammed down on the polished oak desktop. "On to business. I've directed that one of our SSGNs be redeployed to the Arctic. Admiral Thornton? Tell the rest of them what you told me this morning."

"Yes, Mr. President." Thornton cleared his throat. "Last evening, at the President's instructions, we transmitted new orders to the SSGN *Ohio,* then en route for the eastern Med. Four hours later, she rendezvoused with the *Pittsburgh,* a Los Angeles attack sub, just south of Greenland. The two are proceeding north up the west coast of Greenland as we speak, with orders to proceed to the NOAA base and investigate the situation.

"On board the *Ohio* are thirty-two Navy SEALs and one of their ASDS minisubs. We do not believe the Russians have a military presence at their base in the Arctic. Not *yet.* The SEALs have been instructed to resolve the situation, using the threat of force if necessary."

Rubens considered this. Thirty-two SEALs could handle any number of civilians, but how good was the intel that said there weren't any military personnel at the site? Whoever had taken the Americans out of Ice Station Bravo must have had weapons simply to enforce compliance, and the volume of military radio traffic up there suggested a lot of movement and preparation. There were rumors of Russian submarine deployments in the region, and those might have naval troops on board. Besides,

Mys Shmidta was only a three- to four-hour flight by helicopter to the south. If the Russians wanted a military presence on the ice cap, they would have one in very short order.

"I'm not sure a military option is our best choice at this time, Mr. President," Donna Bing said. She hesitated, choosing her words carefully. "Perhaps we should give diplomacy more of a chance here."

"Did you hear those intercepts from our listening station up there?" the President demanded.

"Yes, but—"

"Did you hear them?"

"Yes, sir." She glanced at Rubens, an expression of pure venom.

"The Russians were just waiting for an excuse," the President said. "Just waiting. Damn it, we are not going to take this lying down. If they think they can snatch our citizens out of international waters under some flimsy legalese pretext, they're going to find themselves looking down the barrel of a gun!"

"Perdicaris alive," Rubens said quietly, "or Rasuli dead."

"Eh?" Marcke said. "What was that?"

"Perdicaris alive or Rasuli dead," Rubens said again, more loudly. "One of your predecessors, sir. Teddy Roosevelt in . . . oh, it must have been 1904 or thereabouts. Just before the presidential election, anyway. Ion Perdicaris was a wealthy businessman representing American interests in Morocco who managed to get himself kidnapped by a Berber bandit leader named Rasuli. When Rasuli demanded a ransom from the United States—which harkened back to the old Barbary pirate way of doing business, actually—Roosevelt sent the U.S. Atlantic Squadron to Tangiers with instructions to free Perdicaris or kill Rasuli." He smiled. "Perdicaris was released unharmed in short order. It turned out after the fact he wasn't even an American citizen, but the Republican Party went wild at the news, and the affair helped elect Teddy."

He didn't add that Perdicaris had been released because a weak and vacillating Moroccan government, fearing the arrival of the U.S. fleet, had quietly paid Rasuli the seventy-thousand-dollar ransom. The story was too good to risk muddying the waters with extraneous details.

"Right, right. I seem to remember seeing a movie about that once," the President said.

Rubens grimaced. "*The Wind and the Lion*," he said. "As usual, Hollywood botched it pretty badly. Somehow, a dumpy, middle-aged Greek businessman got transformed into Candice Bergen."

"If you please, Mr. Rubens," Smallbourn said, "I fail to see what all of this has to do with the Arctic situation."

"Mr. Rubens is reminding us, Roger, that we can't give in to ransom demands," the President said. "And that's what the Russians are doing here . . . holding our people hostage in order to gain our compliance. We will *not* let that stand!"

"One of the captured agents, Mr. President," Dean said, "is actually one of my people, a technical specialist on loan to the CIA."

"And you'd like to have a hand in getting her back, eh?"

"Yes, sir."

"What do you suggest?"

"That depends on what you decide to do, sir. However, at a minimum I'd like one of my people up there. He could deploy certain devices with which to track and eavesdrop on the Russians, maybe find out where they're holding the prisoners."

"You have someone specific in mind, then?"

"Yes, sir. His name's Dean. A former Marine."

Collins made a face. "*Charles* Dean?" she said. "I've seen his folder. He's *old*."

Rubens wondered what Collins had been doing going through NSA personnel records . . . and how she'd managed that. He gave her a cool, appraising look. "He's one of my best field agents, Ms. Collins, and frankly, I'll take a tough old Marine with combat experience over a young pup any day. And if you've been going through my filing cabinet lately, you'll know he's just completed his quals with a four-oh. He's *good*. And he gets results."

The President chuckled. "Think your old Marine can keep up with a SEAL platoon, Bill?"

"He'll do whatever is necessary to get the job done, sir."

"The SEALs have experience in deploying all sorts of high-tech gadgets," Thornton put in. "Why do we need your man up there?"

"The SEALs are good," Rubens agreed, "but they haven't been trained in some of our more recent high-tech bits of hardware."

"Mr. President!" Collins said. "I must protest! Once again, this is a job for the Central Intelligence Agency! We have the trained personnel *and* the equipment for covert operations of this nature! The NSA should stick with what it knows . . . signals intelligence!"

"How about that, Charlie?" the President asked. He was smiling. Damn the man, he was *enjoying* this!

"I'm not trying to steal the Agency's thunder, sir. But I do submit that one man, with a portable satellite relay station and some rather small communications pickups, ought to be able to slip in and give us the insight we need into just what the Russians are doing up there." He shrugged. "If the CIA wants to send their own team, that's fine with me. But I *do* want a piece of this, sir."

"How about it, Roger?" the President asked Small-bourn. "Does the CIA have a team they can insert right away?"

"Actually, sir, I submit that we'll get better results with satellite imagery. We don't *need* someone on the ground. Or the ice—"

"With respect, Mr. President, that's not true. At high latitudes, the only satellites we have that can give us close surveillance of the area are those in polar or near-polar orbits. Currently, we have five such satellites . . . and there are two others that might be boosted into new, higher-latitude orbits. We're not talking about geostationary here. To remain above the same spot on the Earth's surface, a satellite has to be at geosynchronous orbit . . . and that's above the equator and over twenty-two thousand miles up. A satellite in a polar orbit is typically only a couple of hundred miles up or so, but it's orbiting the Earth once every ninety minutes or so. That means it's only over a given part of the landscape for a few minutes before it drops over the horizon.

"So with seven spysats in a polar orbit, our satellite surveillance of the Russian base will consist of, at *best*, maybe thirty minutes out of every ninety. That's eight hours out of twenty-four. And that assumes they all have enough fuel on board for course corrections, since to pass over the Russian base, they'll need to be canted a bit off of a true polar orbit, and be precessed so that they keep passing over the same point on each successive orbit. They won't be able to maintain even that much coverage for more than a day or two.

"Besides, the best spy satellite in the world can't see inside those ships. The *Lebedev* is sixty-six hundred tons and longer than a football field. How will the SEALs know where the hostages are being held? And they might not be on the *Lebedev* at all. There are three ships up there. Thirty-two SEALs. What are you going to do, send ten SEALs to each ship?"

"It sounds like you've thought this out pretty carefully, Bill," the President said.

"We try to . . . anticipate, sir."

"Well, goddamn. It works for me. Tell your man to pack his long johns."

"Thank you, sir."

As they continued to discuss the situation, however, Rubens could sense the anger and the resentment among the others—in Collins especially, though that may have been because he knew her best. He still found it hard to believe. The two of them, Rubens and Collins, had been lovers once, if briefly, an episode that he now believed to be the biggest mistake of his life. Collins, he knew, had all the moral sensibilities of a tomcat pissing on the furniture to prove ownership, and she wouldn't be happy until Desk Three was part of her Directorate of Operations.

There was hostility toward the DIA, too; there'd been head-to-head antagonism between the DIA and the CIA over a lot of intelligence issues lately—most memorably the issue of weapons of mass destruction in Iraq, back in '03. As for Bing . . . she was tough to read. Most likely, she was simply trying to secure her own personal empire within the White House basement and would ally with anyone who could give her the power she craved.

The President's injunction to "play nice" would only drive the interdepartmental hostilities beneath the surface, and that only for a time.

The important thing, so far as Rubens was concerned, was that the political infighting and turf wars not be allowed to affect his people, his field agents.

They deserved a hell of a lot better than that.

Menwith Hill Echelon Facility
Yorkshire, England
1340 hours GMT

The Somerset Room was a large mahogany-paneled conference room a level above the Menwith Control Centre, with a long, oval table surrounded by comfortable chairs and the wall opposite the entrance covered by a huge flat-screen monitor. At the moment, that screen, flanked by the flags of both the United States and Great Britain, showed the NSA logo, but shortly it would provide the English end of a conference call, scheduled for 0900 hours EST, 1400 GMT. A row of LED panels above the big screen showed digital readouts for the local times at six different cities in the world. It was twenty minutes to nine, Dean saw, in Washington . . . and 4:40 in the afternoon in St. Petersburg.

Yakutsk would be . . . what? GMT plus nine hours? Something like that. The Arctic base north of Wrangle Island would be GMT plus twelve.

Lia took a seat on Dean's left, Carolyn Howorth on his right. Evans sat across the table from them, with Akulinin next to him. The five of them had talked about the situation into the late evening the night before, discussing the Russian Mafiya, the Russian petroleum industry, and the current international crisis in the Arctic.

It all appeared to be related. Dean was willing to bet his paycheck on that.

Dean was quite taken with Carolyn—CJ, as she insisted on styling herself with her friends. She was quick and she was sharp, one of the infamous Menwith Girls, though she was unusual in actually being English rather than one of the small local army of transplanted Americans. He'd been surprised to learn that she *was* an American citizen, though her parents had brought her over from Yorkshire thirty-eight years before, from a tiny village less than twenty miles from this conference room. The NSA only rarely hired naturalized citizens . . . but they'd made an eager exception in CJ's case. Her expertise in Japanese, spoken, she said, with a slight Kobe accent, had led them to make an exception so that she could work in the public relations bureau at Misawa. Only later had her knowledge of Russian brought her back to the Yorkshire moors and a place on the Russian desk.

And there might have been advantages, Dean thought, in having someone like her on the payroll here in England. The United States wouldn't officially acknowledge her dual nationality, but so far as the Brits were concerned, she was a British subject until Her Majesty personally revoked her citizenship.

"I have some news," Evans said as they took their seats, Styrofoam cups of coffee in front of Lia and Dean, cups of tea for Evans and CJ. "Fischer woke up last night at Barts, and MI5 has been talking to her. *And* we picked up Julie Henshaw at Heathrow. MI5 brought her in as well, and has been having a little chat with the lady."

"Don't tell us," Lia said. "Neither of them knew a thing."

"Nothing worth the asking," Evans admitted. "Fischer knew Braslov as Johann Ernst. She thought he was German and a Greenworld activist, one of the group's founders. She said he had money, a lot of it, enough to take care of her considerable debts, and those of her two friends."

"At least that explains how the Russians recruited them," Dean said. "It doesn't explain how she got recruited for a suicide mission."

"She insists that Braslov told her no one in the GLA building would be armed, for security reasons. Mr. Karr's defense of Dr. Spencer, she said, was most surprising."

"So she was willing to kill a stranger for money," Dean said.

"It's amazing what people will do if they're desperate enough," CJ told them. "If they're *hungry* enough."

"I'm beginning to think that the Russians created Greenworld to serve their agenda," Akulinin said.

"Reverse propaganda," Lia said, agreeing. "They set Greenworld up to do some outrageous things—like assassinate people at a scientific symposium in London—and then they can ignore *all* activist environmental groups when they do something like build a new pipeline through a wildlife refuge."

"Or drill for offshore oil in the Arctic Ocean," Dean put in. "I'm convinced that's what this is all about."

"Proving it will be tough," Akulinin told him.

"Proving it isn't our job," Lia added. "The UN still has to rule on the Russian claim. It's all a matter of international law, right? If the UN agrees they own half of the Arctic Ocean, they can do anything they want with it. That's my take on it, anyway."

"What about the flight attendant?" Dean asked. "Julie Henshaw?"

"Pretty much the same as Fischer," Evans told them. "False-flag recruitment. Someone who called himself 'Johann Ernst' contacted her in London. He claimed to be with Europol, and told her a scientist named Spencer was going to be on her next New York to London flight, Spencer was an important suspect in a big anti-terror operation, and that it was important that Ernst's people be able to track him in London. Sounds like he dazzled her with tales of international intrigue . . . and the promise of a big reward."

"Braslov again," Dean said.

"Or someone else using the same cover, but I'd bet it was him," Evans said. "All Henshaw needed to do was get close to one of Spencer's guards, slip a tiny tracking device into the back of his coat collar, and then alert 'Ernst' when the target left the hotel room the next morning."

"So what's happening to them?" Dean asked. "To Fischer and Henshaw, I mean."

"Fischer is under arrest for murder and attempted murder, plus criminal trespass and half a dozen firearms violations," Evans said. "We're holding Henshaw as a material witness and as a possible accessory to murder and conspiracy to murder, though the government may not be able to make that stick. We may have to release her, though, unless we can find evidence linking her more closely with Braslov."

"You won't find it," Lia guessed. "These people are pros."

"I wonder if you can even prosecute," Dean added. "If she genuinely thought she was helping the police. . . ."

"Well, that's for the courts to decide," Evans said. "For right now, though . . . it looks like it's time to talk with your boss."

The NSA logo on the big screen had just dissolved, and after a connection prompt, Rubens appeared on the screen, seated at his desk. "Good morning," he said. "Miss DeFrancesca, Mr. Akulinin . . . I'm glad to see you both safely back."

"It's good to be back, sir," Akulinin said.

"It's a shame," Rubens said dryly, "that you couldn't bring all of your equipment out with you."

Akulinin winced. "Look, I'm sorry about that, sir," he said. "Things were kind of hot and—"

"We will discuss the matter later," Rubens said, interrupting. "At length."

"Yes, sir."

"Mr. Dean, we received the package with Mr. Karr's

effects. You were right. The tracking device is definitely of Russian manufacture."

"We've been exploring the possibility of going back to Russia," Lia told him. "Braslov appears to have left London for Yakutsk. Charlie thinks he's going on to a Russian petroleum-drilling base in the Arctic."

"A distinct possibility," Rubens said. "And you're quite right, Miss DeFrancesca, and Mr. Akulinin, I am indeed asking you to return to Russia." He raised a small remote control and pressed a button. His image on the screen was replaced by a satellite photo, looking down on a stretch of beach with dark waters laced with waves, cliffs above white sands, and the sprawl of a large and secluded building behind the cliffs. It looked like the mansion of a country estate, complete with the bright aqua-colored kidney shape of a swimming pool, the much smaller blue circle of a hot tub nearby, a series of gardens on manicured lawns, and rising stables in the back.

"This," Rubens told them, "is the private dacha of Grigor Kotenko, just outside of Sochi, on the Black Sea. The place used to belong to a high-ranking member of the Politburo, but Kotenko seems to have acquired it about ten years ago. He uses it several times a month for entertaining important people, but it is currently closed up, with only a small caretaker staff in residence.

"I want you, Miss DeFrancesca, and you, Mr. Akulinin, to gain covert entrance to that dacha and wire it for sound. In particular, we need some keyboard bugs, so that we can keep tabs on Kotenko's computer dealings."

Keyboard bugs were tiny microphone transmitters, half the size of BB shot, that could be dropped loose inside a computer keyboard. Each key, it turned out, made a unique sound print when struck. With those sounds transmitted to a nearby hidden relay and passed on to Fort Meade by satellite, it was possible for the supercomputers at the Tordella Center to reconstruct, keystroke for keystroke, what was typed into the target computer, including e-mail addresses, contact lists, account information, and passwords.

"A routine visit by the plumbers, then," Akulinin said, nodding.

"Black bag work, yes," Rubens said. "You'll be working with Mr. Evans and GCHQ on the details of your insertion, legends, and extraction. We're booking you on a flight to Sochi Monday."

"Well," Lia said, "back to the salt mines."

"Mr. Dean," Rubens said. "I have something special for you."

Dean suppressed a small twinge of disappointment. He'd hoped to be assigned to Lia's op, but something in Rubens' voice told him that that wasn't going to happen. "Yakutsk?"

"No. But you *will* need to pack cold-weather gear, I promise you."

This did not sound particularly promising to Dean, but he nodded and said, "Right."

"You," Rubens continued, "will be hitching a ride on a submarine in two days."

"The NOAA base in the Arctic, then?"

"Yes. And the Russian base near there as well, if necessary. We want Braslov, Mr. Dean. And even more, we want the Americans being held up there released . . . two in particular, a congressman's daughter and an NSA technician."

"Leave no one behind," Dean said. "I understand."

"Spoken like a true Marine."

"Ooh-rah." He recited the battle cry without emotion. He'd always hated the cold. . . .

14

Kotenko Dacha
Sochi, Russia
1510 hours, GMT + 3

GRIGOR KOTENKO WATCHED impassively as the man walked into the room, stopped, spread his arms, and stood motionless, waiting. Antonov had been through this many times before, and he knew the routine. Andre, a man-mountain as heavily padded as a Japanese sumo wrestler, emerged from the far corner to check him for wires or hidden weapons. Yuri Antonov had been with the Organizatsiya for fifteen years, but since Victor Mikhaylov's sudden and untimely death last week, Kotenko was taking no chances. *No* one entered his presence without a thorough search, even after the metal detectors and X-ray scanners downstairs.

It wasn't Mikhaylov's unknown killers Kotenko feared so much, and it certainly wasn't the police, most of whom belonged to him. The majority of his security efforts were actually directed against other Russian Mafiya groups, the circling sharks, as he thought of them. The events at the waterfront in St. Petersburg last week had both wounded the local arm of Tambov and reflected the toothsome possibility of weakness. In such a starkly competitive environment as modern Russia, the other gangs could turn on Kotenko's organization like sharks in a feeding frenzy, maddened by bloodlust.

Within the shadows of the Russian underworld, the wounded, the weak, the indecisive were shown no mercy.

"Mr. Antonov," Kotenko said as Andre straightened up and gave the signal indicating that the visitor was clean. "So good to see you again. What is it you have for me?"

"Something most interesting, Mr. Kotenko. Ah, one of your people took it from me downstairs. . . ."

Antonov was a small, nervous individual with a goatee and a receding hairline that gave him a passing resemblance to Vladimir Lenin. He did not, Kotenko knew, have Lenin's strength of purpose, or his sheer force of will. Antonov did, however, know how to follow orders.

"Yes, yes," Kotenko said. "Security, you understand?"

Dmitry, one of Kotenko's personal assistants, walked in carrying a capacious metal toolbox. Antonov had brought it with him from St. Petersburg, surrendering it to Kotenko's trusted people outside for a careful search.

"This is the box?" Kotenko asked.

"Yes, sir. We found it close to where one of the assassins was hiding. We believe he forgot it as he fled the scene."

Carefully Kotenko took the toolbox and began removing its contents. There wasn't much . . . a length of climbing rope tightly bundled and tied; some devices obviously designed to slip over a person's boots or hands with protruding spikes to help him or her climb walls or telephone poles; some cinches, straps, and buckles that likely were rappelling gear; five thirty-round magazines manufactured by Heckler & Koch, loaded with 9mm ammunition. Of more interest was a set of low-light binoculars with a single light-gathering tube, obviously of military manufacture.

And a communications terminal complete with folded satellite antenna, battery, and encryption box.

"Have our people in St. Petersburg looked at these?" Kotenko asked, examining the binoculars. They might be worth fifteen thousand rubles on the open market. They were certainly much better than anything in the Russian military's inventory.

"Yes, sir," Antonov said as Kotenko set aside the binoculars and began looking at the satcom gear. "They say it is obviously CIA issue. The communications equipment is something called an AN/PSC-12 com terminal, I'm told. Our friends in China might be quite interested in purchasing it."

"Indeed." Kotenko picked up the encryption device, a black box the size of a pack of cigarettes. He knew little about the technology—one employed others to do the knowing with complicated gadgets like this—but he did understand the *price* of technology. The satellite terminal itself might be worth some hundreds of thousands of rubles to governments that might from time to time find themselves the target of American intelligence—China, yes, but also Iran, Syria, Pakistan, North Korea, Venezuela . . . oh, the list of America's enemies was *quite* long.

But the true treasure here was this small and seemingly innocuous black box. There would be codes stored within the computer chips inside, codes that would allow the owner of the box to turn it on its makers and listen in on *their* secret communications.

And that bit of technology was almost beyond price.

Almost. Grigor Kotenko made his very comfortable living by acquiring priceless items, putting a price on them, and finding people able and willing to pay. Normally, these days, he trafficked in corporations and in the future of Russian oil and gas production, but he traded in military hardware as well.

There was also a danger, however. He examined the case of the device closely, searching for any words, logos, or imprints at all. He didn't expect to find them. . . .

"Dmitry!"

"Yes, sir!"

"This device has been screened for radio emissions?"

"Yes, sir. There are no transmissions. Everything in the tool kit, and the case itself, is dead."

Devices such as this frequently included global positioning trackers and transmitters. Its manufacturers might also have placed very tiny listening devices or other intelligence-gathering sensors inside the case, and there was always the possibility that the tool kit had been *deliberately* abandoned at the warehouse, in order to lead its owners straight to him. In the world of espionage, nothing was ever quite what it seemed.

So long as it was not actively transmitting to the Americans, it was probably safe, however.

Probably . . .

He set the device back inside the tool kit along with the other items he'd removed, closed it, and signaled to Dmitry.

"Put this in the safe."

"Yes, sir."

Kotenko's safe was a heavy walk-in downstairs, with walls three inches thick. If the device *did* start transmitting, the signals could not possibly penetrate those walls.

"They checked the box and everything in it for RF transmissions in St. Petersburg, sir," Antonov said as Dmitry walked out of the room with the tool kit. "The devices all are inert."

"I don't pretend to know how these devices work, Mr. Antonov," Kotenko said. Turning, he walked toward the large double doors leading out onto the western deck. "But I do know there are devices called transponders that will patiently wait to send out a signal, but which do so only when they *receive* a signal. Until then, the device could well be, as you say, inert."

He pushed open the doors and walked outside, with Antonov and the ever-watchful Andre following behind. It was mid-afternoon, and the westering sun glared from the broad expanse of the Black Sea. Laughter, male and female, sounded from somewhere nearby.

Kotenko walked to the railing. The back deck overlooked his large pool two stories below, where six of his girls were entertaining two senior officers of Gazprom and a member of the Duma, all of whom had been invited to the Sochi dacha for a working weekend.

At the moment, it appeared to be most enjoyable work. Swimsuits had been discarded some time ago, and shrill feminine laughter chimed from the patio. Expressionless servants silently came and went with bottles of vodka, the vital lubricant of all Russian business meetings.

"In any case," Kotenko continued, watching the pleasant scene below from the railing, "I intend to take no chances. I suspect that the communications equipment is from the American NSA . . . possibly on loan to the CIA, but not necessarily."

"The NSA?" Antonov asked. "What is that?"

"An even larger, more secretive, and more powerful American spy agency than the CIA. The fact that many people have never even heard the name proves how good they are. Did our people carefully check the St. Petersburg shipment for tracking devices planted by the intruders?"

"Yes, sir. Every square centimeter!"

"And it was clean?"

"Some slight radioactivity, but no radio signals of any sort."

"Hmm." Kotenko chewed for a moment on one end of

his bushy mustache, thinking hard. "Those . . . intruders on the waterfront," he said after a moment, "were American. The equipment they carried proved that." If the break-in at the warehouse had been engineered by one of the rival gangs of the Organizatsiya, they would have been using Russian, German, or Japanese devices . . . or less highly advanced American equipment, the sort of stuff in current use by the American military. That might include the light-intensification binoculars—he was pretty sure that such devices were in common use by American Special Forces like the SEALs and the Army Rangers—but the satellite communications equipment was not in widespread use, he was certain. Not yet.

CIA? Or NSA?

The CIA was the organization most likely to carry out covert operations—"black ops" he thought was the American term—in foreign countries. The NSA primarily handled electronic eavesdropping, employing a variety of listening devices both on the ground, in aircraft, and in spy satellites. Still, there were persistent rumors that the NSA also ran covert operations like their CIA brothers.

In the long run it didn't matter which organization was behind the operation. He did *want* to know, however, if only because Grigor Kotenko liked to know exactly who his opponents were. Knowing your enemy, knowing who he was and how he thought and what his strengths and weaknesses were, all was a long part of the path to victory.

The CIA and their operating methods were well known to people in the Organizatsiya like Sergei Braslov, who'd once been GRU, Russian military intelligence. Some of their successes were known, but so, too, were many of their failures.

The public knew very little about the NSA, however, and that spoke volumes for their efficiency, as well as for their potential deadliness in the arena of international espionage. A successful spy mission was the one of which no one ever heard.

Kotenko survived because he took no chances. He prospered because he could see angles other people could not and he had the muscle to take advantage of that.

In fact, Kotenko had believed for some time that the NSA was trying to get a line on him for intelligence purposes, and the St. Petersburg affair had been arranged to give him the upper hand. He'd recruited a low-level enforcer in his organization—Alekseev—to approach an employee at the American consulate in St. Petersburg with information on the beryllium shipment to Iran, and then he'd carefully orchestrated the trap at the waterfront warehouse.

That ambush *should* have netted a couple of American agents for deep interrogation. Some of the people working for Kotenko had learned the fine art of interrogation with the KGB, in the basement of the infamous Lubyanka Prison in Moscow during the Soviet era. They enjoyed their work and were quite good at what they did. The information they extracted from prisoners could be most valuable.

And afterward, if there was anything left, the prisoners might prove to be profitable in other ways, either as insurance or for ransom.

But the ambush had misfired. There'd been at least two Americans, as Alekseev had promised, but they'd arrived at the warehouse separately and the men led by Mikhaylov, concentrating on Alekseev and the woman with him, had missed the second agent. That second agent had been able to help the woman escape from the trap . . . but evidently he'd left behind the tool kit in the chaos of the firefight.

No matter. Kotenko thought he could still make a handsome profit from the affair.

"The special Rybinsk shipment at St. Petersburg," he said after a moment's thought. "Is it safely away?"

"Yes, sir," Antonov told him. "It left for Bandar Abbas two days ago, as scheduled."

"Then it's the Iranians' problem now. Andre!"

"Yes, sir."

"Alert the staff. We will be going to first-level security here at the dacha. We may be having . . . visitors."

"Immediately, sir."

He would also transmit further instructions to Braslov, though he would use Antonov to do so, using a onetime satellite phone, and from a location far removed from the dacha, just to be sure. The enemy might soon be taking an interest in Operation Cold War, as well as in his activities here in Sochi.

His opponents in this game, whether they were CIA or NSA, were not magical, whatever their reputations might be. They were good, *very* good, but there were limits to their powers, and to what they were able to pull off with their technology. The Americans were feared, and justly so, for their technological prowess in the military arts, but technology could only take you so far.

In this game, you needed—what was the American expression?—"boots on the ground," that was it. The Americans would need to put boots on the ground to get at Kotenko and his operation. When they tried it, he would cut them off at the ankles.

Meanwhile, he had work to do. The Duma representative from St. Petersburg and the Gazprom industrialists needed to be convinced that their best interests would be served by a closer alliance with Tambov and what Kotenko could offer them. At the moment, he saw, looking down from the deck, his girls were doing their very best to demonstrate one aspect of Kotenko's generosity. His guests seemed to be enjoying their visit quite a lot at the moment.

All three visitors were married, and all three had solid reputations as stolid, sober, and principled businessmen of the post-Soviet era, the new Russia. Vladymir Malyshkin, there, looked a little less than stolid at the moment, with a vodka bottle in one hand, Tanya nude on his lap, and Natasha's bikini briefs draped over his bald pate like a bright green aviator's cap.

Kotenko trusted that both of the film crews hidden in the house were getting all of this.

In an hour or two, he would go down to the pool and join in the fun. In a few days, at the end of their visit, he would apprise them of some of the *other* benefits to be found in a closer alliance with Grigor Kotenko—such as the promise that the contents of certain videotapes would not be made public.

In the meantime, he had special instructions to give to Yuri Antonov.

Baffin Bay
73° 54' N, 75° 48' W
0920 hours, GMT – 6

Dean sat on the hard, straight-backed seat in the Sea King's cargo compartment and tried not to think of the next few minutes. He wanted this part of the trip to be *over*.

His journey had begun two days ago with a flight on board an aging C-2A Greyhound COD out of Lakenheath for an eleven-hundred-mile flight to the deck of the USS *Harry S. Truman*, cruising the North Atlantic south of Iceland. "COD" stood for "Carrier On-board Delivery," and the ugly little Greyhound bounced him down onto the carrier's flight deck in the middle of a rain-swept night.

He was on board just long enough for a meal and a friendly argument with the senior chief assigned to escort him, an argument over the carrier's name. President Harry *S* Truman was notorious for not having a period after the *S* in his name, which the President jokingly had claimed was not an initial but his middle name. According to Senior Chief McMasters, though, most official documents, the Truman Library, the *Associated Press Handbook,* and, frequently, even Truman's own signature all used a period . . . as did the carrier's blue and orange crest on the quarterdeck, with its motto "The Buck Stops Here."

Dean told McMasters that he was not convinced and was going to need to do some research on the question when he got back to civilization. The good-natured banter helped Dean keep his mind off the inevitable end of his journey.

Within another two hours, the COD had been refueled and he was bouncing once again through a stormy night for another thousand-mile flight to Nuuk/Godthab Airport on the rocky west coast of Greenland. That time, he didn't even get to deplane—not that there was much to see by the cold, near-Arctic glow of sunrise at 0300, local time.

Then the COD flew him north, *far* north, up the coast to icebound Thule Air Force Base overlooking Baffin Bay 950 miles north of Nuuk. There he was hustled immediately across the tarmac to a waiting helicopter, an SH-60F Ocean Hawk, for the final leg of his flight.

By this time it was the middle of the night by both his watch and his stomach, both of which were still on GMT, but a dim, gray, and heavily overcast morning according to the light, though McMasters had reminded him that the sun never set at this time of the year north of the Arctic Circle. They packed him onto the helo, which promptly lifted off from Thule and flew a straight-line course almost due west, low above the choppy waters of the bay.

Soon the cloud deck lowered even more and it began to rain. The aircraft shuddered with heavy gusts of wind, and lightning flared off to the south.

Just freaking great. . . .

On board the *Truman,* they'd packed him into a wet suit, over which they'd placed layers of thermal clothing, a parka, a helmet, and a life jacket, creating a fashion statement that made it tough to move and almost impossible to go to the bathroom. Somehow, though, he'd managed over the past several hours, but when the Ocean Hawk's crew chief began strapping him into the harness, he started having serious doubts.

During his Marine career, Dean had fast-roped out of helicopters numerous times, and more than once he'd taken an unscheduled dip in the drink. This time, though, there could be no room for error.

What was bothering him at the moment was a remembered scene from an old Tom Clancy novel.

As best as Dean could remember it, the hero had been a CIA officer trying to track down a rogue Soviet submarine. At one point in the story, the officer had been lowered from a helicopter down toward the deck of an American submarine somewhere in the Atlantic. When high winds and rough seas—plus the fact that the helicopter was bingo fuel—had forced the helo crew to abort the operation and start winching the hero back up to safety, the officer had hit the safety release on his harness and dropped into the ocean.

That hero had, of course, survived his dunking in the frigid Atlantic waters and gone on to win the day in the finest tradition of literary and cinematic heroes everywhere. The waters beneath the Ocean Hawk this morning, though, were bitterly cold, colder even than the water into which Clancy's fictional hero had fallen. If Dean hit the freezing water of Baffin Bay, he would have a few minutes at best before hypothermia numbed him into insensibility and he drowned.

The Ocean Hawk was hovering now, and the crew chief slid aside the big side-panel door. Spray from the aircraft's rotor wash swirled past the cargo compartment, salty and cold.

At least the rain had stopped.

"We're dipping our tallywacker now!" the crew chief said, shouting into Dean's ear above the thunder of the helo's rotors. "Think of it as ringing their doorbell!"

"Yeah!" Dean yelled back. "Or fishing! Fishing for submarines!"

The chief laughed and clapped Dean on the shoulder.

Suspended beneath a length of cable, lowered from the Ocean Hawk's belly, was a dipping sonar, a device sending out intense pings of sound through the water. Normally, it was used to find lurking submarines underwater, pinpointing them by echolocation. This time, though, as the chief had suggested, it was a pre-arranged signal for the submarine to surface.

Nothing happened for several minutes. Dean, despite his layered Arctic clothing, suppressed a sudden shiver, though whether it had been brought on by the cold or from high-stress anticipation, he couldn't tell. Then one of the sailors on board the Ocean Hawk pointed out the open door. "There! There she is!"

Dean followed the man's pointing finger and saw a white rooster tail of spray on the surface several hundred yards away. A dark, slate-gray shape sliced upward through the foam, becoming the squared-off cliff of a submarine's sail, its forward hydroplanes extending from either side like small wings. As the vessel continued to rise, a second shape emerged from the spray aft of the sail—an Advanced Seal Delivery System, or ASDS, a miniature submarine just sixty-five feet long and riding on the bigger submarine's afterdeck like a black, torpedo-shaped parasite.

In another moment, the deck appeared, immersed in a broad, V-shaped wake. The SSGN *Ohio* was 560 feet long overall, with a beam of 42 feet; it was startling how tiny the sail and the ASDS looked by comparison with that dark sea monster's awesome length and mass.

In another moment, the Ocean Hawk had reeled its dipping sonar back on board and repositioned itself above the surfaced submarine. Dean leaned over, looking down out of the open door, to see the *Ohio* nested within the disk of the helo's rotor wash. Men scrambled out of an open deck hatch forward of the sail, and he could see two officers in the tiny, open cockpit on top of the sail, shielding their eyes as they looked up at the Ocean Hawk's belly. Several of the seamen on the forward deck carried long, slender poles.

"Don't worry about those poles!" The crew chief shouted to be heard above the roar. "They're going to reach up with them and hit your cable before you touch the deck! We've built up an electrical charge in flight, and if they don't bleed it off, it could knock you on your ass!"

Dean nodded understanding. He'd seen this maneuver done before at sea, especially during stormy weather.

They were signaling from the deck, waving him on.

"Okay, Mr. Dean!" the crew chief bellowed. "Out you go! Good luck!"

"Thanks for the lift!"

"Don't worry about the lift! It's the *drop* that scares the shit out of me!"

Gripping the cable attached to his harness, Dean stepped into emptiness. Immediately the prop wash caught him, buffeting him back and forth as he dangled, like bait on a fishing line, beneath the hovering Ocean

Hawk. The ear protectors on his helmet shut out much of the roar, but it still felt and sounded like being caught inside a wind tunnel. Below him, five men in heavy, olive-drab parkas, bright orange life jackets, and safety lines waited with upturned faces. Two of them jabbed at him with static discharge poles.

Of one thing Dean was certain: he was not going to release the harness and drop into the sea. If the Ocean Hawk's pilot decided to reel Dean back in, he'd be *quite* happy to accede to their judgment.

He was starting to drift past the submarine's hull. He could see one of the men below, however, talking into a headset, and the helicopter's pilot adjusted, bringing Dean back and gently down. The fear wasn't as bad as he had thought it would be; somehow, the wind and the pounding of the rotors and the shrill whine of twin high-powered turboshafts and the biting cold all combined to numb the brain and anaesthetize the mind. He dropped lower . . . still lower and then felt gloved hands grabbing hold of his boots and legs and hauling him down to the deck.

"Permission to come aboard!" he shouted as they helped him with his harness.

"Granted!" the chief in charge of the deck party called back. "Welcome aboard!"

In another instant, the cable was reeling away up into the cargo deck of the Ocean Hawk, and the helicopter, dipping its nose, began arrowing away through leaden skies back to the east, toward Thule. One of the sailors guided Dean with a hand on his shoulder aft toward the open hatch in the deck. "Mind your skull, sir," the man told him. "It's a tight fit."

The hatch led down a vertical ladder to the *Ohio*'s forward torpedo room, where several more sailors waited to receive him. He heard some murmurs among them. "So *that's* our spook, is it?" some asked.

"Bond," another voice replied with mock seriousness. "*James* Bond. . . ."

"Shaken," Dean told the watching sailors as he started stripping off life jacket, helmet, and parka and passing them off to waiting hands, "not stirred." That raised a laugh. Someone draped a blanket over his shoulders. Another man offered him a mug of steaming coffee, which he gratefully accepted. He heard the hatch clang shut overhead and someone speaking over an intercom, saying, "Forward torpedo room hatch secured!" The compartment was surprisingly warm, the air fresh, though carrying the mingled scents of oil, salt, and too many men in a confined space.

A lean, pale blond youngster in khakis and a lieutenant commander's rank insignia stepped forward. "Welcome aboard the *Ohio*, Mr. Dean," he said. "I'm Lieutenant Commander Hartwell, the boat's exec. If you'll come with me, please?"

"Now hear this," a voice sounded over the sub's 1MC speakers. "Now hear this. Dive! Dive!" An alarm klaxon sounded, a computer-generated version of the classic *ah—* oo*gah*! of the movies, followed again by the voice calling, "Dive! Dive!"

A modern submarine's true element was the dark silence of the ocean depths, and no skipper wanted to leave his command exposed on the surface for longer than could possibly be helped. As the exec led Dean aft, he felt the deck tilt slightly beneath his feet as the *Ohio* returned to her proper realm.

15

Zhemchuzhina Hotel
Sochi, Russia
1712 hours, GMT + 3

LIA AND AKULININ TOUCHED down at Adler-Sochi International Airport in the early afternoon after an uneventful flight from London. They passed through customs with passports listing them as husband and wife, picked up their luggage in the baggage claim, and caught a cab for the long ride up to Sochi. The airport was located in Adler, just five miles from the Georgian border, but Sochi was almost fifteen miles to the northwest, along the E97 highway that ran along the Black Sea coast.

According to the legend provided by GCHQ, they were Mr. and Mrs. Darby, John and Lisa of Mayfair, on holiday to this rather posh resort region on the Black Sea.

They noticed quite a lot of construction on the hillsides south of the city. Their driver was the talkative sort, running on without stop about Sochi having been chosen as the site for the Winter Olympics in 2014. It was, he proclaimed in heavily accented Russian interspersed with even worse English, just the economic boost the city needed, and everyone was soon going to be rich. Lia studied the new construction with a more cynical eye and wondered how deep the Organizatsiya had burrowed into the local landscape.

They checked in at the front desk, argued a bit with the desk clerk over whether their reservation had been for smoking rather than nonsmoking, then went up to their room. As soon as the door was shut, Lia pulled what looked like a compact from her handbag and began walking around the room, studying the tiny LED readout as she passed the device along the walls, over the lamps and TV, across the head of the big king-sized bed, across the big mirror in its ornate frame over the dresser. "Lovely room, John," she said in a bright voice. "I think the travel agency picked a good one this time."

"Nice view of the ocean," Akulinin said from the window. He, too, was carefully scanning the glass doors onto the balcony with something like a small PDA. They continued to exchange uninformative chitchat until they were reasonably sure that there were no hidden listening devices in the room. Their argument at the front desk had been designed to get the desk clerk to make a last-minute change, just in case foreign tourists were automatically dropped into a room wired for sound or video. If they'd found anything, they were prepared—by means of a dead cockroach sealed in a small plastic bottle—to demand yet *another* room change.

But their room appeared to be electronically, as well as physically, clean.

Of course, the bad old days of the Soviet regime were long gone and tourists were no longer the targets of paranoid suspicion and KGB surveillance. The new and capitalist Russia desperately needed foreign currency and was doing her best to promote a lively tourist trade. The chances were good that no one was spying on the two spies. At least, not *here*.

Still, many of the old ploys used by the KGB were still

employed in the new Russia—especially where business-people were concerned. The honey trap was an old favorite. The traveler might come back to his room one evening to find a lovely and willing young woman waiting for him in bed, complete with a story about how she'd bribed a maid to let her in just so she could meet him, or how the people with whom he was working had hired her for his pleasure, or how she'd accidentally ended up in the wrong room. Sound recordings and video footage would then be used to blackmail the traveler. If Russia was no longer as interested as she once was in political or military espionage, *industrial* espionage was still big business. It was amazing what a business traveler might reveal about a new technical process in order to keep a wife or a boss from seeing a certain compromising and decidedly X-rated video.

And the Organizatsiya was always on the lookout for useful information to sell to the highest bidder or for the payment of a few thousand euros or dollars from a horny and gullible mark. One reason Akulinin and Lia were here posing as a married couple was to make the two of them a less obvious target than the traditional lonely businessman.

"So is everything in there to your satisfaction?" Jeff Rockman's voice said in Lia's ear.

"I got weak positives off the wall outlets and the phone jack," she said. "As usual." Her detector picked up copper wiring as well as electronic circuits. "But I think we're clear."

"I've got nothing," Akulinin said, stepping back inside from the balcony. "It really is a great view, though."

"We'll need you to put down your eyes so we can cover your room," Rockman told them. "And you have a visitor coming up. I just gave him your room number."

A knock sounded at the door.

Akulinin peered through the spy hole, then opened the door. James Llewellyn walked in.

"Good afternoon," Llewellyn said with an affable grin. "How's the old married couple, then?"

"Jet-lagged," Lia replied. "And in no mood for games."

"Understood." He glanced around the room. "We're secure?"

"Yes."

"Capital."

"As secure as we can be, anyway."

"Yes, well, that's what keeps the game interesting, don't you think? You can never be *sure*."

"What's interesting," Akulinin said with a grimace, "is waiting to hear if you guys ever recovered that tool kit. You said you had a team on it that night, but then we got hustled back to England so quickly we never heard what happened."

"Ah," Llewellyn said. "As it happens . . . no." He set his laptop computer on a desk in one corner of the room and opened it. "But, actually, that's a bit of good news. Hang on a tick. I think you'll be interested in what I have here." He began booting up the computer.

"They weren't able to recover the damned thing and that's *good* news?" Akulinin said. He looked bleak.

"He's been afraid they're going to take it out of his paycheck," Lia put in.

"Yes, well, the thing is, we *were* able to track it for a time," Llewellyn said. "Used a satellite to query the satcom's imbedded GPS. We were able to plot its movements over the course of two days, from St. Petersburg to Moscow to someplace near Donetsk. The last time we got a signal from the unit, we think it was airborne and moving south."

"Donetsk is more or less halfway between Moscow and Sochi," Lia said. "You think it was on its way here?"

"A distinct possibility," Llewellyn told them. "We're now certain the gang that jumped you in St. Petersburg was with the Tambovs. Grigor Kotenko is a high-ranking Tambov chief, and he was closely involved in the beryllium sale in St. Pete. Those were probably his enforcers on the waterfront. He specializes in high-tech items, remember, and the black box alone from the AN/PSC-12 would be worth millions to the right buyer."

"Tell me about it," Akulinin said. "Rubens is going to have me shot when I get back to the States."

"Only after he skins you alive," Lia told him.

Llewellyn grinned. "Maybe they'll just take it out of your pay. In any case, we couldn't find the kit on the waterfront where you said you must have left it. The sensors you two left in the area showed the whole place was crawling with people for hours after you left, so it's a fair bet they found it and looked inside. If they reported it to Kotenko, he would have wanted to see just what it was that had so unexpectedly fallen into his hands."

Lia looked at Llewellyn. "So does that mean Kotenko is in Sochi now? I thought the dacha was closed except for a housekeeping staff."

"We thought it was," Llewellyn said. "But several days ago, we saw signs that the place was open for business. Here." He typed a set of commands into the laptop, and a full-color photograph came up on the 17-inch screen, a shot apparently taken from a boat offshore. The camera angle looked up from the water, framing a large two-story villa on a hilltop. Snowcapped mountains—the Caucasus—rose behind, almost lost in a blue haze. The house, its walls and roof brightly colored in tropical aquas, reds, and yellows, looked deserted. He hit a key and a second photo opened up, this one taken from either a satellite or a high-flying aircraft, looking down on the same building. The grounds, the large deck, the balconies, all were deserted.

"Those first two are from a week ago," Llewellyn said, pointing to the date and time stamps on the photos. "You can't tell for sure from two photos, but our agents watching the place reported no activity at all, save for a gardener, a pool caretaker, and two security types. Then, three days ago, we got this."

He brought up a third photo, again taken from overhead. This one showed two cars in the driveway at the front of the dacha, an open table umbrella on the poolside deck, and a number of human figures around the pool. Five security men were visible around the property's perimeter, two of them with dogs on leads.

"My God," Lia said, looking close. She hit a key several times, zooming in closer on the scene. "Is that an *orgy*?"

"Kotenko appears to have been, ah, entertaining some guests this past weekend," Llewellyn said. "We're checking our sources in Moscow, and going through some backlogged cell phone intercepts to be sure, but we think he's brought in some VIPs from Gazprom. Probably for some high-level . . . I think you Yanks call it 'wheeling and dealing'?"

"Looks like that's not all they're doing," Akulinin said, studying the screen. "Damn. That does complicate things a bit."

"Indeed. We were counting on you two having the place more or less to yourselves. But if Kotenko is in residence, he'll have a small entourage with him. Bodyguards. Office assistants. Maids and butlers. Secretaries. And, from the look of it, girls from one of his brothels in town."

"Yeah. Looks like it's a hell of a party," Akulinin said.

Llewellyn typed another entry, and a number of architectural drawings came up—blueprints on the dacha. "We got these from the company in Moscow that built the place," he told them. "The same company made a number of alterations to the house after Kotenko bought it. Notice here . . . on the first floor, and here, in the basement directly below."

"Looks like it's wired for Internet," Lia observed, studying the wiring schematics. "And what's all this in the basement? Looks like they added structural reinforcement."

"Right the first time. They reinforced the floor, there, with load-bearing beams."

"A safe?"

"That's a good bet, Lia. Something damned heavy, anyway. We think this area on the first floor is Kotenko's office . . . and that eight years ago he installed a heavy floor safe, right here."

Lia nodded. "So . . . if we can't sneak in without being seen, we might make it look like a burglary."

"That was our thought," Llewellyn said. "I brought some specialist tools for you from St. Petersburg."

"Wait a second," Akulinin said. "You guys are jumping way ahead of me here. A burglary? I thought this was just a quick in-and-out to plant bugs."

"Ideally," Lia told him, "we could sneak past a couple of security guards, gain entrance to the building, plant our surveillance devices, and slip out again and no one would ever know we'd even been there."

"Right," Llewellyn said. "But with that many people on the property, it's more likely that you'll be spotted."

"Exactly. If we pretend to be burglars, though, they might not think to look for bugs afterward. At least, not the kind of bugs *we'll* be leaving."

"And if you're burglars," Llewellyn added, "the safe, obviously, becomes your target."

Lia watched realization unfold behind Akulinin's eyes. "Ah. Got it," he said. "If Kotenko has the satcom unit, there's a good chance that he'll have it in that safe. We might be able to get it back after all." Akulinin pumped his arm happily. "Yeah! The new kid gets a chance to redeem himself! I can live with that."

"I'd still rather go in without a crowd on the premises," Lia told Llewellyn. "Any chance we could just kick back and wait for a few days, maybe hope Kotenko goes back to St. Petersburg?"

"No, Lia," Llewellyn said. "Mr. Rubens was *most* insistent. Something big is happening either in Siberia or up in the Arctic. He wants to be able to read Kotenko's mail as quickly as possible."

"We should have done this as soon as we heard Kotenko was behind the beryllium shipment," she said. She was thinking that she and Akulinin might have had a better command of the situation in St. Petersburg if there'd been some hard intelligence from Kotenko's dacha before they'd inserted.

"Yes, well, that *was* on the to-do list, don't you know. But it wasn't quite so urgent then."

"That's the government for you," Akulinin pointed out. "Hurry up and wait . . . and then you find they needed it done yesterday."

"So when do we go in?" Lia asked.

"Some of our local assets are still getting into place," Llewellyn said, "and we need to coordinate with your Puzzle Palace. Besides, if you're jet-lagged, a good night's sleep would be just the thing, eh?"

"Sounds heavenly," Lia said.

"Tomorrow night then?" Akulinin asked.

"Tomorrow night," Llewellyn agreed. His fingers clattered over the laptop's keyboard again, bringing up more photographs and diagrams. "Now, let me show you what we've worked out. . . ."

Beaufort Sea
75° 18' N, 129° 21' W
1732 hours, GMT – 7

A shadow, whale-lean and 560 feet long, moved through the eternal night of the abyss, six hundred feet beneath a ceiling of solid ice, invisible and silent.

The *Ohio* had remained submerged as she threaded her way through the Parry Channel south of the barren Queen Elizabeth Islands, emerging at last in the iced-over deeps of the Beaufort Sea. Dean followed the vessel's progress with interest in the big plot board at the aft end of the control room, where an enlisted watchstander marked the *Ohio*'s position each hour, connecting the most recent navigational waypoint with the last.

They were now some 820 miles from NOAA Arctic Meteorological Station Bravo, about twenty-eight hours at their current speed. Officially, an *Ohio* missile boat had a maximum speed of twenty knots; in fact, her actual speed was closer to twenty-five, and Dean was pretty sure she could manage even better than that in a hell-bent-for-leather emergency dash.

Dean was in the *Ohio*'s tiny wardroom, seated at the table with Captain Eric Grenville, Lieutenant Commander Hartwell, and a third man in a black acrylic pullover and no rank insignia. The third man had been introduced simply as Lieutenant Taylor. Mugs of coffee, each adorned with the *Ohio*'s logo, rested on the table before them.

"We should be able to maintain flank speed for most of the way," Captain Grenville told Dean, "*if* we don't run into major ice problems."

"What would be a major ice problem, sir?" Dean asked.

"Pressure ridges," Grenville told him. "Places where ice bangs together and creates a kind of mountain range, but sticking down underwater, instead of up in the air.

That doesn't look very likely at the moment, and now that we're clear of the continental shelf, we can stay deep enough to avoid anything that's likely to show up."

Hartwell took a sip from his mug, then added, "We've been coming to dead slow every so often to get a good sonar picture. Sonar's pretty useless above fifteen knots or so. Too much noise. So we dash along at flank, stop, listen, then dash some more. And we'll need to slow down for the final approach, of course."

"So they don't hear us coming?" Dean suggested.

"Exactly," Grenville said, nodding. "Intelligence says there may be Russian subs operating up there. We'd rather our appearance be a surprise."

That was news to Dean, but then, the National Security Agency wasn't usually concerned with Russian naval movements unless they showed up on SIGINT intercepts. Word on the arrival of Russian submarines had probably reached the *Ohio* via naval intelligence, the DIA, or, just possibly, the CIA.

Dean sipped his coffee. True to the traditions of the submarine service, the stuff was pretty good. "Will Russian subs pose a problem for your operation, Lieutenant?" he asked.

Taylor gave a thin smile. "I don't think so."

"I was wondering if I could come along."

Taylor exchanged a quick glance with Grenville. "Negative. My people know how to work with one another. As a team."

"So do the Marines, Lieutenant."

Taylor's hard expression barely changed. "You're a Marine?"

"I was. In my misspent youth."

"Still not a good idea, sir."

From the hard edge to Taylor's voice, Dean knew that this was one argument he would not win.

Although no one had told him specifically, he was reasonably certain that Taylor commanded a platoon of Navy SEALs. The *Ohio* SSGN conversion had specifically allowed the upgraded boats to carry up to sixty SEALs or other special ops forces, but on this mission SEALs were by far the most likely passengers. SEALs—the acronym stood for the three realms in which they operated, SEa, Air, and Land—were the Navy's premier commando force. Their training was unbelievably rugged, and according to some, they were the toughest warriors on the planet.

Dean held a deep respect for the SEALs but couldn't resist a good-natured jibe. "When I come ashore at that base," he told Taylor, "I do *not* want to see one of your damned signs waiting for me."

The SEAL Teams had evolved out of the old Navy UDTs, the Underwater Demolition Teams, which had been born in the Pacific in World War II. The Marines had prided themselves at always being the first ashore, but on island after island they would hit the beach only to find hand-lettered signs upright in the sand identifying a UDT recon element that had slipped ashore the night before. It was a tradition that had continued all the way through to Vietnam.

Taylor actually smiled. Dean hadn't been sure that the hard-faced man *could* smile. "Maybe you shouldn't have told us you were a jarhead," he said. "When you were just another spook, we didn't know *what* to make of you."

The Teams, Dean remembered, had long maintained a tradition of close work with the CIA, but also preferred to develop their own local intelligence networks where possible. The Teams were close-knit and band-of-brothers tight and tended not to play well with others.

"His ID says he's CIA," Grenville said. "Maybe we should just leave it at that."

Dean said nothing. NSA operatives rarely admitted that they were from the No-Such-Agency when they were in the field, even to friends and allies.

"What exactly is your mission here, Mr. Dean?" Hartwell wanted to know.

Dean reached into the pocket of the dungaree shirt he'd been given to wear when he'd come aboard, and extracted a photograph laminated in clear plastic. He handed it to Grenville.

"Nasty scar," Grenville said as he looked at the man in the photo. He passed it to Taylor.

"Sergei Braslov," Dean told them. "Also goes by the name 'Johann Ernst.' Used to be GRU. Now he may be working with Russian State Security, but he's also working for the Russian mob. He may be at the Russian base up here, and he may be involved in whatever happened to our people at the NOAA ice station. What we do know, beyond a doubt, is that he was behind the murder of another government operative, someone who was also a friend of mine."

Taylor nodded, and his eye met Dean's for just a moment. *He knows,* Dean thought. *Comrades-at-arms, and all of that. Or maybe he just knows what it's like to lose a buddy.*

"If you find Braslov," Dean continued, addressing Taylor, "we want him alive for interrogation. The Russian mafia is putting together something pretty big. We think they're trying to corner the whole Russian oil production network. Braslov may be able to give us some insight on that."

"Okay. So the mafia takes over Russian oil production," Hartwell said. "So what? No skin off our noses, right? What's the big deal?"

"It *is* a big deal," Dean told him. "Remember how gas prices soared in '08? They will again, especially if the Russians start playing games with the market. Gas prices at five dollars a gallon. Higher in Europe. High oil prices mean the cost of *everything* goes up. High prices mean more unrest, turnovers in governments, even revolutions.

"The Russian mob has been running their economy into the ground for twenty years. If they do the same thing to the Russian oil industry, it will have global repercussions. Bad ones. Half of Europe depends on Moscow for oil and natural gas. If Russian production goes under, it will be devastating.

"And Washington is afraid they're going to try to grab half of the Arctic Ocean, probably so that they can begin high-volume oil and gas exploitation up here. We know Canada and Denmark will fight their Lomonsov Ridge claim. A war over oil rights is going to shake the world market, too, maybe bring on a general economic collapse."

Taylor slid the photograph back across the table to Dean. "And finding this one guy is going to stop all of that?"

"Maybe not. But he just might have the key to figuring out what the Russians are really up to."

Grenville looked thoughtful, then stood and walked around behind the table to a wall safe. He punched several numbers in on the digital keypad, pulled open the door, and extracted a thick manila folder marked "Secret."

"Your home office transmitted your clearance to see this stuff," he told Dean, selecting several laser-printer color copies and pulling them out of the folder. He grinned. "Turns out your security clearance is better than mine. Have you seen these yet? Courtesy of the NRO."

The first print showed three large ships in the ice, a shot obviously taken from an oblique angle from high overhead. Black water was clearly visible around each vessel, and Dean could see disturbances in the water caused by station-keeping thrusters.

The next two zeroed in on one of the ships, massive and red-hulled. One showed the entire length of the ship from her starboard side, from far enough back that the entire vessel was visible, sitting in a large hole of black water surrounded by ice. She had a massive, blocklike forward superstructure and a large, open deck aft. Her name, in Cyrillic letters, was easily legible on her raised prow—*Akademik Petr Lebedev*.

"A civilian scientific research ship, sixty-six hundred tons," Grenville said. "Launched in 1989, the second in her class. Designed for physical oceanography and ocean floor sampling. See that mast just forward of the stack, like an oil derrick? Used for drilling core samples."

The next photo was a close-up, focusing on the *Lebedev*'s afterdeck. Individual crewmen could be seen, bundled up against the cold as they worked around a stack of long, slender tubes, each around thirty feet long, Dean guessed. One of the tubes hung off an A-frame over the stern, apparently caught as it was being lowered into the ice-free water next to the ship. A second tube was being lifted clear of the deck by one of five starboard-side cranes. Dean could even make out the face of one man who appeared to be in charge; he had his arms up, his gloved hands twisted in an obvious "come on, keep coming" gesture as he directed the operation.

More photos showed other details of a large-scale Arctic expedition—close-ups of the other two ships, an ice breaker and a cargo vessel—as well as a helicopter, small prefab structures on the ice, and piles of supplies and heavy equipment. Time and date stamps on each of the printouts indicated they'd been taken three days before in two passes about ninety minutes apart.

The NRO, or National Reconnaissance Office, was one of America's sixteen separate intelligence agencies and was responsible for IMINT, or imagery intelligence—photographs shot by spy satellites, in other words. Headquartered in Chantilly, Virginia, it was officially part of the Defense Department, but was staffed by employees from both the NSA and the CIA, as well as by military personnel and civilian contractors.

"No," Dean said. "I hadn't seen these." That much was true, though Rubens had told him about the Russian base on the ice during his long-distance briefing at Menwith Hill.

"What's the matter?" Hartwell said with a chuckle. "Don't you guys talk to one another?"

"You'd be surprised what we don't even tell ourselves," Dean replied. He studied the photo of the activity on the *Lebedev*'s afterdeck more closely. "What are they doing? Pulling core samples?"

"According to the message transmitted with these photos," Grenville told him, "the pipes appear to be the business end of an oil-drilling rig. However, there's no sign of a derrick or platform, and the water at that point is over two thousand meters deep. So the whole thing is pretty much a mystery."

"You can see that they're stringing those sections of pipe together and feeding it over the transom," he said. "The pipe sections are too thin to be a seabed pipeline."

"I was wondering if it was a pipeline myself," Grenville said. "But the ship isn't moving, so she's not paying it out astern. Besides, the water is pretty deep at that spot—almost half a mile. A regular pipeline would have to be a lot thicker, with lots of insulation to keep the oil warm enough to flow." He shook his head. "It would also need some hellaciously big pumps, and we're not seeing anything like that."

"It might also be a natural gas well," Dean said, "but that would still require a derrick." He remembered what Lia had told him a few nights ago about the movement of the ice. "There's something here that's just not making sense."

"Well, we should be at the NOAA station by twenty-two hundred hours tomorrow," Grenville said. "We'll surface there . . . and maybe then we can start getting some answers."

Dean nodded. "You're not expecting any problem with breaking through the ice?"

Grenville smiled and shook his head. "Believe me, the ice is the least of our worries. The stuff's so thin we won't even need to look for a lead."

"I heard it was two or three yards thick."

"Normally, yeah. But the ice cap has been unusually thin for, oh, eight or ten years now. The people preaching global warming aren't just blowing smoke. In August of 2007, over half of the usual summer ice cap was just . . . gone. The Beaufort Sea, the Chukchi Sea, and the East Siberian Seam all the way to well beyond the North Pole, the whole damned region was completely ice free. First time that's ever happened since we started paying attention to the Arctic."

"But that's where they built the NOAA station."

"Right. The sea froze over again the next winter, of course. Right now, though, it's only maybe two feet at the thickest, and with lots of melt holes. The climate guys think even more of the ice cap will vanish this summer. One reason they put Bravo where they did was to monitor the summer breakup of the ice."

Dean thought about the Greenpeace kids and their movie. *That* would have been some good documentary footage on global warming . . . shot as the ice cracked open beneath them.

"Sounds like the ice cap is melting faster than even the doomsayers are claiming."

"The Canadians are actively expanding their fleet," Hartwell put in. "Eight new patrol vessels just so they can safeguard maritime traffic going through the Northwest

Passage. And they're building a big new naval base to support them."

The Northwest Passage, of course, had been a fabled ice-free sea-lane from the Atlantic to the Pacific, the object of hundreds of exploratory attempts as far back as the 1500s and continuing through the Arctic explorations of the nineteenth and early twentieth centuries. That passage had been a myth . . . but as the Arctic ice cap dwindled year by year, the myth had come closer and closer to becoming a year-round reality. The same was true for the Siberian passage from Europe to the Far East by way of the Siberian sea-lanes.

An ice-free Arctic might one day prove to be a boon to global trade . . . if not for the local ecosystems.

Dean thought for a moment about the man Tommy Karr had been protecting. *What was his name? Spencer. Yeah.*

That the Arctic ice was vanishing was undeniable. Was human activity to blame, however, or was it part of an ongoing and completely natural cycle, as Spencer claimed? The answer might never be known with certainty . . . and so far as Dean was concerned, the answer might not even matter. The Arctic *was* on its way to becoming an ice-free ocean, one way or another, and either way, humans would have to learn to live with the result.

The Russians, apparently, were trying to get a jump on the rest of the world's population, however, by staking out their ownership boundaries early. If they could enforce their claim to half of the newly exposed ocean at the top of the world, they would have clear access to an incredible bounty of oil and natural gas—enough to challenge the long-standing near monopoly of the sheiks and strongmen of the Middle East.

Enough to *replace* them as a global source of petroleum as the Middle East reserves inevitably dwindled. . . .

"So what are you going up there for, Captain?" Dean asked Grenville.

"Our orders are, first, to ensure the safety of distressed American citizens in the area and, second, to assert our rights to passage through international waters."

"Any sign of those distressed Americans?"

"No. But there's been helicopter activity near those Russian ships . . . and nothing between the ships and the nearest Russian ports. Intelligence thinks they're being held on the *Lebedev*."

"Which is where you and your men come in, I suspect," Dean told Taylor.

"That's why we're here," the SEAL said.

But Dean found the man's grave confidence somehow disturbing.

As a former Marine, Dean was no stranger to combat; while war was never a *good* option, sometimes it was the best of a raft of genuinely bad possibilities. As a Marine scout/sniper he'd accepted the intensely personal issue of killing a *particular* individual rather than randomly, justifying what amounted to murder with the knowledge that he was saving the lives of brother Marines.

But a global war over the oil and gas hidden beneath the melting ice would serve no one . . . except, possibly . . .

The jokers in this game were the leaders of the Russian mafia, and that was what made things so dangerous. They didn't care whether there was a war or not. In fact, a good old-fashioned war, even a limited naval engagement, might well present them with unparalleled opportunities to make more money. They might broker deals with foreign companies, invest in military-based industries, control the financial institutions bankrolling military construction, hoard reserves of vital strategic materials like . . . oil.

The insight stunned him momentarily. Everyone so far had been assuming that the Organizatsiya was simply carrying out business as usual, a kind of neocapitalism gone wild. But what if the Russian mafia or even just a few of its key leaders were actively attempting to start a war, operating on the theory that war is always good for business?

Dean wondered if the idea had occurred to Rubens already, and wanted to discuss the idea with him. Unfortunately, Dean's communications implant couldn't find a satellite on board a Navy sub six hundred feet beneath the polar ice. He would have to wait until they surfaced, then hope he could get a clear channel.

He thought the idea important enough, however, that he decided to ask if he could borrow a computer in order to write a full report, to be broadcast back to Fort Meade as soon as the *Ohio* surfaced.

So far, the rest of the world—including America's intelligence community—had been two steps behind the unseen enemy. As with al-Qaeda, there'd been a tendency here to think of that enemy as a *government,* with a government's concerns, responsibilities, and vulnerabilities. When that enemy instead was, like al-Qaeda, a criminal network, the problem became infinitely more difficult.

And infinitely more deadly as well.

16

"*POLYNYA*, CAPTAIN!" THE EXEC called out. "Thin ice!"

"I see it," Grenville said, face pressed against the starboard-side periscope. "Sonar! What have you got on the roof?"

"Control, Sonar," a voice came back over the intercom speaker. "The roof appears flat, Captain. No ridge echoes or keels for at least one hundred yards. Signal Sierra One is remaining steady, bearing one-six-niner, range approximately two hundred yards."

Dean stood next to the periscope well, watching the TV monitors high up on the port side of the control room, aft of the side-by-side helm and planesman stations forward. A camera mounted on the scope was revealing what the captain was seeing through the eyepiece of the Mk. 18 scope, which was now angled so that it was looking straight up, toward the underside of the "roof," the layer of ice now twenty yards above them. Details were indistinct, but there was definitely a hazy glow of light up there—sunlight, meaning that the ice over this particular patch of ocean was quite thin.

There were two periscopes, mounted next to each other, port and starboard. The port scope was a Type 2 attack scope; starboard was the Mk. 18, a much more sophisticated instrument with low-light capabilities and built-in cameras. Grenville pulled back from the eyepiece and checked another monitor on a nearby bulkhead, this one showing an almost flat line—a readout of the inverted topology of the ice overhead. For the past few days, the line had looked like an inverted mountain range, but the current display showed a long stretch of flat—and therefore thin—ice. Submariners referred to such thin-iced stretches by their Russian name: *polynya.*

"Rig ship for surface, ice," Grenville called.

"Rig ship for surface, ice, aye, aye," the Diving Officer of the Watch echoed.

"Forward planes to vertical orientation."

"Forward planes to vertical, aye, aye." The *Ohio*'s forward diving planes were mounted to either side of her sail, rather than on her bow as with the newer *Seawolf* and *Virginia* boats. Moving them to an up-and-down orientation let them cut through the ice, rather than risking being bent by the impact.

"Okay, gentlemen," Grenville said. "Down scope! Let's put her on the roof."

"Now hear this; now hear this," the COB, or Chief of the Boat, said over the shipwide intercom. "All hands brace for surface, ice. All hands brace for surface, ice!"

The periscope slid back safely into its well. "Blow main ballast, Mr. Dolby."

"Blow main ballast, aye, aye, sir," the diving officer replied.

Dean heard the shrill hiss of water and air venting from ballast tanks, felt the faint surge of elevator movement beneath his feet and in his gut as the *Ohio* began rising straight up. He felt more than heard the crunch as the top of the sail impacted squarely against the bottom of the ice, felt the *Ohio* stagger in her movement, then resume her ascent with a slight, crackling shudder.

"Shore party," the COB called, "break out cold-weather gear and report topside."

Dean turned to the captain. "Permission to go ashore, sir?"

"Granted. But watch your ass out there."

Twenty minutes later, Dean was on the ice, trudging toward a forlorn cluster of prefab huts. The air was surprisingly warm, though the wind had a bite to it; the sun was low above the northwestern horizon in this land of the midnight sun, even though it was nearly 2200. The sky was a deep, clear blue. The *Ohio*'s sail cast long shadows across the ice at his back.

Several Navy SEALs were already at the NOAA base, clad in black dry suits and holding assault rifles with the trigger guards removed, so they could be fired while the SEALs were wearing heavy gloves. Taylor's SEALs—sixteen of them—had boarded the ASDS hours before, slipping ahead of the *Ohio* to perform a surface reconnaissance. They'd located a *polynya,* broken through the ice, and deployed into the NOAA base, determining that it was abandoned. They'd lowered a sonar beacon through the hole in the ice—Signal Sierra One—to guide the *Ohio* in on the deserted encampment.

Lieutenant Taylor was standing next to a flagstaff planted in the ice outside the main building. The white, blue, and red-barred flag of the Russian Federation fluttered in the stiff breeze above him. Dean watched as the man pulled a diving knife from somewhere under his heavy parka and sawed through the line securing the flag. In an instant, the flag fluttered away on the wind, trailing a loose four feet of line. Another SEAL standing nearby produced an American flag, neatly folded in a triangle. The two men used the remaining rope to secure the flag, then hauled it quickly to the top of the staff and tied it off.

"Well done, Mr. Taylor," Dean said.

"Thank you sir," Taylor said. "*Our* base is secure."

"And no sign of the enemy?"

"Nothing, sir. No sign of our people, either."

"I'd still like to have a look."

The door to the main building was hanging open. Dean stepped inside and immediately made a face. "God, it stinks in here!"

Taylor, behind him, nodded. "Yessir. Too many people in too small a space for too damned long."

"Like on board the *Ohio*, huh?"

"Hell, at least everything on the *Ohydro* has a place and is squared away," Taylor said, using a nickname that went back to the sub's service as a boomer. "This is a damned rat's nest."

Dean agreed. The hut was cluttered with human debris—clothing hung up to dry, a camera sitting next to a chess game in progress and a plate with half a sandwich. Much of the stench was from a long-untended chemical toilet in the back of the room, but the air was also thick with the mingled stinks of perspiration, wet clothing, oil, stale food, and mildew. Curtains that had divided the sleeping quarters had been ripped down and left on the floor. Radio equipment at the opposite end of the room had been smashed, apparently with rifle butts.

Dean stepped away from the SEALs and tried switching on his personal transmitter. "George, this is Charlie. Do you copy?"

He could hear static behind his ear and a faint, dopplering whistle.

"George, Charlie. Are you there?"

"Reception up here sucks, man," one of the SEALs told him. "Satellites are too close to the horizon."

"I guess so." He would have to transmit from the *Ohio*'s much larger UHF antenna later. He switched off the unit in his belt and continued exploring the base.

A storeroom in a nearby building was a charnel house, the air thick with the stink of blood. Someone had gone down the passageway, methodically shooting the sled dogs in their kennels. The act appeared random and cruel . . . until Dean suppressed his anger and thought it through. The Russians evidently had been here on a quick in-and-out to grab the Americans. They hadn't been able to take the dogs along, so they'd shot them rather than leaving them to starve in their cages or freeze on the open ice.

At the far end of the passageway, near some carefully stored snowmobiles, there was a rusty stain on the floor that looked like more blood. Dean studied it for a moment. It might have splashed out of a nearby cage—there were plenty of bloodstains on the wall above the dead dogs—but it looked more like someone had fallen here, bleeding. The stain streaked across the floor, as though smeared by someone dragging a body, and all of the dogs were inside their cages.

Dean used a tiny digital camera to record everything, including the gruesome contents of the cages and the long smear on the floor. Other supply sheds and buildings scattered about the compound appeared to have been searched but seemed to be intact. Eventually, he returned to the main building.

"Mr. Dean?" Taylor said, holding something up as he stepped into the building. "You might be interested in this."

Dean accepted the device, which looked like a small

transistor radio. There was no tuning knob, however, just a knob for volume and on-off. When he turned it on, he could hear a squeal of atmospherics and, just barely, a voice, though the static was too bad to understand the words.

"Where'd you find this?"

"Jones found it underneath that mattress over there," Taylor said, pointing. "It may be nothing, but . . ."

"But the fact that it was hidden makes you wonder, doesn't it?" Curious, Dean popped a back panel off and looked at the batteries. They were double-As, but the words printed on the casings were spelled out in Cyrillic letters.

So, what was someone on the NOAA expedition doing with a single-channel radio powered by Russian batteries?

Dean could think of only one reasonable answer to the question.

"Let's check the personal effects," Dean told the SEALs. "Whose bunk was this?"

Each of the bunks, racked two high in the cramped sleeping area, had a pair of small steel lockers next to it. Methodically, three of the SEALs began going through each, removing the contents and bagging them.

There wasn't a lot—wallets, personal items such as rings and jewelry, toiletries, packs of cigarettes, sewing kits, socks and underwear, and the like. The radio had been found under one of the bottom bunks, so the owner had kept his personal items in one of two small lockers close by. ID cards in the wallets gave the names of the owners.

Steven Moore, Dean knew from his briefing, was one of the Greenworld documentary filmmakers.

Randy Haines was one of the NOAA meteorologists.

And one of them, Dean knew, was a traitor. . . .

The Art Room
NSA Headquarters
Fort Meade, Maryland
1515 hours EDT

William Rubens sat at his desk, staring at the computer screen. The e-mail, on a special, secure feed from Menwith Hill, had come through from decryption only moments before. Lightly he touched the screen, as though wondering if the message would vanish.

"Thank God," he murmured as he began to read the message again. He shook his head. "Thank *God. . . .*"

Major Richard Delallo recovered and safe, the decoded message read. *He ejected into the sea south of Kotka, Finland. He was unconscious when he hit the water, but he was pulled out by Finnish fishermen, who took him back to their village. There was some delay in getting word back to Lakenheath. Major Delallo's flight suit was sterile for the op, and the fishermen thought he might be Russian. It was several days before they contacted the UK embassy in Helsinki.*

Pilots flying covert ops such as Ghost Blue's always went in sterile—meaning no flags on their flight suits, no name tags, nothing that could identify them as American or British.

Major Delallo will be flown to USNH Bethesda later today. He is suffering from the effects of exposure, hypothermia, and frostbite but is expected to make a complete recovery. . . .

The message was signed *Col. Copely, RAF,* the name of the vice commander at Lakenheath Air Base.

Rubens sagged back in his chair, letting the relief wash through his body. It wasn't the *political* aspect of Delallo's rescue that was affecting him . . . but the knowledge that his decision to send Ghost Blue to St. Petersburg had not resulted in someone's death.

Outwardly, Rubens always maintained a level of control and composure that some thought cold. He didn't rattle, he didn't express his worry, and he didn't apologize for sending good men and women into harm's way when the situation demanded it. Composure—even coldness—was part of the territory, the price necessary to keep Desk Three running at peak efficiency.

But he'd also seen Delallo's personnel file—and knew the man had a wife and two daughters, currently living in base housing at Lakenheath.

Rubens made a mental note to make arrangements to have the family flown back to Washington, so they could be with the major as he recovered at the Naval Hospital in Bethesda.

With a mental sigh, Rubens deleted the message, then checked the time.

One operator had been recovered alive . . . but two more were about to insert at Solchi.

He wondered for a moment if he should go down to the Art Room and supervise the insert personally but then decided against it. He had good people. They knew what they were doing.

And he couldn't afford to let them know that he was worried. He worked at his desk for almost an hour before deciding to go down anyway.

Kotenko Dacha
Sochi, Russia
2310 hours, GMT + 3

The Kotenko dacha was built on the western face of a mountain overlooking the Black Sea. Llewellyn and an assistant named Vasily had driven Lia and Akulinin to a spot on the road above the Kotenko dacha after it got dark. From the hillside below the road, but well above the eastern side of the property, they could look down on the house and its grounds, which were spread out for their inspection, well lit and apparently well guarded. Lia held a set of electronic binoculars to her eyes and studied the scene. "Okay, people," she said quietly. "Everybody online? Gordon, do you copy?"

"We copy," the voice of Jeff Rockman said in her ear from a workstation back at Fort Meade. "Good voice. Good picture."

"Dragon, do you copy?"

"Copy, Lia," Llewellyn's voice said an instant later. "We can see and hear just fine." Llewellyn and Vasily, with the handle Dragon, had parked the van beneath some trees a quarter of a mile up the road and were linked in through the vehicle's satellite communications suite. Both the team in the van and the runners back in the Art Room could see the scene transmitted from Lia's binoculars, as well as hear the two of them through the mikes mounted on the collars of their combat blacks.

"Let's have a closer look at that gate," Rockman said.

"Here you are." Lia pressed the zoom function on the camera, and the scene expanded, centering on the main gate where a paved driveway entered the property. A blond man in civilian clothes, but holding an AKM assault rifle, stood guard. Nearby, another armed guard followed the inside of the perimeter wall, a German Shepherd tugging at the leash in his hand. The gate was open and, as Lia watched, a car drove up and stopped beside the guard, who spoke briefly with the driver before waving him through.

A security camera watched it all from a telephone pole beside the driveway.

"I see two dogs," Akulinin said, peering through his own binoculars. "The other one's at the far side of the property, above the cliff."

"We see him," Rockman said. "Let's have a look at the party in the back."

From the hillside above the east side of the mansion, the two agents could see about half of the back deck, which extended from the west side of the house almost all the way to the cliff above the sea. The swimming pool was brightly lit, the blue light shimmering and wavering as it reflected off trees and walls. A dozen people or so were visible, engaged in laughing conversation. Most were casually dressed, though the people sculling in the pool or lounging in the hot tub were nude.

"I don't see Kotenko," Lia said. "Gordon, are you getting IDs on these people?"

"The bald guy talking with the tall blond is Vladymir Malyshkin," Rockman said. "He runs the exploratory division of Gazprom's oil subsidiary. The guy with thick glasses and his arm around the brunette over by the diving board is Sergei Poroskov, a member of the St. Petersburg Duma, and a major shareholder in Gazprom." There was a hesitation as Rockman called up more data on his monitor back in the Art Room. "Yeah . . . all of the men are movers and shakers, either with the Russian government or in the Russian oil and gas industries. The guy skinny-dipping with the two chicks in the pool is CEO of a major construction company."

"What about the women?" Akulinin asked.

"I think they're the floor show," Lia said.

"Kotenko owns a string of gentlemen's clubs in half a dozen cities," Rockman said, "and he's also into producing, um, adult films. Like Lia says, they're probably part of the entertainment."

"Well, as long as they're *very* entertaining," Lia said, "and keep it on the back deck, we should have clear sailing inside. Ilya? Break out the dragonfly."

Akulinin pulled off his backpack and extracted a plastic case the size of an encyclopedia. He opened it, revealing a delicate device, mostly wire and gauze but with a core the size of a pencil. He switched it on and the filmy wings unfolded, quivering in the slight breeze. "How about it, James?" he said. "You have a signal?"

"That's affirmative," Llewellyn replied. "We're good to go."

"Right then. Here goes." Akulinin raised his hand and gave the device a gentle shove, lofting it into the air like a paper airplane. The gauze wings caught the breeze and the device soared higher, circling out into the darkness above the dacha with a faint rasping flutter of its wings.

"Okay," Llewellyn said. "We've got good signal, good picture."

"We have positive control," Rockman put in.

The flier faded into shadowy invisibility against the night. Lia and Akulinin stayed hunkered down on the dark and brush-covered hillside as the team in the Art Room flew the probe from the other side of the Earth, guided by real-time imagery transmitted from the tiny camera in the dragonfly's nose.

The Art Room
NSA Headquarters
Fort Meade, Maryland
1625 hours EDT

Chris Palatino had been hired by the National Security Agency for one reason. He was *very* good at playing video games.

The winner of the Extreme Gamer competition at the Origins gaming convention two years before, he'd been approached by a recruiter for a defense-related corporation. Only later, after Palatino had passed the security clearances, was the true nature of the job made clear: he would have to move from central Michigan to Laurel, Maryland, and take a job with the NSA. The money was less than he might have made writing software for a major corporation, but money wasn't Palatino's major interest.

He called it the gamer's ultimate fantasy, and he was living it—an overweight twenty-seven-year-old geek getting paid to remote-pilot micro-UAVs on missions halfway around the world.

"Good hands, Chris," Jeff Rockman told him. Half a dozen members of the Art Room team were standing behind his workstation, watching as Palatino jockeyed two joysticks on the console before him, eyes fixed on the large flat-screen monitor on the wall in front of him.

"I know, man," Palatino replied, though his voice had that dreamy, off-in-another-world vagueness it usually acquired when he was on a mission. "Watch and learn, watch and . . . *son* of a bitch!"

Fifty-five hundred miles away—measured along a great circle route that skimmed south of the top of Greenland and north of the Shetland Islands—the eight-ounce flier had caught a heavy updraft along the side of the mountain that threatened to sweep it into the trees. Palatino gave the device an extra burst of power, flying into a downdraft and using the descent to pick up speed. A moment later he was clear, skimming above the treetops toward the mansion.

The UAV had been designed to operate on software modeled on the sculling motions of a fly's wings. The wings themselves went rigid with the application of a low-voltage trickle of current, twisting and turning to put out some ten beats per second. That was about a twentieth of the beat frequency for a housefly, but these wings were larger in comparison to the size of the body driving them, and included the ability to glide for long distances. Once clear of the downdraft, Palatino canted the wings into a rigid-locked configuration and, twitching gently at one of the joysticks, nudged the device into a gentle glide that carried it across the back deck twenty feet up.

Any of the party guests who chanced to look up might have glimpsed a dark shape reflecting the light from the pool and dismissed it as a large moth or even a bat. The UAV circled the deck area twice as the Art Room team located and counted guests, staff, and guards.

"Okay, Lia," Rockman said after the second pass. "Still no sign of Kotenko, so he may be inside. We've identified twelve guests, five people who are probably staff, and four guards, not counting the two on perimeter patrol with dogs, or the guy at the front gate. It looks like they're pretty well set out there, not much traffic in and out of the house."

"Copy that," Lia's voice came back over a wall speaker. "Let's get this over with, okay?" She sounded tense, on edge.

Rockman pointed at the screen. "The security camera is there," he said. "On top of that pole."

"I see it; I see it," Palatino said. "Gimme a sec. . . ."

He flipped the UAV's wings out of their locked position, and with a soft rattle of sound the device streaked across the roof of the house, angling toward a solitary pole rising just inside the fence encircling the property, not far from the main gate and driveway. Hunched over the controllers, tongue sticking out in an unconscious expression of pure concentration, Palatino brought the tiny UAV to a near hover a foot from the top of the pole, dropping the body into a vertical orientation at the same moment that he extended four wire-slender and hook-tipped legs. An instant later, the device touched the creosote-blackened wood, and the scene displayed on the monitor became still, an extreme close-up of the pole's weathered wood surface. The flier was now resting on the pole, a few inches behind the target camera.

The NSA possessed the technology to hijack security camera networks anywhere in the world, but doing so required gaining access. Many networks used the Internet for their security cam systems, which made the NSA eavesdropper's task simplicity itself.

The security cameras at Kotenko's dacha, however, were on their own, private network, with no outside connections and, apparently, no computers to sort, clean up, or channel the data. That made tapping into the network more difficult. They also used universal cable connections rather than wireless LAN or Ethernet connections and that, too, made stealing the signal harder.

But *not* impossible.

The camera, a small black box with a sunshade extended over the barrel of the lens, was set up to scan the entrance to the property twenty feet below. On the display, the cable emerged from the back of the camera, ran down the side of the pole a few inches to where it was stapled to the wood, then extended out into the night in the direction of the house.

"Damned primitive crapola," Palatino muttered. "Haven't these people heard of wireless networks?"

"That's okay," Rockman told him. "That's why the dragonfly has a sting. Go ahead. Take a bite."

On the pole behind the camera's field of view, the remote-operated flier edged a couple of careful sideways steps, bringing it to rest directly above the cable. Targeting brackets appeared on the big wall display, centering on and closing around the cable, and flashing when the device had locked onto the target. There was a tiny whine of servomotors, and a slender needle, like a mosquito's sucking proboscis, extended down from the device's head, delicately piercing the cable.

"Okay," Rockman said, looking at another monitor. "We have a signal."

At Palatino's touch, a second needle bit the cable just below the first. A window opened in the lower left-hand portion of the big screen, showing the grainy, low-light black-and-white image currently being transmitted by the camera.

The remote dragonfly probe was now wired into the dacha's security camera system.

"We're recording," another Art Room technician reported.

"Okay," Rockman said. "Nothing's happening. Get about a twenty-second loop."

The seconds passed. "Got it. Ready to repeat."

"Good. Okay, Lia, Ilya. We're hooked into the network. You can proceed."

"Moving," Lia replied.

Kotenko Dacha
Sochi, Russia
2340 hours, GMT + 3

Lia led the way as the two agents scrambled down the slope, making their way toward the dacha property. Both of them wore black head-to-toe, with light-intensifier goggles over their faces, which gave them the look of curious four-limbed insects.

For this op, they were going in semi-sterile, which meant that with one key exception, all of their equipment, everything except their communications implants, anyway, was available through commercial European markets or low-security military sources. The exception was the satchel Lia carried at her hip, which carried the bugging devices they intended to plant inside the dacha.

Once they disposed of those, they would have nothing on their persons that would identify them, if the worst happened, as agents of an American intelligence organization.

They reached the base of the hill and worked their way to a point close to the property entrance. Black figures crouching against black shadows, they waited for long minutes, watching the solitary guard at the gate. He looked bored and not particularly attentive, but Lia wanted to wait for the best opportunity.

"Gordon, are you ready to transmit?"

"We're ready here, Lia," Rockman replied. "Waiting on your word."

"Copy."

That opportunity came ten minutes later, as the headlights of a car swung across the driveway, illuminating the guard and the open gate in a glare immediately stopped down by the automatic filters inside their LI goggles. The car pulled up alongside the guard, who leaned over to look inside, then stepped back and saluted. The car, a long, black sedan, eased past the guard and onto the drive. "Now," Lia whispered.

The two figures separated from the shadows and slipped into the clear-cut zone outside the wall, angling toward the gate.

The Art Room
NSA Headquarters
Fort Meade, Maryland
1654 hours EDT

"Now," Lia's voice said from the speaker.

Jeff Rockman looked up at the display on the monitor, which now showed two inset windows, both with identical images from the security camera. On both, the guard at the front gate could be seen standing a few feet from the wall, shifting his weight from foot to foot and managing to look dead bored, even though his face could not be seen.

"Okay," Jeff said. "Insert the recorded signal."

There was the faintest flicker of static on the left-hand window, and the image of the guard seemed to jump to one side by about a foot. Several seconds later, a black figure entered the lower edge of the right-hand window, easing between the wall of white-painted stone and the guard's back, then vanishing. A moment later, a second figure came into view, stealthily slipping behind the less than fully attentive guard.

By physically tapping into the length of cable on the security cam pole, the Art Room had been able to record a twenty-second segment of video, which they were now feeding into the security network while blocking the real-time signal from the camera. Somewhere inside the dacha, a presumably bored security guard was looking at the monitor, which showed absolutely nothing unusual happening outside the front gate. If he'd noticed the static or the shift in the guard's position, chances were good he'd shrug it off to a fault in the cable . . . which wouldn't have been far off the mark.

There were any number of ways to penetrate a secure target such as the Kotenko dacha. The best and simplest, however, was generally through the front gate. The dogs patrolling the perimeter were trained to pick up strange scents and alert their handlers if they detected the trails of intruders coming over the wall . . . but at the main gate the ground would be a jumble of crisscrossing scent trails, of guards, of automobiles, of guests coming and going. Even if the dogs were well enough trained to alert their handlers that intruders had passed that way, the handlers would probably discount the warning. After all, *everyone* went through that way.

There were motion sensors and sound detectors along the base inside the wall, but again, the security personnel would be alert to intruders coming over the wall elsewhere around the perimeter, not coming through the main gate where the guard's scuffings and pacings, the noises from car engines, and the conversations as the guard challenged each arrival all rendered sonic data useless.

As for the lone guard, he was standing on the driveway inside the open gateway, his AKM carelessly slung over his shoulder, his night vision utterly blasted by the headlights of the car that had just passed through. He didn't see the two figures in black approach the wall behind him, or notice as, one after the other, they slipped silently past his back. He wasn't paying careful attention to the night around him because after all . . . that was what dogs and security cameras were for.

Watching from fifty-five hundred miles away, Rockman breathed a sigh of relief. "Okay, Lia," he said. "You're off the monitor. You weren't seen."

"Okay," she replied. "We're approaching the house."

"The flier is on its way."

On the pole overlooking the driveway entrance, the UAV broke off an inch-long section of its own head, leaving the piece attached by its two slender probes, then launched itself into the air. With a soft flutter of hard-beating wings, it arrowed through the night and came to rest on the outside sill of a second-floor window.

"I feel like a damned Peeping Tom," Palatino muttered, shifting the remote device to walking mode and moving it higher until its camera could peer through the glass.

"Yeah, but it's peeping in the line of duty," Rockman told him. "Let's have a look."

The room beyond the glass was darkened, but the probe's CCD visual pickups could resolve images in almost total darkness and could operate in the IR as well as visual wavelengths. At the same time, two slender wires, like antennas, extended from above the camera and rested against the glass, picking up faint vibrations.

The room might have been dark, but it was definitely occupied—rather enthusiastically so—by two people sharing a large bed.

"Oops," Sarah Cassidy said, smirking. "I don't think we want to go in that way."

"Go to the next window," Rockman told Palatino.

The next window was also a bedroom, but this one appeared to be empty. Rockman passed the word to Lia and Akulinin, who were already climbing up a pilaster to reach the second floor.

This part of the dacha had a roof extending out from the second story over a trellis-enclosed porch. The Deep Black insertion team had already made the assumption that the first-floor windows would be protected by some sort of security system but that the second floor might be clear. Targets who were lazy, cheap, or both sometimes left obvious holes in their security. Unfortunately, that was not the case here. Sensors inside the slender body of the flier had already detected the trickle of electrical current through a slender wire inside the closed window. If the window was opened or broken, the current would be interrupted and an alarm would sound. Rockman passed the news to the team.

"We're on it," Lia said.

Kotenko Dacha
Sochi, Russia
2358 hours, GMT + 3

"We're on it," Lia murmured. In one hand she held a small device similar to the unit she'd used to look for security systems at the warehouse door on the St. Petersburg waterfront. The LED readout indicated an electrical current, and as she moved it around the edge of the window, she found the point where the sensor wire on the glass connected, through a metal contact, with a wire inside the window's frame.

That was the weak point, the point of attack.

The flier clung to the wall a foot away, watching, looking like an odd and science-fictional mingling of large insect with small robot, its wings now folded along the length of its body and hanging off behind like a stiff, gauze cloak.

"This is a guy who takes his security seriously," Akulinin whispered, double-checking the electrical circuit.

"*Any* security system can be breached," Lia replied. "Jeff? We need the drill right here."

In response, the flier moved to the spot she was indicating with her finger. Again, a slender needle extended from beneath the robot's head, touching the white-painted frame of the window. There was a faint whine as the drill bit chewed into the wood.

"Okay, Lia," Rockman's voice said a moment later. "We have a complete circuit."

Akulinin tried lifting the window. It appeared to be locked. Extracting a jimmy tool from a thigh pouch, he inserted the flat blade between window and frame at the bottom, gently applying a steady downward pressure. There was a creak, but the window remained shut.

"Shit," he said. "The damned thing's locked."

"Try the direct approach," Lia suggested.

"Yeah." He ran a gloved hand over the glass. "It might be damned noisy, though."

The two listened for a moment. The sounds of laughter floated clearly across from the other side of the house, followed by a loud splash as someone hit the pool. "Laminated glass," Lia said. "Should be more of a crunch than a crash. Go ahead. Give it a try."

"You're the boss." He reversed the pry, wrapped the handle in a piece of cloth, and slammed the tool into the glass.

The window was plastic-coated and shatterproof, but the glass crazed and yielded under a second, harder blow. The two agents held their position for a moment, listening carefully for a full minute, waiting for some indication that they'd been heard.

Another splash sounded from the rear deck.

The security system wires attached to the inside of the pane were broken, but the needle drilled into the window frame by the robot was now shorting the contact, tricking the system into thinking the circuit was unbroken. Using the cloth to protect his already-gloved hands, Akulinin pushed in the now flexible sheet of fragmented glass, working it in and out until it popped free of the frame.

Replacing the jimmy, Akulinin drew his weapon and wiggled through the opening, headfirst. Lia followed.

"We're in," she said. She glanced around the room, verifying that it was, indeed, empty . . . though rhythmic creakings and moans were coming from the room next door. Her LI headset revealed the space clearly in monotone shades of green. "Tell us where we need to go."

"Straight ahead," was Rockman's reply. "Through the bedroom door and to your left."

Silently the two agents slipped forward through the darkness.

17

**Kotenko Dacha
Sochi, Russia
0007 hours, GMT+3**

DOWN A DARKENED HALLWAY, then right to a flight of stairs. Lia descended while Akulinin covered her from above, then returned the favor, holding her SIG-Sauer P220 gripped tightly in both hands. The weapon had been threaded to receive a sound suppressor, and the ungainly length of the thing extended beyond the ball of her hands like a police officer's baton.

"There's a security camera in the hall in front of you to the left," Rockman whispered in their ears. "Wait one . . ."

The broken-off piece of the dragonfly probe still attached to the cable on the pole at the front gate now gave the Art Room a physical connection with the dacha's security network, with the parked van as a communications relay. Back at Fort Meade, they would be running through a number of camera views, calling up the correct one, and feeding it a twenty-second loop of an empty hallway.

"Okay, Lia," Rockman said. "The hall is empty and the camera is happy. You're clear to move."

Stealthily the two agents turned the corner and walked down the hall. Lia noticed a half sphere of darkened glass mounted on the ceiling—the security cam—and resisted an unprofessional impulse to wave. A few feet farther on, light spilled from beneath a closed door.

Damn. . . .

"We're at the door to the office," Lia whispered. "Do you have a camera inside?"

"That's negative, Lia," Rockman replied. "It looks like there may be a hookup for another camera on the circuit diagram, but it's switched off."

Akulinin tried the doorknob, which turned easily, and gently edged the door open. Beside him, Lia slipped a length of fiber-optic cable through the opening, with the near end attached to her cell phone monitor. Twisting the cable gently between her fingers, she turned the end this way and that, checking out the room's interior.

A man sat at a computer monitor, his back toward the door. The image resolution was too low to let her read over his shoulder, but he appeared to be about ten feet away, his fingers clattering over a keyboard.

There was no one else in the room within the reach of the fiber-optic viewer, though she did see another of the black hemispheres on the ceiling. Why was the security camera turned off?

Then the answer came to her. The man at the desk was almost certainly Grigor Kotenko, and as the head of one of the more powerful families within the Organizatsiya, he would be afraid not only of outside enemies breaking into his personal fortress but also of traitors among his own people. The camera's position on the ceiling would have let his own security people see what was on his monitor; switching it off while he was working gave him an extra bit of peace of mind.

It also suggested that Kotenko was more afraid of betrayal from within his own organization than he was of outsiders, an interesting bit of intelligence.

The figure at the desk turned his head just far enough that Lia glimpsed the shaggy corner of his walrus mustache.

"I see Kotenko," Lia whispered. "Back to the door. I can take him from here."

"That's a negative, Lia," a new voice, Rubens', replied. "Find another way."

She bit off a silent expletive. She had the bastard in her sights . . . the thug who'd given the orders that had ended with Tommy's death. It would be *so* easy to take him out. Two taps to the center of mass, a third in the back of the head . . .

"Lia, Ilya," Rubens said. "If the op is to succeed, we need Kotenko alive."

Lia closed her eyes, forcing the muscles of her hands and arms and jaw to relax, bringing herself back from the edge. God, she wanted to kill the man . . . but Rubens was right. She and Ilya had come here tonight to plant bugs that would give Desk Three an unparalleled window into the Tambov group's operations. If Kotenko's people came into the office later and found their boss dead, American intelligence would have to start all over again as some other crime family came to the fore, or as another leader within Tambov—Braslov, perhaps—took over.

In the long run, they could do a lot more damage to the Russian Mafiya—and not just the Tambov group—if Kotenko survived this night.

"Okay," she whispered. "Ilya, you're up. Remember, Russian only."

"*Da,*" he murmured, and grasping his H&K P9S in both hands, he eased the door open with his shoulder and rolled through.

Lia followed, breaking left and cutting across the room as Akulinin moved right, lunging at Kotenko's back. Attempting to sneak in quietly invited disaster—a squeak to a floorboard, a flicker of movement glimpsed from the corner of an eye . . . even a psychic awareness of someone else present in the room. Kotenko heard the movement and began to turn, one hand snapping toward the top drawer of his computer desk, but Akulinin was on him in three swift strides, reversing the pistol in his hand as he moved, grasping it at the meeting of muzzle and sound suppressor, and swinging the butt around from the side, aiming at the base of Kotenko's skull.

But Kotenko raised his arm, blocking the swing, and for a terrible moment Akulinin and the Mafiya boss struggled in front of the computer desk. Then the office chair scooted out from beneath Kotenko and he fell, heavily. Akulinin's arm came up, then slashed down, the pistol butt striking the man's head with a sickening crack.

Lia held her position at the far side of the office, her SIG-Sauer pointed at the half-open door, covering Akulinin as he checked the pulse at Kotenko's throat, then peeled back one eyelid, then the other.

"He's out," Akulinin said in Russian. If the camera was off, there might yet be microphones online. "Breathing's okay."

"Gordon!" Lia whispered. "Any response?"

"Negative," Rockman replied in her ear. By now, the Art Room would have penetrated deep into the dacha's security network, and would be alerted if an alarm sounded. It was just possible that an open microphone in Kotenko's office had picked up the sounds of a struggle. If so, guards might be on the way already.

They would have to hurry.

Once he was sure that Kotenko was in no physical danger, Akulinin pulled plastic zip strips from his combat harness and bound the man's wrists, knees, and ankles. A fistful of facial tissue went into his mouth, with a length of packing tape to secure it awkwardly beneath the brush of his mustache. Another strip of tape went over his eyes. If he regained consciousness in the next few minutes, they didn't want him seeing what the two intruders were doing.

Lia, meanwhile, pulled out the small induction device that registered the surge in electrical current from any active microphones and swept the room, paying special attention to the camera fixture on the ceiling and to the desk and computer itself. While power was flowing to the computer and its peripherals, of course, it looked like there weren't any active mikes.

Good. They should have a few minutes then.

"*Harashaw,*" she said, still speaking Russian just in case Kotenko was faking unconsciousness with an unusual flair for theater. "Room is clear."

"There's the safe," Akulinin said, also in Russian. "Get the door."

Lia walked to the door and closed it, then snapped off the light. With their LI gear, there was more than enough ambient light through the room's one large window for them to work. Next, she went to Kotenko's computer, sat down at the chair, and took a look at the monitor.

The screen saver had come up—a blatantly pornographic image of a bored-looking woman lasciviously entangled with two young men. When Lia moved the mouse, the image was replaced with a screen full of text and several small, inset diagrams.

It looked important. Her Russian was good enough that she could tell it was a technical report about something called Glubahkii Koladeets, or Deep Well, and which was abbreviated elsewhere as "GK-1," a term that seemed to refer to a specific place or base. The overall project was called Operatsiya Holodnaya Vayeena . . . Operation Cold War.

She scanned down the screen quickly, trying to pick up

the important bits. Work at GK-1, she saw, had been delayed by the high concentrations of *metan* something. *Metan* was "methane," but *what* was the following word? It looked like it might transliterate as "clathates," but she couldn't pin down the meaning.

Well, they might be able to make something of it back at the Puzzle Palace.

It would have been possible, of course, to flash the entire contents of Kotenko's hard drive to Fort Meade, or to simply burn a CD of any likely-looking documents. However, there were almost certain to be security measures in place that would, at the very least, alert Kotenko to the fact that files had been copied, if not passwords and firewalls designed to prevent exactly that. They didn't have the time to track down the man's computer security system or bypass it, and they couldn't risk alerting Kotenko that his hard drive had been raided. She did take a moment to photograph the screen with her cell phone camera, being careful to dial the speed down to a thirtieth of a second in order to avoid having large, black scan lines show up across the screen. Then she reached behind the computer tower and yanked out the plug.

The monitor winked out immediately, taking the page of data with it. Kotenko would wake to find the computer off and assume the intruders had pulled the plug just in case it had an open mike.

Next, she pulled a small, plastic case from her equipment pouch. Inside were several hundred minute bugs, each roughly spherical, perhaps a millimeter across, and flat enough to slip through the spaces between the keys on a computer keyboard. She sprinkled them across Kotenko's keyboard, careful not to allow them to bounce. A few remained stubbornly visible, but she clattered her fingers across the keys, repeatedly hitting several until all of the stragglers vanished down through the cracks.

Next, she looked around along the walls of the room until she found an outlet. When she found one out in the open, she knelt in front of it, swiftly unscrewing the front plate, then pulling the outlet itself free at the end of a length of wires.

She used a small tester to check which wire was which, then took a microrelay and clipped it to the wires, as far back as she could reach. Finally, she stuffed the wires back into place, replaced the outlet and cover, and screwed the plate back on. The whole operation took less than two minutes.

Returning to the keyboard, she softly said, "Gordon, ready to test."

"Copy, Lia. We have signal."

"Starting with the letters, then . . . *ah* . . . *beh* . . . *veh* . . . *geh* . . . "

One by one she struck each Cyrillic letter on the keyboard. The tiny sensors worked together to pick up the distinctive sound of each key as it was struck and transmit it to the relay in the wall.

The microphones themselves were sound powered and activated, while the relay drew on the electrical current in the house. The relay, using the electrical wiring of the entire house as an enormous antenna, was powerful enough to transmit each sound to the waiting van; before Llewellyn left the area, he would plant a larger satellite relay on the side of the mountain, where it would continue to receive transmissions from Kotenko's keyboard and send them on through the satellite uplink to Fort Meade.

There the Tordella Center supercomputers would identify each separate key from the distinct and unique sound it made when struck and reassemble a complete readout of what Kotenko was typing at his workstation fifty-five hundred miles away. The system would let them pick up passwords and activation codes, which in turn would allow them to study and bypass his security systems and, soon, to be able to record his entire hard drive, read all of his mail, and track down every one of his electronic correspondents without ever again coming close to the Black Sea dacha.

With the keyboard bugs online and double-checked, Lia turned her attention to bugging the rest of the office. Another tiny microphone went inside the telephone handset on the desk, while a microcam—hidden inside the barrel of a working ballpoint pen with the lens disguised as a clear plastic clicker—went on the highest bookshelf, positioned so that it gave the Art Room a view of both the computer and the door. Another pen, this one masking a backup relay unit, went into the sofa behind the cushions.

Akulinin, meanwhile, was working at the safe. A flat case with an LED readout was placed just above the combination dial, and as he slowly turned the dial right or left, lights winked on to indicate the fall of tumblers inside. Within a couple of minutes, there was an audible thump and he operated the handle to pull the heavy door open.

"*Udacha!*" he cried, reaching in and retrieving the lost tool kit. "Success!"

Lia gave him a thumbs-up and began going over the room, checking to see if anything had been left undone or disturbed. Akulinin took the time to write out the combination to the safe, together with the letters *P* for *prava,* or "right," and *L* for *leva,* or "left." He dropped the paper on the floor in front of the open safe before checking through the shelves inside.

There was money, a great deal of it, in three briefcases, in rubles, euros, and U.S. dollars. There were a number of engineering charts and reports, all of which fitted—barely—inside the tool kit. And there were a number of plastic jewel cases, each with a CD cryptically labeled with Cyrillic notations. These went into various pouches in Akulinin's combat blacks.

A groan from the bound and prone Kotenko warned that he was beginning to come around. After one last, swift check, Lia and Akulinin went to the door. "We're done," she whispered.

"Passageway outside is clear," Rockman told her. "Still no alarm."

She opened the door. "We're moving," she said. "Ready for exfil."

"Satlink is in place," Llewellyn told them. "We'll be waiting at the primary."

With luck, Kotenko would assume that one of his rivals had broken in and cleaned out his safe. The paper with the safe's combination could only have one logical explanation—that someone inside Kotenko's personal retinue, or, just possibly, one of his houseguests, had discovered the combination and given it to the intruders.

That ought to make life inside the dacha interesting for the next few days.

"Lia!" Rockman's voice called in her head. *"You've got company!"*

The Art Room
NSA Headquarters
Fort Meade, Maryland
1721 hours EDT

The big display screen in the Art Room showed the layout of the Kotenko dacha as a series of architectural floor plans. Two points of light, one following the other, moved along one of the hallways. On a nearby monitor, ranks of inset windows showed the overhead views of empty rooms and hallways set in pairs, one with the monochromatic image of what someone watching from the security office was seeing, the window next to it showing the real-time image of the same scene.

In one real-time window, Lia and Akulinin, anonymous figures in their combat blacks and LI goggles, could be seen moving through one of the corridors.

And in another, a solitary figure could be seen just coming in from the back deck, a bulky, muscular man built like a professional wrestler. The Deep Black records department had already identified him as Andre Malenkovich, a onetime Moscow street criminal now in Kotenko's employ as bodyguard and personal assistant.

And Malenkovich had just entered the same hallway now being used by Lia and Akulinin. The computers managing the imaging session had just thrown a third light onto the architectural schematics, showing the bodyguard just one bend in the hallway away. In another few seconds he would round a corner and come face-to-face with the Deep Black insertion team.

"Turn around!" Rockman told Lia and Akulinin. "Back the way you came! There's a janitor's closet ten feet behind you! *Hurry!*"

Malenkovich was almost up to the corner. . . .

Kotenko Dacha
Sochi, Russia
0022 hours, GMT + 3

Akulinin reached the closet door and turned the knob. *Locked!* . . .

Lia bit off a curse as she turned, pulling her sidearm from its holster. The door to Kotenko's office was eight feet farther up the hall; keeping her weapon with its heavy sound suppressor trained on the bend in the corridor ahead, she started backing toward it. Akulinin did the same.

"He's stopped!" Rockman told them. "Two more people just came in from the pool! I think he's talking to them!"

Which might give them another few seconds. The hallway came to an abrupt end behind them, with the only way out going around the corner and squarely into Malenkovich. They didn't have time to pick the lock on the closet, but just possibly they could hide in the office. Lia reached the office door first, opened the door, and slipped inside. Akulinin followed.

"He's around the corner," Rockman told them. "He's coming toward the office door!"

Not good. Lia looked around the office. There wasn't much in the way of places to hide; worse, Kotenko was now awake, struggling against the plastic zip strips binding his wrists and legs and making desperate mmphing noises into his gag. As the two NSA agents reentered the office, though, he went still. He probably couldn't see anything more than human-shaped shadows against the light spilling in from the hall, but he knew they were there.

And so would the bodyguard in another moment.

"Bad guy is definitely headed for the office," Rockman warned. "There's nothing else in that arm of the hallway for him to go to unless he's looking for a mop."

"*Oknah!*" Lia said, lowering and roughening her voice to a growl for Kotenko's benefit. There was no sense in telling him that one of the intruders was a *woman*—and possibly letting him begin to connect the dots all the way back to the St. Petersburg warehouse.

Oknah—the office window. It was large and looked west out over the Black Sea. During daylight hours, Kotenko must have a hell of a view.

And right now, that was their only escape route. Akulinin understood her terse exclamation. Lia pulled back the drapes as he holstered his pistol and experimentally hefted the toolbox he was carrying. "*Beregeess'!*" he warned, and slammed the long metal case squarely into the window like a battering ram.

Like the window upstairs, this one was safety glass, laminated in plastic. There was a loud thud, but the glass barely gave under the blow. Swiftly Lia raised her sound-suppressed SIG-Sauer in a two-handed stance. The weapon coughed sharply as she triggered three rounds in rapid succession into the pane; the glass crazed around three neat impacts, and Akulinin smashed the window again with the tool case.

This time, the glass bulged out, then disintegrated in a spray of rounded fragments. At the same instant, the door swung open and Kotenko's bodyguard burst into the room, his own weapon already drawn.

Pivoting sharply, her P220 still in a two-handed grip, Lia squeezed off three quick shots into the center of the man's considerable mass. He howled, staggering backward into the hall, and Lia put two more rounds into him as he collapsed, just to make sure. Outside, in the corridor, a woman screamed.

Akulinin used his gloved hands to peel away some of the remaining glass. Then, stooping, he patted the bound Kotenko on the shoulder. "*Dobreh nochee,*" he said, grinning, wishing the crime lord a good night. Lia scrambled through the window and Akulinin followed.

They dropped a few feet onto the back deck, where a dozen men and women stared with gaping mouths as the two insect-faced agents clambered through the broken window. Ignoring them, Lia raced to the low stone wall rising at the edge of the deck. Beyond, there was a narrow stretch of ground, and then the hillside dropped steeply away toward the road along the seaside, heavily covered with brush and small trees. Vaulting the wall, she dropped feetfirst over the edge and began sliding rapidly down the hill.

Akulinin followed. As she bumped and rolled through loose earth and leaves, she heard shouts and screams from above, and a sharp-barked command to halt: "*Stoy!*"

"Dragon!" she cried as she slid, trying desperately to keep from losing control. "Change of plan! Pickup at extraction two!"

"Got it, Lia," Llewellyn said. "We're on the way!"

They'd plotted three separate pickup points, allowing for the possibility that they'd have to leave by a different route than the one they'd taken going in. Gunfire cracked from above and behind, and she heard the snap of bullets among the branches above her head.

The trouble was that Llewellyn had the van on the road above the property, while Lia and Akulinin were plunging through brush and loose dirt toward a different road, some fifty yards below Kotenko's dacha. Llewellyn would have to drive like a maniac to pick up a crossroad two miles to the south, then double back along the seashore to meet them.

And the bad guys were in hot pursuit. Lia heard the deep-throated bark of a German Shepherd and the shouted orders as more guards spilled out onto the deck or began descending after the fleeing Deep Black agents.

The trees were bigger toward the bottom of the slope, a tangle of open woods, with scattered boulders, some as large as a small house, tucked in among the trees. Lia came to a jarring halt as her boots hit a tree trunk; the slope had leveled off enough here for her to stand and begin picking her way down the rest of the hill on foot.

Akulinin reached the road first, dropping to the ground and facing back up the hill with his handgun at the ready. Lia dropped down beside him. Someone above them opened fire with an assault rifle, spraying away wildly on full-auto, but with no clear target. Bullets whined high above their heads or thunked into tree trunks; the two agents held their fire. Even sound-suppressed rounds might give away their position, and in any case, at this range they wouldn't hit anything save by sheer luck.

They could hear thrashing sounds from above as men crashed down the slope after them. Several bright lights flared among the tree trunks, the shafts of light probing among the branches and brush. Lia nudged Akulinin in the ribs and pointed to the right. Together, the two began moving southeast along the hillside. If that crowd took the straight route down, they'd be on top of Lia and Akulinin in another few moments. Even in the dark, the men might be able to follow the double trail of skid and scuff marks down the slope.

And there were the dogs.

How many pursuers were there? During the circuit with the dragonfly, the Art Room had identified six guards outside—including the dog handlers and including the man at the front gate—but there might be more inside. It was a big place, and Kotenko might easily be paranoid enough to maintain a small personal army up there.

Lia and Akulinin worked their way silently about a hundred yards farther up the road and crossed over to the far side. That gave them a good view of the edge of the woods beneath the cliff, and the guards would have to leave the cover of the trees and come out into the open if they wanted to cross the road.

Behind Lia and Akulinin, a low surf hissed along the beach. The sky was overcast, hiding the moon, but her LI goggles showed the waves in oily tones of green and black. *A shame we didn't bring a getaway boat*, she thought. *Or a submarine. . . .*

"Dragon!" she called. "We're on the southwest side of the road now, just above the beach."

"We're just turning onto the coast road," Llewellyn replied. "Three kilometers, maybe three and a half. . . ."

Which meant perhaps one or two more minutes. And the flashlights were *much* closer now, darting and bobbing among the trees at the base of the hill, a hundred yards away. A guard emerged from the shadows, moving along the edge of the road. A second appeared a moment later, tugged along by an enthusiastic dog.

Akulinin braced his pistol, sighting along the barrel. "I could try for a long shot from here," he said.

"Negative," Lia told him. "All that'll do is tell them where we are, and give them a chance to surround us."

"Damn. . . ." He lowered the weapon. "Those dogs *will* find us. . . ."

"We'll worry about that when they get closer." Lia was angry, and the words came out more harshly than she'd intended.

She was angry at herself, though she was having some trouble identifying just what it was that had made her so mad. They'd done everything right, so far as she could tell, taking the op step-by-step.

But in this kind of work, any operation that ended with shots being fired was a failure, at least on some level. The opposition should never have even known they were there. It was the op on the St. Petersburg waterfront all over again . . . and the second op in a row for her to end in a firefight. This was getting old very, very fast.

The two men and the dog were closer now . . . about fifty yards away. They were walking slowly, and the man in front had a flashlight that he was using to examine the bushes and shadowed recesses on both sides of the road. Other men were spreading out in the distance, some going down to the beach, others following the road to the northwest.

And she could hear the crack and snap of still more

searchers in the woods directly across the road now, moving unseen among the trees.

"Dragon!" Akulinin whispered. "Any time now would be *very* good!"

"Another kilometer," was the reply. "Can you show me a light?"

"Negative!" Lia replied. "We have bad guys right across the road from us, and more coming along the road! If we move, they'll spot us!"

The tactical situation, she realized, was deteriorating to the impossible. Even if the van arrived right now, there were enough gunmen about to lay down a deadly barrage.

"Listen, Dragon," Lia said. "I think we need another plan. You can't come in here without getting killed!"

"Already got a plan, m'lady!" Llewellyn replied. "Sit tight! We'll have you out of there in a mo'!"

The two walking down the road were twenty yards away. The dog, its nose to the earth, whined, then growled.

"Can I take them *now*?" Akulinin whispered.

Something dropped out of the night.

Even with the LI goggles, it was hard to see what it was, but it looked like a bird or a bat, and it was swooping low in front of the two guards with a flutter of wings, making both of the men shout and duck.

It took Lia a second to realize what was happening. The dragonfly! Someone back in the Art Room had brought the dragonfly in as a diversion!

At almost the same moment, a vehicle came careening up the road from the southeast, traveling *backward* at a high rate of speed. Lia could see the taillights glowing brilliantly in her goggles, followed by the sudden flash and glare of the brake lights.

The guard with the flashlight raised his assault rifle.

"Yes!" she told Akulinin. *"Now!"*

They opened fire together, sending a fusillade of 9mm

rounds slamming into the two guards, and both collapsed in a tangle at the side of the road. The dog, its leash trailing behind it, bolted toward them and was in mid-leap when the dragonfly slammed into its back. The animal yelped and turned, snapping at something no longer there. The dragonfly swooped once more . . .

And then the van was there, the back door open, with Vasily leaning out and waving them on. More men were crashing down through the woods on the other side of the vehicle, and somewhere up the road a burst of automatic weapons fire cracked against the night.

"Don't forget your tool kit!" Lia called as she dove for the back of the van, lunging in headfirst.

Akulinin didn't answer as he landed heavily beside her, but she saw that he did, indeed, still have the heavy metal box with him.

"*Go! Go! Go!*" Vasily was screaming as more gunfire cracked and thundered close by. Lia heard the clang of bullets piercing metal, but Llewellyn, in the driver's seat, had floored the accelerator and the heavy vehicle peeled rubber as it sped up. Through the open back doors of the van, Lia got a glimpse of running figures on the road well behind them, until Vasily managed to slam both doors shut.

There were bullet holes in the windows of the back door and more in the side of the van, just above their heads. That had been *entirely* too close. . . .

"Hang on!" Llewellyn called back to them. "Next stop, the Georgian border!"

Lia lay on the floor of the van, trying to slow the galloping pace of her heart.

Behind them, the dragonfly swooped far and high out over the Black Sea before suddenly inverting and plunging at high speed into the water. On the security camera pole at the dacha entrance, the piece of hardware left behind by the probe burned as its magnesium casing ignited, a tiny, hot star at the top of the pole that left nothing behind but a severed length of cable and a charred spot on the wood.

This time, no incriminating hardware would be left behind.

18

USGN *Ohio*
Arctic Ice Cap
82° 34' N, 177° 26' E
0915 hours, GMT – 12

DEAN SAT AT THE WARDROOM table, staring into the
screen on his handheld PDA. Rubens' lined face stared
back out at him. "I know, Mr. Dean," Rubens was saying.
"But the President was most insistent. We treat this as a
terrorist hostage situation."

Captain Grenville had let Dean use the wardroom for
his communications session with Fort Meade. The *Ohio*
had shifted position some seventy miles to the north of
Ice Station Bear, taking her closer to the Russian ships
parked in the ice. An hour ago she'd surfaced in a
polynya, rising just enough to extend the sub's communications mast and establish a link with one of the National
Security Agency's dedicated comsats. The image on
Dean's handheld tended to fuzz and break up at times—
atmospherics were still playing hell with RF signals, and
the satellite was quite close to the horizon—but at least
there was nothing *on* the horizon to block the signal completely.

"But suppose the hostages aren't there any longer?"

Dean said. "Suppose they've been moved to the mainland?"

"Fourteen, fifteen people, plus their guards, would need a fairly large transport," Rubens told him. "Something the size of a Hip at least."

"Hip" was the NATO designation for the Russian Mi-8 helicopter, an old design going back to the early 1960s, but still common both throughout the Russian Federation and with numerous Russian military export customers.

"And there's one of those operating off the *Lebedev*," Dean said, nodding.

"Right. But satellite reconnaissance has picked up no air traffic at all between the Russian base and the mainland. It's nine hundred miles at least to the nearest land base; that's a flight time of six and a half hours for a chopper . . . and an Mi-8 would require at least two refuelings en route. It doesn't have air-to-air fueling capabilities, so it would have to land on ships with helipads. We have some holes in our satellite coverage up there, but none big enough that we wouldn't have seen an operation of *that* size. If the Russians had moved our people to the mainland, we'd have spotted it."

Dean didn't have the same faith in high-tech magic that Rubens did, but he was willing to accept that Desk Three was satisfied that the Americans were still at the Russian ice base. But he could see a lot of problems blocking any attempt to get them out.

"Is there any way of imaging those ships to get an idea of where our people might be held?"

We've been collecting a lot of satellite recon data," Rubens told him, "especially from the IRSAT series. We've been building up a coherent picture over the past couple of days. Here. . . ."

The image on Dean's handheld screen changed from Rubens' face to a photograph of the *Lebedev*, taken from overhead and to one side. The picture then changed, becoming fuzzy, green, and somewhat translucent, as the ice and water around the vessel turned black and certain parts of the ship, her engine rooms in particular, glowed in mingled tones of white, yellow, and pale green. A number of light green dots were scattered in irregular clumps through the ship.

"Infrared imagery," Rubens said. "Heat. IRSAT is sensitive enough to pick up the heat radiated by a living human body, even behind walls. The detector's not sensitive enough to pick up warm bodies on the lower decks, but the walls of the superstructure are pretty thin. We're picking up sixty human signatures here."

"That's less than half of the *Lebedev*'s complement."

"Correct. But we can see where people are congregating in the superstructure. The bridge. Berthing quarters. Mess room. And here. . . ." A red disk winked on, highlighting a tight clump of green dots near the aft end of the superstructure. "And here. The supply lockers."

"Interesting."

"We count sixteen human-sized heat sources in this one area. Our ship experts believe these would have been stores lockers, which are empty now, after months at sea. Good places to quarter a large number of supernumeraries."

"Hostages, you mean," Dean said. "And their guards. Okay. I'll buy it."

"You'll need to use that special equipment to try to confirm their location," Rubens told him as the image was replaced once more by his face. "I've already spoken with Lieutenant Taylor. You will accompany the SEALs on board the ship. Just try to stay out of their way. Let them do their business."

Dean groaned inwardly, however. No military commander liked being micromanaged, and none liked it when spooks, no matter how high up they were on the org chart, told them they had to drag along unwanted baggage. He kept his feelings to himself, however, and simply nodded at the handheld's optical pickup. "Of course."

"We've had a breakthrough, of sorts, thanks to Lia and the new man, Akulinin."

"Their op went okay then?"

"Well enough." Something about Rubens' expression on the tiny screen told Sean it hadn't been as simple as that. "They're both okay. They made it through to the Georgian border, then to Turkey. They're still in Ankara, waiting for a flight back to the U.S."

"I'm glad to hear it. What did they find?"

"The three ships up there in the ice are part of an operation called Deep Well, or GK-1," Rubens told him. "It's a new and experimental drilling process for oil."

"Pretty much what we thought, then."

"Yeah. The unexpected part is the drilling platform."

"They're using the ship, right? The *Lebedev*?"

"No. Or, rather, not directly. The drilling platform is underwater."

"So. *Literally* 'Deep Well.' How the hell did they pull *that* off?"

"Lia found a report on Kotenko's computer that let us piece things together."

The screen cut to a series of schematic views, plans and elevations of something that looked more or less like a conventional ship with a slender midships section between much larger bow and stern sections. Dean was strongly reminded of the FLIP, or Floating Instrument Platform, an odd-looking vessel used by the Scripps Institution of Oceanography since the 1960s. Like FLIP, the Russian undersea oil platform appeared to be designed with ballast tanks that let it rotate ninety degrees into a vertical position, bow high. It could then be anchored by cables to piers sunken at the planned drill site, and then, unlike with FLIP, ballast and trim tanks could submerge the structure to any desired depth, all the way down to three thousand feet. The drilling rig ran down the length of the vessel, from bow to stern; feeder tubes could be raised to the surface on flotation buoys to take on air if necessary, though he saw provisions in the blueprints for desalinization plants to make fresh water, and hydrolysis units to break oxygen out of seawater. Other tubes could be raised in order to pump oil or natural gas up to a waiting tanker.

"GK-1 is a prototype," Rubens continued, "a test bed for new technology and proof-of-concept. The bugs Lia planted in Sochi have led us to a Houston company called Wildcat Technologies." More schematics appeared of a design identical to the Russian structure. "They call the thing Deepsea. It's an oil rig anchored to the sea floor at a depth of anything from a few hundred feet to half a mile down. Teleoperated robots and something like the Canadian arm used on the Space Shuttle let them take drill segments passed down from a ship on the surface, piece them together one after another, and add them to the drill train."

Dean studied the schematics for a moment. "So . . . it doesn't need anything at the surface at all? The whole thing's entirely underwater?"

"Obviously, once the structure's in place, it needs to be serviced by ships on the surface. During the drilling operation, a vessel like the *Lebedev* lowers the drill sections down to the rig, but once the well is producing, the design allows supply ships to come and go without needing to shut down the operation between visits. A relatively small crew lives on board the submerged rig. Docking ports here . . . and here allow miniature submarines to ferry personnel and supplies to and from the surface. The whole thing can be self-sufficient for a couple of months at a time, maybe longer."

"Like one of our nuclear missile subs," Dean said. "They can stay submerged for months. I don't see any engines, though."

"The structure is designed to be towed into place. No engines, except for station-keeping thrusters. Oil or natural gas brought up from the sea floor is pumped into large collapsible bladders secured to the hull until they can be transferred to a tanker. The bladders increase the structure's buoyancy as they fill, of course, but that's counteracted by progressively flooding onboard ballast tanks."

"So the whole drill rig can't be affected by waves or storms, and they can carry out long-term drilling operations underneath the ice." Dean nodded. "Slick."

"Exactly. Icebreakers give access from the surface when they need to send down supplies, or to fill a tanker. When a well gives out, they just attach guide cables from above, release the anchor cables below, and float the structure up to a hole cut in the surface ice, where it's righted. Then they tow the whole thing to a new location."

"So what's the payoff?" Dean asked. "It sounds expensive."

"It is. The big oil companies have been using semi-submersible rigs since the 1960s, using ballast tanks to partially sink the rig, but this idea required a lot of new technology. The project was initiated ten years ago, with the idea of developing an oil platform immune to storms."

That made sense, Dean thought. There'd been several nightmarish accidents when storms had toppled conventional oil rigs on the surface. He remembered reading about one, the *Ocean Ranger,* a drilling platform that had sunk in a storm in the North Atlantic in 1982, killing all eighty-four people on board.

"There's also a considerable public relations bonus if

it works," Rubens went on. "Environmentalist groups have been targeting visible drilling operations off of Los Angeles, and in the Texas gulf. If the drill platforms are out of sight, they're out of mind. That was the idea, anyway.

"But the real advantage, of course, would be for drilling underneath the Arctic ice cap. A couple of the global oil giants have been working on the technology for some time, now. They've known for years that the North Slope fields extend pretty way out into the Arctic basin. They just weren't sure how far, or how extensive they might be. The Russians have been doing exploratory drilling up there for at least fifteen years now. According to the data Lia found on Kotenko's computer, it's a bonanza."

"You said this is an American design?" Dean asked. "Did the Russians buy it, or did they steal it?"

"We're . . . investigating that. We've come across an interesting tidbit. One of the Greenpeace people at Ice Station Bear used to be a mid-level manager at Wildcat Technologies." A new image came up onscreen, a dark-haired, bearded man with a worried look on his face. "Harry Benford. According to some of the intelligence we developed in Solchi, he evidently was working for the Russians. He might have provided them with the Deepsea engineering specs."

"Something's not right here," Dean said. "When I was at the ice station, we found that little one-channel radio receiver in the bunk belonging to either Steven Moore or Randy Haines. Seems like it's pushing things a bit to assume that there were *two* Russian spies at the base."

"I agree. It would have been easy enough for Benford to plant the radio in another bunk, especially in all of the confusion when the Russians arrived at the base. Of course, it's also possible that Wildcat was cutting a back-room deal with Moscow."

"Oh?"

"We've been doing some checking. Wildcat is in deep financial trouble right now. The company put a lot of money into R and D for this thing, but the oil companies that might have purchased Deepsea are holding off on investing in the new technology."

"God. Why? This looks like a really decent idea."

"Because it is so damned expensive. Because a lot of the technology is still unproven. And the way things are going with the Arctic environment, it may be they just need to wait a few years for all of the ice up there to melt. Then they could build cheaper, traditional ocean-rig platforms."

But the Russians, Dean thought, might not want to wait for that to happen.

"Anyway," Rubens went on, "there are laws that would block the transfer of some of this technology to another country. The Justice Department will be investigating to see if any of those laws were broken by Wildcat . . . or if this is simply a case of simple industrial espionage."

"I see." Dean considered the situation for a moment. "So we're going to take them down."

He didn't like this. It was inevitable, perhaps, that as oil reserves dwindled around the world, as war continued to wrack the Middle East, as the demand for oil increased, those countries dependent on petroleum for economic and political stability would begin to squabble among themselves over what was left. It was a depressingly Malthusian scenario.

"Just so you know, Dean," Rubens said, "this is not about oil."

Damn. Sometimes Dean swore that Rubens could read minds. "No, sir. I didn't say it was." *Not out loud, at any rate.*

"Espionage aside," Rubens continued, "it's the President's assumption that the Russians have a perfect right to drill for oil up here. That's not the issue. They do *not* have the right to hold American citizens hostage, to take over American science stations, or to claim half of the Arctic Ocean as their own personal backyard."

"I understand, sir."

"And they especially don't have the right to kill or capture my people."

That, of course, was the telling point—especially to a former Marine. Presidents and politicians might take their countries into war for the most selfish, shortsighted, vainglorious, or otherwise idiotic of reasons . . . but the men on the front lines didn't fight for political causes. Not really. They fought for their buddies, the other grunts in the trenches with them. *That* had most likely been a basic principle of war even before Narmer united Egypt.

"If Braslov's up here, I'll find him," Dean said.

"Good. *Alive.* I'll also want you to keep an eye on the people the SEALs rescue, make sure they all get out okay. Two of them are intelligence operatives, remember— Yeats and McMillan—and McMillan is one of ours."

"Yes, sir."

"According to the diplomatic communiqué, two of the hostages are injured, one of them seriously."

"Jesus. What happened?"

"No details yet, but the Russians reportedly have both of them in the hospital facility on board one of the ships. They also have a body."

"Of who?"

"According to the Russians, the dead guy is Kenneth Richardson. He was the leader of the Greenpeace film crew at the NOAA ice station. They say the NOAA CO shot him twice, and that another Greenpeace guy smacked the CO in the face with an iron bar."

"That's the badly injured man?"

"Commander Larson, yes."

"And the guy who hit him?"

Rubens' mouth twitched in an almost smile. "Harry Benford."

"Well, well, well. The possible spy."

"Benford is the other man. Apparently, Larson shot him in the arm before Benford was able to hit Larson."

"And if Benford was working for the Russians, maybe he set the whole thing up."

"That is the belief of the analysts we have working on the intelligence developed by Miss DeFrancesca and Mr. Akulinin," Rubens said. "The Russians were looking for an excuse to move in and grab the NOAA station. Quite possibly, they'd already realized that we were spying on their base from one of our met stations nearby. A murder is reported—a murder supposedly committed by the leader of the scientific expedition, no less—and the Russians, claiming that region as their legal jurisdiction anyway, move in. They probably hope to use the incident in support of their official claim to the Arctic basin."

"It sounds pretty tangled."

"It is. And untangling it will not be your job, for which you can be duly thankful. But you're going to have a damned full plate. Whatever goes down, I want you to make sure we have Braslov alive. If they've separated our intelligence operators from the rest, I want them found and freed. Whatever it takes."

"Yes, sir." No man left behind.

"And remind the SEAL platoon commander that there are two wounded men *and* a body, probably in the ship's sick bay. We'll need at least the wounded men for questioning, if we're to make sense of this mess."

A knock sounded on the wardroom door. "Mr. Dean?" a very young voice called from the other side. "The skipper says for you to get ready for the shore party. They're getting ready to go."

"I'll be right there," Dean called back. He looked at Rubens' image again. "It's time for me to go, sir."

"Right. Good luck, Dean," Rubens said. And the image winked off.

CFS *Akademik Petr Lebedev*
Arctic Ice Cap
82° 34' N, 177° 26' E
0920 hours, GMT − 12

A sharp rap sounded from the door to Golytsin's office. "Come."

One of the naval marines assigned to the *Lebedev* opened the door and stepped inside. "Sir!" He handed a message flimsy across to Golytsin. "This just came in from the *Dekabrist.* It has been decoded."

Golytsin accepted the message. "Very well."

The marine saluted, turned, and left. Golytsin read the flimsy.

FROM: COMMANDING OFFICER, CFS DEKABRIST

TO: F. GOLYTSIN, CFS AKADEMIK PETR LEBEDEV

SONAR DETECTED SOUNDS OF UNIDENTIFIED SUBMA-RINE SURFACING IN ICE AT 0810 HOURS. LOCATION UNKNOWN BUT SUSPECT INTRUDER TO BE WITHIN 20 KILOMETERS GK-I. REQUEST SHOOT-FIRST ORDERS IF INTRUDER SUBMARINE APPROACHES PERIMETER.

SIGNED: KIRICHENKO, CAPTAIN FIRST RANK

Brief and to the point. Golytsin frowned, wishing there'd been a bit more information . . . like a *bearing,* for God's sake.

But at least the waiting was over. The Americans were here.

They'd been expected, after all. The diplomatic message announcing the capture of fourteen American scientists and Greenpeace activists would have arrived on the desk of the American President several days ago. There'd been time for an American submarine to be redeployed north.

The problem, though, was that American submarines were so hellishly quiet. During the Cold War—the *original* Cold War that had so focused the military might of both the United States and the old Soviet Union— American technology had consistently outstripped the Russian Navy's attempts to keep pace. The Walker spy ring, operating from 1967 to 1985, had helped tremendously, had in fact been responsible for a whole new generation of ultra-quiet Russian submarines, but that hadn't significantly helped the Soviets track American subs.

Golytsin had been part of the Soviet naval intelligence team working on the information provided by the Walker ring. He'd also commanded two Russian submarines during the early 1980s, and he knew something about American submarine technology. It was good, very, *very* good. Time after time, American attack subs had picked up Soviet missile boats as they exited their lairs in the White Sea or along the north coast of the Kola Peninsula and trailed them, often just a few tens of meters astern, sometimes slipping close enough to photograph details of the Soviet craft's hull through the periscope, and the Russian sonar operators had never heard a thing. A number of the better than two hundred thousand encrypted messages deciphered with Walker's help had been top-secret reports on the movements of Soviet submarines, and their astonishing accuracy had alerted the Red Fleet's high command to the problem.

Feodor Golytsin was one of the few men alive who knew just how difficult it was to track an American submarine, *especially* under the Arctic ice, where bizarre sonar echoes came ringing back from every direction and subs could play hide-and-seek among the *polynyas,* keels, and subsurface ice ridges.

And it had been Golytsin who'd recommended that the *Dekabrist* be deployed to the area around GK-1, as a bit of added insurance. The Americans, he'd argued, were certain to arrive, and the chances were good that they would arrive by submarine. Any submariner could tell you that the best way to catch a sub was to use a sub.

Those idiots back at Severomorsk HQ had hesitated. They feared a confrontation with the United States and didn't see the GK-1 project as one of Russia's vital national interests. What they didn't understand was that Russia couldn't possibly lose in this new round of international brinksmanship. If the Americans managed to sink the Russian boat, as some of the Northern Fleet's admirals feared, it would simply be wood to the fire of Russia's case before the court of world opinion: the Arctic Ocean properly belonged to Russia, and the United States was unfairly using its superior submarine technology to bully Moscow into yielding.

If, on the other hand, a submarine battle ended in a Russian victory, Moscow could simply claim that it was legitimately defending its own interests from the bellicose Americans. More to the point, the Americans were notoriously weak when it came to accepting necessary military losses. American military leaders were as afraid of open war in the Arctic as their opposite numbers at Severomorsk, and the American President would be reluctant to commit to yet another unpopular war. The Americans would . . . what was their delightful expression? Cave. That was it. The Americans would cave.

Either way, Russia would win.

And with the GK-1 project now fully in place, when Russia won, the Organizatsiya would win as well, would win to the point that, soon, the Tambov group would control *all* petroleum and natural gas production and sales across the Motherland, with an annual income to be measured in the *trillions* of rubles. Russia, and with her, Tambov, would again become a major player on the world stage.

And Feodor Golytsin would at last have his revenge over certain men, politicians prominent under both the Soviet regime and the new Federation, who'd been responsible for him freezing his ass for three bitter years in the gulag.

Captain First Rank Kirichenko was a good man, Golytsin knew, experienced, and a cunning tactician. If anyone could beat the Americans at their own game beneath the ice, it was Valery Kirichenko. But Golytsin needed to be sure Kirichenko knew what was at stake.

Turning to the computer keyboard on his desk, he began composing his reply to the *Dekabrist*'s commanding officer.

USGN *Ohio*
Arctic Ice Cap
82° 34' N, 177° 26' E
0942 hours, GMT – 12

Dean met the others at the air lock leading to the *Ohio*'s aft deck and the waiting ASDS, located in a cramped compartment aft of the control room. A heavy, watertight door stood open as one SEAL passed a bundle of equipment through to a waiting SEAL inside, and he, in turn, passed the bundle up the ladder to someone out of sight overhead.

Taylor gave Dean a dark look as he walked in, and Dean knew that he resented what he thought of as micromanagement on Dean's behalf.

This would require tact and diplomacy. Perhaps a preemptive strike. . . .

"Mr. Taylor," Charlie Dean said, "I know you don't like the fact that I've been assigned to operate with your platoon. I regret that . . . but I had nothing to do with the order. I hope you'll let me prove that I *can* be an asset on this mission."

"That's one you're going to need to prove to me, Mr. Dean," Taylor growled. "I don't like being told who's coming along on *my* op. I don't like having to leave one of my men behind because I have to make room for a damned tourist. And I *damned* sure don't like babysitting a fucking suit. You understand me?"

"I hear you." So had every man in the SEAL unit preparing to board the ASDS, plus Captain Grenville and Lieutenant Commander Hartwell and three enlisted ratings helping the SEALs with their gear. This was going to be tougher than Dean had expected. "You will not need to babysit me."

Taylor ignored him. "You will be responsible for your own equipment. *And* you will follow my orders to the exact letter. Copy?"

"Copy," Charlie Dean said, his irritation evident in his voice.

"All right. Just so we understand one another. You'd better get suited up, suit."

"I think that's enough tantrum, Mr. Taylor," said the captain. "And please try to remember that you're just a fucking lieutenant."

That comment was a conversation stopper. "Yes, sir," Taylor replied in a normal tone of voice.

They had a combat dry suit for Dean, a one-size-fits-almost-all worn over warm clothing. Unlike a standard wet suit, which allows water from the outside to get in between skin and suit and become warm with body heat, the dry suit worked by keeping cold water out. It was colored in a gray and white camo pattern that would be conspicuous on the ice but help the wearer blend in on board a gray-painted ship. The rig included a combat vest, boots, and a hood. Dean decided that if he actually fell into the water, the weight of his fashion statement was going to take him straight to the bottom.

"We won't be doing a lot of swimming," Taylor told him. "The dry suit should keep you alive for the swim up from the ASDS to the ship. Just stick close, do what you're told, and be ready to hotfoot it up the boarding ladder when we tell you."

"In broad daylight?" Dean asked.

"This here's the land of the midnight sun, cupcake. It's *always* broad daylight, at least for the next few months. But Captain Grenville here is going to create a small diversion for us."

Grenville nodded. "We'll be listening for our cue through our sonar system. When we get it, we'll surface alongside the *Lebedev,* about a hundred yards off her port side. That should keep them looking at us and not at you, and should also mask any noise you make going aboard."

"After that," Taylor added, "it's all up to us. Your boss said you have some gadgets that will help. Whatcha got?"

Dean was kneeling at the pack he'd brought on board, uncasing a bulky weapon with an oversized muzzle and a rotary cylinder. Reaching into an ammo case, he pulled out a blunt projectile.

"Forty mike-mike grenades?" one of the SEALs said with a dark chuckle. "Ain't nothing new about those."

"There is about this one," Dean said. "It's a tiny UAV. Has a camera in it that will send live-feed video, both visible light and infrared. It'll help us keep track of where the bad guys are, and where our people might be."

"I was told the hostages are on the main deck, in the aft superstructure," Taylor said.

"And they might get moved as soon as the Russians know we're on deck."

Taylor nodded. "Okay, Dean. Maybe you're a keeper after all. Just stay the fuck out of our way, right?"

"Ooh-rah," Dean replied, the battle cry of the Marines.

"Shit, man," Taylor said, grinning. "This is the Navy SEALs. It's *hoo-yah!*"

The SEALs began filing into the airlock and up the waiting ladder.

19

ASDS-1
Arctic Ice Cap
82° 34' N, 177° 26' E
1010 hours, GMT – 12

IT WAS, DEAN THOUGHT, LIKE being locked in a steel closet.

And fifteen Navy SEALs were locked inside with him.

The Advanced SEAL Delivery System was the latest evolution in using miniature submersibles to handle covert insertions of special operations teams. For decades, there'd been fierce turf battles between Navy SpecOps and the submarine force over the design of such craft.

The original SDVs, or SEAL Delivery Vehicles, had been wet subs, meaning that the SEALs on board rode in a water-filled compartment. After hours inside their cramped conveyance, they arrived at the Area of Operations cold, wet, and tired—a no-good way to begin a critical covert op. Requests for *dry* delivery vehicles had repeatedly been scotched by the submarine service, which insisted that all such vessels be under its control.

Eventually, though, the ASDS had surfaced as a compromise. In the forward compartment, Dean knew, were two men, a pilot/commander who was a Navy submariner and a SEAL copilot who handled navigation and sonar. It was an awkward division of responsibility, at times, but the two officers had cross-trained in each other's jobs in case one or the other was incapacitated.

The aft compartment was large enough—just—for sixteen men and their weapons and equipment, and it had the added capability of becoming a hyperbaric chamber if there was a diving medical emergency. Between the two compartments was a spherical lock-out chamber with watertight doors above and below, and fore and aft. The design, drawn from the earlier DRSV deep-rescue submersibles, allowed the ASDS to dock with a variety of submarines, or for swimmers to exit or enter the minisub while it was underwater.

Dean sat on the narrow bench, his knees touching the knees of the SEAL sitting opposite him, his shoulders pressed against those of the men to either side. His weapon, ammo, and the UAV controller were inside a watertight pouch resting on the deck beneath his feet. Each man wore a Dräger rebreather unit on his chest, and held in gloved hands a full-face mask that included built-in short-range radio transceivers. Short flippers were strapped on over their boots and would be discarded as soon as they reached the *Lebedev.*

Bathed in the sullen red light illuminating the narrow chamber, Taylor was standing at the forward end of the compartment, his hand pressed against the side of his head, listening to a small receiver plugged into his ear. "Okay, men," Taylor said after listening intently. "We're passing under the *Lebedev.* Remember the op plan. Teams two and four, deck security. Team three, secure the hostages. Team one, water security and tactical reserve, once we're on deck. Dean, you're team one, with me. Everyone with me?"

He was answered in a subdued chorus of affirmatives.

The *Lebedev* almost certainly had hydrophones in the water that would pick up loud noises, at least, so conversation was kept low and to a minimum.

"Okay," Taylor continued. "Masks on!"

Dean pulled the diving mask on over his head, making sure the straps were tight at the back. The faceplate was triangular, covering his mouth as well as his nose and eyes. He checked the controls on his rebreather pack; air was flowing, though it had a faintly bitter chemical taste to it.

"Radio check," Taylor's voice said in Dean's ear. "Sound off. One-one, okay."

"One-two, right."

"One-three, check."

The SEALs ran down the line, identifying themselves by fire-team number. Each of them wore a tightly fitting hood over his head, with a short-range radio receiver next to the ear, a microphone pressed up against the throat. They would be able to talk while underwater.

"One-four, okay," Dean said.

"Two-one, ready to rock."

There were no portholes, of course, or TV monitors. Dean was aware of the faint vibration through the deck and the curved bulkhead at his back as the craft's powerful electric motor drove it forward. Moments later, the deck tilted up sharply, and he felt the vibrations lessen.

"We're at ten to twenty feet," Taylor told them. "Twenty yards off the *Lebedev*'s starboard side. Commander Hartwell says we're sending the signal now."

Lieutenant Commander Hartwell was the SEAL officer forward, acting as copilot, navigator, and sonar operator for the ASDS. A coded sonar chirp would be easily picked up through the *Ohio*'s new Lockheed Martin AN/BQQ-10(V4) sonar-processing system, alerting the sub that it was time to surface and commence the diversion.

Minutes dragged by as the deck rocked gently beneath Dean's feet. The minisub's commander must be juggling his trim and ballast tanks, trying to keep the ASDS at a motionless hover beneath the surface.

"Right," Taylor said, still listening to his earpiece. "The *Ohio* is surfacing."

And Dean could hear it now, a kind of heavy, crackling thunder filtering through the thick steel hull of the ASDS, sounding both muffled and very close.

"That's our cue," Taylor said, removing the headset. "Let's get wet! Hoskins!"

"Sir!"

"You make sure our . . . ah . . . guest makes it to the roof."

"Aye, aye, sir!"

The SEALs stood in the cramped compartment, gathering up their gear in tightly secured satchels, checking straps and buckles on one another, making sure everything was cinched tight and that there was no loose equipment to tangle, trip over, or fall. The SEAL behind Charlie Dean turned him around and tugged at several straps, then checked the settings on the Dräger unit secured to his chest before clapping him on the shoulder and motioning him forward.

Dean waited in line, then, as the SEALs, two by two, entered the lock-out chamber. Since the ASDS was hovering just a few feet beneath the surface, they didn't have to lock the doors and pump water in and out of the chamber each time. Instead, the air pressure inside the submarine kept the seawater from entering the lock-out chamber; when it was Dean's turn to go, he ducked his head to step through into the spherical compartment and saw black water lapping in the open, circular hatch in the deck. Hoskins, the SEAL assigned to get him to the surface, pointed and gave him a gentle shove. Careful not to snag his baggy suit on the hatch combing, and with his water-proof gear bundle clasped tight in one hand, Dean stepped into the water, sliding down a pole extended from the side of the hatch for the purpose, letting himself sink.

Deep, blue-green water closed over his head, and he felt the sharp bite of the cold at exposed portions of skin at wrists and ankles. The dry suit kept the rest of his body dry, however, and the temperature overall seemed cool but not cold. For a scary instant, claustrophobia threatened to close him in and paralyze his breathing, but he forced himself to stay calm and to continue to pull in each breath at a slow, steady pace. His Marine training kicked in, and he began to move to one side, getting out from under the open hatchway above him.

Air rasped through his face mask, dry and cold. Unlike a standard SCUBA rig, the Dräger unit received his exhalations without releasing a telltale column of bubbles.

The red lighting inside the ASDS had allowed the men's dark adaptation to kick in during the hour-long cruise after releasing from the *Ohio*. Dean found himself adrift in a surreal blue-green cosmos with crystal-clear visibility, but where it was almost impossible to judge scale or distance. The ASDS loomed directly overhead; to his left was a curving steel cliff extending for some distance into the depths—the underwater portion of the *Lebedev*'s side. Beyond the ASDS, there appeared to be a ceiling of tortured, convoluted ice, the surfaces smooth and rounded but piled and folded into fantastic geometries that teased and tricked the eye.

The surface of the water around the ship appeared clear of ice, however. Sunlight blazed and danced with the movement of the water, with shafts of light entering from above almost parallel to the surface. Below, the blue-green emptiness deepened into midnight black, a yawning gulf far beneath Dean's gently stroking swim fins.

Toward the aft end of the *Lebedev,* Dean could see the vast and shadowy shapes of the ship's massive screws, along with several cables that appeared to descend straight down into blackness. In the opposite direction, toward the bow, he could just make out a shadowy something snug against the *Lebedev*'s side, but details were lost in the blue-green haze of ice-roofed water and scattering sundance from above.

Dean was having some trouble. Though skilled with rebreathers as well as standard SCUBA gear, thanks to Marine training decades before, he'd never used a full-face mask, and each time he breathed out, he tended to loosen the mask's seal with his face slightly. Icy water had already seeped in between the mask and his face and was collecting now at the bottom of the faceplate, salty at his lips. Awkwardly, one-handed because he was still holding his gear, he tried to clear it, pushing down on one side, turning his head, and exhaling hard to force the water out.

"Team one!" Taylor's voice said over the underwater radio. "Deploy. . . ."

Dean felt a sharp tug at his elbow; Hoskins hovered at his side, jerking his thumb up toward the surface. Dean's mask still wasn't clear, but he nodded and followed the SEAL toward the gleaming, shifting light, knowing he could remove the mask once he broke the surface. Several gentle kicks were sufficient to propel Dean toward the rust-streaked steel cliff ahead, then straight up along the *Lebedev's* side. In another moment, his head broke the surface.

He and three other SEALs had surfaced directly alongside the ship, which towered over them now, the side black against an intensely blue sky. They were so close that the chop of the water bumped them up against the metal; anyone on deck wouldn't have been able to see them without leaning out over the starboard rail.

Hoskins and another SEAL had taken up positions in the water several yards out from the ship, kicking gently to stay on the surface while holding submachine guns to their shoulders, the weapons trained at the railing above. They were the fire team one water security element, carrying special CAR-15s modified for use in seawater, with sound suppressors on their muzzles and with laser-sight targeting modules attached to their rails. "Water security," in this instance, meant staying in the water to provide cover for the rest of the SEALs as they went up the side. They'd already pulled out the tight-fitting plastic plugs in muzzles and receivers that kept the salt water out of the weapons and were training them now on the ship's main deck.

A black rubber boat had been inflated and secured to the ship's side with a length of white line and a powerful ceramic magnet with a mooring eye. Some of the SEALs had already removed fins, face masks, and Draeger units and tossed them into the boat, freeing them for the ascent. It was amazing how swiftly the evolution was proceeding. These men, Dean realized, had practiced this sort of maneuver time after time after time, until they had the closely choreographed movements down perfectly.

"Ladders up," a voice said.

"Deck clear," said another.

Dean turned in the water and saw that two more SEALs had used long, telescoping poles taken from racks on the outside hull of the ASDS to raise a pair of boarding ladders up the side, hooking the upper ends of the ladders over the *Lebedev*'s gunwale. As soon as the narrow chain ladders were in place, the SEALs of teams two and four were on their way up, moving swiftly and with an elegant and death-silent economy of motion.

"Fire team two, on deck!" a voice called over the radio. "Target! Engaging! . . ."

"Team four, on deck! Moving aft! . . ."

The assault on the *Lebedev* had begun.

The Art Room
NSA Headquarters
Fort Meade, Maryland
1825 hours EDT

"There they go," Rockman said. "Right at the water-line, about three-quarters of the way aft from the bow. See them?"

Rubens placed his hands on Rockman's workstation desk and leaned forward, staring into the big screen as if by sheer force of will he could influence the events unfolding there. Yes, he could see them, tiny antlike shapes moving up the huge ship's rounded side.

The scene being transmitted to the Art Room was real-time, images picked up by the NIKOS-4 reconnaissance satellite launched into a polar orbit from Vandenberg just two days earlier. The scene showed an oblique view of the *Lebedev,* looking down on her starboard side from about forty-five degrees above the horizon. Beyond the *Lebedev,* the *Ohio* had just surfaced, her conning tower showing as a narrow, black square protruding above the ice. The other two Russian ships were farther off, almost half a mile distant.

From the wall speaker, bits of radio transmission, captured by the NIKOS satellite and transmitted back to Fort Meade, sounded against the crackle and hiss of background static.

"Fire team two, on deck! Target! Engaging! . . ."

"Team four, on deck! Moving aft! . . ."

Rubens thought he could see one of the antlike figures advance on another, see the second figure crumple to the deck. But the details were lost, and he wasn't entirely sure what he was seeing.

It was frustrating, really. Desk Three and the Deep Black operation were built on the supremacy of technology, the ability to use sophisticated sensor platforms such as NIKOS to penetrate an enemy's strongholds and reveal his secrets. Rubens was always mindful of the dictum of one of his favorite authors, a science fiction writer named Arthur C. Clarke: *Any sufficiently advanced technology is indistinguishable from magic.* The National Security Agency and the Art Room performed astonishing feats of magic on an almost daily basis.

And none of that could help now. Up there on the Arctic ice, satellites in geosynchronous orbit, orbiting above the equator in step with Earth's twenty-four-hour rotation, were simply too close to the horizon to be useful for surveillance. You needed spysats in a low polar orbit to see what was going on down there, and those passed across the entire span of the sky within a minute or so. The image on the screen was already dwindling as NIKOS-4, at an altitude of 120 miles, raced toward the southeastern horizon.

"Damn it, can't you zoom in any closer?" he asked Rockman.

"A little, I think. But we're pushing the limits of our resolution now. . . ." Rockman entered a set of commands on his keyboard. The view rushed in closer, but still not close enough. He could just make out figures moving on the *Lebedev*'s deck, but the details tended to blur and fuzz out at the extreme limit of NIKOS-4's resolution.

"Here," Rubens said. Reaching into his coat jacket, he produced a laser pointer and switched it on. He let the red dot dance around a portion of the *Lebedev,* on her starboard side up near the bow. "Any ideas about what *that* is?"

Whatever it was, it had not appeared on any of the ship plans and schematics the Art Room had been able to pull up for the *Lebedev* or her sister research vessel, the *Akademik Sergei Vavilov.* It appeared to be a temporary structure hung over the ship's side, something like an enclosed vertical tunnel or ladder shroud, with what looked like a swim platform at the level of the water, close by the ship's waterline. Rubens had never seen anything like it.

"That platform," Rockman said, thoughtful. "Might be for small craft tying up alongside the ship."

Rubens nodded. "Makes sense. Boats must go back and forth between all three ships, and that's how they get on board."

A logical assumption . . . but Rubens was worried. Assumptions based on insufficient data *always* worried him.

If the satellite had been directly above the *Lebedev,* the men and women here in the Art Room would not have been able to read newspaper headlines over someone's shoulders, as the popular myth had it, but they would have been able to distinguish Navy combat dry suits from Russian parkas, spotted weapons, detected ambushes, and maybe seen clearly the structure hanging over the *Lebedev*'s starboard bow. But the satellite was too close to the horizon for that now, and in another few seconds it would vanish over the curve of the world.

Whatever was going to happen now was in the hands of those Navy SEALs, the skipper and crew of the *Ohio,* and one NSA agent.

The image on the screen broke into shifting, jumping pixels, then re-formed as empty ice. It was tracking over the edge of the ice pack now. Rubens saw the dark blue of open water, and broad leads where the ice cap had cracked open. As he watched, ice gave way to deep blue, open water, and a patch of brilliant glare where the sun was reflecting off the sea and into space.

"NIKOS-4 is passing over the horizon, sir," a technician reported from another station. "We've lost transmissions from the *Ohio*."

"How long before the next satellite reaches the AO?" he demanded.

"That would be NIKOS-1," Rockman said, consulting his monitor. "Fourteen minutes."

Fourteen minutes. An eternity in combat.

And Rubens was as helpless to affect the outcome as he would be if the boarding action were taking place on the far side of the moon.

Damn!

Arctic Ice Cap
82° 34' N, 177° 26' E
1026 hours, GMT − 12

Treading water close beside the *Lebedev*'s waterline, Dean wondered if he was about to make a fool of himself. It had been years since he'd even climbed an obstacle course cargo net, and his recent round of quals had stressed the purely physical—push-ups, timed runs, and target shooting—rather than acrobatic activities like climbing chain ladders.

"Dean!" Taylor's voice crackled in his hood. "You're up next!"

He swam over to the rubber boat and clung to the side as he pulled off his fins and breathing equipment, dropping them with the rest of the SEAL swim gear in the bottom of the boat. He then sidestroked his way carefully to the nearest ladder, slung his waterproof pack over one shoulder, and, with Taylor steadying the ladder at the bottom, started up. *No doubt about it,* Dean thought. *I'm getting way too old for this.*

With Taylor holding the ladder taut, though, the climb

wasn't as bad as Dean had feared. He was breathing heavily by the time he rolled over the starboard rail and dropped onto the starboard companionway, but he was able to unsling his satchel and break out the Master Blaster, unfolding the stock and locking the foregrip in place.

There was a dead man on the companionway deck in front of a door twenty feet away, one of the *Lebedev* sailors gunned down by silenced shots from one of the first of the SEALs to come aboard. There was no room here for gentlemanly conduct or proper rules of war. SEALs relied on total surprise coupled with a concentrated focus of overwhelming firepower and violence to achieve their aim . . . and a random sailor unexpectedly strolling out onto the starboard side companionway for a smoke couldn't be allowed to sound the alarm.

The SEALs, once on board, had split into separate elements and dispersed, moving both fore and aft to secure the Russian vessel's main deck. "Team four!" sounded over the radio. "Multiple targets, port! Engaging! . . ."

Dean heard a kind of sharp clicking and recognized it as shots fired from the sound-suppressed H&K, coming from the other side of the ship's main deck superstructure. Shouts and screams followed, the sounds of spreading panic.

Gripping the grenade launcher, Dean hurried aft.

Golytsin's Office
CFS *Akademik Petr Lebedev*
Arctic Ice Cap
82° 34′ N, 177° 26′ E
1027 hours, GMT − 12

The ship's general alarm shrilled from the intercom speaker overhead, bringing Golytsin to his feet. Someone pounded on the door. "Sir! The ship is under attack!"

Only moments before, the report had come down from the *Lebedev*'s bridge: an American submarine was surfacing just a hundred meters off the port side. Golytsin had been preparing to go outside to see the spectacle for himself when the alarm had gone off.

The ship under attack? From the submarine?

"I'm coming." He reached into a bottom desk drawer and extracted his sidearm, a PM—Pistole Makarov—still in its holster and slung from a web belt. His parka was on a coat hook by the door.

Down the main port-side passageway, through a watertight door, and out onto the deck, where a blast of cold and keening wind cut into his face like myriad thrusting needles. A dozen or more of the *Lebedev*'s crew were already along the port railing, staring out into the glare of the ice. There was the American submarine there, her sail black against the ice. An American flag had been unfurled above the conning tower, so there could be no mistaking the vessel's nationality. He could even see two tiny human figures in the weather cockpit in front of the flag and more figures on the submarine's forward deck, putting down a gangplank to the ice.

Well, well, he thought with grim surprise and something approaching admiration. *Perhaps the Americans have grown some balls after all.* But, while surprising, the surfacing of that submarine didn't constitute an *attack,* as such. . . .

"Sir!" Lieutenant Alexei Stilchoff gripped his upper arm. "Sir, you should get below! *Now!*"

"Alexei! What the devil's going on?" Golytsin demanded. Stilchoff was the commanding officer of the contingent of naval infantry stationed on board the *Lebedev.* He was an old hand, a veteran of the Chechnyan War, and not easily flustered or scared.

Stilchoff pointed aft. "American commandos! They're already on board!"

Golytsin looked back along the port-side railing toward the *Lebedev*'s fantail. Even as Stilchoff turned and pointed, a pair of gray-clad figures appeared around the corner of the superstructure aft, *menacing* figures with compact submachine guns held rigidly against their shoulders as they moved forward with the deadly grace of predatory cats. Nearby, one of Stilchoff's men fumbled with the AKM assault rifle slung over his shoulder, dragging back the charging lever and raising the weapon to take aim. At the same moment, Stilchoff grabbed the butt of his holstered PM, trying to drag the pistol free of its holster.

Before either man could complete the move, however, triplets of bullets slammed into them both, knocking them back a step, sending them crumpling to the deck in untidy sprawls. Golytsin hadn't even heard the shots as they were fired.

Golytsin was still standing in the open door leading onto the deck outside. At the instant Stilchoff and the other man were hit, Golytsin jumped backward, pulling the heavy door shut, hearing and feeling the clang of bullets striking it outside. With his right hand, he pulled out his own PM, and stood leaning against the bulkhead for a moment, breathing hard. God, that had been *close*!

He chambered a round in his pistol but didn't even consider trying to engage those two invaders. They would be American commandos from that submarine . . . most likely U.S. Navy SEALs, who were widely regarded even in countries other than the United States as the best, most deadly small-unit fighters in the world. To attempt to face those two men outside in combat was nothing less than suicide.

He pulled a radio from the pocket of his cold-weather gear and pressed the handset button. "Captain Mironov!"

"Mironov here."

"We have American commandos coming onto the fantail. I recommend you put men with machine guns on the wings of the bridge, and in the main passageways."

"Commandos? How many?—"

But Golytsin switched off the radio. *Let the command staff figure this one out.*

The prisoners. They were here to free the men and women from the American research station—a hostage rescue.

He needed to get down there, get down there *fast.*

Fantail
CFS *Akademik Petr Lebedev*
Arctic Ice Cap
82° 34' N, 177° 26' E
1028 hours, GMT – 12

With his grenade launcher in hand, Dean moved aft onto the *Lebedev's* fantail. Long lengths of metal pipes or tubes were stacked along the fantail, evidently drilling sections waiting to be lowered to the GK-1 somewhere below. The A-frame gantry loomed overhead, one pipe section still secured to the arm by a heavy wire rope.

A football field's length away off the port side, the *Ohio* had emerged from the ice, her black island standing above a tumble of ice blocks shouldered aside as she'd surfaced. A number of Russian sailors had gathered along the port side of the *Lebedev* to stare at the risen apparition. Now, though, SEALs moved down the deck, weapons held against their shoulders as they moved. Two Russians, both of them naval infantry judging from their uniforms, lay dead on the deck. The rest, unarmed, were fleeing, scattering forward along the deck or ducking back into doorways.

One of the key tactical considerations for this op, Dean

knew, was just how many armed troops were on board what was ostensibly a civilian research vessel. According to her published specs, the *Lebedev* was supposed to carry 128 men. Most of those would be ordinary sailors, even merchant seamen, with little or no knowledge of weapons. A few would be Russian naval infantry; some might even be Spetsnaz—Russian Special forces—depending on how important this expedition was to the Russian government and military. But the chances were good that only a few—fifteen? Twenty?—would have military weapons or training.

Standing orders would be to engage enemy forces capable of resisting but to minimize other casualties. Still, there were only fifteen Navy SEALs on board the *Lebedev* now and one former-Marine-turned-spook. They had to seize the initiative and hold it; if they let the enemy recover their breath and their wits, the SEALs could find themselves up against some very serious opposition indeed.

Dean might not be a SEAL, but he should be able to help with that. Kneeling on the afterdeck in the shadow of the huge A-frame crane, Dean pulled the UAV control board out of its watertight plastic case. The device was the size of a large paperback that unfolded flat at the press of two buttons, with a built-in swing-up screen, a small keypad, and a two-inch-high joystick that popped up when he unfolded the panel. He switched the device on and made sure he had a clear signal from the Sky-HUNTIR, then set the unit on the deck and picked up the MGL-140.

Taylor appeared on the fantail next to Dean, a gray apparition, still dripping, an H&K in his hands. "Well? How about that special spook stuff, Marine? You said you'd have something to show us."

Dean was already training the six-shot grenade launcher on the dazzlingly blue zenith of the sky. "Taking care of that now, sir," he said, and he squeezed the trigger.

The MGL-140 grenade launcher gave a sharp cough as it sent a 40mm round streaking into the sky. Dean set the weapon down and quickly picked up the controller, his thumb on the joystick. Seven hundred feet overhead, the grenade Dean had fired came apart as it reached the top of its trajectory, the expended propellant cartridge falling away to expose a small, battery-driven pusher-prop and an unfolding ram-air parafoil the size of an unfolded newspaper.

One of the rounds originally developed for the MGL-140 was called HUNTIR, a somewhat tortured acronym standing for High-altitude Unit Navigated Tactical Imaging Round. Fired by a Marine on the ground, the HUNTIR flew into the sky, deployed a small parachute, and drifted back to earth like a flare . . . but instead of burning magnesium, it carried an onboard CMOS camera aimed at the ground, transmitting whatever it saw in real time. It gave ground forces a badly needed tactical advantage in places like Iraq, where you never knew what was waiting for you behind that wall up ahead, on the next city block, or on the other side of the next hill.

The problem with HUNTIR, though, was that it only transmitted for about eight seconds, and if you didn't place the round perfectly above the right piece of real estate, you might miss seeing what you needed to see. The National Security Agency, looking for new and innovative ways to gather useful data on the battlefield and during covert insertions, had married the HUNTIR with a self-powered UAV. The result was Sky-HUNTIR, a long-bodied 40mm round that deployed an engine and a parafoil wing at the top of its trajectory. The battery on board would keep the device aloft for up to ten minutes, and an operator on the ground—or, in this case, on the fantail of a ship—could remotely fly the UAV to exactly the right point for useful snooping, or let the onboard computer chip steer the vehicle on a preset search course.

The Sky-HUNTIR was already sending back black-and-white images, though so far they showed nothing but a wildly tilted horizon. Nudging the joystick, Dean brought the flier around in a broad turn, angling the camera in its nose to look back at the ship.

"That's the IR view?" Taylor asked, looking over his shoulder.

"IR overlaid on visible," Dean replied. He pointed at the screen. "We're getting some thermal imaging through the superstructure. Looks like the hostages may still be gathered here."

Large numbers of human bodies radiated heat—quite a bit of it. The ceilings and walls of the *Lebedev*'s super-structure were relatively thin and not well insulated; on the screen, numerous dark blobs of fuzz marked man-sized heat sources, some moving, some clustered together in one place.

Dean tapped on the small keyboard, bringing up a schematic of the *Lebedev*'s upper decks, then had the computer drop the recorded heat sources onto the deck plans.

"Team three!" Taylor snapped. "Hostages are at prime target area. Execute!"

Nearby, the four SEALs of fire team three moved closed on the large watertight door at the aft end of the *Lebedev*'s superstructure from either side.

20

FEODOR GOLYTSIN REACHED the long passageway on the main deck outside the machine shops and stores lockers. This was the aft end of the *Lebedev*'s above-hull superstructure, a long block of large compartments used to support the mechanical aspects of at-sea drilling and bottom sampling.

The aft stores locker had been filled with crates of food at the beginning of the expedition but was nearly empty now. Days before, Golytsin had given orders that the compartment be carefully searched for anything that might become an improvised weapon. Then mattresses had been moved into the compartment, which had sinks and a toilet. The American "guests" could be housed temporarily there, at least until arrangements could be made to put them on board a helicopter, and they could be flown back to Mys Shmidta. A naval infantry guard stood outside the door, gripping his AKM tightly and looking nervous at the growing sounds of battle outside.

"Stand aside," Golytsin ordered. "Open it."

The guard undogged the hatch and stepped back. Golytsin stepped inside, exercising caution in case the prisoners had prepared an ambush inside. The prisoners, however, were gathered along the far bulkhead, slumped on mattresses or the bare deck.

"What the hell is going on?" one of the men demanded.

"Some of your countrymen have decided to launch a hostage rescue, Lieutenant Segal," he said. During the past days, he'd closely questioned all thirteen of the prisoners, and now he knew them all by name. He raised his PM and pointed it at one of the women. "Miss McMillan, you will come with me."

"Now wait just a damned minute!" Tom McCauley yelled, coming to his feet, fists clenched. Fred Masters got up as well . . . and then all of the prisoners were on their feet.

"Stay put, Kathy!" Randy Haines ordered.

"What the hell are you trying to pull?" Steven Moore demanded. "She stays with us, you Russian bastard!"

Golytsin smiled. Moore was one of the Greenpeace moviemakers. It was interesting to see how the two groups had forgotten differences and come together since coming on board the *Lebedev*.

Golytsin brandished the pistol. "I promise nothing will happen to her," he said. "But if the rest of you don't sit down and do *exactly* as you're told, several of you will be dead!"

"It's okay, boys," the woman said. She crossed the deck to stand in front of Golytsin. She still wore the T-shirt she'd had on when she came on board; someone had found her a pair of BDU trousers, however, which were baggy on her. "So what am I, Feodor, your personal bargaining chip?"

"Something like that." He grabbed her upper arm and steered her toward the door. "I suggest the rest of you lie down, cover your heads under those mattresses, and don't move around. Hostage rescues can be . . . very hazardous for the hostages."

He led the woman out into the passageway.

"Where are you taking me?" she asked.

"Somewhere safer than this ship," he told her. He pointed with the PM. "That way."

During the past week, he'd been quite impressed with Kathy McMillan. Threats of torture, of gang rape, of being abandoned on the ice or dropped into freezing water, *none* of those had shaken her resolve to tell Golytsin absolutely nothing.

Golytsin considered himself to be an ethical and moral man. He disliked violence, disliked bully tactics, and had never intended to actually carry out any of those threats on the woman. But she didn't know that, and he'd been impressed by her stolid, almost Russian willingness to confront and endure whatever the future might hold for her.

Still, her silence, and that of one of her companions, Randy Haines, had confirmed for Golytsin that both of them were American intelligence agents, probably CIA. The third man the *Dekabrist* had plucked off the ice, Dennis Yeats, Golytsin was pretty sure was just another NOAA scientist. Haines was almost certainly CIA, but he was also a big man, with powerful arms, and Golytsin didn't trust his own ability to keep control of someone that physically strong.

Those commandos outside could have the rest of the prisoners. McMillan, Golytsn had decided, was more valuable than the lot of them combined.

"Faster!" he urged as they hurried down the passageway.

Fantail
CFS *Akademik Petr Lebedev*
Arctic Ice Cap
82° 34' N, 177° 26' E
1031 hours, GMT – 12

The SEALs reached the watertight door leading into the *Lebedev*'s superstructure and tried pulling the grab handle. "It's locked!" one yelled.

"Blow it open!" Taylor called back.

One of the SEALs reached into a waterproof pouch, producing a strip of cutting charge. But it would take precious seconds to affix the charge and blow the door off of its dogs and hinges.

"Have your men step clear," Dean said. He put the Sky-HUNTIR on an automatic search orbit above the ship and set the controller on the deck, retrieving the MGL-140. "And I mean *way* clear. We can kick the door in with this baby."

Taylor nodded, clapping Dean's shoulder with a gloved hand. "Do it."

At Taylor's direction, the SEALs stepped well back from the door, taking cover around the corners of the superstructure. Dean brought the MGL-140 to his shoulder and sighted on the center of the door.

The MGL-140 had been developed to meet a number of design challenges posed by earlier grenade launchers, like the well-known M-203. Besides being able to launch a tactical battlefield camera, the MGL-140 could also utilize a variety of new munition types, in addition to the large and varied family of 40mm grenades already in the military arsenal.

Among these was the MEI Hellhound round, an impact-detonation grenade with twice the lethal radius of the conventional M433 high-explosive grenade and far more hitting power. The joke was that the "hound" in the round's name stood for "High-Order Unbelievably Nasty Destruction," a rather too-cute acronym, which Dean was inclined to doubt came from real life, but which certainly told the story. Officially, the round was called "hyper-lethal/enhanced blast." The round was the reason the MGL-140's unofficial nickname was Master Blaster.

"Knock-knock," Dean said, and he squeezed the trigger.

The grenade streaked across the open fantail deck and slammed into the steel door dead-center. The explosion engulfed the door; the concussion rang shrill in Dean's ears and slapped against his face and combat vest with a palpable, startling blow. Pieces of the door frame clinked and rattled across the deck as smoke billowed across the fantail. As the smoke cleared, Dean could see that the watertight door had been punched off its dogs and slammed back into the passageway beyond.

"Go!" Taylor yelled. "Go! Go! Go!"

The SEALs dashed up to either side of the opening. One tossed a canister through into the swirling smoke, and a few seconds later a string of thunderous explosions and bright, strobing flashes erupted from inside. The flash-bang was designed to incapacitate anyone waiting on the other side, blinding, deafening, and stunning them with a series of sharp detonations. Dean suspected that if any bad guys *had* been on the other side of that door, they weren't going to be affected much by a flash-bang grenade now, not after the Hellhound had come knocking.

The four SEALs of fire team three clambered over the smashed-in door, following close on the heels of the last of the flash-bang detonations.

"Good shot," Taylor told him. He sounded relaxed, almost chatty. "You know, I trained with the 140 at China Lake for a while. Damned impressive weapon."

Dean placed the launcher on the deck and retrieved the UAV controller. "It's all about force multipliers, sir," he said. Reasserting control over the UAV still circling high above the ship, Dean put the device into a shallow dive, bringing it down closer to the ice-girded *Lebedev*. As he turned the UAV to fly parallel to the ship, from stern to bow, he saw something on the screen, something worrisome.

"Uh-oh," he said. "We've got trouble."

"What?"

Dean enlarged the window on his monitor and zoomed in close. From either side of the bridge at the forward end of the *Lebedev*'s superstructure, open wings extended out over the port and starboard companionways. On the screen, two men in uniform could be seen wrestling something long and heavy out onto the starboard wing.

"What the hell?" Taylor said.

"PK," Dean told him. "Russian machine gun. If they get that thing set up there, they'll be able to sweep the entire starboard companionway."

"Fire team two!" Taylor called over the radio. "Be advised there's a Russian MG being set up on the starboard bridge wing. Watch yourselves!" Team two had been working its way up the starboard companionway toward the bow.

"Copy," a voice came back. "We've got . . . shit! *Shit!*"

The sharp rattle of automatic fire sounded from somewhere forward. On the screen, Dean could see the two Russians on the bridge wing standing behind the PK, which had been dropped into a vehicle mount on the aft wing railing. They were firing sharp, short, controlled bursts down onto the companionway.

Tilting the UAV around, Dean was able to spot two SEALs, crouched on the companionway deck behind an open watertight door. They were using the door as cover, but if they moved, either to fall back or to go around the door to enter the superstructure, the machine gunners above would have them in a clear and deadly line of fire.

"One-one, this is Two-one," a voice called. "Andrews is hit. It's not bad, but we're pinned down, can't move!"

That PK machine gun had just sucked the vital initiative from the SEAL assault.

Dean put the UAV back onto automatic. "I can get that machine gun," he said, picking up the MGL-140 again.

"Do it," Taylor said.

Dean stood up and started forward.

"Where are you going?" Taylor asked.

Dan pointed. "Up there. I need a clear shot."

A ladder led up the aft end of the superstructure to an upper deck, where the *Lebedev*'s single smokestack rose clear of the structure. Forward of that was a drill rig, with another ladder leading up.

"Don't get yourself lost, Marine," Taylor warned him. "When we sound recall, we're gonna have to get the hell out of Dodge *fast*."

"I'll be there," Dean said. And he started up the first ladder.

Main Starboard Passageway, Main Deck
CFS *Akademik Petr Lebedev*
Arctic Ice Cap
82° 34' N, 177° 26' E
1032 hours, GMT – 12

Golytsin urged the American woman ahead of him at a ragged jog. He'd ordered her to turn right when the passageway came to a T intersection, leading her around and past the internal housing for the ship's smokestack, then forward up the starboard side of the ship. Seconds after they made that turn, an ear-wracking boom had echoed down the passageway, followed moments later by something that sounded like Chinese fireworks, only much louder.

The enemy commandos were storming the *Lebedev*'s interior.

No matter. His destination was not much farther ahead.

"Look, Feodor," the woman said. She sounded exasperated . . . and tired. "Give it up! Let me and the rest go and no one needs to get killed."

"People have already been killed, Miss McMillan," he replied, his voice cold. "But it's in a good cause."

"*What* good cause? Oil?"

"Money," Golytsin told her. "Money, and something much more precious."

"What's that?"

"*Survival.*"

"I'd think you would want to survive the next ten minutes."

"Miss McMillan, you really have no idea what the people I work for are like."

"And who would that be?" she snapped. "The Organizatsiya?"

That observation alone confirmed for Golytsin that the woman was with American intelligence.

"Something like that. They are *not* nice people."

"Then why work for them?"

He snorted. "As I say, you don't know them. With Tambov, once you're in, you can *never* leave."

From outside, he heard the urgent, pounding yammer of a machine gun, and he knew the captain had gotten one of the PKs set up to sweep the outside companionway. It wouldn't stop the enemy commandos for long, but it would slow them up long enough for him to get his prisoner to their destination.

And then the Americans could *have* the damned ship, for all the good it would do them.

Drilling Tower
CFS *Akademik Petr Lebedev*
Arctic Ice Cap
82° 34' N, 177° 26' E
1034 hours, GMT – 12

Forward of the *Lebedev*'s smokestack, a miniature oil derrick rose forty feet above the aft superstructure. The *Lebedev*'s mission included taking core samples of the bottom, and the derrick, presumably, was used for drilling into the sea floor to get them. A ladder, steel rungs welded up one corner of the tower, gave access to the top of the structure. Slinging his Master Blaster, Dean grabbed the nearest rung and started up.

He needed to climb about twelve to fifteen feet to get a clear shot. While the ship's aft superstructure was one level high, not counting the smokestack and several small buildings off to one side, the forward half was a solid block rising three stories above the main deck, with the much smaller bridge house on top of that. The bridge wings extended to either side of the bridge, and he needed to get high enough that the forward structure didn't block his line of sight.

He could hear the hammering of the PK, though, and the shouts of Russian troops rallying somewhere forward. The two SEALs were still pinned down, unable to move back or forward, and there was no other way to get at the machine gun that was causing the trouble.

There they were, two men crouched over the machine gun as they trained it on the deck four stories below. As Dean climbed higher, though, one of the Russians noticed him, pounded his partner's shoulder, and pointed.

Looping one arm through a support beam on the derrick, Dean unslung the MGL-140, checked that the next round up was a Hellhound, and brought the weapon to his shoulder.

Through the sights, he saw the magnified image of the two Russians as they swung the PK machine gun around to bear on him. If they fired first, the sheer volume of fire would sweep him from his perch like a fire hose. He squeezed the trigger.

An important innovation on the MGL-140 was the two-stage trigger. You needed to squeeze hard to get to the first detent—an important safety consideration when you were humping a weapon loaded with this much high explosives. After that first tug, though, a relatively light squeeze was all that was necessary to actually fire the round.

What that meant for Dean was that he could actually use the thing, unlike any other grenade launcher, as a sniper's rifle . . . a sniper's rifle with one hell of a kick when the round detonated.

In his sight, the PK's muzzle flashed. Rounds struck the tower just above his head, whining into space and sending a shard of hot metal sizzling past his head and tugging at his ear. At the same moment, Dean fired the MGL, sending the hyper-lethal round hissing downrange.

The grenade struck the bridge wing railing or the PK—he couldn't tell which—and detonated with a savage flash. One of the Russians was torn apart by a round identical to one that had just torn out a thick steel door, while the other was lifted and tossed over the disintegrating railing in a flailing of bloody arms and legs.

When the smoke cleared, the starboard-side bridge wing was completely gone, reduced to tangled fragments of metal on the deck below or tossed into the water alongside. Smoke continued to emerge from the open doorway leading onto the bridge as well, suggesting that the blast had caused damage there as well.

Climbing higher, Dean could see past the bridge and down to the forward deck, where several Russian troops were gathered. Taking aim, he placed a second grenade on the deck just behind them. The explosion thundered across the vessel and sent a column of smoke boiling into the pristine sky.

"Two-one and Two-two are clear," Taylor said over Dean's radio headset. "And team three is bringing out the hostages. Come on back to the fantail, Dean. We're gonna hotfoot it out of here!"

But Dean had just seen something else. Through the MGL-140's sight, he could see a man in a heavy military-style parka emerging from a doorway onto the main deck forward, just beyond the point where the bridge wing had collapsed. He was leading a woman in baggy pants and a T-shirt at gunpoint.

"You didn't get all the hostages," Dean said over the radio link, slinging his weapon. "I'm going after one."

"Dean, get the hell back here! No heroics!"

He didn't reply. Sometimes it was necessary to pretend radio failure.

Using his gloves and his insteps to brake his descent, he slid down the drill rig ladder, hitting the deck hard before breaking into a sprint. He was angry. If he'd had the sense to bring along an M40A1, or one of the other sniping rifles available, he could have taken out the Russian with a single shot from the tower, no sweat, and he or one of the SEALs could have gone forward to recover the hostage. Using a grenade launcher as a sniper's weapon was all well and good, but it didn't count for a damned thing when you needed to be *selective* with your kill. He could have easily taken out the running man . . . but the blast would have killed the woman in front of him as well.

Across the aft superstructure, then, to the corner of the forward structure, rising like an apartment building in front of him. Another ladder led down the starboard side to the companionway. He swung out onto a rung and slid down, his MGL-140 bumping against his shoulder as he dropped.

He hit the deck and started running again, unslinging the grenade launcher as he moved. He might not be able to use the thing against someone using an American prisoner as a human shield, but the sight of the monster weapon might frighten the guy into compliance.

A beanbag round would have been a useful addition to his kit, Dean thought ruefully. They were riot-control projectiles consisting of soft, weighted bags that hit hard enough to knock down a man but not injure him seriously.

It was way too late to second-guess his decisions, however. He would have to make this one up as he went along. He had to slow down to navigate a treacherous part of the deck partly blocked by fallen rails and decking from the collapsed bridge wing. As he reached the forward end of the *Lebedev*'s superstructure, gunfire barked, the rounds snapping past his head.

He returned fire, sending a hyper-lethal grenade into a knot of Russian naval infantry crouched behind and beside a deck funnel. The blast ripped the funnel aside and scattered the men like tenpins. Ahead, a kind of wooden box, man-tall and lined with fluttering sheets of blue plastic, rose at the starboard railing. And as he approached, a man stepped from inside.

Dean had expected Braslov, who was supposed to be out here somewhere, but this man was a stranger. He wore civilian clothing, but with a military parka and with a ramrod bearing that shouted military at Dean.

He was standing behind the woman, his arm locked

around her throat and a Makarov pistol pressed against her temple.

"Do not speak. You will drop that rather formidable weapon," the man said. *"Now."*

At least the guy hadn't added a melodramatic "or the girl dies." Instead, he nodded as Dean placed the grenade launcher on the deck.

"Good. Now kick it over the side."

Which meant he couldn't dive for it if he saw an opening for Hollywood-style heroics. Reluctantly he put his boot on the weapon's heavy barrel and shoved it hard enough to send it skittering into the gunwale. Carefully the Russian used his foot to slide it over the top. Dean heard the lonely splash when it hit far below.

"You will hold your arms out from your body, please. And turn around . . . slowly. Good. Now remove the combat harness and throw it over the side as well."

Dean did as he was ordered. He could see the fear in the woman's eyes, but she stood calmly, not struggling or panicking.

He recognized her now. Rubens had transmitted a file photo of Katharine McMillan, the NSA agent who'd been sent up to the Arctic as a loaner to the CIA. It had taken Dean a moment to connect that photo—of a calm-looking woman wearing lipstick, eye makeup, and neatly styled hair—with this person, scared, dirty, her hair uncombed, salt-matted, and windblown.

"Your radio," the Russian said. "I see the mike at your throat. Lose it. Over the side. I warn you, do *not* speak."

A few tugs were sufficient to pull both the microphone and the earpiece out of his hood. He wondered if the SEALs had overheard the Russian giving him orders and decided they had not. The microphone was sound-powered and needed a very close voice, his own, to activate. Sounds of gunfire were crackling from the stern of the ship; they were probably pretty busy back there in any case.

"You are . . . what?" the man said, his brow furrowed as he looked Dean up and down. "Not a Navy SEAL, surely. You are much too old." He looked at McMillan, then back to Dean. "Might you be one of this young woman's associates, then?"

"Actually," Dean said, reaching for a lie, "I'm empowered to negotiate for her release. What is it you want?"

"No, no, *no*," the man said, shaking his head and waggling the Makarov for emphasis. "You've got it all wrong, my friend. *First* you negotiate; *then* you send in the commandos, after the negotiations break down. You don't do it the other way around. It looks bad, and the insurance adjustors ask difficult questions. What is your name?"

"Charlie Dean." There was no point in playing games.

"And you are . . . what, Charlie Dean? CIA?"

"Something like that. The question remains, what is it you want? Holding this woman won't help you. Killing me won't help you. But perhaps I can find a way to end this . . . standoff to our mutual advantage."

The man chuckled. "Actually, Mr. Dean, as I see it, there *is* no 'standoff,' as you put it." He waggled the pistol again. "I have the cards in my hand, and they appear to be a full house." He brought the pistol back to McMillan's temple, just as Dean had begun calculating his odds if he were to try a sudden lunge. If he could catch the Russian when the pistol was pointed somewhere else, pin the arm, wrestle him down . . .

"You," the Russian continued, all lightness gone from his voice now, "will come with us. Actually, I was thinking of killing you, but it seems to me that holding *two* American intelligence agents might be to my advantage. I know some . . . people who might pay quite well for access to your memories."

Dean raised his hands, palms out. "Take me, then. Two of us would be trouble. Believe me."

"No. I quite like the young lady's company. I considered bringing along her CIA companion, but decided he was too young and strong to be worth the risk. You, however, are *old*. I believe I can handle you, and the girl as well."

Dean laughed at the brazenness of the statement but added a bitter, "You son of a bitch," to the chuckle.

"Exactly. You will precede us down the ladder. Now."

Dean did as he was told. The structure hanging from the side of the *Lebedev* was a wood, plastic, and canvas shelter around a ladder extending all the way to the ship's waterline. At the bottom was a kind of flat pier, attached to the ship's side but hinged so that it moved up and down with the lapping of the waves.

Moored to the side of the pier was something large and rounded, painted a bright yellow and with Cyrillic lettering here and there on the hull. A circular hatch on a raised combing gave access to the thing's interior.

It took Dean a moment to realize what he was looking at. "Jesus!" he said. "A submarine!"

"Exactly," the Russian said, descending the ladder right behind McMillan. "Permit me to show you just what it is we've been doing in this godforsaken wasteland. I think you will be impressed." He waved the pistol again. "Open the hatch and climb inside. No tricks, or I will shoot the woman."

Reluctantly, Dean stooped to obey the command.

21

The Art Room
NSA Headquarters
Fort Meade, Maryland
1841 hours EDT

"NIKOS-1 IS COMING OVER the *Lebedev*'s horizon now," Marie Telach reported. "We've got the target ship on-screen."

This time, the satellite would pass almost directly over the *Lebedev,* giving the observers in the Art Room the closest possible look at what was going on in the ship. Jeff Rockman entered keyboard commands that swung the spysat's cameras up to focus on the approaching vessel, zooming in for a closer look.

Rubens studied the images with care. Fourteen minutes had passed since the last satellite had orbited over the Area of Operations. Anything could have happened in that time.

"Do we have comm pickup yet?"

"Coming through now, sir," Telach reported.

"Three-one, One-one!" an urgent voice called, just intelligible through hissing static. "Get your people onto the bridge. The rest of you, start herding the tangos forward!"

"One-one, Four-three! We have resistance from the bow. Looks like two, maybe three November Indias behind the wreckage of that capstan!"

"Four-three! Take them down!"

"Copy that."

November Indias—"NI," for "naval infantry," the Russian equivalent of Marines. And "tango" was SEAL shorthand for terrorists, in this case a generic term for the enemy. From the sound of things, the SEALs in general had the upper hand, though there obviously were still pockets of resistance. As the satellite drew closer and closer to a point directly over the *Lebedev,* the details of the action unfolding on her deck became clearer.

The scene was a computer-enhanced blend of optical and IR imaging. Rubens could see individual SEALs and Russians on the huge ship's deck now. Heat sources inside the superstructure were vague, dark gray blurs, but the people in the open were easily distinguished, right down to details of uniforms and weapons.

"Can we raise Dean?" Rubens asked.

"We have a channel," Rockman told him. "We can try."

Establishing a direct channel to Dean had posed a serious technical challenge for the Art Room, one that had never been fully resolved. Dean's usual communications gear and bone implant receiver were useless without a clear satellite connection accessible through an antenna coiled up in his belt, so the only way to reach him was through the SEAL tactical comm net.

And using that net for private chitchat ran the risk of jamming up the SEALs' tactical communications in the middle of a firefight—something the SEAL CO would *not* appreciate.

But it was important that the Art Room let Dean know some key information about the Russian operation, information uncovered by Lia and Ilya in Sochi and added to day by day as the National Security Agency's master eavesdroppers continued to look over Kotenko's shoulder as he typed out e-mails and messages on his home computer.

And they would have only a brief window of opportunity as the NIKOS satellite passed overhead—two minutes at most.

"Sparrow, this is Bird Watcher," Marie Telach was saying from her workstation. "Sparrow, Bird Watcher."

Sparrow was Dean's code name for this op. Bird Watcher, obviously enough, was the Art Room.

Static hissed in response.

"Sparrow, Bird Watcher."

"Bird Watcher, clear this channel!" a new voice said, sharp and demanding.

Rubens picked up a microphone and held it to his mouth. "This is Bird Watcher," he said. "We need to get a message to—"

"Bird Watcher, this is Sierra Echo One-one," the voice said. "Your pet spook disobeyed orders and has gone MIA. Now *clear the fucking channel*!"

Rubens replaced the microphone. Sierra Echo One-one would be the call sign for the SEAL element commander, Lieutenant Taylor. Dean was missing?

"There!" Rockman said, pointing at the big screen. "That must be him!"

The satellite was now looking directly down on the *Lebedev*'s forward deck from the zenith. The watchers in the Art Room could see three figures now standing on some sort of platform extending from the ship's side off the starboard bow. It looked like a mooring platform for a small boat against the larger ship's waterline, and there appeared to be an oval hull tied up alongside, bobbing in the water. One figure was standing close beside the *Lebedev*'s hull, and even at the resolution of an image captured from space, the object in his hand was obviously a small pistol. The other two figures appeared to be unarmed, one a woman, one a man. The man had just opened a circular hatch on top of the oval hull and was now climbing down inside.

Rockman continued jockeying the satellite's camera array, keeping the scene on the monitor locked on the mooring platform.

Rubens picked up the microphone again. "One-one, this is Bird Watcher. Dean is being taken on board a small submarine off the ship's starboard bow!"

"Bird Watcher, this is Overwatch," another voice said. "Clear the channel. You are jeopardizing the operation!"

Rubens scowled. Overwatch was the handle for the Special Operations Command HQ team overseeing the SEAL op in the Arctic. The airwaves over the ice suddenly felt uncomfortably crowded.

It would be a mistake to keep pushing, Rubens decided. The opportunity to communicate with the SEALs would come again, if he didn't force the issue now. Right now, the SEALs had their plate full trying to take down a ship full of Russian marines, and Desk Three would not be helping things by screwing up their communications channels.

"Sir!" Telach called from her station. "We've got something new developing!"

"What is it?"

A monitor above her workstation showed the view from another satellite, this one looking down on a barren coastline, ocean surf on a gravel beach, and a long, obviously military airstrip. Two jet aircraft were lifting off from the runway, afterburners flaring. Two more military jets were in the process of taxiing to begin their takeoff roll.

"It's Mys Shmidta," Telach said. "Four MiG-35s are taking off from the base there. Two MiG-31s apparently took off ten minutes ago. They're all headed north . . . toward the *Lebedev*."

"We're getting heavy radio traffic from Wrangle Island," a communications technician reported. "Sounds like they've put a Midas in the air, too."

It had only been a matter of time, of course, before the Russians responded to the assault on the *Lebedev* with military force. Rubens had hoped, however, that they would be a little less efficient, a little slower on the uptake. He did some fast calculations.

The MiG-31 Foxhound was strictly an interceptor, with no weapons that would be of use against targets on the ground. It was also limited in range to less than seven hundred miles—which was why the Russians were scrambling a Midas, the NATO code name for an Ilyushin Il-78 tanker.

The Foxhounds would simply be escorts for the real muscle, the MiG-35 Fulcrum-Fs. The Fulcrum-F was one of their best strike fighters, with movable forward canards giving exceptional maneuverability, and a maximum speed of Mach 2.2 . . . say 1500 miles per hour. They wouldn't push that hard for very long, not without causing some seriously dangerous stress to engine and airframe. Mys Shmidta was about nine hundred miles south of the *Lebedev*; the Fulcrum-F's combat radius was well over twice that.

So make it nine hundred miles at Mach 2. . . .

The SEALs had perhaps forty minutes before some very nasty company arrived.

Mir 1
Arctic Ice Cap
82° 34' N, 177° 26' E
1042 hours, GMT – 12

It was a tight fit down the submarine's hatch. Dean eased himself through and stepped back from the ladder as McMillan's legs dropped into view, following him down. A moment later, the Russian joined them, moving to the far side of the narrow compartment so that he could keep them both covered with his Makarov.

"This is one of your civilian Mir submarines," Dean said, looking around. The overhead was low and cluttered with pipes and bundles of plastic-coated cables. At the forward end, a pair of bubble windows looked out and down into the ocean depths. "Adapted for deep-sea oil work?"

"Very good."

"They were using these things to take tourists down to the sea floor at the North Pole a year or two ago," McMillan said. "The Russians have had a lot of experience with the technology."

Their captor had pulled a small radio from his parka and was speaking into it urgently in Russian.

"Who is this guy?" Dean asked her. He had the feeling he'd seen the man before—in a file photo, perhaps.

"Feodor Golytsin," she replied. "He's some kind of bigwig with Gazprom."

That was it. Dean remembered his briefing with Carolyn, the pretty English woman at Menwith Hill.

"Right," he said. "He used to be a sub driver during the Soviet days, and then got promoted to admiral and given a shore billet. He got into trouble with Moscow and ended up in a gulag for three years."

Golytsin put the radio away. "You seem to know a lot about me, Mr. Dean."

"A little bird told me." Dean shrugged. "Actually, we have quite a sizable file on you. If anything happens to us, there will not be any place on this planet where you can hide."

It was a bluff but a reasonable one. People throughout the world, Dean knew, tended to have an inflated fear of the CIA and other American intelligence agencies and what they could actually do. He was hoping to play on that fear.

"I'm not too worried about that, Mr. Dean. Sufficient money can buy some very good hiding places. Look at Osama bin Laden."

Pointing with the pistol, Golytsin herded them back and away from the minisub's control panel. Reaching over, he began flipping switches in a particular pattern. Dean felt the ventilator system kick on, blowing cold air into the compartment, and felt a faint shudder through the deck as the power system came to life.

Dean watched the switches being thrown, trying to memorize their positions and order as they clicked on. He had a pretty good idea by now of where Golytsin intended to take them. If he and McMillan were to have a chance in hell of getting out, he would need to learn to pilot one of these things, on the fly and with only a single demonstration.

"So what are we waiting for, Admiral?" Dean said. He wondered if using the man's former rank would help forge a psychological bind he could use. A long shot, to be sure, but right now Dean was willing to try *anything*.

The deck shifted beneath their feet as the submarine suddenly rocked from side to side. Golytsin looked up and smiled. "For *that*." Footsteps rang through the compartment from overhead. Someone was clambering around on top of the Mir. With a clang, the topside hatch opened, and a pair of BDU-clad legs appeared coming down the ladder. The newcomer pulled the hatch shut above him, then joined the three of them in the now extremely cramped control room.

Dean recognized this man's face immediately. Sergei Braslov. Former Soviet Army, GRU, MVD, and, more recently, and as Johann Ernst, co-founder of the militant environmental group Greenworld. He, too, held a 9mm Makarov pistol in his hand.

Braslov said something to Golytsin in Russian, and the other man replied with a shrug and two words, "*Da, gaspodin!*" He turned and took his place at the controls of the little submarine.

Dean was trying to get a feel for the social dynamics here. He'd been thinking of Golytsin as the guy in charge of the Russian Operation Cold War, but if he'd just called Braslov *gaspodin*, meaning "sir" . . .

And there was that photograph of Braslov on a beach with Grigor Kotenko, who was very high indeed in the hierarchy of the Tambov group, the St. Petersburg branch of the Russian Mafiya.

Things were falling into place now. Braslov was the plumber, the fixer who made Kotenko's orders materialize. Golytsin was a high-ranking executive in Gazprom, a company targeted for takeover by the Russian mob. He'd served a short term in the Siberian gulag, just long enough to make some key contacts with prominent members of the Organizatsiya; when Golytsin reached out to push a power control forward, his sleeve fell back far enough to reveal some blue tattooing at his wrist . . . and tattoos, especially blue ones, were marks of Mafiya membership. When Golytsin had been freed, Kotenko or other high-ranking mob bosses might have made sure he got a position with Gazprom.

Creating a Mafiya beachhead within the largest natural gas company and the third-largest producer of petroleum in the world.

That left a few questions unanswered as yet. Why was the Mafiya so interested in GK-1? Had they, in fact, organized the project from scratch, or had they simply taken over an existing program? It might not matter. Either way, a sudden infusion of profits from the GK-1 drilling project might be the lever needed to move key power centers within Gazprom, facilitating a takeover of the entire company.

A takeover that would make the Russian Mafiya the owners and the beneficiaries of the largest energy company in the world.

As Golytsin pushed the throttle control forward, the whine of electric motors hummed from the aft end of the compartment. A joystick control pushed forward nosed the Mir minisub into a downward cant; steering the submarine, Dean thought, was a pretty simple seat-of-the-pants exercise, with one joystick controlling up-down and left-right maneuvers and the throttle providing forward thrust.

"Move away from the control panel," Braslov warned.

"I'm not touching anything," Dean replied. Carefully he placed his hands behind his back. "See? I just want to take in the view."

He doubted that Braslov was stupid enough to fire a weapon inside the Mir's sealed passenger compartment; a cracked port or a broken hydraulics line would end the voyage quite quickly. By taking the lead and making decisions for himself, however small those might be, Dean was snatching a tiny bit of psychological advantage from the situation and perhaps keeping their captors just a little off balance.

Braslov seemed about to bark an order, but Golytsin said something in Russian and laughed. Braslov shrugged. "Just touch nothing," he growled.

With his hands at his back, Dean stared out through the curved transparency on the starboard bow of the craft. There was very little to see. The water was lucidly, inexpressibly clear, like deep blue crystal, but there was simply nothing to see in all of that emptiness. As the Mir continued to descend, the blue grew rapidly deeper, darker, and more opaque, until the endless and absolute night of the deep abyss closed in.

Golytsin hit a pair of switches overhead, and a faint glow answered from outside. A few isolated particles danced in the Mir's lights like tiny white stars.

"How deep are we?" Dean asked.

Golytsin glanced at an LED readout on a TV monitor. "Four hundred meters," he said.

"And how deep can we go?"

"Quiet," Braslov ordered. "No more questions."

Electric motor shrilling, the Mir continued its steepening descent.

The Art Room
NSA Headquarters
Fort Meade, Maryland
1902 hours EDT

"Yes, sir," Rubens said. "Yes, sir, I understand. Thank you, Mr. President."

He hung up the red phone.

At least the White House operator had put him straight through to the President this time. Bing was no longer keeping him isolated, at least for the time being.

A map of the Arctic had been thrown up on one of the secondary wall monitors. A bright red triangle showed the position of a flight of six MiG-35s, now better than halfway between the mainland and the *Lebedev*.

At Mach 2, they were ten minutes from the *Lebedev* and the *Ohio*. The President had not been pleased with this latest turn of events. The encounter in the Arctic, what was supposed to have been a quick in-and-out by the SEALs to rescue the Americans held on the *Lebedev,* was fast turning into a deadly confrontation.

Over the past half hour, the Art Room had continued monitoring the situation on board the *Lebedev*. At last report, SEALs had taken over both the bridge and the engine room and a large number of seamen had been sequestered in a forward hold, under guard. Twelve American prisoners had been freed from an empty storeroom aft, and another, the seriously injured Commander Larson, had been found in the ship's sick bay.

Two were still missing—Harry Benford, the traitor, and the NSA employee Kathy McMillan.

With the *Lebedev* under the control of the SEAL assault team, the focus of the operation had shifted to getting the former hostages off of the Russian ship and across the ice to the *Ohio*. A long gangway had already been set up, allowing people to reach the ice off the *Lebedev*'s deck. A similar gangway, with safety lines and stanchions, had been rigged to let them clamber off the ice and onto the *Ohio*'s forward deck.

Everything was going perfectly according to plan, with three serious problems.

Russian MiGs were on the way, perhaps ten minutes out. The SEALs had to get the released prisoners off the ship and across the ice before those aircraft arrived, because when they did, the *Ohio* would be an easy and obvious target.

That was one. The second was worse. Fifteen minutes before, the *Ohio*'s sonar operator had reported a new underwater contact . . . almost certainly a miniature submarine of some sort. Minutes later, however, a second contact had been reported, this one larger, much larger . . . most likely a Russian attack submarine. Because of the difficulties of determining range and bearing in the weirdly echoing undersea terrain of the Arctic ice cap, it was impossible to tell just where the new contact was, or how close. But the chances were good that someone on the

Lebedev had called for help, possibly over an undersea hydrophone system, and the attack sub was moving in on the *Ohio*.

And Charlie Dean had been captured. From the look of things, he and the other NSA employee, McMillan, had been taken aboard a miniature Russian sub and were now heading into the ocean deeps, presumably to rendezvous with GK-1.

"The captain of the *Ohio* reports the last of the hostages are on board," a communications tech said. "The SEALs are evacuating the ship."

"Very well."

But once the SEALs were aboard, the *Ohio*'s skipper would have a deadly choice. If he stayed on the surface, he would be vulnerable to attack by the incoming MiGs. If he submerged, he might drop squarely into the track of torpedoes fired by the Russian sub. Damned if you do . . . damned if you don't.

This was not shaping up to be one of America's better days. . . .

Mir 1
Arctic Ice Cap
82° 34' N, 177° 26' E
1108 hours, GMT – 12

There were lights in the darkness.

Dean leaned forward in an awed silence as the Mir continued its descent. According to the monitor readout, they were now at eight hundred meters, half a mile beneath the ice-locked surface of the Arctic Ocean. And GK-1 was just now coming into view.

The thing was enormous—at least a hundred yards long, perhaps more. Bow and stern had the look of a conventional surface-going ship, but they were joined by a relatively slender center section holding the two together like the bar on a set of barbells. At first, Dean nearly didn't recognize what he was seeing as a *ship*; it was moored in the darkness bow down, which is not the usual attitude for a vessel designed to move along the ocean's surface.

Five massive cables stretched out and down from the bow, vanishing into the darkness below. Several more slender cables reached straight up from the stern, tethering the structure to the *Lebedev* half a mile overhead. Something like a slender needle extended from the structure's bow straight down into the abyss—the drill itself, Dean assumed. On the stern—the highest point on the ship in this position—was a round well or receptacle. Dean could make out one of the drill pipe sections hanging suspended just above the structure's stern. Something like the remote-controlled arm of the Space Shuttle reached out of the stern, bent back at an elbow joint, and grasped the pipe section as though preparing to insert it into the receptacle.

But nothing was moving. Work, it seemed, had halted.

The technical challenges in designing the thing, Dean thought, must have been staggering . . . but the payoff was a stable drill rig that could operate half a mile beneath storms and rough seas, beneath moving ice, and well off the radar of any environmental groups that might oppose drilling on the ocean floor.

"Not much happening," he commented to Golytsin. "What is it, Russian workers' holiday?"

"No. We've run into a . . . snag, I believe you Americans call it."

"Don't tell them any more," Braslov ordered. "They don't need to know."

"It hardly matters," Golytsin said with a shrug. "If Kotenko doesn't order them killed, they'll still never be allowed to leave Russia."

"Methane," Dean said, venturing a guess. "Methane clathrates on the bottom. Isn't it?"

"You're too smart for your own good, old man," Braslov said.

Dean had received a last-moment briefing update from Rubens before the *Ohio* had moved to her new position off the *Lebedev*'s port side. It turned out that a report Lia had seen on Kotenko's computer had concerned immense deposits of methane clathrate discovered on the seabed beneath GK-1. Evidently there'd already been one accident, fortunately rather minor. Work had been suspended until the problem could be resolved.

The update had included a brief discussion of clathrates, also known as methane hydrate or methane ice. Apparently outcrops of the stuff were often associated with stretches of seabed rich in petroleum and also marked fields of natural gas bubbling up to the surface through fissures or geological fault lines in the ocean floor. Methane—natural gas—formed in underground pockets. When it percolated through to the ocean at depths of over about five hundred meters, the cold and extreme pressure of those depths sometimes formed clathrate fields. As Dean understood it, water froze into normal water ice on the sea floor and adhering to it and within it, rather like permafrost, clinging to the bottom instead of floating to the surface. As the water froze, it trapped molecules of methane—CH_4—inside its crystalline structure. A piece of methane hydrate liberated from the seabed to a laboratory counter looked like an ordinary chunk of ice. Set a match to it, however, and the ice *burned* with a hot, bright red flame as the methane was liberated.

Methane clathrates had been advanced as a possible solution to the energy crisis, since it appeared that there was more methane locked up inside seabed deposits of clathrates than there were reservoirs of natural gas under dry land. But they also posed certain risks of unknown magnitude. A few climatologists had actually suggested that periods of global warming in the past had been caused by massive releases of seabed methane. A mass extinction of life on ancient Earth—like the one that had wiped out the dinosaurs, but almost 200 million years earlier and on a far larger scale—had been blamed by some on an explosive release of undersea methane into the atmosphere.

"It could put a real stopper on your pet project, couldn't it?" Dean continued after a moment's silence. "I mean, you drill into the sea floor and find you're drilling through ice. What happened? The drilling broke some pieces off that floated to the surface and ignited?"

"GK-1 sustained minor damage when a large block of methane ice floated up from the bottom and struck one of the anchoring cables," Golytsin said. "Mainly, though, Gazprom called a halt to activities while an assessment was made on the possibility of harvesting methane ice in quantity from the ocean floor."

Some more pieces fell into place for Dean. The organized-crime groups trying to infiltrate Gazprom were doing so through the GK-1 drilling project. Probably the revenue from newfound petroleum was going to give Kotenko and Tambov leverage within the organization.

But now another branch of Gazprom had interfered, stopping work at the GK-1 site while decisions were made about the natural gas resources discovered there. A power struggle? Or simply a delay? It would be interesting to know what was happening within Gazprom's halls of corporate power.

The Mir sub drew closer to the undersea station now, approaching the stern of the submerged and vertical ship. In the glare of the outside lights, Dean saw other Mir submersibles docked with their upper hatches snug against a massive tube, evidently a boarding tunnel or air lock.

"What kind of pressure do you maintain in there?" Dean asked.

"Standard sea level pressure," was Golytsin's surprising answer. "Just as inside the Mir. We haven't had to work with high atmospheric pressures in some years now. We build very *good* in Russia, you see. . . ."

Impressive, given that the outside seawater pressure on the GK-1 must be incredible. Dean did some fast calculations. The pressure exerted by seawater went up by .445 pounds per square inch for every additional foot of depth, he knew. Eight hundred meters was about twenty-six hundred feet and a bit, times .445 . . .

At a rough estimate, the pressure at this depth was over half a ton per square inch. Most of the outside work at GK-1 must be handled by robots or with miniature submarines like the Mir, equipped with mechanical arms. He noticed that there weren't any windows or portholes on the vessel, not even at the lower edge of the stern section, where he expected the bridge to be.

Skillfully Golytsin maneuvered the Mir underneath the docking tube, watching the approach through a TV monitor relaying the view from a camera mounted on the Mir's dorsal hull next to the hatch. For a moment, Dean had memories of space-docking events he'd seen, of Apollo spacecraft docking with Lunar Excursion Modules, or the Space Shuttle connecting with the space station.

There was the faintest of bumps, and a hollow clang. Golytsin threw a series of switches. "We're home," he said.

"The last home *they'll* ever know," Braslov said with an unpleasant grin.

22

**SSGN *Ohio*
Arctic Ice Cap
82° 34' N, 177° 26' E
1112 hours, GMT – 12**

"BRIDGE, RADAR!" AN URGENT VOICE called over the intercom. "Two bogies incoming at very high speed, bearing one-seven-five, range twenty miles! We've got *maybe* fifty seconds!"

"Very well," Captain Grenville replied. He glanced at the southern sky, saw nothing, and turned his attention back to the forward deck. The last of the Navy SEALs scrambled up the gangway. A deck detail of sailors started to haul the gangway in. Grenville picked up a loud-hailer. "Chief of the Boat!"

Master Chief Fuselli, bulky in his Navy-issue parka, turned and looked up at the weather bridge.

"Jettison the gangway!" Grenville called.

Fuselli tossed him a salute and started bellowing orders. In seconds, the lines making the gangway fast had been freed and the long metal bridge had been heaved over onto the ice.

He took another look at the *Lebedev*, just one hundred yards to the north. When the firefight had finally sputtered out, the SEALs had disarmed the crew and herded them into a hold, but it hadn't taken long for Russians hiding elsewhere in the ship to set their comrades free. There'd been a couple of gunshots from the *Lebedev* as the SEALs crossed the ice, but nothing concerted and nothing accurate.

"Lookouts below," he ordered. The two lookouts in their cockpits aft of the weather bridge began securing their posts. One pulled in the fluttering American ensign.

Grenville's major concern at the moment was the fact that he didn't know what the Russians were going to do. Those incoming aircraft might be lining up a bombing run on their very first pass . . . and that would be very, very bad. More likely, they would overfly first, to get an eyes-on look at the ships in the ice and to make sure they knew which targets were friendly, which hostile. Then they would attack if, in fact, they'd been ordered to do so.

Grenville assumed that the Russian pilots had those orders. From their point of view, their people had been attacked first, on board the *Lebedev*. They would assume the commandos had come from his boat. Besides, right now the *Ohio* was the only American target around.

Master Chief Fuselli was the last man down the forward hatch. Grenville heard it bang shut, saw the wheel dog tight.

"Diving Officer of the Watch," he said over the intercom as his hand came down on the dive klaxon button. "Dive the boat!"

He turned to descend into the *Ohio*'s sail but stopped as he heard a low-voiced growl, a distant, trembling thunder. He looked south . . . and then, almost before his brain could register what he was seeing, two sleek high-performance jet aircraft streaked in low above the ice, traveling almost wingtip to wingtip. He had the briefest of instants to take in details—broad, delta wings; canards riding far forward under the cockpits; the glaring flash of sunlight off of canopies; the red-star-inside-white-star roundels on the wings.

MiG-35s, definitely. They passed two hundred yards east of the *Ohio,* streaking past the *Lebedev* and dwindling to specks above the northern horizon. Grenville heard a far-off roar emerge from the dwindling thunder of engines and wondered what it was.

Then he knew. *Cheering.* The crew of the *Lebedev* was cheering.

He descended the ladder into the *Ohio*'s sail.

The *Ohio*'s ballast tanks were already flooding by the time he reached the control room. "Captain on deck!" the Officer of the Watch cried as he walked in.

"As you were. Radar! What're our friends up there doing?"

"Bogies have made a full one-eighty and are coming back at us, bearing three-five-four, range five miles. Looks like an attack run, sir."

"Very well. Diving officer. Take us down. Make depth two-five-zero feet."

"Make depth two-five-zero feet, aye, aye, sir."

Bridge operations on an American submarine were a meticulous choreography of order and order repeated back, each step checked and checked again to make sure a command had been properly heard and was being properly executed.

Grenville could hear the crack and rumble of ice on the hull. Normally, a submarine was moving forward as it dove and the diving planes were adjusted to literally "fly" the vessel into the depths. Starting from a dead stop surrounded by ice was a different matter. All you could do was pull the plug and go straight down.

Those MiGs would be almost on them now, bearing in from the north. What were the Russian pilots going to try to do? What were their orders?

He held the tactical layout in his mind . . . Ohio *here* . . . Lebedev *there* . . . *aircraft* there . . . and he smiled.

If they were trying for an attack run, the *Lebedev* was in the way. The ol' *Ohydro* would have a few more crucial moments to slip back into her natural element.

GK-1
Beneath the Arctic Ice Cap
82° 34' N, 177° 26' E
1112 hours, GMT – 12

The Mir's hatch clanged open and Braslov climbed up the ladder. Dean followed, then McMillan, with Golytsin coming out last. Braslov gestured with his pistol. "This way."

Although the submerged structure was huge, the livable portions were relatively few and cramped, which made sense given the tremendous pressure of their surroundings. Most of GK-1's internal structure was given over to ballast and trim tanks, and to the machinery necessary for turning and maintaining the drill.

The passageway into which they'd emerged was so low that the three men had to stoop slightly to negotiate it; Dean noticed several emergency survival dry suits hanging from a rack along one side of the passageway—available, he assumed, in case there was a need for an emergency evacuation.

The sight of those emergency suits, and the claustrophobic feel of the corridor, drove home to Dean the nightmarish aspects of life on board this facility. It was cramped, it was damp, and it was *cold,* with moisture condensing on every exposed metal surface. Outside those curving steel decks, bulkheads, and overheads, the ocean was pressing in with an inexorable, crushing pressure of better than half a ton over every square inch. If anything went wrong down here, did the crew have any hope of escape at all? With an air pressure of one standard atmosphere on board, they weren't going to be able to go outside without a very long period of pressurization inside an air lock. The only way to the surface in an emergency would be on board one of those miniature submarines docked outside.

As Dean walked, bent forward with his head brushing bundles of pipes and wiring with each step, it was all too easy to imagine those tons upon tons of seawater pressing in from every side.

What a hell of a way to live. . . .

The passageway led them over the control room, rather than past it. A large, open hatchway in the deck gave access to what was obviously the GK-1's control center twelve feet below, a room thirty feet long filled with monitors, workstations, and consoles, and with both a ladder and an open elevator platform against the aft bulkhead leading up to the hatch at his feet. The perspective was odd and took some getting used to; it took Dean a moment to realize that the vessel was designed to ride both like a normal ship on the surface and in its vertical configuration during drilling operations. When the structure was rotated into the work configuration, decks became aft bulkheads, and forward bulkheads became decks.

There appeared to be eight or ten men on duty in the control center, though there were workstations for more than that. A large monitor on the forward bulkhead was showing what looked like a stark black-and-white image of the sea floor, though at this angle it was difficult to be sure. A murmur of Russian voices rose from the compartment.

Braslov gave Dean a hard nudge in the back with the muzzle of his weapon. "Keep moving," he growled.

How many people were on board the facility? A normal drilling rig might have as few as fifty or sixty people on board, while one of the giants might have a population of hundreds. There would be other crew spaces—sleeping quarters, a mess deck that might double as a rec room, laundry facilities, probably lab spaces for analyzing core samples.

They reached a turning in the passageway and a door—set in the bulkhead this time, rather than in the floor. Golytsin produced a set of keys and fumbled at the lock. The door opened, and a young man tried to emerge.

"Hold it right there," Braslov said, pointing his weapon at the prisoner. "Back!"

"Let me out of here!" the prisoner cried. "You have no right—"

"You two," Braslov said, turning to Dean and McMillan. "Inside."

"What's this?" Dean said. "The brig?"

"It'll do for now, until we decide what to do with you. Go on."

Dean followed McMillan inside. It was a storeroom, mostly empty, but with a pile of musty-smelling mattresses at the back, stacked crates labeled with Cyrillic lettering, and shelves of folded sheets and blankets.

"There's a bucket for your . . . sanitary needs," Golytsin said, pointing to one corner. "I'm sorry about the accommodations, but as you can imagine, we're a little cramped for space down here. Someone will bring food to you a little later."

"If you're lucky," Braslov added with a sour sneer.

The door slammed shut, and they heard the sound of Golytsin's key turning in the lock.

Dean looked at their new roommate. "Harry Benford, I presume?"

The man's eyes widened. "Yeah! How did you know?"

"Lucky guess."

"Listen! They're trying to blame me for murdering Ken Richardson! It's a damned lie! I never murdered anyone!"

"Oh? Why would they do that?"

"I don't know! It . . . it was Commander Larson. He shot Ken. Then I hit the commander with a pry bar, took him down. But then the Russians came in and arrested everybody! And they took me off from the others and brought me down here. And now they say they're going to blame *me* for the murder!"

"Sounds like your playmates play pretty rough," Dean said.

"Kathy! You gotta believe me! I didn't kill anybody!"

"Harry, right now we're all in a pretty bad fix. I suggest you sit down, be quiet, and let us think about how we're going to get out of this."

Benford seemed inclined to argue. "They can't do this to us!"

Dean stepped between McMillan and Benford, towering over the smaller man. "Do as the lady says," he growled. "We'll worry about who did what later, after we get out of here."

"Who are you, anyway?"

"Charlie Dean. I'm here to help."

"Looks to me like you're a prisoner just like us! Fat load of help *you'll* be!"

"Sit down and shut up." Dean considered whether or not to let Benford know how much he knew and decided that the information might give them a psychological edge. "Just so you know, Benford, we *know* you were feeding information to the Russians, we know you gave them blueprints to help them build this station—possibly illegally—and we know the Russians planned to use a murder at the NOAA station as a pretext for taking it over. If they knew about the murder in advance, then the murder was planned ahead of time . . . and that strongly suggests that you *were* the killer."

As Dean spoke, Benford's eyes got wider and wider, his mouth open. He tried to interrupt at several points but was unable to do more than sputter protests.

"You . . . you're with them! It's all lies! . . ."

"You can prove your innocence later. Now shut up!"

Sullen, Benford retreated to the back of the storeroom, collapsing on a mattress on the deck with his back to Dean and McMillan.

"I'm Kathy McMillan," she said.

"I know. Charlie Dean."

"Are you—"

He held up his hand, then tapped his ear. "Never say anything," he told her.

Her eyes widened slightly, and she nodded. Dean didn't know if the room was bugged or not, but the oldest trick in the book was to put prisoners in a room where they could talk freely with one another—and listen in from somewhere nearby.

"So . . . is that all true?" she asked Dean quietly. "He was a Russian agent?"

"Looks that way," Dean told her, his voice a low murmur. Even if there were no hidden mikes, he didn't want Benford listening, either. "He had a small, one-channel receiver. We think the Russians gave him a signal and he murdered Richardson to give them their excuse to come in."

"Why'd the Russians blame him, then?"

Dean shrugged. "Probably because it's just not that

plausible that the commander of a NOAA scientific expedition would kill the leader of the Greenworld contingent at his base. Doesn't make sense."

"I don't know," McMillan said. "There was no love lost between those guys. Scientists and nutcase environmentalists. It was bad news, believe me."

"You're not serious!"

She smiled. "No, I honestly don't think Commander Larson would have killed anyone . . . not even someone as annoying as Richardson."

"If it's any consolation, the rest of the expedition people were being evacuated off the *Lebedev* about the time I ran into you and Golytsin."

"That's good." She folded her arms and shivered. The storeroom was cold. Dean went to a storage shelf, pulled down a military-style wool blanket, and draped it over her shoulders. "Thank you. Aren't you cold?"

He shook his head. "This dry suit's almost too warm." He was eyeing the door, the bulkheads, the overhead. "We need to think of a way to get out of here."

"I don't suppose you brought along any James Bond gadgets? A thimble-sized laser to cut through the door, maybe? An origami flamethrower?"

Dean made a face. "Gadgets have their place, I suppose," he said. "But the only thing that's *essential* is right here." He tapped his forehead.

In fact, Dean was wishing he'd brought along something—the components of a binary explosive, for instance, with which he could have shattered the lock. Lacking that, however, the possibilities included finding something here in the storeroom that would help them break out—unlikely—and waiting for the bad guys to show up and overpower them.

"Let's check those crates and see what we have to work with," he said.

SSGN *Ohio*
Arctic Ice Cap
82° 34' N, 177° 26' E
1120 hours, GMT – 12

"You *knew* those guys weren't going to shoot at us, Skipper!" Lieutenant Dolby said. "How?"

Grenville gave a modest shrug. "They zipped past south to north, pulled a major U-turn, and came straight back for us, north to south. But on that bearing, the *Lebedev* was between us and them. At their altitude, they weren't about to drop anything nasty, not without hitting their own people. Hell, they were lucky if they didn't clip the *Lebedev*'s mast."

The *Ohio* drifted once again in her preferred world, the abyssal deep, her screw turning over just enough to give her way.

Grenville picked up a microphone and keyed it. "Sonar, this is the captain."

"Sonar, aye," came the immediate response.

"Talk to me, Chief. What's out there?"

"It's pretty much a hash, sir," Sonar Chief Kevin Mayhew replied. "Ice grinding. Lots of incidentals from the Russian ships." There was a puzzled hesitation. "I . . . I think they're cheering over there."

"You can hear that, Mayhew?"

"That's what it sounds like, sir."

"What about submarines?"

"We had two on the waterfall for a while there, sir. Sierra One-one-five was the midget. The library tagged Sierra One-one-six as a probable Victor III. Right now, they're both shut down. Not a thing on the boards."

"Any sign of the *Pittsburgh*?"

"Sir, they could be right alongside and all we'd hear would be the hole in the water."

"Well, do your best listening, understand? I want to know the moment you hear a shrimp fart."

"Shrimp fart. Aye, aye, sir."

The *Ohio* had been in terrible danger while exposed on the surface. She might pack 154 Tomahawk cruise missiles in her vertical launch tubes, capable of striking targets fifteen hundred miles away, but she had absolutely no way to defend herself against an air strike save by seeking the quiet safety of the depths.

Now, however, she was in far greater danger. It was one of the axioms of submarine warfare: the best way to kill a submarine is with another sub, and somewhere out in all of that ice-noise hash, there was a Russian Victor III waiting . . . and listening.

Victor IIIs were decent attack submarines—about the same size as the American Los Angeles boats but a little lighter, a little slower. Some of them had an odd eight-blade screw consisting of two co-rotating four-bladed props, which gave them a unique signature on passive sonar. Grenville had dogged a Victor or two back when he'd skippered the *Miami* and, earlier, when he'd been the XO on the *Cincinnati*.

Now a Victor was dogging him.

When they surfaced, the surrounding ice had formed a protective bastion. The only way to hit the *Ohio* with a torpedo would be to have it detonate under her keel, and the chances were good that with all of that surrounding sonar-reflecting ice, the enemy wouldn't even be able to locate the *Ohio* well enough to target her.

Down here in the deep, though, it was different. The Victor was listening for them, trying to sort their sound signature out from the same background hash that Chief Mayhew had complained about. And the *Ohio* was listening for the Victor.

The *Ohio* had three major advantages, however, and

Grenville intended to take full advantage of them both. American subs were the quietest in the world; it would take some very good sonar people on the other side to pick her out of the background noise. American submarine technology was the best as well, especially as demonstrated by the *Ohio*'s sonar suite and computers.

And finally, and more important by far, American submariners were the best trained in the world and their sonar operators were capable of seemingly magical feats of sensitivity and accuracy.

If that shrimp did cut a hot one, Mayhew and his team of sonar techs would hear it.

GK-1
Beneath the Arctic Ice Cap
82° 34' N, 177° 26' E
1122 hours, GMT − 12

"Not much here," McMillan said. She slumped back, the set of her shoulders showing her despair.

"Well, you didn't think they were going to lock us in the storeroom with all the guns in it, did you?" Dean said. "But there's stuff here we might be able to use." He held up a one-liter tin of stewed tomatoes, hefting it. "This could make a nasty club."

"Kind of awkward."

"Yeah," Dean admitted, dropping the can back into an open crate. "And it doesn't quite have the same reach as a nine-millimeter Parabellum."

They'd been going through a sampling of the crates stored in the narrow compartment. Peeking into three of them, so far, they'd found only foodstuffs—canned goods and boxes, all of it, and not a single bottle that might be judiciously broken into a makeshift knife. They'd examined the wooden slats of the crates themselves, but the wood was soft pine, each slat only a couple of feet long, and they were fastened together with staples rather than nails. You could do some damage with the things, surely— but not against a couple of alert men holding pistols.

He'd considered bunching a wool blanket up in a big wad and using it as a shield as he rushed the guard. Would a crumpled blanket absorb the kinetic energy of a 9mm round with a muzzle velocity of about twelve hundred feet per second? Or would the bullet slice right through and kill him before he'd taken two steps? Dean wasn't sure, and given the possible consequences, he wasn't about to experiment.

The best plan Dean had been able to come up with so far was to bundle a blanket over a guard when he came in with a tray of food and pummel him into unconsciousness with a can of vegetables. That might work *if* the guard was alone—extremely unlikely if he was carrying food— and *if* he carelessly stepped into the room without ordering the occupants back against the far wall with their hands in plain sight before he entered.

These people were not stupid. They weren't going to make many mistakes, certainly not dumb-ass Hollywood villain goofs.

He leaned back against a damp metal bulkhead. "Well, a fine James Bond *I* turned out to be. Sorry, Miss McMillan." He was still wrestling with possibilities. Maybe if they could cut a thin strip from one of those sheets and use it as a garrote. The trick would be to get the tear started without scissors or a knife. Maybe he could do it with his teeth? . . .

"I'm Kathy. And you're doing just fine."

He found he was almost missing the presence of Jeff Rockman or Marie Telach in his head. With his personal transceiver working, they would be feeding him all sorts of helpful advice about now . . . something involving turning urine and stewed tomatoes into plastic explosives, perhaps.

Of course, even without the problems of maintaining clear communications this far north, there was no way a radio signal could penetrate the thick tempered steel of this compartment, the pressure hull of the facility itself, and half a mile of water, plus the ice on top of that.

He was about as isolated from outside as it was possible for a person to be.

"The way I see it," Kathy mused, "they can't really afford to just out and out shoot us. They need to know how much we know about their operation. About this base."

He nodded. "Not only that; our side knows we're here. They can't make us disappear and hope our people forget about us. They won't."

"You know, I think the Russians, the organized-crime bosses, I mean, have been really scared of bad publicity." She looked pointedly at Benford. "*He* was put in to give Greenworld a bad name, I think. To discredit them, and anything they might say about Russian drilling in the Arctic."

"Makes sense," Dean said. "What can you tell me about Golytsin?"

"He seems to be the guy in charge of all of this. . . . At least he was until the mean one with the scar showed up. Golytsin takes orders from him."

"Braslov."

"That's him." She folded her arms and shuddered. "He's bad news. Golytsin? He made some pretty terrible threats when he questioned me, when he first brought me aboard the Russian ship . . . things like turning me over to the crew if I didn't tell him who I was really working for, or leaving me out on the ice to freeze, but I think it was all bluff. He's been looking after the needs of the prisoners, gave orders that they weren't to be hurt or molested in any way. I think . . ."

"What?"

"My impression is that he's proud of being Russian . . . a patriot, you know? But he sees the people above him being assholes, maybe even doing things that will hurt Russia in the long run. He has to obey their orders, but I don't think he likes it."

"Well, that's something we might be able to use, then. . . ."

Keys rattled in the lock outside. Dean shoved the opened crate aside and stood up. The door swung open, revealing Golytsin and a man in a Russian naval infantry uniform, both of them holding Makarov pistols.

Golytsin glanced at the open crate. "Hungry?" he asked. He pointed the pistol at Dean and gestured with it. "You. Come with me. No sudden movements, please."

"Where are you taking him?" Kathy demanded.

"Never mind." Golytsin gestured again. "Come!"

Hands raised, Dean stepped out into the passageway and watched as Benford and McMillan were locked in once more.

"It's time, Mr. Dean," Golytsin said, "that you and I had a frank chat. *This* way."

23

SSGN *Ohio*
Arctic Ice Cap
82° 34' N, 177° 26' E
1132 hours, GMT − 12

"BRIDGE, SONAR!"

"Go ahead."

"Sir . . . the shrimp just cut a loud one."

"Stay on it, Mayhew. I'm coming over."

The *Ohio*'s sonar room was located just in front of the control room, adjoining it off the starboard passageway forward. Grenville walked down the passageway and stepped into the curtained-off room, a narrow compartment with four console workstations side-by-side, with a large acoustic spectrum analyzer at the far end.

At each station, display screens could be configured to show any of several key elements of the cascade of sonar data entering the *Ohio*'s AN/BSY-1 combat system, pronounced "Busy-One" by the men riding the boards.

Sonar Chief Kevin Mayhew was the sonar watch supervisor. At the other workstations, an ST/1 and two ST/2s sat at their boards, headphones on, their eyes locked on their sonar displays.

"Whatcha got, Chief?"

"An incidental, Captain. Wanna hear?"

"Play it for me."

Mayhew touched a key. His sonar display winked out, then came back on, with a green trace drawing out a horizontal line. Grenville held a headphone to his ear. A moment later, he heard a sharp scrape, a thump, and a hiss as the green tracing zapped up and down like an earthquake seismograph. As the initial sound faded, he heard something in the background, a fluttering rattle . . . like the piece of cardboard he sometimes had attached to hit the spokes of his bicycle when he was a kid.

"Hear it, sir?"

"He bumped the ceiling."

"Yes, sir. And did you catch at the end? . . ."

Grenville smiled. "He throttled up, probably to get the hell out of there, but he did it too fast. He was cavitating."

"Exactly my thought, sir."

Increase your speed too quickly and tiny bubbles built up on the surface of your propeller blades. When they popped, it made a hell of a racket, an effect known as cavitation.

"It's not the *'Burgh*," Mayhew added. "Not a damned rookie trick like that. And we got enough of the engine noise to analyze. It's a Victor III . . . probably the same one we recorded a year ago in the North Atlantic."

"Not such a rookie trick, Chief," Grenville said. "Let's not underestimate him."

If you scraped the ceiling of ice, it was because you were hugging the ice cap, staying tucked in close . . . and the only reason to do *that* was to lose yourself in the scatter of sound bouncing off the ice. In a way, it was like a helicopter pilot flying nape-of-the-earth in order to stay hidden for as long as possible.

Only very *good* sub drivers would try that.

And here was another possibility as well, a chilling one.

That Russian sub driver out there might have brushed against an ice ridge and put the pedal to the metal for just an instant *deliberately*, knowing the American boat would hear . . . and just possibly respond a little too hastily, a little too carelessly.

No, Grenville did not intend to underestimate this fellow.

"Best guess on range and bearing, Chief."

"Strongest registration was starboard side fairwater, sir. Range . . ." Mayhew screwed up his face, as though unwilling to go out on too slender a limb. "Not close, like right alongside close. Maybe one mile. Maybe two."

"Good enough." Grenville picked up an intercom mike. "Control Room, Captain. Helm, come right nine-zero degrees. Ahead slow."

"Helm right nine-zero degrees, ahead slow, aye, aye," was the response.

The *Ohio* was turning directly toward the Russian boat, slowly and quietly. The only question was whether the Russians had spotted them yet.

GK-1
Beneath the Arctic Ice Cap
82° 34' N, 177° 26' E
1134 hours, GMT – 12

Golytsin and the Russian marine led Dean down the long passageway, up a stairway, and directed him at last into a small and nondescript office. It might, Dean thought, have been Golytsin's office while he was aboard the submerged GK-1 platform, but it could as easily have been a workplace for any administrator who needed one. There was a desk and two chairs, a computer and a telephone, but nothing in the way of photographs or decorations, books or paperwork, no *human* touch.

The marine stayed outside as Golytsin closed the door and gestured at one of the chairs. "Have a seat."

"Is this where the torture starts?" Dean asked.

Golytsin shrugged, then dropped into the chair behind the desk and clattered an entry into the computer keyboard. "If you like."

Dean was measuring the man. Golytsin was a little older than him, he thought—probably in his late fifties or early sixties. He had the look of a senior corporate executive.

He also looked lean and fit. If he spent much of his time behind a desk, he also must work out a lot, or get out into the country to work off the fat. Dean thought he could probably take Golytsin in hand-to-hand, but that assumption was by no means assured.

Besides, he still had the Makarov, and Dean's chair was a good five feet from the desk. *And* there was the marine outside.

Golytsin completed the entry, then turned his full attention to Dean. "To tell you the truth, however, I dislike the idea of torture. I'm sure there are things we could do to you that would in quite short order have you telling us everything we want to know . . . or everything you *think* we want to know, anything at all to stop the pain. And yet, what would be the point? At the end, we still wouldn't know whether you'd told us the truth or not. We would, in fact, have to start all over, at the beginning, and go through the whole process again. And again. And yet again. And then *again,* but this time with drugs, questioning and cross-questioning each of your answers. And then do it again with you wired to a polygraph.

"And we keep doing it all again until we can tell from changes in your responses at varying levels of stress whether you are, in fact, telling the truth . . . or making up stories, what you think we want to hear, simply in order to make us stop. That is the trouble with torture, you know. It takes so very *long* to arrive at the truth."

"That, and the fact that you can never be sure you've actually gotten there," Dean agreed. "Have you broken the subject? Or is he a very talented actor? Or might he truly believe what he's telling you . . . but what he believes is a lie because someone lied to him?"

"Exactly! So . . . you can see my dilemma. I very much want to know about you, Mr. Dean. Who you work for. Why you've come here. What you know about this operation. What your employers know. What your employers might plan to do about us in the future. I *could* torture you until you told me . . . but I'd never be sure I was getting accurate information."

"I appreciate your predicament."

In fact, Dean was wondering where this line of conversation was leading. Golytsin evidently had tried threats of torture or sexual abuse to get information from Kathy. Why was he using such a markedly different approach with him?

"I tend to believe, personally, that torture is counterproductive." Golytsin hesitated, then added, "Of course, not everyone shares this belief, you understand. And not everyone cares that it's counterproductive. There are people who enjoy torturing subjects simply because . . . because they very much *like* doing it. My colleague, Sergei Braslov, for instance . . ."

Then it clicked for Dean. Of course! Golytsin was trying different psychological approaches, probing for weakness. With Kathy, he'd seen a woman, vulnerable, alone, a prisoner on a ship full of hostile male strangers . . . and he'd threatened her with rape, or with a cold and hideously lonely death exposed on the ice cap, with no one to help. With Dean, Golytsin was trying to engage him in an almost friendly, chatty relationship—not comrades-at-arms but certainly with the feeling that they all were in this together . . . with just a hint that the *other* guy might be a psychopathic monster capable of anything. It was, in fact, a variant of the old good-cop/bad-cop ploy, where a prisoner would willingly confide in the "nice" interrogator in order to avoid the mean one.

Okay. Dean could play this game.

In fact, Dean thought, he had an advantage over Golytsin. The Russian knew nothing about Dean whatsoever, but Dean already knew some of Golytsin's background. He'd been a submarine skipper. That meant he was smart . . . and he knew psychology. He was also supremely *loyal*—back in the bad old Soviet days, Russian sub drivers were selected almost exclusively on that one factor alone. However, he'd been outspoken enough in his opposition to the war in Afghanistan that he'd been imprisoned. That suggested both a willingness to think for himself and the possibility that his loyalty might lie to his country, rather than to his government.

Feodor Golytsin, Dean thought, was a true patriot, a lover of Mother Russia willing to risk arrest and prison in her defense.

A patriot, but one working for the Organizatsiya, a criminal organization that had already done incalculable harm to post-Soviet Russia.

And at that moment, Dean saw Golytsin's tragic flaw.

"Ah, yes," Dean said, nodding. "Braslov. We have quite a file on him, you know."

Dean saw the flicker of interest in Golytsin's eyes. "File. And you work for? . . ."

"The Agency, of course." Carefully, he didn't specify *which* agency.

"Really? Some of my . . . superiors are of the opinion

that the American NSA has been rather interested in their activities recently."

Dean waved a hand carelessly, as if dismissing the thought. "Don't be ridiculous. The NSA are mathematicians, technicians, and electronic eavesdroppers. They tap telephones. They don't even have *field agents,* for God's sake!"

"No. No, that's what I always thought." Golytsin was looking at him strangely, as though wondering if Dean was being honest and aboveboard . . . , or putting on an act. He would be suspicious if Dean seemed *too* cooperative. "So, Mr. Dean. You claim to be a CIA agent?"

Dean spotted what was either a bit of carelessness . . . or a trap. "CIA *agents* are foreign locals recruited to work for us, one way or another. The people working out of Langley, or running local agents in other countries, are called *case officers.*"

"Quite so. Quite so."

"And I gather you're with Gazprom," Dean said, taking the initiative. "You play with the big boys."

"Actually, Mr. Dean, I believe that *I'm* the one conducting this . . . interview."

"Ah. And would the information you're looking for be for you? For the Gazprom Board of Directors? Or . . ." Dean leaned forward in a properly conspiratorial manner. "Or is it for the Organizatsiya?"

Golytsin looked startled, then uncomfortable. "What do you know about them?"

Dean shrugged. "Enough. I know Sergei Braslov works for them. As I said, we have quite a file on him. And we know he works for Grigor Kotenko, and Tambov. Kotenko would be the guy pulling the strings on *this* operation."

"And why would the American CIA be interested in

them? What happens inside Russia has nothing to do with American foreign interests."

"Come, now, Admiral," Dean said. He paused. "It *was* Admiral, was it not?"

Golytsin grimaced. "Actually, I was deprived of that rank."

"By the Politburo board that censured your stand on the war in Afghanistan. I know. The Soviet leaders of that era had gotten the Rodina into some serious trouble, and you tried to point that out. They didn't appreciate the attempt, I seem to recall."

Anger flashed. "What the hell do *you* know about it?"

Dean smiled. "Enough. We have a thick file on you, too."

"It seems to me you know entirely too much for your own good, American."

"Yes, well, that's been a failing of mine ever since I was a smart-assed kid. Poking my nose in where it's not wanted. I tend to be the curious type."

"You Americans have an expression, I believe? About curiosity and a cat . . ."

"Believe me," Dean said, leaning back and doing his best to express an attitude of calm and relaxation that he was not even close to feeling, "you and your people do *not* want to kill me. Or Kathy McMillan. Enough people know exactly where we are that you can't just make us disappear. Not without exposing your whole operation. To begin with, Russia will lose her claim to the Arctic Ocean."

"The Arctic is ours by right."

"That has yet to be determined. Denmark and Canada, just to name two, do not agree with you. But that's not really the point, here."

"Oh? And what is?"

"The point, *Admiral,* is that you love Mother Russia.

Once, twenty, twenty-five years ago, you were willing to stand up against politicians and commissars and apparatchiks when you saw them making decisions that threatened to destroy your country. Right? But now you're working for people who are sucking the lifeblood out of Russia."

"You do not understand."

"Don't I? Russia has a new chance, not just at life, but for greatness . . . but the Organizatsiya siphons off the profits, discourages new business, scares off foreign investment. Russia is dying, Admiral . . . and the Mafiya is a ghoul feeding off the corpse before it's even properly dead—"

"Enough!" Golytsin brought his hand down sharply on a key. Dean suspected that there was a microphone wired to the computer, that the Russian had been recording the conversation.

But the conversation had veered unexpectedly in a new and unwanted direction.

"Things are not that simple," Golytsin said. His face was flushed, and he was breathing heavily.

"No, sir. They never are." Dean looked around the small office, at the thick steel bulkheads coated with pale green paint. "This is an astonishing facility you have here. Truly remarkable. It's a real testament to Russian ingenuity, science, and technology, and if you're able to develop it, it could help put Mother Russia smack back on the map. A global superpower. *If* Kotenko and his piranhas don't strip her to the bone first!"

"I think this interview is at an end." Golytsin stood.

"Time to turn me over to Braslov?" Golytsin gave him a sharp look, and Dean shrugged. "I know you were trying the good-cop/bad-cop ploy on me. Now it's time to give me to the bad cop, right?"

"Mr. Dean—"

"You're the one with the gun, Admiral. You decide what's right. Just remember that you have to take the responsibility for the outcome of your decisions."

"I do every day, Mr. Dean. *Every day*."

"I imagine you met some people while you were in the gulag. People who offered you . . . what? An opportunity to get revenge over the party-blind bureaucrats and petty martinets who'd put you there? I'd like to know, Admiral. Is that revenge worth the survival of your country?"

"At this point, Mr. Dean, there is not much choice." The anger had faded, leaving behind an expression of sheer emotional exhaustion.

"Bullshit. There's *always* a choice!"

"Really? And what would my choice be down here?" Reaching up with the Makarov, he lightly tapped the steel bulkhead beside him. The steel was thick and gave back only a dull click. "In case you hadn't noticed, Mr. Dean, this is a prison. It's every bit as much a prison as the gulag."

"Help me, McMillan, and Benford get out of here. Get us back to the surface, where we can be picked up by our people. And you come with us. We can offer you asylum."

Golytsin expelled a single sharp puff of air, as though he'd been struck in the gut. "Asylum!" he said. "There is no asylum. Not from *these* people."

"You could tell us what you know about the Organizatsiya. Names. Places. Projects. Damn it, Admiral, you could help us shut these bastards down, and give the New Russia a fighting chance!"

"No, Mr. Dean. It's far too late for that." Reaching over, he opened the door to the room and gestured with his pistol. "Time to go back to your quarters. You're right about one thing, though. Sergei Braslov will want to have a talk with you in a little while. Perhaps you'd care to discuss the Tambov group's role in the New Russia with him and a few of his muscular friends."

"Admiral—"

"No, Mr. Dean. It's time for you to return."

Golytsin and the guard led Dean back down the passageway toward the storeroom.

SSGN *Ohio*
Arctic Ice Cap
82° 34' N, 177° 26' E
1156 hours, GMT – 12

"Captain! Sonar!" Chief Mayhew's voice came over the intercom hushed but sharp with urgency.

"Go ahead, Chief."

"Transients, Skipper! He's opening his bow doors."

"Where?"

"Starboard side, Captain. Estimate range is no more than one thousand yards!"

"Very well."

Grenville was standing in the control room again. The compartment was dead silent, filled with sailors and officers all intently attending to their duties . . . and waiting for the next command from him.

He glanced at the plot board behind the periscope station, where an enlisted rating was using a grease pencil to mark the *Ohio*'s position relative to the *probable* position of sonar target 116. Half an hour ago, the *Ohio* had turned toward the target, moving dead slow. By now, they would be passing the target, starboard to starboard. Grenville's intent was to pass the Victor, then pull a Williamson turn, swinging around 180 and dropping in on the Russian submarine's tail.

If he was opening his bow doors, he was preparing to fire torpedoes. That could mean he'd heard the *Ohio* and was getting ready to fire now . . . or it could mean he merely suspected the *Ohio* was close and was preparing a war shot just in case. Which?

And where the hell was the *Pittsburgh?* . . .

GK-1
Beneath the Arctic Ice Cap
82° 34' N, 177° 26' E
1201 hours, GMT – 12

Golytsin held his pistol aimed at Dean's left side as the young Russian soldier holstered his own pistol and fumbled with the keys outside of the locked storeroom door. The door swung open, and Dean saw Kathy's worried face inside just above a bundled-up blanket, with Benford, looking sullen, standing behind her.

There would be no better time.

Marines learned in survival-training courses that if they were made prisoner, the best times to try an escape were when they were being moved. The guards would be more distracted at those times, would be forced to pay attention to more details, and there was always the possibility of the unexpected. The Makarov was aimed at Dean's ribs, but Golytsin's head had turned as he watched the door open . . . alert to the possibility that the prisoners had elected to use this opportunity to attempt an escape. Dean whipped around to his left, his elbow sweeping Golytsin's wrist into his body, the heel of his right hand slamming up and across and squarely into Golytsin's jaw.

The Russian staggered back a step and Dean followed, his right hand grabbing Golytsin's right hand and turning it sharply inward, a jujitsu move that made it impossible to maintain a grip on anything in that hand. The pistol dropped, clattering onto the steel deck.

The naval infantry guard was grabbing for his holstered weapon when Kathy lunged through the door and hit him full in the chest. It had scarcely registered on Dean that she was clutching one of the blankets in front of her, using it as a shield. When she collided with the guard, there was a clatter and a number of large aluminum cans scattered across the deck. Dean dropped to his knees, scooping up the pistol Golytsin had dropped, then coming back to his feet just as the guard slammed backward into him.

The three of them, Kathy, the guard, and Dean, went down in a thrashing tangle of limbs and wildly rolling cans of stewed tomatoes. Somehow, Dean was able to roll out from under and get on top, the Makarov in his hand swinging up, then down with savage force, striking the guard in the side of the head with the weapon's butt just as the man managed to pull his own pistol free.

The guard sagged back to the deck, unconscious. Dean rose shakily to his feet, the pistol aimed now at Golytsin, standing several feet away. "You okay?" Dean asked Kathy as she scrambled clear of the blanket and got to her feet.

"Yeah."

"What's with the cans in the blanket?"

"Improvised ballistic armor," she said. "I thought it might at least deflect a bullet if he got off a shot."

Dean was very glad she hadn't had to put the idea to a test. It *might* have worked . . . or the 9mm round might have slammed straight through blanket, tomato cans, and Kathy and scarcely even slowed down.

"Put the guard in the room. And gather up those cans. Benford! You help her!"

"You can't get out of here, you know," Golytsin said.

"I'm damned well going to try. And you have a choice."

"What choice?"

"You can get into that room. We'll lock you in with this guy. When they let you out, you can quite truthfully say the Americans overpowered you and escaped."

"Or?"

"Or you can come with us. The offer's still open."

Golytsin was clearly thinking about it as he stood there, rubbing his wrist where Dean had nearly broken it. Benford and McMillan together dragged the unconscious guard inside the storeroom, tossing in the blanket and the errant cans. Kathy retrieved the guard's pistol and the keys.

"Time to make your decision," Dean told him. "Loyalty to your new masters? Or loyalty to Mother Russia?"

Golytsin turned and entered the storeroom. Kathy began to close the door . . . and then he glanced around suddenly and said, "Wait! I'll come!"

"Good man. C'mon."

"You're thinking of the Mir subs?"

"You have a better idea?"

"No. The Mirs are kept charged and ready to go at all times. They're the closest we have to lifeboats in this place."

After locking the storeroom door, the four of them hurried down the passageway, rounding the ninety-degree bend in the corridor and skirting the opening in the deck leading down into the facility's control center. The waiting Mir subs were just ahead.

"Everyone grab a dry suit!" Dean called. "We'll need 'em topside!"

And then a sharp cry came from behind.

"Stoy! Ruki v'vayrh!"

SSGN *Ohio*
Arctic Ice Cap
82° 34' N, 177° 26' E
1204 hours, GMT – 12

"Weps," Grenville said softly. "What's our war-shot status?"

"War shots loaded in tubes one, two, three, and four,

Skipper. Inner and outer bow doors closed. Four Mark 48 ADCAP torpedoes ready for firing."

"Open bow doors two and four," he said. "But manually."

"Open bow doors two and four manually. Aye, aye, sir."

Using the hand cranks was slower, but it could be done in complete silence. He didn't want the Victor out there hearing the *Ohydro* getting set to shoot. Tubes two and four were on the port side of the vessel, on the side farthest from the Victor now, but they would be the first to bear as the *Ohio* came out of the Williamson.

A minor point. In modern submarine warfare, you didn't have to be aimed at the other guy to have a chance of hitting.

But it *did* help. Especially at close range.

"Captain, this is Chief Mayhew."

"What is it, Chief?"

"I know this is out of order, sir, but . . . can I talk to you for a sec, here in Sonar?"

"Be right there."

It couldn't be super-urgent for Mayhew to sidestep the usual formalities of command protocol, but it did sound important. Grenville walked forward up the starboard passageway and stepped into the sonar shack.

"Whatcha got?"

"Sir . . . I don't really have *anything* . . . but it's kind of a . . . a feeling, okay?"

"A feeling."

"Yes, sir. We're still getting occasional transients from Sierra One-one-six, okay?"

"Yes. . . ."

"And we're getting a lot of background from, from . . . all over. Ice grinding overhead. We have some biologicals. *Lots* of noise from the ships on the surface. In fact, half the problem is just hearing the Victor's transients over all the background—"

"What's your point, Mayhew?"

"Sir . . . look here." He pointed at one of the two display monitors above his workstation. It had been reconfigured to show a waterfall.

"Waterfall" was the term for a particular type of sonar display. It looked like a green TV screen filled with static, but with some of that static just orderly enough to begin to sketch out white lines against the green background. Across the top were compass bearings; down the left side were time readouts, recent at the top to older at the bottom. The waterfall made the universe of sound surrounding the *Ohio* visible and tracked each source over time. Each line drifted at an angle across the screen, its bearing changing as the *Ohio* moved relative to it or it moved relative to the *Ohio*.

"Ignore these three, Captain," Mayhew said, indicating the three brightest and most slowly moving lines. "Those are the three ships topside. *This* is Sierra One-one-six." He pointed to another line that, over the past few minutes, had drifted sharply across the *Ohio*'s starboard side.

"Not much there," Grenville said.

"No, sir. We're close enough to pick up some noise from his screw, and some from his power plant. Down here . . ." He pointed to a bright patch on the line. "That's when he opened his bow doors."

"Yes."

And thank God a Russian torpedo hadn't followed a moment later. The other captain was hunting still, not sure where the target was.

"This is what I wanted to show you, sir."

Mayhew indicated an area of random static, a vague patch somewhere behind the Russian sub. Random static . . . but somewhat less of it than elsewhere on the screen. . . .

Grenville's eyes widened as he realized what he was seeing. *"Shit!"*

"I think—," Mayhew started to say, but Grenville's hand was already on the intercom mike.

"Helm! This is the captain! Hard left rudder! *Now!*"

24

GK-1
Beneath the Arctic Ice Cap
82° 34' N, 177° 26' E
1205 hours, GMT − 12

DEAN SPUN, DRAGGING BACK the slide on the Makarov to chamber a round. At the far end of the corridor, perhaps eight or ten yards away, a man in civilian clothing was aiming a sidearm at them. "*Stoy!*" the man shouted again. "Stop!"

As Dean moved, the man fired, the shot a thunderclap in the steel confines of the base passageway. The bullet struck the overhead, ricocheted with a screech, then ricocheted again off a bulkhead somewhere at Dean's back.

"*Jesus!*" Dean ducked reflexively, even though the round had already screamed past. Taking aim, he triggered a round as well, and heard the bullet bouncing off one of the walls before rebounding from the bulkhead behind the other man. Something clattered on the deck ahead of Dean . . . the spent round, spinning as it burned off the last of its energy.

This was, he realized, a deadly shooting gallery. Handguns simply weren't accurate beyond a range of a few yards unless the shooter was well trained. Here, though, the massively thick steel bulkheads served to channel shots all the way down the passageway . . . with the effect of making this a little like a shoot-out inside a sewer pipe.

Sooner or later, even the worst shot would hit something. Dean needed to end this *now*.

He fired three more shots in rapid succession, not trying for accuracy so much as for a storm of bouncing, ricocheting rounds that would force the Russian gunman back behind the shelter of the far bend in the passageway.

The ugly little Makarov was uncomfortable in Dean's hand, the grip considerably thicker than what he was used to. A disengaged part of him recalled that the design enabled the shooter to handle the weapon easily while wearing heavy gloves—a necessity in the cold, long winters of Russia.

The other man dropped to the deck, writhing. A pipe running along the overhead suddenly spurted a stream of water. A second man appeared and snapped off another shot that came shrieking down the metal corridor, then pulled back out of sight. Behind him, Dean heard a sudden gasp, a cry of, "*Ah!*"

"Who's hit?" Dean called.

"It's Golytsin!" Kathy said.

"I'm okay!" Golytsin said. "Into the submarine! Into the submarine!"

Two men appeared around the bend in the passageway, grabbed their comrade, and dragged him back out of sight as water continued to spray into the far end of the corridor. At least, Dean thought, it wasn't coming in with a force of half a ton per square inch; it must be a broken internal water supply.

"You can't get away, American!" a voice yelled.

Braslov.

For answer, Dean fired twice more, deliberately aiming at the bulkhead far down the corridor in an effort to bank the shots around the corner. He heard a shriek with the second shot.

Behind him, the others had scrambled down an open hatch in the deck. Dean fired one more shot blind, then jumped into the opening, pulling down one circular hatch and dogging it, then the second.

Golytsin was already at the controls, flipping power switches and bringing the little submersible to life. "We need to leave *now*," he told the Russian. "Before they figure out how to stop us."

"Coming online now," Golytsin replied. Dean could hear the rising hum from astern. "Cutting the connectors now . . ."

There was a jolt and a sudden dropping sensation as the deck tilted sharply forward. The whine aft shrilled louder, and then the deck started to level off as Golytsin wrestled the submarine level.

Dean dropped the Makarov onto one of the narrow seats provided for passengers on the craft and squeezed forward between Kathy and Benford, peering over Golytsin's shoulder.

"Are you okay?" Dean asked the Russian.

"For now."

"Where'd you get hit?"

"His side," Kathy told Dean.

"It just grazed me." Golytsin shook his head. "I didn't think the idiots would open fire inside the facility!"

"The walls seem pretty thick," Dean said.

"Yes, but the water pipes, hydraulic lines, and wiring conduits are all *quite* vulnerable," Golytsin replied. "We could have crippled the base!"

"I wish we had," Dean said. He was looking at a TV monitor mounted high up on the forward bulkhead, above and between the two thick quartz portholes. The screen showed the view aft, the brightly lit stern of the upended

Russian ship now receding slowly astern. "Can they come after us?"

"They might," Golytsin acknowledged. "We'll just have to see. . . ."

The portholes forward showed only impenetrable blackness. The deck was tilting again, however, this time with the bow nosing higher. They were beginning their ascent: eight hundred meters, half a mile . . .

Dean glanced around the compartment and saw three sets of bright blue survival dry suits on the deck aft where the others had dropped them.

"Let me take the helm, Golytsin," he said. "You three should get into your dry suits . . . and, Kathy? Check his wound. I don't want him bleeding to death. Is there a first-aid kit in here?"

"Port-side bulkhead," Golytsin said.

Dean was still wearing the neoprene dry suit he'd donned for the assault on the *Lebedev*. Once they reached the surface, it would be best if they could stay snug and dry inside the Mir, but he didn't know how long the little vessel's life support would last, or how well it might ride on the surface. If they did have to abandon ship, the others stood a much better chance of surviving if they were properly garbed.

A neoprene dry suit was designed to prevent hypothermia; Dean's suit had proven that much already. He'd been miserably hot over the past hour, especially with the athletic exertions of the past few minutes, and was sweating heavily inside the thing.

"Keep hold of this," Golytsin told him, moving aside so he could take the joystick. He pointed at a digital readout. "That is our angle of ascent. Keep it between twenty and forty degrees."

"Right, Admiral."

Golytsin looked pale and drained and was clutching

his right side. Dean could see blood slowly spreading beneath Golytsin's hand.

Dean hoped they could find the *Ohio* up there. Even with a survival suit, Golytsin wouldn't last long on the ice—or in this cold chamber—not when he was already going into shock.

The Mir continued its climb through darkness.

SSGN *Ohio*
Arctic Ice Cap
82° 34' N, 177° 26' E
1208 hours, GMT – 12

Captain Grenville had been wondering what had become of the *Pittsburgh.*

The Los Angeles–class attack submarine had accompanied the *Ohio* all the way up to the Arctic. They'd passed messages back and forth, of course—by radio when they both were at periscope depth and could raise a mast, and by hydrophone while at depth—but once they'd entered the AO, the Area of Operations, all hydrophone communications had ceased. Anything one of the American subs could hear underwater could be heard by Russian subs, and at an extraordinary distance.

Standard operation orders, therefore, required a communications blackout. According to the ops plan, the *Pittsburgh* was to have begun orbiting the AO ten miles out each time the *Ohio* surfaced, providing perimeter security against the Russian attack subs that were known to be in the vicinity.

Grenville stared at the patterns on Mayhew's waterfall, realizing that what they represented was a slight decrease in noise—even the background noise of grinding ice and distant ships—just astern of the Russian Victor.

In short, Grenville was seeing what amounted to a

sound-absorbing hole in the water, and the only thing that might do that was the anechoic, sound-absorbing paint on the outer hull of . . .

"The *Pittsburgh*," Mayhew said softly. "It's *gotta* be."

"Agreed," Grenville said. He put out a hand to steady himself against an overhead beam as the *Ohio*'s deck tilted with her turn. The *Ohio* had been passing the Victor, from bow to stern and off her starboard side, but not on a perfectly parallel course. Grenville had been intent on executing a maneuver known as the Williamson turn, cutting behind the Russian Victor and coming around on an exact reciprocal of his initial course—which would put him squarely in the Russian's wake.

But it appeared now that the *Pittsburgh* was already there. Grenville had broken off to port in order to avoid a head-on collision with the other American sub in the area.

He watched the patterns of sound shift on the waterfall and hoped he'd given the order to turn in time.

Mir
Beneath the Arctic Ice Cap
82° 34' N, 177° 26' E
1209 hours, GMT – 12

Dean held the Mir in its climb. For the past couple of minutes, he'd been listening to the swish and zip of clothing being changed behind him and trying *not* to picture Kathy stepping out of those baggy pants and wiggling into her survival suit. She was, he thought, quite attractive.

He found himself thinking about Lia instead. Safe in Ankara, Rubens had said yesterday. Was she back in Washington yet? Or still overseas? . . .

"This doesn't look too bad," Kathy's voice said a moment later.

He risked a glance back over his shoulder. Golytsin

was slumped in one of the seats, the leggings of his survival suit on, but the rest bunched up behind his waist and back. Kathy, in another blue dry suit, knelt in front of him, looking at an angry red slash just below his rib cage. She had the sub's first-aid kit open and was applying a wad of sterile gauze.

"I told you," Golytsin said. "Just a scratch."

"Yeah, a scratch bleeding like a stuck pig," Kathy said. "But this should stop the—"

"It hardly matters," Benford said. "He's going to die anyway. You all are."

Dean looked past Kathy and the Russian. Benford was standing all the way at the aft end of the compartment, stooped slightly under the low overhead, and he had a Makarov pistol in his hand.

SSGN *Ohio*
Arctic Ice Cap
82° 34' N, 177° 26' E
1209 hours, GMT – 12

"We're cavitating, Captain!" Mayhew said.

"Captain, Con!" a voice called over the intercom at the same instant. "We're cavitating!"

The damage was done. "Helm! Maintain turn! Come to new heading two-six-zero! Ahead half!"

"Helm maintain turn to new heading two-six-zero, aye! Ahead half. Aye!"

Even at a creeping pace of four knots, the sudden turn had been enough to make noise in the water. The trouble was that the *Ohio,* over 560 feet long and with a submerged displacement of 18,750 tons, did *not* stop on a dime or turn inside her own length, and Grenville had to goose the old girl to give her rudder some bite to the water.

The cat was well and truly out of the bag now, dripping wet and making a hell of a racket . . . but that was better than scoring an own goal by ramming the *Pittsburgh*.

The question now was what the Russian was going to do about it.

SSN *Dekabrist*
Arctic Ice Cap
82° 34' N, 177° 26' E
1209 hours, GMT – 12

"*Got* him, Captain!"

Captain First Rank Valery Kirichenko looked up as the sonar officer called over the intercom.

"Talk to me, Lieutenant."

"Sir! We have sounds of propeller cavitation to starboard, bearing two-five-zero, range approximately five hundred meters. Target aspect changing, and appears to be turning away from us, to port. I'm getting increased power plant noise as well. I believe he is accelerating."

"Excellent! Stay with him!"

Kirichenko's orders required that he find and neutralize any enemy submarines operating within a twenty-kilometer perimeter around the GK-1 if hostilities commenced. The *Lebedev* had passed him the word hours before that American commandos were boarding the ship and that an American Ohio-class submarine had surfaced alongside.

The Americans had made it so easy . . . but then the game had turned dark as the *Dekabrist* slipped closer to the enemy. The American vessel had suddenly submerged, making the challenge of finding her that much more difficult. He knew approximately where the enemy vessel was, but not precisely. He'd hoped the sounds of scraping ice and opening bow doors would have enticed

the Americans into doing something rash—and noisy—
but there'd been nothing.

Until now.

"Helm!" Kirichenko ordered. "Come right eight-five
degrees, to new heading two-five-zero! Increase speed to
twelve knots!"

"Yes, Captain!"

Five hundred meters. They'd been so close! But the
American sub was turning away, which made her an easy
target.

"Stand by to fire torpedoes one and two," Kirichenko
said. "On my mark! . . ."

Mir
Beneath the Arctic Ice Cap
82° 34' N, 177° 26' E
1209 hours, GMT – 12

"Everyone stay calm," Benford continued. "But you
will do as I say. Or you'll all die sooner, rather than later."

"Harry!" Kathy cried, pulling back a little from
Golytsin. "What do you think you're doing?"

"I'm *not* going to jail for murdering Richardson!" he
said. "The damned Russians double-crossed me . . . tried
to put the blame on me. Well, they're not going to get
away with it!"

"We're not trying to blame you," Dean said. He was
kicking himself. That was *his* pistol, the one he'd carelessly dropped on a seat after coming on board the Mir.
He was trying to remember . . . how many cartridges
should be left?

He didn't know the Makarov well, but he knew the
Walther PP series and he'd read once that the Russian
Makarov was based on the tried-and-true PP design.

Walthers had eight-round magazines, so the chances were good that the Makarov had an eight-round mag as well.

But how many rounds had he fired in the short, savage firefight on board the GK-1 just now? There'd been his first shot . . . then three quick ones. . . .

He couldn't be sure—things had happened so fast— but he was pretty sure the pistol only had one shot left. *Maybe* two . . .

"Yes, you are!" Benford cried. There were tears on his face now, and his hands were shaking. *Not* good . . .

"Harry, it'll all be okay!" Kathy told him. She started to rise, but he swung sharply, pointing the pistol at her.

"*Don't move,* you little bitch! Damn it, no one believes me! It . . . it wasn't supposed to be this way! I did everything they wanted me to do, and then they always wanted more! And now they want to double-cross me! Well, *I'm* giving the orders now!"

"Listen here, Benford," Dean said.

"No, *you* listen!" The pistol swung back to point at him. "You . . . you just get me to the surface, understand? *And get me out of this fucking box!*"

The stress, Dean thought, must have been building on the man for days. From the sound of it, he was having a bout with claustrophobia as well, first locked up in that stores closet on the Russian platform, and now crammed into the Mir. That and his fear at being caught for the murder . . .

The trouble was that if he fired that pistol in here, it could very easily kill them all. The hull of the Mir was as thick and rigid as the hull of the GK-1, designed to withstand the incredible pressures of the abyss . . . which meant that a bullet fired in here would bounce wildly around the crowded compartment until it hit someone— or cracked one of the quartz viewing ports forward, or smashed some piece of equipment vital to their continued survival.

"The pressure on the hull outside, Benford," Dean said, keeping his voice low and level, "is roughly one half ton pressing down over every square inch. Do you know what will happen if you put a hole in one of our viewing ports with that thing?"

"Don't make me find out!"

"Give it up, Benford! Put the gun down!"

"No!"

"If you think it's cramped in here now, wait until twenty tons or so of seawater blast in through a porthole and smash you into a grease spot!"

"Shut up!"

Dean met Kathy's eyes. He flicked his own gaze forward, to the place where she'd laid her pistol when she'd changed clothes. It was lying on a shelf on the starboard side, a few feet forward of Golytsin's chair and well out of her reach . . . out of Golytsin's reach, too, assuming he could move fast enough to grab it.

Dean glanced aft again to meet Kathy's eyes, then ahead to the pistol again. She gave a barely perceptible nod.

If Dean could throw the Mir into a violent maneuver, knocking Benford off his feet, Kathy might be able to grab the other pistol and regain control.

Of course, Benford's weapon might go off when he fell. The odds were not real good at the moment . . .

And then something collided with the Mir, knocking it sideways with the violence of a sledgehammer blow and sending Benford slamming against a bulkhead.

"What the hell?"

Kathy looked up at the TV monitor over Dean's head and pointed. "Look!"

Dean glanced up, then looked again. Another submarine, bigger than the Mir, an ugly bug of a submersible painted dark red and with a pair of insect's arms spread wide, had just slammed into the Mir's aft port quarter.

And Dean saw Braslov's leering face in the cockpit canopy.

SSN *Dekabrist*
Arctic Ice Cap
82° 34' N, 177° 26' E
1210 hours, GMT – 12

"Fire number one!" Kirichenko said.

The weapons officer brought his palm down on the firing button at his console. Kirichenko felt the slight bump through the steel deck, heard the hiss of compressed air forward.

"Number one fired electrically, sir!"

"Fire two!"

Again, a bump and a hiss.

"Number two fired electrically, sir! Both torpedoes running true and normal."

"We have operational control of both torpedoes," a *michman* seated at the weapons console announced.

"Estimate impact," the weapons officer said, looking up at the clock high on the bulkhead, "in thirty seconds!"

SSGN *Ohio*
Arctic Ice Cap
82° 34' N, 177° 26' E
1210 hours, GMT – 12

"Torpedoes in the water!" Mayhew yelled over the intercom. "Two torpedoes, 650s, range seven hundred yards, closing astern! Estimate impact in thirty seconds!"

Grenville was just entering the control room again.

"Release countermeasures!" he barked. "Helm! Hard right rudder! Ahead full!"

"Release countermeasures," the weapons officer announced, "aye, aye! Countermeasures released!"

"Helm to hard right rudder, aye, aye! Ahead full, aye, aye!"

There was no panic, no urgency . . . just men performing their assigned jobs, according to long training and experience, with cool efficiency. Grenville was proud of them.

If the two torpedoes coming in on the *Ohio*'s tail were 650s, they were the largest in the world—650mm wide and over 9 meters long, with warheads weighing close to one ton apiece. They would be wire-guided and wake-homing, and they were *fast*. Driven by a powerful closed-cycle thermal propulsion system, they could travel at fifty knots for up to 60 kilometers . . . or cruise at a more sedate thirty knots for a full 100 kilometers. As they sped from the Russian sub's bow tubes, they trailed slender wires behind them, allowing the Russians to steer them toward the target. When they were close enough to acquire the target on their own, the Russians would cut them loose and they would home on the sound of the *Ohio*'s screw.

The *Ohio* couldn't outrun them, not at what amounted to point-blank range. By popping countermeasures, however, a pair of canisters releasing clouds of sound-reflecting bubbles astern, the *Ohio*'s maneuver might be masked for a critical few seconds. The Russian skipper, Mayhew thought, had pushed things too close. The *Ohio* was barely seven hundred yards away—damned close for a pair of 650mm torps, he thought—and they might well miss on their first pass.

Of course, the Russian weapons officer would steer them around on their wires until they reacquired . . .

"Captain!" Mayhew called again. "Torpedoes in the water!"

"I *know,* Mayhew, I know—"

"No, sir! *New* torpedoes! It's the *'Burgh*! He's just popped two ADCAPs and is slamming them right up the bastard's ass!"

SSN *Dekabrist*
Arctic Ice Cap
82° 34' N, 177° 26' E
1210 hours, GMT – 12

"Torpedoes running, Captain!" the sonar officer called.

"I know, Lieutenant. Our torpedoes—"

"*Enemy* torpedoes, sir! Coming in from dead astern!"

"What?" Where in hell had a second American submarine come from? . . .

SSN *Pittsburgh*
Arctic Ice Cap
82° 34' N, 177° 26' E
1210 hours, GMT – 12

"Both torpedoes running hot, true, and normal, Skipper! Time to target, twenty seconds!"

"Very well." Captain Peter Latham, CO of the USS *Pittsburgh,* glanced at the clock on the bulkhead. This was going to be damned close.

Ordered to cover the SSGN *Ohio,* the *Pittsburgh* had been lying back, staying quiet and staying out of sight. They'd been following the damned Russian for hours, ever since they'd picked him up near the location of the remote weather station. He'd clearly been hunting for the *Ohio,* but the op orders for the American subs had been to go weapons-free *only* if the Russians made hostile or provocative moves.

There was a lot of latitude to orders like that, and making the wrong decision could wreck a man's naval career—assuming it didn't kill him first. But firing a couple of torpedoes could definitely be construed as "hostile," no matter how the weekend quarterbacks in Washington chose to interpret things later.

The *Pittsburgh*'s advantage here lay in the fact that she'd been squarely behind the Russian boat . . . and therefore in the Russian's blind spot. Between wake turbulence and the sound of your own screw, it was almost impossible to hear anything from directly astern, even the shriek of incoming high-speed torpedoes.

"Both torpedoes have armed," the weapons officer said. "Both torpedoes have now acquired the target."

"Very well," Latham said. "Cut the wires."

"Cut the wires, aye, aye."

"Helm, come left four-zero degrees!"

"Helm come left four-zero degrees, aye!"

"Down planes, one-five degrees!"

"Down planes one-five degrees. Aye, aye, sir."

It wouldn't do to be too close to the Russian when those ADCAPs hit. Explosions under the ice could be unpredictable at best.

Latham kept watching the clock, counting down the seconds. . . .

25

Mir
Beneath the Arctic Ice Cap
82° 34' N, 177° 26' E
1210 hours, GMT – 12

ANOTHER SAVAGE JOLT ROCKED the Mir as Braslov's submersible slammed into them from astern. Dean pulled the joystick hard over to the right, at the same time shoving the power control all the way forward. The electric motor whined as the Mir twisted hard to the right; the deck slanted sharply, and Benford fell, toppling clumsily into the seated Golytsin and the kneeling McMillan. On the TV monitor overhead, the other minisub swam out of the camera view, but they could hear the bumps and clatters as its keel dragged across the Mir's upper hull.

Dean chanced a quick glance over his shoulder. Kathy was wrestling with Benford, struggling for control of the pistol. Dean snapped the stick over to the left and hauled back, praying there was enough oomph in the electric motors to pull off this sudden a maneuver. Minisubs were not jet aircraft, and the sluggishness of the Mir's response reminded Dean of the bumper cars at an amusement park he'd gone to as a kid.

The *Mir* came left and started to climb, directly into Braslov's submarine. . . .

SSGN *Ohio*
Arctic Ice Cap
82° 34' N, 177° 26' E
1210 hours, GMT − 12

"Ten seconds to impact!" Mayhew called over the intercom.

The COB put an intercom mike to his lips. "All hands! All hands brace for impact!"

Thunder boomed through the *Ohio,* the force slamming Grenville hard against the Mk. 18 periscope mount. A second explosion followed hard on the heels of the first, the twin detonations ringing like hammer blows. *This is it!* he thought as the deck heeled far over toward starboard, threatening to invert the boat.

Only as the *Ohio* began swinging back toward a normal orientation did Grenville realize that the explosion had not been that of a Russian torpedo detonating against the *Ohio*'s hull.

"Torpedoes passing close astern!" Mayhew warned. "They're homing on the countermeasures!"

Grenville heard them now, the high-pitched whine of torpedoes passing very close to the *Ohio,* sounding close enough to touch. . . .

The *Pittsburgh*'s ADCAPs had struck their target first. The Russian torpedoes, still racing toward the *Ohio,* had taken the bait and homed on the cloud of bubbles, punching through and into the clear, cold, empty water beyond.

Grenville and the officers and men crowded into the *Ohio*'s control room collectively held their breath as the whine dwindled into the distance.

"Con, Sonar!" Mayhew called. "I have major flooding and breakup noises close to port!"

"Helm, reverse turn," Grenville ordered. "Come left one-eight-zero degrees!"

"Reversing turn, helm left one-eight-zero degrees! Aye, sir!"

He tried to picture what must be happening on board the Russian sub right now, just a few hundred yards to port. The 'Burgh's ADCAPs must have winged squarely into the Russian boat's stern, tearing out the main ballast and aft trim tanks, the engine room, the generators . . . maybe even the nuclear power plant. Forward, men would be struggling in absolute darkness as freezing-cold seawater blasted into compartment after compartment.

It was every submariner's nightmare, no matter what the uniform they wore or flag they sailed under.

Grenville's concern now was to steer away from the collapsing wreckage lest the *Ohio* become tangled in the debris . . . and also to put some distance between the *Ohio* and those Russian torpedoes.

The torps would have been wire-guided. If the enemy weapons control officer had already cut them loose before the 'Burgh's ADCAPs hit, they would be operating under a search program, one that would swing them about in a large circle until they reacquired their target, or found a new one. If the wires had still been attached, though, when the Russian sub exploded, all steering commands had suddenly ceased. Depending on what the final set of programmed instructions was telling them, the torpedoes might go into automatic search mode, or they might simply continue running, descending into the depths.

Until Grenville knew which was the case, he intended to put as much maneuvering room between his command and those Russian torpedoes as he could manage.

Mir
Beneath the Arctic Ice Cap
82° 34' N, 177° 26' E
1211 hours, GMT – 12

Braslov's minisub was twice to three times the size of the Mir, an ugly, cigar-shaped monster perhaps eighty or ninety feet long. It had the blunt, rough-hewn character of a construction vehicle, and Dean imagined that it was used for heavy lifting around the GK-1, hauling and attaching sections or drill tube. It mounted two shrouded propellers aft, plus smaller directional thrusters for tight maneuvering.

Its sheer size, however, gave Dean and the Mir an advantage. As the larger submersible passed overhead, Dean brought the Mir's bow up and around to the left. Reaching down with one hand, he slipped his arm into the open framework of the controller for one of the Mir's mechanical arms. As his hand closed on the squeeze-grip handle inside, there was a whine of servomotors and the arm on the Mir's port side jerked spasmodically, then extended itself, grippers wide open.

He missed. He'd been trying to jam the Mir's arm into one of the propeller shrouds on the other sub, but there was no kinesthetic feedback to the thing, and he couldn't feel what he was doing, or judge distance and reach. The Mir's arm flailed wildly, banging uselessly off one of the construction sub's tall rudders.

He tried coming right again, tried getting above the other craft.

Behind him, Golytsin and McMillan continued struggling wordlessly with Benford.

The shock wave struck, slamming into the Mir from above and from the left. Dean heard the roar, like far-off thunder, but the jolt ringing through the Mir's hull was sharper and more insistent. The Mir tipped hard to port as loose gear and equipment crashed from storage racks and a water pipe somewhere on the port side broke with a shriek of high-pressure water.

The Mir very nearly flipped over, but somehow Dean brought the stubborn little craft back onto an even keel. He heard a loud thump behind him. When he glanced back, he saw Benford flat on the deck, evidently unconscious, with Kathy standing over him, the Makarov in her hand. Golytsin, bare-chested, was getting up off the deck, his hand pressed against the oozing wound in his side.

"Nice maneuver," Kathy told Dean. "Give us some warning next time!"

"Wasn't me," Dean told her. "Shut off that water pipe! Golytsin! You know how to work the arms on this thing?"

"*Da.* . . ."

"Then help me! Get up here and take that sucker apart!"

Braslov's construction craft was just ahead, apparently dead in the water. Dean could see a large, white numeral 4 painted on the upper starboard side.

"What was that explosion?" Kathy wanted to know.

"Damned if I know," Dean said. "It wasn't us; that's all I know. Golytsin! Can you disable that bastard's props?"

"If you get me close enough to the stern, yes."

He was studying the other craft narrowly in the glare from the Mir's outside work lights. It didn't appear to be damaged, but it wasn't going anywhere at the moment. It appeared to have a very slight negative buoyancy, but it was still upright, still intact under the terrible, crushing pressure outside.

He cut the forward power back by half and pulled the Mir into a tight turn until the other minisub's stern was directly ahead and below. Dean didn't want to spend too much time here; other Russian construction subs might have launched from the GK-1 and be in the vicinity.

But if he, Golytsin, and Kuthy could cripple Number Four, that would be one sub, at least, that would not pursue them to the surface.

Nomer Chiteereh
Beneath the Arctic Ice Cap
82° 34' N, 177° 26' E
1211 hours, GMT – 12

Braslov groaned and opened his eyes. That had been an underwater explosion, and one close by. A smear of blood glistened on the control panel in front of him—*his* blood. That explosion had slammed him forward, momentarily stunning him. He raised a hand to lightly touch his forehead; it came away wet with blood.

No matter. He'd suffered a lot worse. The important thing was . . . what was the condition of his submarine? Quickly he looked around, checking monitors, checking readouts. The hull was still intact, power still good, trim still good . . .

And the Mir with the Americans on board was swinging around onto his tail.

Braslov grinned. That would get them nowhere.

He reached again for the controls.

Mir
Beneath the Arctic Ice Cap
82° 34' N, 177° 26' E
1211 hours, GMT – 12

With Golytsin working the controls, both of the Mir's mechanical arms extended, reaching toward the other craft's starboard side screw. Before Dean could grab hold, however, the propeller suddenly spun to life, the shroud pivoting as Braslov put the craft into a sharp turn.

Damn!

"Okay. We'll just have to try to race him to the surface," Dean said. He brought the *Mir*'s nose up and rammed the power handle full-forward. "I don't suppose there are torpedoes on this thing?"

"No," Golytsin said. "No torpedoes."

Sluggish, the *Mir* began climbing.

Behind it, the construction submarine turned a clumsy circle, then began to give chase.

Beneath the Arctic Ice Cap
82° 34' N, 177° 26' E
1214 hours, GMT – 12

Three miles away, the two torpedoes fired from the Russian submarine *Dekabrist* continued their flight through the lightless deep, continuing to descend as they raced through the water at fifty knots. Though the American submarine captain was not yet certain of the fact, there'd been no backup programming directing the weapons into a search sweep. They would continue to drive into the depths until they either ran out of fuel and sank . . . or hit the bottom.

Groaning like a dying man, the wreckage of the *Dekabrist* settled toward the bottom as well. They could hear the sounds in the sonar rooms on board both the *Pittsburgh* and the *Ohio* as steel bent and twisted. Now and then, a compartment sealed off from the rest of the vessel would give way under the steadily increasing pressure, a sharp, chilling *pop* as seawater inexorably forced its way inside.

The bottom here was eighteen hundred meters down . . . just over a mile.

It would take the *Dekabrist* a long time to get there.

Mir
Beneath the Arctic Ice Cap
82° 34' N, 177° 26' E
1218 hours, GMT – 12

Dean checked the aft monitor. Sure enough, Braslov was on their tail, and coming fast. Dean could see the work lights on the construction sub like four dazzling stars in the night, the bow of the sub a vaguely seen insect's face between them.

"He can move faster than us," Golytsin told Dean. "Especially in ascent. More power, and larger ballast tanks."

"Great. Fucking *great*. . . ."

"But the Mir is more maneuverable," Golytsin continued. "And more rugged."

"How much more rugged?" Dean wanted to know.

"Mir can outdive him by perhaps twenty percent."

"Meaning it can take more pressure on the hull?"

"Yes. Wait . . . you're not—"

"No," Dean said. "I'm not going to try to lure him beneath his crush depth. That would be crazy."

"Yes."

"I'm going to try to ram him. Kathy! You've got Benford secured?"

"Yeah," Kathy replied. "There was some rope in this locker back here."

"Okay. Strap yourself down."

"No seat belts, Charlie."

"Then hold on, damn it. Golytsin! Where are the ballast controls on this thing?"

Golytsin pointed.

"Flood the ballast and trim tanks," Dean said. "And kill the forward lights! Let's see if we can discourage the bastard!"

He pulled over on the stick, bringing the nose of the Mir up even higher, then over and around. Like a jet aircraft in a stall, the little submersible hung suspended for a moment, then nosed over, beginning to descend.

Ahead, the four work lights on the construction sub grew brighter, and seemed to stretch farther apart.

"God in Heaven," Golytsin said, eyes widening. "What are you doing?"

"Playing dolphin to his shark, Admiral."

"You'll kill us!"

"Where's your faith in good old, solid Russian engineering, Admiral?"

At twelve knots, the Mir slammed into the construction sub, bow to bow. There was a savage *bang* that rang through the hull, followed by the scrape and tear of metal.

And all of the lights went out.

Nomer Chiteereh
Beneath the Arctic Ice Cap
82° 34' N, 177° 26' E
1218 hours, GMT – 12

Braslov had been puzzled when the Mir's work lights winked off, then decided the American was hoping to lose his dogged pursuer. *Idiot! Nomer Chiteereh* had sonar and would be able to hunt him down easily even in the pitch-blackness of the depths.

Braslov was reaching for the sonar switch when he caught a shiver of movement in his forward view port. The Mir was just ahead, coming into the illumination cone of his own work lights.

His full attention was yanked back onto the other craft. It was close . . . impossibly close, and swelling to fill the forward port as though racing down to meet him.

The shock threw Braslov out of his seat, slamming him to the deck as the construction submarine heeled far over to port. The sound was an explosion of raw noise, the shock indescribable. Several internal pipes gave way, and streams of ice-cold water blasted into the construction ship's compartment.

Braslov struggled to get up, to get back to the control panel, but the deck was now a bulkhead and threatening to become a ceiling, and it was all he could do to cling to the deck grating as the submarine heeled over.

Then salt water hit wiring, and the interior lights flicked off, came on, then flickered off once more, leaving Braslov in the deepest, most profound darkness he had ever known. . . .

Mir
Beneath the Arctic Ice Cap
82° 34' N, 177° 26' E
1219 hours, GMT – 12

"Golytsin!" Dean shouted. "Blow all ballast!"

"Give me a moment! I can't see!"

"We don't *have* a moment!"

An alarm was shrilling, and a recorded voice was saying something in Russian. The outside lights were off, but he could still hear the whine of the motors, and the instrument lights and LED readouts were still on.

A moment later, the Mir's emergency lights switched themselves on. "You see, Admiral?" Dean said brightly. He reached out and thumped the console with his fist. "You Russians know how to build these things solid!"

"Don't hit that too hard," Golytsin warned. "Not until we know the full extent of the damage!"

Dean was pretty sure the man was cracking a joke.

Golytsin hauled down on a large handle, and there was a sudden jar as several hundred kilograms of iron suddenly dropped clear of the Mir's keel. He pulled another handle, and they heard the shrill hiss of pressurized air forcing its way into the ballast and trim tanks. As the water was forced out, the Mir rose faster.

"Emergency surface," Golytsin explained.

"Yeah, but there's ice up there," Dean said. "What happens when we hit it?"

Golytsin smiled. "Where is your faith in good, solid Russian engineering, my friend?"

The Mir rose rapidly up from the abyss. . . .

Beneath the Arctic Ice Cap
82° 44' N, 176° 50' E
1219 hours, GMT – 12

Some five miles away now, the first of the Russian 650mm torpedoes slammed into the seabed. Had the ocean floor consisted of soft mud and sediment, like so much of the abyssal plain elsewhere, the contact detonator likely would have failed to go off and the weapon would have buried itself harmlessly in the ooze.

Unfortunately, large stretches of the seabed in this region were covered by and penetrated by immense shelves of ice, methane ice clinging to the ocean floor like permafrost.

The detonator triggered and nearly one ton of high explosives went off.

With no oxygen to support combustion, the methane clathrates on the floor couldn't ignite, but the blast did break a very great deal of ice loose and send it rocketing toward the surface.

It also liberated a large amount of methane gas—several

hundred million tons of it—from the sea floor, the bubbles rising in massive clouds out of the deep.

Mir
Beneath the Arctic Ice Cap
82° 33' N, 177° 45' E
1225 hours, GMT – 12

"How long before we reach the surface?" Kathy asked.

"We're passing two hundred meters now," Dean told her, glancing at the instrument readout screen. "Maybe . . . another minute?" He looked to Golytsin for confirmation.

"Something like that," the Russian replied. His hand was on the ballast control. "But I'm going to begin slowing the ascent now. You're right, of course. We don't want to hit the ice ceiling too hard."

"It would be nice to be able to break through," Dean said. "But if we happen to hit a thick patch . . ."

"Exactly. Even with recent climatic warming, the ice is as much as a meter thick in places, and the Mir might not be able to break through. There is also the chance, a small one, that we could come up beneath the keel of the *Lebedev* or one of the other ships up there. So we will come up close to the surface, and attempt to find a *polynya.*"

"Do you think Braslov will be able to come after us?" Kathy asked.

"I don't know," Dean said. "We hit him damned hard. If we're lucky, he's on his way down, now, while we're going up." He sighed. "Just one problem."

"What's that?"

"My boss is going to kill me. I was supposed to bring Braslov back *alive.*"

Nomer Chiteereh
Beneath the Arctic Ice Cap
82° 34' N, 177° 26' E
1225 hours, GMT – 12

The construction submarine *was* sinking, as water continued to leak in from a ruptured seal, dragging the craft down tail first. In total darkness, drenched in icy water, Braslov struggled upward toward the forward part of the compartment. If he could just reach the controls and trip the main circuit breakers, perhaps the emergency power circuits were still good. He needed to blow ballast and surface . . . or at least try to regain neutral buoyancy long enough for them to come out and rescue him from GK-1.

His arm felt like it was broken. The cold was a living thing, leeching the heat from his body, leaving him trembling and exhausted.

Almost there . . .

The methane cloud struck from beneath, totally unexpected, a sudden shock slamming into the construction submarine's belly and stern. Braslov had the sudden sensation that he was rising, and then the submarine flipped end for end and he hurtled into the forward end of the compartment, screaming as he slammed into the control panel. Water cascaded over and around him, stunning him, immobilizing him.

And above the roar, he could plainly hear the shriek of metal as the tortured vessel began to tear open amidships. . . .

Mir
Beneath the Arctic Ice Cap
82° 33' N, 177° 45' E
1231 hours, GMT – 12

"I can see light!" Dean said, peering up through the view port. "I can see the surface!"

"Let me have the controls," Golytsin said. "I'll see if I can find open water."

The Mir was drifting toward the surface slowly now, the weight of the water in its ballast tanks counteracting the lift induced by the release of the heavy keel plates. Under his guidance, one of the electric motors was coaxed to life, and the Mir began to respond. . . .

The cloud of methane, expanding enormously as it rose out of the constricting pressure of the depths, caught the Mir, sending it rocketing upward as the vessel rode the shock wave for a moment. Then, with a savage jolt, the Mir dropped through a methane bubble, hit water beneath, then hit another bubble. For several interminable seconds, the Mir tumbled in the frothing sea, its occupants slammed from deck to overhead and bulkhead to bulkhead like rag dolls.

Water came thundering in. . . .

Nearby, the bubble mass struck GK-1, ripping the anchoring cables free. The drill train, extending into the depths, snapped, then snapped again, again, and yet again as the shock wave worked its way up out of the abyss.

The shock wave ruptured ballast and trim tanks, flooding the forward section first. Unimaginable stresses clawed at the ship, and the relatively slender and unarmored midships section ripped apart as conflicting forces tried to draw the stern higher while dragging the bow down.

Then watertight seals ripped open and the ocean came pouring in.

The Art Room
NSA Headquarters
Fort Meade, Maryland
2032 hours EDT

"My God!" Jeff Rockman said, staring at the big screen on the wall. "What in hell is *that*?"

The view, a real-time image of the Arctic ice around the Russian base, showed an awesome transformation, worked in an instant. The ice crazed like shattered glass, then appeared to blur. At the same moment, geysers erupted around all three of the Russian ships, still holding position in the ice, and from the open-water footprint left behind by the Ohio as well.

"What is it?" Rubens asked, leaning forward. "A volcanic eruption?"

The geysers were growing in size. The *Lebedev* was swallowed whole. The cargo ship was ponderously rolling over onto her port side. In places, solid ice was breaking open now as enormous blocks of ice shattered and broke free.

"I don't know," Marie Telach said. "But it's *big*." The view receded several clicks as the magnification on the spysat's optics was cut back. The polar ice cap seemed to recede suddenly as the curve of the Earth itself was revealed. Below, a vast stretch of the ice cap was *smoking*.

"Whatever it is, it's affecting an area of over three hundred square miles," Rockman said, his voice awed. "Too big to be a nuke . . ."

Rubens nodded his understanding and sighed. "I'm guessing . . . it's Dean."

Mir
Beneath the Arctic Ice Cap
82° 33' N, 177° 45' E
1235 hours, GMT – 12

Dean recovered consciousness first. The Mir was riding on the surface; he could tell by the way the deck swayed and rocked as the stubborn little craft bobbed with the surface chop.

"Come on!" he shouted. He pulled Kathy's head out of the water, slapped her face until her eyes fluttered open. "Get up! Get up!"

Nearby, Golytsin struggled to his feet. Benford, still bound hand and foot, struggled in the aft part of the compartment, panicking as water rose steadily around him. "Help me! Help me! Don't let me drown!"

"Golytsin!" Dean yelled. "Get Benford. Cut those ropes! We've got to get out of here!"

Dean cracked the dorsal hatch, blinking as sunlight streamed into his face. He looked around, feeling curiously out of place. There was no ice visible at all . . . only mile upon mile of intensely blue and open ocean.

"Let me," Golytsin said. "There is an emergency raft. . . ."

Dean stepped back out of the way as Golytsin climbed the ladder, leaning out of the hatch to free the raft. The Mir was flooding slowly, settling gently by the bow as water continued to pour into ruptured flotation tanks.

"Quickly!" Golytsin called from outside. "Into the raft!"

Dean helped Kathy climb the ladder, then Benford, his hands and feet free now. Dean took a last look around, then climbed the ladder after them. Golytsin and Kathy helped him slide off the back of the Mir and into the raft.

"What happened to the ice?" Kathy asked, looking around. "My *God*! What happened to the ice?"

The ice wasn't completely gone; there were still numerous floes. But where before there'd been an uninterrupted plain of solid, windswept ice and blowing snow, now there was a horizon-to-horizon expanse of open water littered by blocks of ice.

"I don't know," Dean replied. "Admiral? You guys didn't have a nuke or two on board that underwater base, did you?"

"No. No nukes. I think . . ."

"What?"

"I don't know how it happened, but I think there must have been a release of gas from the bottom. A very *large* release."

"Methane?"

Golytsin nodded. "We know the sea floor here was covered in methane clathrates. That was why we were forced to stop drilling, while Gazprom decided what to do." He shivered. "Something must have triggered an enormous explosion. . . ."

Nearby, with a loud gurgle, the Mir was slipping at last beneath the surface of the water.

It would have a long fall to the bottom.

"Are we . . . are we going to die?" Benford asked at last.

"I don't know," Dean said. "How about it, Admiral? Does this thing have an emergency beacon?"

"It should have triggered automatically, as soon as I triggered the inflation release."

"Then all we need to do is wait for someone to pick up the signal and send help," Dean said. "Anyone want to take bets on whether we get picked up by the Americans first, or the Russians?"

"Russians," Golytsin said. "Definitely the Russians. We are well inside Russian territorial waters, after all!"

"Says you," Dean said. He looked up into the impossibly clear blue sky. "My bet is on some high-tech gadgets listening for our signal." And the people running those gadgets.

It was cold, and the wind was beginning to pick up. The four of them huddled together in the raft for warmth.

Dean found himself face-to-face with Kathy. "Pretty good, James Bond," she said. Her lips were blue and she was shivering, but she managed a smile.

"Nah," Dean said. "If I were James Bond, it would be just you and me together in this thing, alone."

And they drifted with wind and current, beneath an endless day. . . .

EPILOGUE

Bethesda Naval Hospital
Bethesda, Maryland
1520 hours EDT

"HOW'RE YOU FEELING, CHARLIE?"

Dean sat up a bit straighter in the hospital bed. He'd not been expecting Bill Rubens himself to come down to see him.

But, then again, he thought, *Rubens is that kind of guy.* He was tough, he could be a son of a bitch, but he *cared* about his people.

"Doing better, sir," Dean replied. "They say maybe another week . . ."

"Well, don't rush things. We want you back at Desk Three all in one piece. Understand?"

Dean nodded at the grisly joke. He'd come close to losing his feet, his ears, and his nose to frostbite. The four of them, Golytsin, Benford, McMillan, and Dean, had drifted in that open raft for forty hours before they'd been rescued.

The rescuers had not, as Dean had hoped, been the *Ohio* or the *Pittsburgh,* and after being pulled from the water he'd been relieved to hear that the two American submarines had survived the devastating explosion under the ice cap. Both had been slammed into the underside of the ice and sustained serious damage. Both had limped south through the Bering Strait, ending up at last at the Bangor submarine base across the sound from Seattle. The freed American prisoners had been taken off the *Ohio* while the SSGN was still north of Alaska, flown by helicopter a few at a time first to Point Barrow, then back to the Lower 48 for a full debriefing.

The four castaways in the rubber life raft had been plucked from the freezing waters by the *Algonquin*, an Iroquois-class destroyer, operating in the Arctic in conjunction with a Danish frigate, the *Peter Tordenskjold*. The two had been deployed north to show their respective flags and to contest the Russian ice-grab claims, reasserting their rights to free passage through international waters. NSA monitoring stations and satellites had picked up the distress locator signal in the raft; Rubens himself had talked to the Canadian ambassador in Washington, requesting that the little international flotilla be diverted to search for survivors.

All four had been suffering the beginnings of severe frostbite by the time they'd been rescued. "How are the others doing?" Dean asked.

"They think they'll be able to save Golytsin's left foot," Rubens said. "Right now our . . . associates with the Agency have him at an undisclosed but secure medical facility, and are talking to him about Mafiya activities in Russia and in the United States. Turns out turning him was quite an impressive intelligence coup. As good as bringing in Braslov would have been."

"Listen, about Braslov—"

Rubens held up a hand. "It's not a problem. There was no way you could have brought him out as well as the others. You brought us Golytsin. Well done.

"Benford is at a different secure location, discussing

things with the FBI. Again, it turns out the Russian Mafiya has penetrated deep into a number of American organizations and corporate structures. We're learning a lot. He's promised to testify in exchange for leniency."

"Leniency? The man murdered Ken Richardson in cold blood, and assaulted an NOAA officer with a crowbar!"

"Life might be considered leniency in some circles, especially when the alternative is the death penalty. So would transfer to a regular Federal penitentiary, instead of the ADMAX facility in Pueblo."

"And Kathy?"

"She's doing just fine," Kathy said from the door. She was wearing a blue hospital robe and fuzzy slippers. "Now awaiting her official transfer to something called Desk Three. And how's my James Bond?"

"On the mend, I'm told."

" 'James Bond'?" Rubens asked, one eyebrow rising.

"Don't ask."

"I won't. I just wanted to drop by and see how you two were doing. Oh, and you might be interested in this. . . ."

He dropped a newspaper on Dean's bed. It was folded to page 5 and had a one-column article circled. Dean picked it up and scanned it rapidly.

Dr. Earnest Spencer, a U.S. government climatologist, had given a speech at a Press Club luncheon in Washington the day before, claiming that the large-scale release of methane gas beneath the Arctic ice cap the previous week—apparently a completely natural phenomenon—had released the equivalent of two years' worth of human-produced greenhouse gasses into the atmosphere. He pointed out how lucky everyone concerned was that that enormous volume of gas hadn't ignited in the atmosphere.

While global warming was an incontrovertible fact, he said, human responsibility for that warming was still very much an open question.

"I don't know, sir," Dean said. "It didn't feel very warm when we were bobbing around in that raft."

"I imagine not. Of course, Al Gore is back on TV saying the gas release is a global disaster. About a quarter of the ice cap appears to have been broken up by the outgassing, and the pieces are melting much faster than expected. There's now open water all the way to the Pole, they say."

"And our involvement in what happened is—"

"Classified," Rubens said pointedly. "*Highly* classified. The submarine battle with the Russians never happened. The loss of their experimental drilling facility and two of their research ships is a tragic accident . . . an accident which also destroyed one of our NOAA research weather stations, by the way."

"Someone already had me sign a paper," Kathy said.

Rubens nodded. "We don't want people to know we were in a pissing match with the Russians; they don't want people to know they might have triggered the outgassing with their drilling."

"And the Mafiya?" Dean asked.

"Stopped cold," Rubens said, "at least for the moment. Golytsin's interrogation suggests that the Tambov group was using both honey-trap tactics and the promise of billions of dollars of new income to pull key members of the Russian Federation Duma into line. Some of those politicians are having second thoughts about the whole thing now. Kotenko had promised that all of the world environmentalist concerns would be crippled when Greenworld was revealed as a terrorist organization, but the reports of the gas explosion in the Arctic have kind of driven Greenworld to the back page all over the world. And we now have Kotenko's computer under constant electronic surveillance. We think we may be able to put pressure on some of those Duma members and strengthen the campaign against the Mafiya. At least that's our hope."

"Sounds like it's not over, though."

"No. In some ways, the Organizatsiya is a more deadly enemy than al-Qaeda. They don't go around blowing up skyscrapers . . . but they don't mind selling nukes to al-Qaeda or anyone else who wants one. Anything for a buck, or even just a ruble." He looked around. "Well, I've got to get back to the Puzzle Palace. You two enjoy your vacation. There's going to be a lot for you to do when you get back."

He left, leaving Kathy at Dean's bedside.

"I'm glad you're okay," he said.

She grinned. "Same for you . . . Double-oh Seven."

He made a face. "Listen, I should tell you before the teasing goes any further . . . I *am* in a relationship right now." Lia, the last he'd heard, was now back at Menwith Hill with the new kid, Ilya Akulinin. But they both would be back in Maryland soon.

"So?" She shrugged. "Doesn't mean I can't tease you. Or even see you once in a while, right?"

"No," he replied. "No, it doesn't."

"Mr. Rubens said he wanted to bring me into Desk Three, that you could show me the ropes and everything. He seems to think we'll be dealing with the Russians again soon."

"Of that," Charlie Dean said, "I have no doubt whatso-ever."

He had a feeling that, for Desk Three and the National Security Agency, at least, the new Cold War was not yet over.

Coming soon from *New York Times* bestselling author

STEPHEN COONTS

THE ASSASSIN

A Novel

ISBN-10: 0-312-99446-X

ISBN-13: 978-0-312-99446-4

A bloodthirsty terrorist. An international
uprising. A deadly race against time...

"Exciting....The action moves swiftly to its Hollywood ending."
—*Publishers Weekly*

Available in August 2009 from St. Martin's Paperbacks